MARC BOLAN KILLED IN CRASH

A Musical Novel of the 1970s
by **IRA A. ROBBINS**

Cover design by Kristina Juzaitis

ISBN-13: 978-0-9842539-4-4
ISBN-10: 0-9842539-4-7

www.trouserpress.com

Twitter: @IARobbins @TrouserPress #marcbolankilledincrash

Facebook: trouserpressmagazine

Also by Ira Robbins:

Kick It Till It Breaks: a belated novel of the 1960s (Trouser Press Books, 2009)

———————————————————

For her support, suggestions and love, this novel is gratefully dedicated to Kristina Juzaitis.

Trouser Press Books

"I write a song because I want to. I think the moment you start writing it to make money you're starting to kill yourself artistically."

Pete Seeger

"John and I literally used to sit down and say, now, let's write a swimming pool."

Paul McCartney

Thinking back on it now, I didn't become a bitch overnight, leastways I don't think I did. I didn't scheme any scheme or dream any big dreams. I just took what life placed in front of me and ended up a different person. I can't really claim any credit for what happened. Perhaps I stayed the same while the world shifted around me.

Put it this way: I was blind to the possibilities laid out for me and then I stumbled into them. So you can all piss off. Change is natural; dealing with it is anything but. Shit, I was just a little kid — what did I know?

BOOK ONE

Face your fears

This Is Where It All Ends

THE MUSIC blasting inside the small office on the seventeenth floor was always so loud that people in the hall routinely paused conversations as they passed. How the occupant was able to conduct telephone conversations in there struck many as a mystery, but he in fact did, seated behind a dented metal desk, surrounded by the records, cassettes, souvenirs, awards, fashions, detritus and marketing tchotchkes of the record business. A phone shouldered to his ear, a feathered hat perched above it, a cigar in his mouth, he went about his job unperturbed by the jet-propulsion laboratory of ambient sound he inhabited, exhibiting an uncanny ability to isolate a speaking voice in a telephone receiver from the din enfolding him.

The person on the other end of the line, however, was having difficulty making out words over the background noise. The nuisance of repeatedly being asked to repeat himself, a growing problem among high-decibel rockers who had not yet discovered the long-term benefits of ear protection, might have led a reasonable adult to adjust the volume in the office, but this one had clear and firm priorities, and music was at the very top — so, no.

"*International Musician* magazine, eh? Yeah, I get a comp from you guys. Try to read it, but y'know…Sure. I said *sure*. What would you like to know? To *know*?"

Eon Clean shifted the receiver to the other ear and set about igniting the cigar in his hand with a Billy Joel lighter.

"Shit, I haven't thought about her in years. Haven't. No, years. No. Hey, would you like me to shoot you a cassette of demos for this amazing band we've got in the pipeline? They're from Seattle. Seattle. *Seattle*. It's gonna be the next Liverpool. *Liverpool*. Never mind. Forget it."

Exhaling a nimbus of smoke, he tossed the lighter onto a mess of papers in a basket marked "COMING." Next to it, a *Playboy* daybook displayed 1989 Playmate of the Year Kimberley Conrad in all her blonde glory.

"Yeah. OK. Rockit LA. Yeah, I knew her. Knew her. I knew her when she was

1

just plain Laila Russell. *Russell*. We had, y'know, a thing. A thing. A thing. Affair? Don't put words in my mouth. No, not from the south. Mouth. Mouth! Fuck. No, not an affair. N-o-t-a-n-a-f-a-r-e. A thing. Fling? No, a *thing*." He blew out a cloud of smoke, imagining the numbers she could have done in the States had MTV been around back then.

"Cute kid. Is she dead or something? *Dead*. She's not? Good. *Good.* Sure, sure."

"Hold on, what? *WHAT?* Hang on a tick, let me turn down the music." He switched off the 400-watt Sony tube amplifier, leaving the room silent save for the tinnitus whoosh of air conditioning. The sudden sonic vacuum was noticed by a publicist meeting with a product manager across the hall; she checked the fluorescent lights over her head to see if there'd been another blackout.

Clean plopped back down in the burn-scarred executive chair he'd had special ordered and pushed a suede loafer against the desk, leaning the chair back at a precarious angle.

"Wow, that was a long time ago. We were just kids. Yeah, she did one tour over here, but it wasn't really happening for her in the States. But then none of those glam bands really made it here. Bolan, one single. Bowie, it took a while to get his skinny ass off the ground, sales-wise. But Slade had a rough time of it, Alex Harvey did a bit of TV... a couple of tracks clicked for the Sweet, but not the ones they wanted, right? And Cockney Rebel — he might have been a huge star at home, but the fact of the matter is Steve Harley couldn't get himself arrested if he took a dump on the White House roses. What a talented guy. Just too British."

"The Kinks? Yeah." He switched the receiver to his other ear. "Yeah. Rockit LA." He picked up a stack of messages and idly thumbed them as he listened. "No, American, born and bred. I picked up a bit of an accent living in London in the early '70s. Yeah, it was an amazing time. Paid my dues, don't you know, learning the biz from the ground up. Worked in a record shop. Right around the time Virgin was getting going. Yeah, I know Richard a bit. Quite a charmer. I'd like to work for him someday. That's off the record. Right."

"What did you say your name was again?"

"And what sort of piece are you doing on her? Who gives a crap this late in the

2

day, man? I mean, really, c'mon, it's been, what, like fifteen years since she was big, and now you're doing an article on her? How old were you in 1975?"

"Shit, I've got a jock strap older than that."

"Chaz Bonapart? Yeah, that's a sad story. I used to like his records, but then he really lost the plot. Sad to see an old-timer fall so far down the ladder of success. I see his name in the trades now and again, managing some loser or another. Sad."

"Lyrics? What do lyrics have to do with anything?"

"Yeah, I remember those songs. Catchy enough, but they did squat over here."

"Did I do *what*? That's a strange question."

"What? No. No. Look, I really can't go on the record about this shit. Like I said, a good kid. But you're barking up a dead tree here, pal. I can't help you. There's legal things involved. And my memory of those days is a bit fuzzy. Sorry. Look, if I think of anything, I'll call you. Alright. *Alright*. Yeah."

He put down the phone and reached for the power switch on the amplifier. The tubes began to glow and, in a minute, the music was back on, full blast.

Lost and Found

"I SAY, erm, miss, is that seat taken?"

The seat in question, across the carriage, was occupied by a leather knapsack and what I took to be some of its former contents. The gentleman's enquiry was directed at the top of a head bowed in a book: neat brown hair, cut short at a sharp angle.

The speaker cleared his throat and tapped his brolly on the floor as if he were a circus ringmaster urging an elephant to mount a plinth. In response, and with a theatrical sigh, the head tilted back, although not far enough to meet his gaze. "All yours, guv'nor."

Oversized red plastic specs, large bright eyes, smooth, pale skin, thin lips with a slight upturn at the left that suggested a wry smile, independent of mindset or intent. Tasteful makeup. I took it all in at a go. The smashing balance of prim and plucky continued downward: tailored white shirt and knotted tartan tie, red wool mini, no tights. Leather boots; red laces up to the knee. Smart, I thought. *Very* smart.

"Erm...."

She was staring directly at him with a look equally free of curiosity and concern and nary a move in response. The gent waved at the offending bag, then turned around, his cheeks reddening with irritation and despair. Just about the right mix, I thought. Welcome to bloody old England, where the goal is to fail a bit less and put up with what remains a bit better each year.

She sighed, placed a finger on the page and did a slow pivot from his face to her bag, as if weighing what possible connection they might have. And then again. A breeze of citrus, wood and spice floated into my nose.

"Oh, right. Sorry." Can a voice be said to drip with insincerity? Carefully laying the book on her lap, she leaned over, shoveled the loose bits in and dropped the bag at her feet, every movement expressed with ultimate disdain.

4

I glanced at an advert over her head, hoping to inspect her face without being caught. But she must have seen and ducked back down to her reading. I moved my gaze to the paperback in her lap, which I decided, without a shred of evidence, must be *Lolita*, a book I'd read a bit of in the library. A young heartbreaker recognizing and admiring herself in a novel, seeing the potential of her power — perhaps as yet untested — over men expressed in words. I imagined her reviewing a parade of gentlemen callers, weighing them on the scales of benefit and bother and finding each in turn well short. Me, I wished somebody — anybody! — would fancy me the way Humbert did Lo. Even if he was ancient and creepy.

She wasn't much older than me, but despite the clear evidence that we were both young English females seated on a warm, close eastbound Tube in the late afternoon of the last day of March 1972, she might as well have been a member of a different species space-warped in from a far-off planet.

I felt a green pang of envy that a girl could look so sharp. I would never have the nerve. Or the imagination. Clothes did nothing for me. The magical transformation from goose to swan that was always on offer in the shops and magazines never took when I tried the clobber on; rather than improve or disguise my shortcomings, clothes just hung on me, more shapeless box than clingy wrapper.

I reckoned this girl *knew* things. In my tatty brown jumper and blue denim flares, ripped plimsolls and khaki book bag, I was merely a bog-standard example of Teenasaurus Gawkus, a thawed-out fossil from the time before things got groovy. If only *I'd* got groovy along with them. She was strictly 20th century fox, all high style and frosty pose. I'll be surprised if people like me aren't soon shipped off to a desert island as a cosmetic contribution to London's greater good. Perched on the sill separating supreme confidence from offensive arrogance, she looked like a preview of next year's model, cool Britannia's thrilling future. Maybe we would all be gorgeous, fearless and proud someday, fitted with top gear, clear skin and Yankee teeth.

She might be snobby, I thought, but then she probably had full rights to it. Superiority is its own reward. Wish for it now, have it tomorrow. And bring it home, free and clear, not on hire-purchase.

I glanced from an older bloke — who'd been staring at the same page of *The Mirror* so long that he had to be illiterate or asleep with his eyes open — to a black girl painting her eyelashes with a bristly brush (I would never dare that, I'd put an eye out) and then focused on a tourist family. The man had an *A–Z* in his hand and was squinting — holding his specs up over his eyes — at the map over the doors. "I hope this is the right train. I can't find Lie-chester Avenue on this damn map." The two children (boys, maybe four and six) looked fidgety; their mum weighted with resignation. With a weary sigh, she sought to help. "Let me have a look. I'm good at reading maps." The man's retort was irritable and curt. "No, you're not."

The train slowed suddenly, causing the family to stumble with no serious harm. The parents looked concerned, as if it might happen again, but the boys began throwing themselves about and falling down for sport. The father grabbed the older one's arm roughly and pulled him up, which set off an air raid siren of crying and wailing. I couldn't watch anymore.

As we neared Leicester Square, the Americans began chattering excitedly but ultimately stayed put. The girl closed the book and closed her eyes with the grace of a curtain coming down on a play as the heat and the gentle rocking of the Underground worked its narcotic power on both of us.

"...Cross – St. Pancras, alight for connections to the Metropolitan, Northern, Victoria, Circle Line and British Rail." The driver's announcement jerked me back to consciousness. I looked at the door for a sec and then faded back to black. I still had a ways to go.

But the girl did not. "Bloody hell, where are we?" She was suddenly awake and seized with alarm. (So, she *could* be rattled. Comforting to know.) She squinted at the window, her head pivoting quickly, her coolness well and truly gone. "Is this King's Cross?" she said. "Oh, *Christ!*"

That brought me around. I suppose I could have just murmured "yes," but that felt too wan, inadequate to the drama of the moment. In as serious a voice as I could muster, I announced, "As a matter of fact, quite." She didn't look in my direction, just pushed by the Yank family — who had begun to disembark but with no great dispatch — and scrambled out the door. The Americans followed, shouldering aside a woman attempting to board, who gave the dad a haughty up-and-down and an indignant "I *beg* your pardon."

The book, which had been thrown from her lap, was abandoned to the floor near my feet. I reached down to pick it up, thinking I might be able to catch up and return it to her, but my sack fell off my lap in the process; I got myself in a tangle on the floor and was sitting stupidly on my arse as the train doors closed. By the time I had the book in hand (it was not *Lolita* after all, but one called *A Separate Reality*) and spotted an open window, I realized it was beyond my athletic abilities and sure to brain someone if I'd given it a go. Plus, she was nowhere in sight.

The same was not true of her bag, which I now saw was also on the floor of the carriage. As the train rattled out of the station and into the dimly lit tunnel, I flashed on a family memory. I'd got separated from Dad once when I was little: we were coming back from Wimbledon, where he'd gone to see a man about a dog (his words, not mine) and taken me along because Mum was out for the evening and he was in charge of me. Coming back, we ran for a train at Tooting Broadway that would have had us home in enough time to support the fib he was going to tell her. He could've been thinking of her, or of the ten quid he'd dropped, but he clearly wasn't thinking about me, lagging behind, unable to keep up with those long legs of his. Without turning to check on my proximity, he jumped into the last carriage, just ahead of the closing doors. Once inside, he turned around to see me, still on the platform, hands on knees, staring in terror as the brakes hissed in preparation of departure. He yelled through the glass for me to take the next train and he'd wait for me at Victoria. (Do I need to mention that he had the tickets and I had all of tuppence in my pocket?)

Glancing at a sign warning about suspicious packages, I reached for the bag as if it were mine, and when the train stopped at Caledonian Road, I shouldered it and strolled off like nothing was out of order. I found a bench and waited, but there were no trains. Something was clearly poxy with the Underground. I spent the change in my pocket on a Cadbury Fruit and Nut, which passed the time but gave me a headache. I probably should have found an official some-body and handed the bag over for conveyance to the lost property office. But I didn't. Chalk it up to curiosity or — if the lie I told myself were true — the belief that I'd be able to locate her quicker and return it, while the city berks would just park it on a shelf and wait for her to come calling. But how would she know to look there?

I got on the next train, the bag on my shoulder, as calm and casual as you please. No one had to know what I was doing. I was just heading home.

In the Bag

DAD WAS peering from behind the net curtains by the door as I came up the walk. If he'd seen me, I'd probably have to explain the mystery bag. He wasn't always on high alert, but he had a good working knowledge of what I had, and I certainly hadn't left the house with two bags. I had a story sorted in my head before I put the key in the lock.

"Hello, luv." Something was wrong, but my course was set so I leaped right in.

"Dad, see, there was this girl at school…"

But he wasn't interested in any of that and cut me off before I could get my fable out. "I'm glad you're home. You're late, and I was getting a bit anxious." He glanced about, as if he needed a cue for what was coming next. I shrugged.

"Right, we've got to get to Dagenham and see your aunt Ruth. She's had a fall, and she's in hospital. I don't know how serious it is, but we've got to go and see what she needs. I've packed a bag for you and put it in the car, so we're off. Do you need the loo or a cuppa?"

"No, I'm alright, Dad. Just let me…" I rushed down the hall and did a quick check of the bag he'd packed; there was no telling what he guessed a teenager needed for hasty travel.

I dig Aunt Ruth. She's more like my nan, 'cause she's pretty old. She's really Mum's aunt, and the one East Ender in the family, a real character. She talks like Alf Garnett on *Til Death Us Do Part*.

I put my school bag on the bed and chucked the one I'd found into my wardrobe, next to my shoes. I was dead keen to see what was in it, to figure out how to reunite it with that girl, but that would have to wait. I pulled open the bag he'd packed and added a few girl things he'd neglected. Then I changed into a warmer shirt and grabbed a heavier jacket. Dad hadn't said how long we'd be gone.

"Laila, come *on*!"

9

Laila. That's me. Dad give me that name because I was born the day after the Russkies shot a dog called Laika into space. He was fired up about the CND that year, and I guess he thought it would be cool to show solidarity with the Soviets and their space stuff, even though we were worried about them starting World War III with the Americans. Y'know what? He could have just bought a badge. Or sent a few pound notes to Moscow.

He and Mum had a loose-bowled beagle they named Lenin, but that was only for us. When people came over or if the subject came up in conversation, the dog was called Lenny. I swear that poor thing must have got a complex from all the confusion. He didn't answer to anything that didn't come in a bowl or involve a need to go outside. I guess it never crossed Dad's mind that people would assume he meant the Beatle, not the Commie. Too literal by half.

Did that satisfy his red boffin sympathies? Not quite. When I came along, he had another bright idea. Mum must have been knackered after twenty hours of labour and, in the telling, Dad was too excited to properly consider her feelings. For a quiet, gentle kind of bloke, he never paid her much mind when it came to things other dads would reckon were too important to decide without proper discussion. I've always thought that if it were him flat on his back with the stuffing kicked out of him, she would have given me a regular name: Rose or Helen or Margaret.

But he was dead set on Laika. Fortunately, either out of fear or species loyalty (I doubt it involved any concern for my future feelings in the matter), Mum was able to prevail upon him before my birth was officially recorded and got the spelling changed to make the tribute less obviously canine or Russian. So Laila it was. Thank God for that. Y'know what "laika" means in Russian? *Barker!* That would have been dead awful. Sometimes I think he wouldn't have much minded if I did have four legs and a tail.

The worst of it? He never bothered to tell me that the poor mutt, sent from Russia without much love, never made it back home from her space adventure. That bit I had to learn for myself.

Turned out one random shitter was all they could handle. When I arrived, the pooch went to live with Aunt Ruth, who called him Winston. (Sometimes I've wished they'd packed me off and kept the dog.) She saw him through a sudden decline and death when I was four or five. I doubt Mum was too upset about that, but Dad talks wistfully about good old whatsisname to this day.

Lucky for me, the kids in school aren't much bothered about the space race, and my teachers haven't spent much time talking about it. We're all happy to leave all that space stuff to the Yanks. Ever since that stupid record came out last year, kids in class have been calling me "Lay-la" and winding me up with dramatic readings of that stupid line: "You've got me on my knees." Thanks, Eric. I could have done without that.

Mum always called me Bunny. I liked that. But then she went and died.

That got Dad's full attention. And so from the time I was seven I've been at the centre of it, although most of the time I do the looking after. After she died, things went off for him and he's never been quite right since. The dole pays our rent and puts food on our table, allowing him to mope around the house, watch the football and pretend to be busy.

His name's Cliff, like the singer. Dunno which one's older, so that could be who he was named after. Or, if not, then someone else entirely. Mum, Catherine, called him Chives. I've no idea why. I love him and all, but even I have to admit he's kind of a shit father. Not the truly terrible kind that winds up in nick or on the cover of the Mirror sporting three days of stubble, a bloody nose and a torn shirt, with six little buggers in filthy rags pulling at his trousers — he's not a serious drunk or a drug-taker, and he's never raised a hand to me — but I think he signed on to parenthood expecting Mum to manage the details, not get hit by a motorcycle. Her dying didn't instantly turn him into a model parent the way my being born did her. In his telling, which is all I have to go by, his twenty-two-year-old superwoman of a wife (I was born two days before her birthday; Dad said she thought of me as an early present, I liked that) brought me home from the hospital, had a cuppa and a kip and had the whole business of motherhood sorted by the time the sun came up.

I'm tall for my age and I've been told I've got a good figure. People always take me for a bit older than I am. The other girls in my form are less developed; some don't have any curves at all. From the back they could be boys. I could stand to lose a half a stone; I'll have to see about that.

There are a few total slags in school, but it's hard to be jealous — they'll be pushing prams and wiping snot soon enough, and who in God's name would want that? Boys in class say stupid stuff and clutch their hands out toward my chest like they're mongs, but other than my monthly visit, I don't get what any of it is for. I doubt they do either. If they really want to squeeze something, the corner shop is open 'til half six. I don't see the point. I've tried it on myself, and it feels ridiculous.

I might be something if only I had the bottle — and, I guess, the brains and the cash — to present myself better. Dad thinks I take after Mum, but I can't see it in the pictures we have. She's pretty. He's more funny-faced, but handsome in his way. Still, the features he gave me don't do me any favours. My nose is too small. And my eyes are big and a bit far apart. In the mirror I might have just caught a fright. When I get in a state my face twitches like a rabbit, nose jumping up and down, mouth dancing to the left — hence my pet name.

"Face your fears, bunny." That was the last thing Mum said to me. Leastways, I think it was — I wasn't keeping track of everything she said on the off chance she might be about to die. She might have told me something else after that. I prefer to recall her parting shot to me as a dose of useful maternal wisdom, not a trivial remark about the weather or a scolding about dirty fingernails.

"Crackers, Laila, get a move on!" From the tone and volume of his voice, I had about two more minutes to get it together and fly down the stairs in time to prevent the local version of a nuclear meltdown. I reckoned it was even money that we'd actually get in the car, but less likely that he'd get us there without finding some reason to turn back and leave poor old Ruth to fend for herself. As it was, he'd be useless when we got there, so I'd be up to my eyes in it. Whatever *it* might turn out to be.

"Laila, you're really getting on my wick. Can we just go now, please? *Crackers!*" I was tempted to give it back to him, but I would have felt bad about it, so I decided not to bother. (And what put it in his head that "crackers" is an all-purpose swear word?) One of us was going to be the victim here, and it might as well be me. It wasn't always, just sometimes. I tried not to let the wankers at school push me into being a twat at home.

12

I always feel that bad things are coming, that it would be better all 'round if I just ducked out of the way. I suppose that makes me a coward, but so what. I can't see the point of standing in the steamroller's path when I can just move out of the way. If that makes me feel pathetic afterwards, well at least I've not also been flattened.

I tried to get with it, the teenaged girl thing, really I did. I look at the magazines in the shop at the top of the road, but I have never understood a word. I read an article called *All About Kissing* the other day that told me nothing useful about something I definitely needed to know more, if not quite all, about.

Honestly, I didn't get any of it. Lipstick is sticky and hard to put on straight. It gets on everything, especially pale shirts and jumpers. I grasped that boys took notice of it, but that didn't make putting on or wearing makeup any easier.

I kissed a boy from school at a party a few months back, and it was alright I suppose, but not something I needed to do all the time. Afterwards, I had worked on my technique using the inside of my elbow, but it tickled and felt stupid. And when all was said and done, there was other stuff that interested me a lot more than putting my mouth places it probably oughtn't to go.

I thought back to the girl on the Tube, the way a hummingbird at the zoo might make you think about nature, and how some things are this way and others are that. How does one even work out the details of a look like that? I could spend a month thinking about it and still get it all wrong. I'd read all the rules and theories — when to wear horizontal stripes and what colors make your bum smaller — but clearly there was loads I didn't know about looks. She must have been born to it, like boys who are already dead good at football in primary school.

"Be down in two ticks, right. Swear to…" I knew he wouldn't like it if I finished that sentence, so I didn't. Instead, I looked to see where my shoes might have got themselves to.

The Call-Up

"SO THAT was your brainstorm blitz of a marketing plan, you miserable tit? To leave a clue about the next single on the Piccadilly Line and see if word of it would spread, like lice in a Brixton infant school?" Flecks of spit sprayed the bowed head of the object of this invective, who stared at her toes through a pricey pair of Shutdowns, the specs trendies called "sod-off shades" for their mirrored black implacability. Amanda Charles looked up, mouth open to deliver a reply that she could not form.

"You young ones... appalling with your casual disdain and...arrogant disregard." Rubbing his bald head, he paced back to his side of the desk. "And would you *please* take off those blasted specs. Where the fuck do you think you are?"

She obliged, placing them on a glass table to her left. "Mr Guy, it was an honest mistake. *Honest.*" Her voice was shaky, a plea for understanding when none was on offer.

He thundered back. "A mistake, to be sure, but what exactly would make it worthy of being deemed honest? What could *possibly* accord such dignity to your incompetence? That you meant to do it? That you *didn't* mean to do it? That you only tried to hide this catastrophe from me briefly rather than indefinitely? I fail to see why honestly abject stupidity deserves to be forgiven."

Head down, eyes focused on the carpet, one small, fair hand gripping the antique chair's arm as if she might fall off, she stifled a sob. "I'm sorry."

"Stop. Just stop. Much as it might amuse me to continue plucking off your flimsy wings, I do have more urgent matters than your well-earned dressing-down. Let's be done with it. You've been paid through Friday, so that's that. I don't see how you've contributed anything that deserves compensation since then, so don't expect anything from us. Now clean out your desk and piss off. And be bloody quick about it."

She didn't respond instantly, but then it hit her, and the tears flowed freely.

She was smart, young, beautiful and clever, but in London's current economic slump, those advantages offered no assurance of satisfying and reasonably lucrative employment. Burgher Management Ltd. (friends and enemies alike referred to the company as BuggerMan, but never to Frank's face) was her first job. For all she knew, it might be her last.

"I'm s-sacked?"

"Quite. You're done. You've buggered things up royally and I won't keep you in a position to do any further damage. Now, push off."

Before she could rise, in strode Chaz Bonapart. Dressed in an approximation of street clothes, he might have passed for a regular bloke, if said bloke had plush lips, gorgeous eyes, magnificent hair and routinely caused hysteria among certain elements of British society. Unlike the Americans of his profession and acclaim, who tended to be unnaturally tall, with enormous heads, he had a loaf of average size and was closer to short; it took custom-made stage shoes, five-inch snakeskin platforms with internal risers, to make him at least *appear* to tower. The rest of it was down to bearing; a lean frame carried with the posture of a Guardsman and the self-assurance of a headmaster. With pale skin that shaded toward the grey of the undead, he displayed little in the way of health, energy or vitality. That job fell to his eyes. Since childhood, what allowed ordinary Arthur Trundle of Whitechapel to become Chaz Bonapart radiated directly from those two grey-blue spheres, which could — at their owner's direction — convey pleasure, understanding, kindness, anger or mischief.

"Here, what's all the shouting about?" He nodded at his manager, who was now parked like a sated pasha behind his enormous Louis XIV desk.

Interrupted by Chaz's arrival, Amanda had not yet done as bidden. Tipping his head ever so slightly in her direction, Frank enunciated his reply like a newsreader. "Afternoon, Chaz. Miss Charles was just about to take her leave. Permanently. She no longer works for you."

They both looked at Frank — Amanda ruefully, Chaz bemusedly. "Is that so? And why would *that* be?" He flashed a grin, a luxurious display of teeth and lips that could mean just about anything, or — as in this instance — nothing. "You disloyal little harlot. And without so much as a 'tara' to her favourite rock deity?" The friendly cheek would have been easily understood as ribbing

15

between chums if they knew each other, but Frank was careful to insulate the staff from his stars, and Chaz had spoken with Amanda no more than three times in the eight months of her employment. It was unlikely he knew her name or what she did in the organization. "Have you found a better opportunity beyond our magical kingdom? Don't tell me, I don't want to hear about it." He put a hand to his brow and feigned a theatrical swoon. They all laughed, and the mood lifted. That was what stars did with nothing at stake. But then, when it suited them to be hard or cruel, they could open a trap door that led down to hell.

Amanda sniffled and looked at both men, stuck between Frank's sincere disdain and Chaz's phony jocularity. She began to rise, but Chaz motioned her back down. Her non-answer made for an awkward silence, which Frank ended. "She did something frightfully stupid and so is no longer in your employ."

"Oh, come on now, how bad could it be? Did you catch her humming "Stay With Me" at her desk? Did she steal one of your silk ties to wear as knickers?" Chaz let out a hearty chuckle and assessed both of their faces without reaching any conclusion about the situation. There was no way to tell if he was taking it all in or just playing a game.

"I'll tell you later. For now Amanda needs to leave. And she knows why."

Amanda straightened in her chair and turned directly to Chaz. She gave him a thin smile and turned her most sincerely innocent face his way. "Actually, I don't," she cooed.

Frank had no desire to have Chaz to muck up a matter that was already sorted, but he was powerless. "Bloody hell, give it a rest" proved a useless parry to Chaz's meddling.

Chaz liked her look and thought it would be a shame not to see her around the office any longer. Frank took things too seriously sometimes. "Actually, Francis, I'd like to hear what she has to say." Chaz's use of Frank's Christian name was never a good sign. And especially not when uttered with the exaggerated calm of a nursery school teacher.

Amanda reached out for the sunglasses and cradled them protectively in her lap. "My bag was lost on the Tube this afternoon. It had notes from last week's meeting about 'Prime Number.' Mr Guy evidently believes that's ruined everything for you, and I truly am sorry for my cockup, but really? I bet some Paki cleaner's binned it by now." She recalculated the mood of the room and tried a dollop of sneer. "Mr Guy reckons it went straight to St. John's Wood and is, as we speak, being studied by a crack team of Mickie Most's marketing genii."

The men stared in shock at the girl's temerity. The absurdity of what she was saying had less impact than her audacity in saying it. Chaz chuckled at the thought of Most's Marketing Genii. He imagined a glass office door with the words stenciled in a trendy typeface. He wondered how to spell it. She pressed on, emboldened by the sound of her own voice. She stood up and positioned herself at an angle to the door that left her immediate intentions a tossup between coming and going. Sliding the Shutdowns back up her nose gave her an added jot of confidence. She checked Frank for displeasure at the gesture and was satisfied at the frown crossing his face. Chaz, however, didn't react at all to the opaque discs covering a good bit of her face.

"Mr Guy never gave me a chance. He just decided I was useless full stop. I expect I'm done here, but I can't say I know why. I've worked really hard for you, Mr Bonapart." She looked to Chaz, who had no idea if that was true. He ventured an arched eyebrow, a mild look of disapproval and a tiny shake of the head. Signal received; Frank switched gears with seasoned aplomb.

"Look, Amanda. Perhaps I've been a bit hasty. Gi's us a minute, would you?" She nodded and walked out, head up, shoulders back. Once the heavy doors were closed, Frank turned to Chaz and said, "Jesus Christ, man, do you have to be such a pushover for every well-assembled bit of crumpet wot fancies you?"

"No, I don't. And why do you have to be such a miserable fuck? It doesn't flatter you. Did Joe run off with the gardener?"

"Chaz, really, we're running a business here, not an orphanage for wayward girls. If we were a bank, and a trainee teller left a bag of your readies on the lift, you'd be pretty brassed off, wouldn't you?"

"Sorry? Wouldn't be my problem, now would it?"

Frank was nearly shouting. "If she'd left your best topcoat on a bench in Hyde Park, you'd be upset, no?"

17

"Oh, balls, she didn't do that. And what if she had? You leave piles of cash on the table every time you go out to eat, and what've you got to show for that other than a thickening middle? You're out of order, mate."

Frank got up and walked around to stand directly in front of Chaz.

"Here's the bottom line, *mate*: the ambitious marketing plan we put together, at no small expense, for your next single could now be in anyone's hands. I can't go to the label and demand they commit thirty-five grand to fund a promo campaign that could be completely derailed by her carelessness. And without that push, your single is going to be deader than bleeding Winston Churchill."

"And how exactly is sacking her going to fix that?"

Frank hated when Chaz came on all lord of the manor in matters that neither concerned him nor even, if challenged, actually interested him. This kind of meddling was just a pain in the bollocks, and he'd had his fill.

"It's not, but at least I can tell them straight that we did something about it. And she won't have an opportunity to do it again." He rubbed his mouth, buying a moment to contain his irritation. It poured out all the same. "And are you sure she didn't just give it to the other side? How do we know she's not in their employ?"

"Don't be daft."

That snapped the remaining tip off of Frank's composure. "I can't believe the idol of millions is wasting time on the employment of a £50-a-week dogsbody, admittedly a stylish and pretty one. Why don't you just let me sort things out and you stick to the rock star stuff, yeah? What you're good at?"

If Chaz even considered the suggestion, he would never abide by it. In a firm end-of-discussion voice, he announced, "Here's what you're going to do: Tell CBS we may have to hold the release. A week or two won't mean anything to them. They've got their hands full with that Paul Simon album anyroad. Give her the a few days to find the bleeding bag. If she comes up with it, she keeps her job. And a small rise to make up for your rotten temper, you twat. If she comes a cropper, cancel the single, forget her name and we'll get started on Plan B. Got it?"

Shocked at the clarity and thoroughness of the orders, Frank swallowed and blinked. He knew the score. "Right. Consider it done. I'll walk her out."

"And be sure to say this was all your bloody idea, not mine," Chaz laughed, no longer at all interested in whatever this nonsense had all been about. He wondered what the girl's name was again.

"Very well, your lordship." Frank left Chaz in his office and found Amanda puffing furiously on a fag in reception.

"A word please." He pointed at her hand.

She stabbed out the smoke and followed him outside.

"Right. I expect I've been a bit hasty here. I'm sorry. I'd like to keep you on for now, if that's alright, and give you a chance to locate the purloined papers before we make a final decision about your future."

"As you wish."

"Turn it up this week and we'll forget all about this little row. I'll add a fifteen percent rise to make it right. How's that sound?"

"So I'm not sacked?"

"Not for the moment, no."

"Very well, then. I reckon that's best for both of us." It was amazing, Frank thought, how she was able to combine relief and smugness into a most annoying version of gratitude, colored with the implication of privilege, as if she presumed to have her failures not just forgiven but erased. The do-over generation, that's what they were becoming. And no good would come of it.

AMANDA WAS HOME, drinking wine and worrying a bit about how she might recover her bag, when she remembered that her parents were expecting her. She was already several hours overdue, and they were all the way up in Newcastle, so there was no chance of just turning up late. But it wasn't her fault, not this time, it was all down to that blasted bag. As she picked up the phone to call, she realized their new telephone number was written in her Filofax. Which was in her bag…

After sulking for a good quarter-hour, Amanda called Directory Enquiries in Newcastle and obtained the number. There was not even a glimmer of surprise in Mr Charles' voice when he sleepily answered the telephone and heard his daughter's voice from 250 miles away. "Your mother is very disappointed," he said, knowing full well how little impact that would have on her.

"I'm sorry Dad, but I'm in a terrible spot. I'm off my head about it." He noticed more conviction in her voice than she usually mustered for parental excuse-making, and that worried him. Holding the Trimphone to her right ear with her left hand, she picked up a brush and put it through her hair absentmindedly.

"No, of course I understand how upset Mum must be. Would you be a dear and explain it to her?" He'd get it sorted, he always did. "I promise I'll be on the train first thing in the morning, and I'll be to you lot by afternoon. Monday's a holiday, so I can stay two nights and be back to work Tuesday. Alright? Can you check the schedule for me? Alright? See you tomorrow."

She put down the phone and got into bed.

And That's the Truth, Ruth

THE AUNT RUTH visit turned out to be more of a false alarm than a real ordeal. She wasn't too poorly, and she was ready to go home from hospital as soon as we arrived. We stayed a day and a half. She only needed a bit of handholding and concern, a pot of tea and a few minor house repairs, which Dad attended to with surprising competence.

I like Ruth. She reminds me of Mum, although I don't suppose they were really anything alike. She's not my auntie, in fact, she was Mum's auntie. She's a lot older and a real East Ender, with all those weird rhymes I never understand, like, "Would you fancy some Tommy Tupper?" and "I'll just close the burnt cinder" and "with all the rain pissing down, be sure to wear yer weasel and stoat so's you don't catch a frock and frill." Dad knew some of it, but for me conversations with Ruth could be a puzzle that didn't always get solved.

For me she's a reminder that Catherine Russell was a real person, not just a name and a fading memory. I like spending time with her, but I think this visit did Dad in a bit. He rabbited on for the entire ride there and then fussed over her like an old hen all weekend. I got the feeling Ruth was ready to see the back of him after a short while. Or maybe it was me she was wishing away. Who can tell with pensioners? It's probably on account of what happened to Mum. It must still haunt her.

The best part of the trip was a photo Ruth gave me. I'd never seen it before, and she made a point of getting me alone, as if it was a big secret from Dad.

"I want you to have this, luv. It was taken on the first day of Catherine's job as a teacher. It's outside a school in Streatham, the one where she met your dad. But don't show it to him. It'll make him moody."

I stared at it. Mum looks like a bit like an older me, with a smile that can fix anything. Her hair is back, and she's got on clothes that were probably in style a decade earlier. My heart broke looking at it. I gave her a hug, burying my gratitude and sadness in her bony chest.

"Dad gave me a photo — from a different school, maybe five years later. They're standing together and he looks more like a teacher than she does."

"I don't recall that one, luv. I wonder…"

I could see it clearly in my head. I've stared at it a million times. She's showing a bit of leg, and her white shirt has a few buttons undone. He's wearing the teacher uniform —white shirt, loosely knotted necktie, rumpled trousers, wingtips and the all-but-mandatory academic brown corduroy blazer.

The photo was actually the second secret thing Aunt Ruth gave me. When I turned twelve, she handed me a list Mum had given her. I don't think she was keeping it for me, or from me, it was just in a shoebox she happened to look in while cleaning out a wardrobe one day. In a crap novel, it would have been sealed in wax with a note reading, "Do not open until your 12th birthday" or locked in a safe deposit box with a mysterious key delivered by a solicitor.

It was nothing like that. It was just an old sheet of foolscap that was found and given to me, evidently months after its excavation (Aunt Ruth could be a bit dotty). Mum had — in her happy young schoolteacher way, cleverer than your usual sort — put down a list of lessons (in alphabetical order, mind) that, Ruth said, she planned to teach me when I got older. As if she somehow guessed she mightn't be around to guide me to adulthood in person.

She'd typed it on the back of a '60s political flyer; the ink was a bit thin in spots, especially in the creases. There was a wine ring in the lower right corner. Her name was written at the top: Catherine Russell.

A few of the — what would you call them, fortune cookie phrases? doubled up on letters, as if she couldn't decide which one she believed in more solidly. There weren't any items done for "q" or "z," which I suppose is understandable, and the ones for "K" and "X" seemed to bend the rules a bit. A few I didn't understand at all, but I found one for "E" terribly ironic, tears flowing at how quickly her life was erased.

- Assess your advantages
- (Your) body will betray you
- Creativity is competition. (Competition can be creative.)
- Doubt is d-u-m-b and destructive

- Don't look down (on people)
- End things efficiently
- Face your fears
- Gladness leads to greatness
- Have a heart; hurl it at the one you love
- Imagine what's inside
- Jail your jealousies
- Know your (k)needs
- Live your lies
- Make time for misery
- Never a need to be nasty
- Outlaw the obvious – own your oddness
- Pull the plaster
- Remember who you are
- Stay silly
- Tell your tale
- Undertake the unthinkable
- Victory of vengeance has no value
- Worry is a waste
- EXamine the complex
- EXperiment. relaX
- You can only be you

The only one of the those she got around to sharing with me in person was "Face your fears." I remember the first time she said it to me: I was five or six, and we were about to leave for a seaside holiday, probably Brighton, but I'm not sure. She put me in the bath and told me to put my head underwater so's I'd be ready for proper swimming lessons. I couldn't do it. It turned out facing one's fears was a lot easier said than done. Fear is a powerful force, and until you work out what the worst possible outcome could be, the imagining of how bad it will be is the real problem. I've given that a lot of thought each time I've backed down or chickened out. It always makes me feel crap, and it always sticks me back in that awful dim green hospital passage, waiting for Dad to arrive, unable to bring myself to go in and witness the final moments of her life. I thought about what she'd tried to teach me after that, but thinking it did not enable me to do it. I know I couldn't have done anything for her. But I hate to think of her all alone, thinking in her fear and pain that perhaps no one loved her. That was a lot for me to carry around, especially after reading that Shakespeare bit about cowards dying a thousand deaths.

We got back home Sunday in time for tea. I wasn't thrilled that the visit didn't get me out of school, but I was anxious to get back to the bag in my wardrobe. And I kept thinking about the smart girl who must have gone spare over losing it. But first we went out to the chipper, a treat I usually enjoy but not when I'm on pins and needles. I was so distracted that I back-shook red vinegar on my white jumper, leaving a pink circle in a rather embarrassing spot (but only one, thank goodness). Dad didn't even notice. I would've died if we'd run into anyone on the way home, but luckily we didn't. When we got home, I ran it under cold water and rubbed it with soap.

"Dad, do you think Aunt Ruth is going to die soon?"

"Laila, why would you say something like that? She's getting on, but she's right as rain. Don't you worry about such things." He settled into the big chair in front of the telly and quickly nodded off. I watched for a few minutes, news of more labour actions. Christ, nothing — or nobody — in this country works.

I CLOSED MY door, fetched the bag out from my wardrobe and set it down on my bed for a look. I kicked off my trainers and got to work, unloading the contents in neat rows. I spent a while emptying a tartan plastic makeup case: Max Factor and Mary Quant Youthquake lipsticks in seven different shades of red, fake eyelashes, mascara of several sorts, blush, eyeliner, nail polish remover (but no nail polish; odd, that), tweezers, a small round mirror that was too dusty to use for anything as obvious as reflection, hair brush, man's comb, mints. Black, blue and red biros. Silk Cuts, a lighter. Oh! de London perfume. A toothbrush. I delicately removed a greasy Wimpy wrapper (that went straight into the rubbish) and tissues with bleary makeup traces but nothing disgusting. They went in the bin as well. I went and washed my hands. Just to be safe.

There were two square foil packets imprinted with the name Durex. There was something squishy inside which I didn't care to open and inspect. Binned those

24

as well, carefully hidden under the tissues. I had a suspicion about what they might be and promised myself to take it all outside before Dad saw to it. Not likely, but you never know.

The wallet was in a zipped outside pocket. Brown leather, worn through at the corners. I set it down and stared at it, imagining what it might contain. I blew my nose and felt my left ear close up. As I took things out, I made a mental note of where they had come from so I could put it all back correctly. There was a surprising amount of dosh — four of those new £20 notes — plus some tickets for the Underground, a London Rail timetable for Newcastle, a ticket stub for T. Rex at Wembley and a folded-up advert for Hammersickle Blowtorch, a hair salon, that looked to have been through the wash.

There were calling cards, but all of the names on them were men. One was for a bloke named Harvey Goldsmith; I imagined ringing him up: "Hullo, you don't know me, but I found a pretty girl's bag on the Tube and I was wondering if you can please tell me the name and address of anyone who fits that description and might have your card? No? Well, thanks anyway." That would be pathetic, even for me.

I was starting to think this was the sort of brain-teaser I would never solve. After a quick sneezing jag closed my other ear, I dug back in and found a brown folder with a string tie. I put it aside and returned to the inner life of the bag, where I discovered a pocket that hadn't been there before. I slid my hand in and drew out a small diary, covered in soft brown suede. Beautiful, really. I was turning it over in my hand, enjoying the feel of it when my door opened.

"Hallo, luv, wh'ave you got there?"

Dad was in my doorway, a rumpled mess, rubbing his eyes and scratching his head like some mangy old hound (but, to his human credit, using a hand rather than a hind foot). It was moments like this that I truly loved him. I looked down at the bed, then up, then down again, as if I was seeing the girl's gear for the first time. I tried to come up with a likely lie but opted for the truth. He'd understand. Or at least he wouldn't care. So long as I turned up for tea and brought home passing grades, he pretty much left me to get on with it.

"A girl on the Tube left this behind the other day and I picked it up to return it. Only I've not had the chance, what with the visit to Aunt Ruth and all."

"Good girl. Make sure you do. Night." He pulled the door closed.

He won't remember any of this in the morning, so I won't get grilled about why I hadn't turned it into the left property office. I wouldn't have had a proper answer for that, so it was just as well.

I glanced at the bin to remind myself to empty it later. Then it was back to detective work.

There it was, neatly written on the back of the diary:

AMANDA CHARLES
17B TETCOTT ROAD
LONDON SW10

"Amanda Charles." I said it out loud, marveling that she not only had a name but that I now knew what it was. Sounded posh — public school, old money, new gear, chauffeurs, swank invitations, all that. I joined my imaginings with the image I could conjure of her on the Underground and tried to work out whether in real life she more resembled what I saw or what I didn't see.

I went and fetched the *A–Z* off a shelf in the kitchen so I could see where in SW10 that was. It took some searching until I found it, just off the King's Road in Chelsea. The pages of the journal offered no further clarification — it was all numbers and phones and dates and names of cities. Maybe she was an air hostess, or an underworld spy. Or a travel agent. That one would be disappointing. I wanted her to be something important so I could properly enjoy my small brush with posh.

That left the folder. Now that I knew who the bag belonged to, I could see about returning it. I had no reason to nosy any further into her things. No reason at all. But I was too curious about Miss Charles not to.

Inside was a single sheet of Savoy Hotel stationery, a lovely robin's egg blue with elegant printing at the top. The handwriting beneath it, however, was in red and far less elegant — the scratchings of an impatient child, different size letters sloping this way and that, busy with underlines, scribbles and exclamation marks. Surely not what I expected from the stylish sophisticate I'd seen on the Tube. I must have read it a dozen times trying to work out what it was about.

The Savoy

The Strand, London WC2

Title "Prime Number"

CBS 8-2183 (pic sleeve)

Release Date – 16 June 72 !!! (double confirm with Tessa at the press office)

~~OGWT: 30 June~~

TOTP - 15 June*******

coordinate with.... release party. would C like?????

~~Trafalgar Square~~

~~London School of Economics~~

~~Oxford??~~ (Frank – nothing out of town)

~~Selfridge's shoe department~~ (not avail...)

Rib Room on the Thursday???? *

~~Harrod's √√√!~~

Carlton Tower YES! – frank ok for the * rib room –Chauncey, maître d' okay says £300 to arrange

>>>> store thing at HMV???? Later on maybe

>>>> Pre-release leak to Radio Caroline and Lafferty at the Telegraph??

– Send Peel handwritten note

1/2 page Ad buys in Melody Maker, Music Weak (NOT Sounds!!!),

what about the states???

>>>> badges, stickers, posters university berk to explain "prime numbers" (aha!)

album (maybe) title: A Bible of Bumpf (Toilet Paper Bible in the US)

A to Zed

THERE WERE, I discovered, eighteen A. Charleses in the telephone directory, none of them at the right address. She might live with her parents. She could have moved houses or have a married name. So I couldn't ring to arrange the bag's return. And I wasn't keen on wrapping it up and putting it in the post. Then again, I didn't want to go to Chelsea. I had schoolwork to do. I thought again about dumping it on someone in the Underground and letting them deal with it, but I worried they'd nick the good bits and chuck the rest. And then, I suppose, there was always the chance of a reward.

Now that I had worked out the paper was about a record, I wanted to learn whose. I stopped by the newsagents up the road and bought *Melody Maker* and *Music Week* — maybe the "1/2 page Ad buys" were in there. They weren't. But the bloke said there were other music papers, so I scoffed the lot — *NME, Sounds, Record Mirror* — and took them home for a closer look. *Melody Maker* had an article called "Blind Date With Chaz Bonapart" in which he said that hearing the chorus of Genesis' "Happy the Man" might oblige him to "rethink" a song he was working on called "Five Seven Eleven." When I realized that five, seven and eleven are all prime numbers it hit me that perhaps that title could have turned into "Prime Number." Makes sense, right? Maybe maths was good for something after all.

Pop music to me is noise — not the sound, actually, I just don't pay much attention to it. I have a Roberts wireless in my room, but I only turn it on when I don't want Dad to hear what I'm doing, or I've had it with his snoring. Telly? I watch the music shows now and then just to shrink my clueless-prat rating, but I never remember what I've seen. They try so hard to look weird. I don't need to be reminded that I don't fit in with my own kind.

Sometimes I think isolation from that standard element of teendom makes me faintly cool, in a backwards sort of way. If you can't join 'em, make them feel like their club is too stupid to join. Or that you suspect it might be — even though you wish they liked you for something, no matter what that might be.

So while I've heard of Chaz, I can't say that I know what his records sound like, or why he's supposed to be better than Bovril. I guess he's good-looking, in a young dad way, although he dresses completely mad.

I looked at the paper again, guessing that what I had in my possession might be a very big deal, a major concern to a tower block office suite of important people I'll never see in the flesh. I mean, it's not every day that a big star releases a single. Maybe this one'll become a smash hit, the kind of number couples play at their weddings in the year 2000. I closed my eyes and imagined — solely on the basis of the title and my education — how it might go...

"You're a prime number, baby" (and the girl singers go "five, seven")
"We're two you can't divide" ("eleven")
"I watch you sleep, baby" ("forty-seven")
"We can only multiply" ("you're my pri-yum...")
"Let me be your number-one"
"We'll have fun under the sum" ("twenty-three")

I giggled at the thought of it, and even stood up to take a bow for my own cleverness.

As I stared at the purloined notes, my curiosity passed my ignorance on the way to a meeting with lonely indignation. How come nothing exciting ever happens to me? Perhaps now it had. This could turn out better than a polite handshake and a fiver from a snappy dresser who won't remember my name for as long as it'll take her to say it. She must be well off to be carrying all that money. I wasn't a thief nor was I preparing for the teenaged blackmailer Olympics, but I still wanted to see what my find would bring me.

I always believed I couldn't do things, and that put me off trying. Children who go for karate lessons — they don't know if they're going to be kicked sense-less, they just do as they're told. By the time they're ten, some of them have worked out that they can punch with impact. The rest merely learn how much it hurts when you get hit.

Face your fears, bunny. That was Mum's advice. I hadn't ever really taken it because it was easier to fail and let her forgive me. But it had begun to feel pathetic to go there in my head every time I had to make a decision. Enough. Alright Mum, I'll go round and do the deed in person. As scared as the idea

29

made me feel, I rather fancied that I could be someone — even for just a few minutes — in the eyes of such a person. I knew it wouldn't mean much to her (maybe not even to me), but I still had a small rush of pleasure at the thought.

"DAD, I'M SORRY but I can't. I've got to go." Amanda took a small bite of toast and a last sip of tea, grimacing at the eggs and rashers going cold.

"Oh no, luv, you've only just got here. And we've not seen you in ever so long." Mrs Charles gave a pleading look at her husband for encouragement but got none — "We want to hear all about your exciting life down in London."

Amanda rolled her eyes and made a dramatic show of burying her face in her hands. After several changes of plan necessitated by the trains running on a holiday schedule, she'd finally turned up late Monday afternoon, but had immediately gone out for a drink with one of the few schoolmates she still knew in Tyneside. Her mother and father knew better than to make an issue of it; she'd pop off home in a mood if they did. But he needed to say something, if only to prevent his wife's later recriminations.

"Oh, come on, girl. What's so important in London that you can't stay two nights with your old mum and dad? Why not have a nice rest and stay another day? Your mother would appreciate it, I'm sure."

"You look like a twig, luv."

"Mother, I'm fine. Really. But I can't stay. I need to find my bag. I don't want to lose my job. They're all counting on me."

"Where do you plan to look for it? Perhaps you could run an advert or have your publicity friends do whatever it is they do to spread the word." Amanda wondered why she even bothered. Maybe they meant well, but Christ, if they would only shut up and let her get on with it. What did they want from her? "No, I've got to get this sorted. I've got to get back so I can turn up at the left property office as soon as it opens in the morning. If it's not there, I don't know what I'm going to do, but I know I can't get anywhere sitting here in Newcastle with you lot. Plus, if I don't find my bag I've got to buy all my toiletries again. I can't go around without makeup or scent." And then there was the small matter of the £80 she'd "borrowed" from petty cash.

"Oh, dear. Would a tenner help? I'm sure Dad would be happy to give it you."

She ignored the offer and flashed her father one of those smart grins that would buy his loyalty and keep mother from ringing every five minutes. She loved them, sure, like you're supposed to and all, but they were from another world, and could be thick sometimes. "No, that's alright. I'll be fine."

She regretted telling them about the bag, the job, any of it. She resented agreeing to this visit. "I've got to ring work and then Stephen and tell him I'll be on the next train." Rather than endure their looks of disdain for her sort-of boyfriend, she checked her watch and made a rough calculation of distance and travel time.

Without mentioning her current location, she asked (well, told, really), the receptionist to inform Mr Guy that she was off in search of her "purloined pocketbook" and would be in "later in the day," by which she meant tomorrow. She also had a whispered row with Stephen about the importance of collecting her in a taxi at St. Pancras.

It was a long shot there'd be any joy at the lost property office on Baker Street; given the current state of the unions and government bumbling she'd count herself lucky just to find it open. Regardless. Her mother was doing the washing up; her father had relocated to the settee with his pipe and paper.

She needed the timetable that was in her bag; her provincial parents, who never went anywhere, surely wouldn't have one. "Oh sod it, I'll just go down to the station and see what's next to London. There's got to be one soon that'll get me home." Amanda grabbed a jacket off the hook and slipped into it. Grabbing her case, she flew through the door without saying goodbye.

RISING EARLY AFTER a fitful night of plotting and fretting, I moaned to Dad that it was *that* time of the month (I seriously doubt if he knows whether or not I get my period yet, but it's a handy all-purpose excuse and guaranteed question-preventer) and so I'd have to stay home. It's amazing what men's discomfort at girl business can get you.

I got into the shower at eight and came out freezing; the electric fire in my room couldn't melt an ice cube. I pulled on pants, a striped jumper and boots to avoid advertising that I was bunking out of my educational obligations for a day. The white shirt would have been a dead giveaway, so would the blue skirt. It was fun to wear my own kit on a weekday for a change

It was getting on, and Dad hadn't gone out or taken a nap. I picked up the copy of *Jackie* that'd come in the mail (the subscription was a birthday gift from Ruth, as it happens, but I had never renewed and it just kept coming, year after year) and read some rubbish about David Cassidy. I was getting antsy waiting for my opportunity when I finally heard snoring and started my engines. I scribbled a note saying I felt better and decided to go to school after all.

I put the bag inside a Debenham's sack so it wouldn't look as if I'd made it my own and headed off to Chelsea. There were delays noted on a chalkboard due to the construction work at Hammersmith that'd been under way for as long as anyone could remember. Tetcott Road was a good walk from the Tube station, but I finally found it. And a lovely spot it was, at the bottom of a terraced street that ended in a bright green park. One side of the road was a row of white houses; antique shops lined the other. Very posh, I'd say. With a sharp intake of breath, I gathered up my courage and knocked.

No answer.

I tried it again to the same result. It dawned on me that she might not be home but bugger me if I knew what to do about it. Plus I needed to pee. I considered simply leaving the bag on her doorstep, but that was a crap idea. Instead, I scrawled a note saying I had the bag and would return and crunched it halfway into the mail slot and went off in search of a loo. There was nothing on the King's Road; I had to walk all the way to Fulham Road, where I came upon a Marks and Sparks.

Having spotted my salvation, I threw away the Debenham's bag. The toilet must not have been seen to in ages — it looked like a shithole and smelled worse — but I was still grateful. I swear I didn't roll out more than the usual handful of paper, but instead of going down, the flush set my piss flowing over the side onto the tiles. My Docs had been pissed on before, but I didn't move quickly enough to grab up the bag, and it got a good soaking.

Now I *really* had a problem. I tried not to panic and thought for a minute. I took off my jumper (fortunately I had a T-shirt over my bra, and a bra to have a

T-shirt over) and wrapped it around the bag, pressing on it to dry it as much as possible. I left it in the bin and headed for the park by the flat to air out the bag. It wasn't too cold out and there was a bit of sun. I made do.

I tried the bell again, with no joy. I considered giving up, but then I'd have to go through this all again, and I'd already come all this way. I decided to keep at it. But first I needed some food. I had two quid in my wallet, and there was a Wimpy bar near the Tube, so I walked all the way back and had a greasy burger. I sat there for a long time, grateful for the warmth, and then walked back to the park. The sign said it closed at dusk, which suited me — I had no intention of being there past teatime. If I couldn't complete my mission by then, I'd need another plan.

STEPHEN WAS NOT at St. Pancras when Amanda arrived at 3:32. That was hardly a shock: arriving places on time was of little import to him; the fact that it might be to people who relied on him, whose feelings about it might have some impact on how they felt about him, didn't trouble him either.

Amanda knew he was not the best sort of friend, but he had top-quality drugs and was a sharp dresser, great to be seen with, which was high on the list of things that mattered to her. He could be a miserable shit, but that was no missile crisis; she could match him pain for pain, and often did. If the span of self-awareness runs from clueless to full-on narcissist, he inhabited the mid-field — clever enough to censor himself when he was about to say something that didn't flatter his image but equally inclined to say things meant to provoke or offend.

She waited ten minutes, no more — that was her rule — and then headed off to Baker Street, hoping to find the left property office still open. Amazingly, it was. She strode in, head back just enough to raise her chin and lower her eyes, a museum-quality display of imperious condescension, carriage that conveys privilege and grants the bearer a subtle edge in any exchange.

She approached the counter, took a deep breath and explained her situation all in one go to the aged Jamaican man positioned there. When she was done, he shrugged and disappeared through a metal door. After a time, he returned, and shrugged again.

33

"What line did you say that was?"

The query was meaningless; the answer was already fixed.

"What? Piccadilly."

"Sorry, Miss. I don't have it. Until someone turns y'article inna London Transport, there's nuttin' I can do about it."

"No, you don't understand." She began to repeat her speech, but he stopped her with a lowered head, a raised hand and another maddening shrug.

"Sorry, Miss."

With that she crumpled. Pushing her arms down as far they could go, palms up in desperate supplication, she whined, "Oh *please*, you have to help me. I'm not the sort to lose keys or leave brollies in restaurants." She set her jaw to indicate the sincerity of that sentence, notwithstanding its inaccuracy. "You have to help me. You just have to." A tear lined her cheek.

The man offered a kindly look, but then his face hardened. "Sorry, Miss. I can't conjure up your bag for you. I'm no Merlin. Perhaps you should learn to be a bit more careful wit' your tings next time," he scolded.

Her shallow reserve of humility and patience emptied, she shifted abruptly into rage. "*No!!!*," she shrieked. "My life is in that bag, and I'm in a terrible fix. I don't care about the money, I'm sure that's gone, and it wasn't just a few bob. But there's all the rest. I could lose my job. Do you know who I work for?"

The man, all deep-set eyes, greying hair and worn-in wrinkles, could have been seventy or fifty. He shrugged. "I'm sure I don't. Wouldn't make no matter anyways. Everyone alla same to me. I am sorry you're inna fix, Miss, but I don't have your bag. And I'm not the one what left it onna train."

"Right, thanks for pointing that out. Like I don't feel bad enough already. Look, if I leave my number, will you ring me up the instant it comes in?"

The clerk smiled pleasantly but shook his head. "This is the lost property office, girl, not your mum's house. You would do well to check back every few days. We're open half eight to half four, Monday to Thursday; noon to five Fridays. Closed on Bank Holiday."

34

"Why aren't you open every day, like the Tube? I had to wait all weekend and that bleeding holiday to come here, and now you're being completely useless."

He repeated the schedule slowly. "Half eight to half four, Miss, Monday to Thursday. Noon to five Fridays. But don't be turning up at five expecting to get in. If there's a line, we close the doors fifteen minutes early." He picked up and set aside a newspaper open on the counter.

"Bloody jobsworth," she muttered. "Do they pay you extra to be such a fucking useless tosser or do you...you do it for free, just to get back at people like me?"

"There ain't no call for such language, Miss."

"Christ Almighty. No one wonder this country is going down the bloody sewer. No one can be arsed to do their bloody job." She turned on her high heels and went down the stairs into the bustle of Baker Street.

He shrugged and looked at the queue. "Next?"

There was now nothing for Amanda to do but wait until the morning and capitulate to Mr Guy, who would doubtlessly ratchet up the misery ante for her second sacking. Then it would be on to the dole, for as long as it took to relocate a suitable form of employment. A glorious future to contemplate.

She hadn't paid any mind when the BBC raised an alarm about a million people on the dole a few months back; that was for other people. Heath was supposed to get that sorted, but he was useless, that's what her father said. Now there was the distinct possibility that she'd have to sign on.

It was grey and getting on to sundown by the time she finally debarked in Chelsea. Her walk down the King's Road, even skipping the off-licence, was long; it'd be nicer to take taxis, but her pay packet didn't support that luxury. It would cut too far into her weekly budget: £48 minus Tube fare, food, booze and rent equals clothes.

And clothes were the crucial element in the equation. Miss Charles took her appearance as seriously as others take love, money or happiness. She saw it as her creative expression and her social advantage. With the figure of a tall fourteen-year-old boy, she could wear anything and make it look good. She favored styles she'd seen in photos of Jean Shrimpton (who she liked to think

35

she resembled), Jean Seberg, Marianne Faithfull and Peggy Moffitt — a version of the swinging '60s she updated with exaggeration and juxtaposition. As a child, she'd read *Vogue*, not *Girls' Own*, and devoted the money other kids spent on records to fabrics and patterns. She wouldn't admit it to anyone and had sworn her parents to secrecy on the subject, but she was a dab hand at sewing, and had made a good bit of what hung in her wardrobe.

Reaching her door at the end of Tetcott Road, she noticed a piece of paper sticking out of the mail slot. It was probably for the people who lived on the first floor; they were late with the rent more often than she was (or so the landlord said; he was a dodgy sort), so she tossed it aside and reached in a pocket for the key.

The sound of rustling caused her to spin around for a peer into the evening murk. There'd been a rise in petty crime in the borough recently, and the council had put up posters about it. The lights from Westfield Park were not very bright, but she could see a small figure rushing out of the darkness. Amanda recoiled, but the figure stopped a few feet away, clutching the gate. "Pardon me, Miss Charles?"

Amanda could make out a girl, poorly outfitted, panting, pointing, jabbering and — unbelievably, she thought, as she made it out — clutching her lost bag, which looked (and smelled) a lot rougher than the last time she'd seen it.

She took a few steps forward and shouted, "Give me that, you dreadful little thief!" She reached for the bag, tugging it toward her with one hand while shoving Laila away with the other. At the end of an awkward dance and stagger, they landed on the ground in a tangled heap, the bag beside them.

"Owww, bloody hell, I've skinned my knee." Laila sat up and clutched her leg. Amanda leaped up and opened the door. She reached inside and turned on a light, which illuminated the young ruffian sitting on her walk.

"You're a right mess," she said, pointing at Laila's shin. She pitched the bag inside the flat, turned on the light and then looked back at Laila, who was juggling equal measures of fear, excitement and pain. "You'd best come in." She leaned down to offer a helping hand. Laila clasped on, stood up and followed Amanda inside.

The subsequent effort to clean and bandage Laila's bleeding knee was of the three thumbs two left hands variety, a painful ordeal with plentiful quantities of scotch tape and a paper serviette in lieu of anything clean or useful (like a simple plaster) that any remotely competent adult might have provided. Laila knew she'd have to pull it all off before getting home, and worried how much worse it might be as a result of these incompetent ministrations, but she still appreciated the effort and the attention. It almost felt maternal.

Once the bandaging was done, Laila thought she might at least be offered a cuppa. "It was quite decent of you to bring my bag by. I still don't get how you came by it, but I won't pursue that. What's done is done."

Despite her relief, there was nothing about this episode that inclined Amanda to be nice to this teenaged nuisance. Flashing a magnanimous grin whose purpose was to end conversations, settle matters, push people away and leave everyone with a good feeling of having been seen right by, Amanda opened the door and angled her body to encourage egress.

"My name is Laila." She extended a hand and, after a momentary pause, received a flimsy shake. "Like the song? How funny." Laila grimaced. "Thanks so much. Now, if you don't mind, I have to get on with..." So much for a cash reward, even a proper expression of gratitude. As she was being frog-marched out of the flat and back into the night, Laila summoned up all the courage she had and timidly asked the question that had been on her mind all day. "Wossit like, then, working for a pop star?"

Amanda's face fell and, almost imperceptibly (given the paleness of her skin), drained of color. She pulled Laila back inside and kick-closed the door. "You looked in my bag?" The element of incredulity in her voice surprised and stung Laila, but it also opened a wellspring of indignation, borne of the time and trouble spent returning the wretched thing.

Amanda, who had not thought to inspect the returned bag, turned it out on the floor and dropped down to paw urgently through the contents, an attempt to confirm a mental inventory made impossible by the fact that she had no clue what it might have held in the eight months she'd owned it. She made a disgusted face. "What in God's name is that smell?" With a quick check to empty the zips and pockets, she carried it outside to the bin and dropped it in.

That gave Laila enough time to gather her wits. "How do you think I found you, you silly cow? ES bleeding P? Of course I opened your bag." Laila was shocked to hear herself going at this incredible creature, who was not proving to be cool at all. In an aggravated whine, the sound a child would pitch at a mum who'd just packed off a favourite toy to the church for its Sunday sale. "But, but... why'd you have to read my stuff? Some of that's totally hush-hush."

"So now it's our precious little secret, innit?" She had no idea what burst of bravado would spill from her mouth next. It was terrifying, but exciting as well. *This must be what Superman felt when he discovered he could fly, she thought. And, don't be a total prat, all you did was say something a little mean. Not exactly a superpower.*

Amanda could scarcely contain her unhappiness at being compromised by a, by a... "little girl. How dare you? None of this is your concern, you just happened to be the beggar who grabbed my bag. That doesn't put you in my world. Or his. You're just a messenger, and your messenging job is well and truly done."

She cast a newly suspicious look Laila's way and then changed course and put on a beneficent smile. She picked a couple of coins off the floor and handed them over. "That's for your trouble. I trust you'll understand the need for, erm, discretion."

Laila was acquainted with casual ingratitude — Dad said "please" and "thank you" without fail but expected her to fill the domestic hole left by her mother and took her doing the household chores for granted. That never felt fair, and on the rare occasion when she asked for a favour, the scales always came up short on her end. It wasn't that she had failed to do this bit of washing up or hoovering, it was that doing those things didn't earn her enough credit in the adult world. She felt mildly cheated all the time and was used to it. But this posh girl's smug idea that she could be bought off with a few coppers was a short sharp shock, and her face flushed in anger. Caught unprepared with any instinctive response that might have helped, Laila ran out, stopping to pull the crap bandage off her knee and fling it back through the open doorway.

Face Like a Fist

FRANK LEANED back in the armchair and flicked ash into a brass bowl the shape of a crown. He released a plume of smoke with a languorous sigh and reached across his face to scratch an ear with his pinky, narrowly missing an eyebrow with the orange ember.

The face of Francis Christopher Guy looked, for all the world, like a fist. The clenched and bony compression made it a bumpy sphere of imminent thrust. Atop narrow eyes, the brows bore in on a large nose and a small mouth. His bald head — nobbly and scarred, waxed to a luminescent shine — was the thing people noticed and remembered. That and the prominent incisors that made him look a bit lupine.

In most circumstances outside the boxing ring, the fist serves more effectively as a threat of incalculable violence than as a means for actually delivering it: nobody wants to be hit, and the level of that instinctual fear — which typically decreases with actual experience — controls the value of its promise. A young tough might welcome the presentation of knuckles as a challenge, an opportunity to prove himself, while a milquetoast might gladly hand over his wallet in the hopes of evading a pounding. An all-mouth-and-no-trousers wolf might be chased away from a lamb by the balled hand of a third party, where a more confident and determined attacker will stand his ground and do battle, the rough and tumble merely being a cost of doing his business.

In fact, Frank was unanimously described by friends as a great bloke. Business associates thought him a fair-deal sort of guy, a straight shooter. *You always know where you stand with 'im, they'd say. Never the one to start bovver or take undue advantage. You can be assured of a fair shake from Francis.* He was quite well liked in the music industry, an odd attribute for one who could inspire fear. He could be tough as anyone. As Frank himself was given to saying, in the rare times when he'd been underestimated, "I was raised polite not pathetic."

A small bird tattoo on his neck fluttered up toward his left ear. He wore an expensive watch and custom-made boots with an extra inch on the heel that leaned him forward ever so slightly when he walked. On his right thumb was a heavy ring of braided platinum and white gold, a gift from his lover.

It was no secret that Frank fancied men. Women fancied Frank, and rather than shut them out he would enjoy their social company and then make his apologies, call it a night and drive home to Joe. They had a house in Sussex, a few miles past Cotchford Farm, the onetime Christopher Robin pile in the Ashdown Forest owned by Brian Jones. He'd died shortly before they moved in, but that place had been well beyond their means at the time.

AS IF A GEAR had been turned, Chaz put down his drink and turned to face his manager. He relished these private meetings in Frank's handsomely appointed office; better than a headshrinker session, he often said, but a lot dearer. He leaned in, speaking quietly. "I don't want to be admired for what I've done. In the past. That has no meaning for me. I need to show the world what I can do now. I need to *be* the genius people say I was. Am. I'm lashed to a ghost that looks like me. What's gone by means nothing to me now. I won't be a bloody antique, Francis, I won't."

Frank flashed back over the years of hard slog up and down England's motor-ways in Blue Bulldog. The clubs Frank had to threaten to burn down to extract payment. The pillocks he'd bullied to get the band a decent sound mix. A real horror show, it was, up and back from Bristol to Glasgow, Hull to Blackpool. Broken axles, useless bassists, cancelled gigs, crooked promoters, diabolical weather. Nights of total despair, gigs played to nearly empty rooms, the train of drug and girlfriend problems, crap food, guessing how much petrol it would take to reach the next stop. Then one day, without warning or explanation, the clouds parted, and it all got easier. Blue Bulldog was the same band, but its result improved. Top venues that wouldn't give them a look in suddenly had prime weekend slots open. Journalists turned up at gigs. Audiences grew.

Things got good. Then things got great. Result started exceeding effort, first too slowly to bank on, then too fast not to. Massive. Brilliant. It'd been a right ride and when Frank determined that the time was right to jettison the band and take its singer solo, his carefully drawn plans worked as smartly as a

Special Forces raid. After all the hard, hopeless graft, Chaz had his pick of labels, producers, sidemen, gigs, birds. With Frank as a career guide, he was ushered into a glittering city paved with bank notes, where nothing couldn't be had and everything was his for the taking. Frank's shrewd instincts and the advice of an accountant with global connections kept the money faucet pouring into a secure pit that couldn't be squandered, lost, taxed or wasted. It just kept growing and growing, a glorious beanstalk to the sky...

Until...

Until the unfortunate intersection of:

    a) Frank's past association with Reg and Ronnie Kray
    b) A teenaged niece of theirs who always wanted to meet a rock star
    c) A self-important rock star who, all too predictably, ignored the warning to absolutely, positively — no ifs and or buts — keep it in his pants with this one.

That was a fucking disaster. Frank had to get on his knees — literally — in front of Reg to make it right and stave off the bloodshed. And hand over a small fortune to pay for the young lady's future education. If only the cunts on Fleet Street had been of an equally forgiving nature. ***Rocker Robs the Kray-dle*** wasn't even the worst of it. Pages and pages of newsprint circulated in the millions turned Chaz from beloved icon to tarred pariah. They'd even discussed leaving England, but Scotland Yard — which could not find anyone willing to be interviewed on the subject yet pressed an inquiry all the same — strongly discouraged that. If there was any cold comfort in this catastrophe, Chaz finally grasped the truth that he could not follow Frank's direction selectively, it was all or nothing if he wanted to keep at it.

Months after the inevitable career collapse, once the shock had worn off and the guilt drifted away, Frank and Chaz both came to understand that scandal was not the full extent of their problems. Like any canny observer of rock mores, Frank knew that sitting out the penalty on the sidelines for a bit would put the mess behind them, readying Chaz to mount the triumphant comeback. No, the bigger worry was the torpid state of his music, which had got a great launch off the Blue Bulldog pad but was now in danger of being overtaken by the glam girls, prog wankers, art-rock poseurs and pop promoters. He wasn't moving forward creatively and standing still meant falling behind — a dire development route in the fickle sea of teenage loyalty. With platform shoes raising the stature of a new generation, the weeklies and the radio lost their taste for hard rock, making Chaz and his kind a relic of loon pants and manly chest-beating. The '60s were done, the guard was changing, and only a few of the great bands made it through. The Stones and the Who could still get away with being themselves, but lesser lights fell out of favour and were left outside to fend for themselves when the cultural door slammed shut. Chaz grasped what was happening but could not sign on to Frank's vision of reinventing himself. While Led Zeppelin, the Kinks, Bowie, Status Quo and others worked it out for themselves, Chaz railed bitterly at what he considered a personal affront to time-tested and righteous (that is, *his*) values.

FRANK'S PAST, before he'd found Chaz, had also been a difficult campaign. Abusive drunk for a dad, in and out of nick, a very young mum who tried her best but finally couldn't cope with raising two sons on her own and handed the boys off to a sister in the Midlands, a dull realm where intelligence and ambition were discouraged, if not downright shameful, and toughness was the only measure of a lad's character. A couple of years in the Army, an abortive stint as a trainee at an advertising agency and then a dive into London's criminal demi-monde, working in the East End for Ronnie Kray alongside another hard geezer who somehow made the leap from clubland to the legitimate music business, a route Frank watched with keen interest. He kept his eyes and ears open, picking up angles and ideas while keeping body and soul together. Burying our kid, a junkie, at twenty-two, and the sorrows that followed that. A couple of scrapes with Old Bill, nothing serious, a loving but violent affair with a dockworker that ended on a bloody note. Rock and roll was never his thing, but he understood that there was money to be made and that appealed to him. He could look after himself, but he wanted more than the streets could ever provide. He wasn't looking when he found Chaz, he didn't even have a particular service in mind to offer; it just happened, a perfect fish leaping from the sea into his lap. In a flash, he saw what could be done (if not how to do it) and he grabbed on for dear life. Mutual need wrapped around a big, impossible dream made the sale so easy.

Having a pint with some mates at his local in the East End one rainy night, Frank happened to catch what was only the third gig by BaRRy and the BuLLdogs since Chaz — not yet calling himself that — took over as "the new BaRRy," the original one ("with the big Rs," as his bandmates joked behind his back) having pissed off for the steadier wages and hours of an office clerk in advance of a blessed surprise. As Frank watched them slog through poxy blues-rock numbers, he couldn't take his eyes off the singer, who was reading lyrics off a sheet of A4. Even with no idea what role he might take, he knew he wanted in. This lot had stumbled down a gold mine but couldn't see the gleaming treasures it contained. Even if they had, they lacked the tools to bring its riches to the surface. By the time he had drained his pint, Frank had conjured up an alchemical vision for the nice-looking lad in the homemade Savoy Brown T-shirt.

Frank all but pulled "the new BaRRy" bodily out into the fog and drizzle during the interval. While the future Chaz wondered if he should (or even could) fend off the poof's advances, Frank — who was far too buzzed to want anything as common as a shag — made his pitch. "I've never done this before, mate, I'll tell you now. I don't have the first idea how to go about it. But I'll tell you two things, and you can kill me dead if I'm lying. One, I can suss special when I see it, and, two, I've never lost a battle in my life." Arthur, for that was his Christian name, would have laughed at the Peter Lorre melodrama were it not for the burning fury in Frank's eyes. He could see that this hard cunt was serious. A gay shag was now a certainty, and he wondered how much it would hurt.

Frank recognized the unfounded fear in Arthur's face and laughed. "Shit, mate, that's not it at all. Did you...? No, no, I don't want to get a leg over, I want to make you a fuckin' star." Arthur's tension drained off and was replaced by mounting excitement, like the hard-on he got watching a girl strip off for the first time and appraising what was about to become his. This random stranger wanted him to succeed even more than *he* did, and the boy — who was no fool — couldn't help but believe he might. His composure fully regained, he shifted to rocker cool, Terry in *The Wild Ones*. He shrugged. "Go on."

"I promise you I will give it my all. If you've got what it takes, and my guess is that you 'ave, I will do whatever it takes to make your career dreams come true." Arthur, who hadn't considered that he could *have* career dreams until this very minute, had only been in the band for a fortnight and — after meeting Frank — wouldn't stay another.

They came up with his stage name together, flipping through old books in a stall on Portobello Road. Frank, who knew nothing about fashion, sent the lad shopping with a mate who did, and got him dressed in gear that made him look smart. (Well, *smarter*. Funds were not unlimited.) They got to know each other a bit, talking about this and that over pints in the Fire and Brimstone. And then they got to work.

At first, Frank was useless at being a personal manager. Despite the bits of his past that should have prepared him, he lacked the innate instinct for looking after someone other than himself: the ego-stroking, money-getting and problem-sorting. But he had a sharp, shrewd mind and an exquisite nose for bullshit, and he soon cracked it. Hard graft, a publicity campaign that took full advantage of Chaz's looks and the men's interlocked ambitions slowly paid off. Chaz Bonapart entered the new decade a bona fide star, with albums in the charts and a huge, loyal following. It was a fine time to be alive.

A year in, Frank sensed danger, a shadow looming over the yellow brick road. Change was in the air, and what Chaz was doing musically was not so different from a dozen other good-looking geezers. Plus, it was getting old-fashioned. A new generation of pretty young things had come calling, young boys who made a nation of young girls feel safe by wearing *their* clothes onstage (while shagging them senseless in dressing rooms.) The glam bands that popped up in the feathery wake of T. Rex, David Bowie and Mick Jagger played at pooftery, trying on their girlfriends' makeup for a harmless thrill. Sure, some of them would have it off with boys now and again, but they weren't actually queer. In a modern version of blackface, they just played at gender rebellion, bending the rules to prove their fey daring, taking the piss by being fabulous.

Chaz's looks and charisma would guarantee his stature only so long as the punters didn't grow up. He was already too vain to grasp how Peter Pan it all was, so it fell to Frank to do the worrying for the both of them. He kept his concerns to himself, but they did keep him up at night sometimes.

He was taking a bored flick through a porn mag when it occurred to him that his greatest value to Chaz, his secret weapon, as it were, was the ability to see his star in purely sexual terms. Not that he meant Chaz to become a gay icon — that would be far too limiting. Songs and guitar solos were all well and good, but that was workaday stuff. The punters had plenty of choices, and Chaz was far from the most talented or accomplished artiste on offer. It was Chaz himself — the hair, the eyes, the mouth, the trousers and all that promised — that aroused a new stirring in Frank's fiscal vision. Gently but firmly, and without ever revealing his purpose, he pushed Chaz out of the bluesy cock rock that drew in male fans — who could only admire him as a musician, not as a man — and toward jolly pop designed expressly for the knicker-wetters who would come to desire him with every cell of their nubile bodies.

The image overhaul wasn't difficult. Frank got a friend of a friend in to rethink Chaz's look, pushing past wan English ideas of macho — John Wayne would have picked his teeth with Chaz — toward panto androgyny (which, paradoxically, only served to raise his heterosexual popularity). It wasn't a totally daring or original move, but it was a big change for Chaz. Others were getting up to the same thing — the male preserve of rock and roll was suddenly awash in eyeliner, Qiana, satin and towering platform boots — and a lookalike audience was voting at Boots.

The days when long hair was as good as a band badge were gone. Now a splash of facepaint was the mark of musical allegiance. Derisive, then dubious, Chaz finally allowed himself to receive a half measure ("just for a larf") and was transformed into a right queer in all but reality.

The look was easy, but the songs weren't. Mutating the music to be boppy, twee and concise instead of heavy, rousing and endless was direct but painful, like passing a stone. Once it was done — which meant replacing musicians and producers and turning Chaz's head around — it was done. But lyrics were a separate matter. Chaz had never written for little girls (except in terms of their appeal and utility, but that wasn't quite *for* them, was it?) and wouldn't entertain the thought of singing anyone else's words.

After a couple of quick successes that Frank wrote off to past momentum and canny marketing, reality set in. Chaz was willing to overhaul the sound of setlist standards like "Boilermaker," "Two Tons of Rock," "Sloppy Thirds" and "Let Me Lay It on You (Hard)," but the lyrics said nothing of value to the Janes and Elizabeths and Millies who held the keys to his future. Someone would have to come up with new ideas, and it was obvious that it would not be Chaz.

Frank took another drag and exhaled silently. *Christ*, he thought, *what a git. Not even thirty-five yet — leastways not so far as his fans know — and he's whingeing like an OAP.*

The two men, in their shared state of comfortable intimacy, could not have looked less of a piece. One was a colorful flower, marvelous if a bit past youth's fresh bloom; the other a suited-up spiv, who looked distinctly out of place amid the tasteful opulence of his own office. Frank was compact and fit, with broad shoulders wrapped tightly in a bespoke suit of silver-grey flannel which would have flattered almost anyone else, but only made him look harder, a thin disguise that only amplified the menace he could not avoid conveying. Perhaps there was a pile of discarded suits in a tailor's somewhere, ripped seams and dark stains of unstated provenance waiting to be brought back to life.

Lines around his eyes and mouth added years to his thirty-six. The East End accent, its mark of a street life spent rough delivered in a thick, booming voice, moved with deliberate patience through words, shaping each carefully. Even when he was just talking shite, which he rarely did, people paid close attention. Few dared take him for granted; he could have spoken with a lisp and dressed in bunny costumes but his message, intended or not, always came across loud and clear. This was a man you would not test without the utmost confidence that your bollocks were a good bit bigger than his.

"My cupboard is bare. I rummage around for an idea, something to get me going, and there's nothing there, nothing that excites me enough to work on. I might as well be making stone soup — I can go through the motions and still wind up with nothing anybody'd fancy. Everything seems old or phony to me. I can't write another one like 'Power Button.' It's just not in me any longer. And I wouldn't know how to sell out even if I allowed myself to sound like everyone else. I couldn't even do a convincing *Top of the Pops* LP."

That felt like an opening to Frank, a way to counter this rubbish with mockery. He couldn't bear to indulge self-pity, which experience promised would be gone and forgotten, replaced by the more reliable preening arrogance, in short order. But maybe not this time. Frank sensed a deeper lack of confidence, one he could understand if not tolerate. Like one of those heart transplants, the reinvention hadn't quite taken, and Chaz's creativity was unsuited for the new shell he was wearing.

"You're an ungrateful cunt, you are. You've got it all and yet you want more. You're the one with all the gifts and you can't even see it." The disgusted complacency of the exquisitely bored got under Frank's skin, although many others surely thought the same of him. More importantly, he needed to prod the patient a little and see where the sensitivity lay.

"Sorry?" It was not an apology, but rather a request to repeat the last bit. "Call me names if you must, mate, but don't forget that I'm the source of your bank manager's slavish devotion. You could be more respectful."

"Sorry, guv," Frank replied, hunching up his shoulders and mocking the servile tone of a movie gangster's henchman. "I didn't mean nuffin' by it." He smiled, wondering if Chaz caught the irony.

These Friday afternoon chats had been going on for years, whenever both men were in London. Nowhere else, it had to be here in Frank's office. The talks were an important part of their collaboration, a rhythmic governor for the consideration of matters great and small.

For Chaz, it was an oasis from the madness, a chance to take stock with a trusted ally. For Frank, it was often a lobbying opportunity, a relaxed setting to nudge things in the right direction, float prospective opportunities and take his client's emotional temperature. As a breed, rock stars were like race cars or prize stallions: highly tuned machines that needed to be guided by someone who could see the whole track and field. They were, as a rule, diabolically poor judges of their own condition and in constant need of attention, both overt and covert. It was the rare star who could keep a clear head as the air got thinner.

Frank reckoned he understood what was gnawing at Chaz, but he could not grasp how success — as measured in chart positions, expenses, advances, grosses, all that — had lost its magic. In Frank's estimation, being a pop star was as good as it gets. Some might think it a lightning bolt of superpowers shot down from the heavens, like in the comics, but he knew it didn't work that way. He'd lived through the scuffling, the maddening frustration, the hard, thankless graft of going around and around, waiting for the golden ring to suddenly appear for the grasping. He knew what life was like in the before time, but he'd outgrown it, and was now focused on the challenge of keeping the rocket ship in flight, on a safe trajectory to wherever.

But Chaz wasn't wrong about the lack of inspiration. The creeping undertow of his outlook, mixed with the evidently impossible task of addressing a different audience and doing so credibly, had done him in. His latest effort — which Frank had heard a few nights earlier, on a cassette of three long-delayed demos — was dismayingly out of character, pretty much out of bounds altogether. Instead of welcoming a likely new realm of fans, Chaz had chosen to shit on them, and himself. "Let Me Go," "Grip of the Tongue," "The Futile (or was that *feudal*? Chaz was an atrocious speller and all Frank had to go on was handwritten on the tape box) Lord" and "Screw You All, This Is Rubbish."

What initially sounded like a cloud of disgruntled malaise that would surely blow over had become a full surrender to self-pity and disgust. Frank knew that "Screw You All, This Is Rubbish" would never be released, but what if it was? The BBC would ban it straightaway and no one would argue the point. The point of pop music was to make kids happy, not inconsolable. These oddly tuneful expectorations could not imaginably matter to any but his most myopic and morbid fans, the kind who would go through his doctor's rubbish looking for medical waste and lap up even the sourest milk issued from the house of Bonapart. But they were a small group, with no real financial impact. After an unsettling report from the chartered accountant, Frank saw the need for a prompt and sizable uptick in Chaz's income, especially with the likelihood of an ugly faceoff with Inland Revenue come October.

Frank tried the reassurance mode, one of many settings on his star-coddling machinery. "We — you'll — get it sorted out. It's just a matter of unlocking your gifts and getting your creativity back in synch with the punters. What about that song you worked on in Ibiza last month? What was it called — 'Jeweleria'?"

Chaz snorted and drained his drink. Setting down the glass, he slumped lower in the chair. "I would have finished that song had it merited finishing, but it didn't. There was something off from the start, like a rocket shot on the wrong path to the moon. I couldn't make the needed adjustments and it's sailed off into space, never to be heard from again."

The fireplace crackled, incinerating the memory of Chaz's failure. "Did you listen to the new batch of songs?"

Frank wasn't ready to pull that pin. "Oh Chaz, I'm sorry, I started to, but then Joe and I had a row, and I couldn't give them my proper attention."

"I bet."

"Tonight. Swear."

He frowned and looked down. "I'm not exactly sure how I feel about them. I could use your feedback. I think I'm pushing boundaries a bit, and it might be a risky move. Not feeling tip-top in the songwriting department, more like they're writing me than the other way 'round."

"You'll be alright, you will. I'm sure these are great, and I've no doubt there'll be better ones coming. We'll get your engines roaring in no time. *In no time,*" he repeated, a little more loudly. Frank had gotten used to the problems with Chaz's hearing and occasionally thought to stave off his shame over asking for repeats.

Chaz looked at him sharply. "Bollocks. They're my bleeding engines, and 'we' shan't be doing anything about it. I'll sort myself out, thanks all the same."

Frank thought it best to just ignore the scolding, take it as nothing more than an annoying but necessary display of brio, what his shrink called an "ego defense mechanism." Lessons learned in advertising still served him well and made him feel a bit like a chess player who had committed a book of secret plays to memory. He already had a catchy slogan rolling around pleasingly in his head: Elevate Your Expectations (EYE). He knew it would be a hard sell, but long shots didn't worry him. Others could dream things up but had no clue how to put them into action; Frank had both ends sewed up, which kept him in good with his clients, especially the one currently staring at him, awaiting the presentation of an idea worth twenty percent off the top.

A log popped loudly, launching a cascade of sparks from the fireplace onto the stone floor before it. Neither man bothered to check if a stray ember threatened to set the room on fire.

"Are you still bothered about Bolan? Last month? That was quite the display."

"T. Rex at Wembley? Yeah. Probably crap, really, but fucking massive."

Frank knew exactly how massive, down to the shillings and pence of T-shirt sales. An absolute fortune was made that night. And a wealth of even greater possibilities. Although he'd stayed away, he recognized the shaman's magic, a gift that transcended the usual parameters of talent or effort. Bolan sang nonsense, minced about like a showgirl, played guitar like a wanker and had a vast audience that would gladly follow him into the sea. A lifelong partisan of reason, Frank took the hard lesson — logic doesn't always make sense.

Chaz, however, got it all wrong. He took others' success as a personal affront. Getting back in the good graces of Britain's youth was never going to happen for a deep thinker worrying about securing his stature in the cultural landscape. It was there for the taking by the most confident, arrogant bastard that could passably carry a tune, dress well and wiggle a bit onstage. Chaz was no longer that dragon-slayer. Frank was only half listening as he catalogued his anxieties.

"...what works anymore. I'm writing songs even *I* don't want to sing. I can't even imagine what would suit me any longer. I used to pounce on ideas like a trained pig on a truffle hunt, but now..."

"French truffles, eh?" Frank recalled the ill-advised months of tax exile in France that had saved a few guineas but proved unsustainable. A few words of poorly pronounced French was the only long-term benefit Chaz had to show for it.

"*What*? Nothing bangs on me clearly any longer. In restaurants, I have trouble picking what I want to eat. At least my todger still knows which way is up."

Frank wondered if *he* was the one who needed to raise his expectations. Chaz was in greater need of a jump-start than he'd thought.

The fire glowed quietly. They refilled their drinks and settled into a drowsy silence. Then Chaz had another go at it, from an angle that animated Frank's anxiety even more than "Screw You All, This Is Rubbish."

"Dunno, mate. I'm feeling awfully aimless, and in an aimful time at that."

"Aimful? I don't think that's a word."

"What?"

"Is that a word?"

"Is what a word?"

"Aimful."

"How should I know? I'm no more of a uni swot than you are."

"There's a dictionary on that shelf if you care to check."

Frank didn't even bother looking, just yanked a thumb over his shoulder, more at the window than the books.

"No, thank you all the same."

"What you mean is you've lost your way. For a tick. I get it. Not exactly a global crisis."

"Not exactly a what?"

"A global crisis."

"You're bloody right it's a bloody crisis. I'm fucked. It feels like everyone else is sorted and well on their way to a high old time and I'm still staring in the wardrobe, wondering what to put on before I go out."

"'S not like that, mate. You're just having a bit of — what do they call it" (he knew full well what they call it) "self-doubt, yeah?"

Chaz let out a long sigh, redolent of exhaustion and despair. He wanted his pain to be truly appreciated, and Frank's blasé reassurance was getting on his tits. His head hung down for a moment. "And, really...really, why do I do this?"

"That's not a question I've ever thought to ask you, and I'm a bit surprised you would. I mean, isn't it obvious?"

Chaz frowned. "Is it obvious? No, it bloody well isn't. I've had the fame and the birds and the money and all that, but the hit-making thing, it's not just a machine that you turn on and let it run. I – I – have to put some real graft in to it, and I don't see the point anymore. The rewards are fine, but when I'm thinking up bollocks to sing, there has to be something in it, some goal that I'm aiming for. The rewards can't be the all of it. Gigs, sure that's for the dosh, but making up songs and cutting records, there's a bit of an art to it, innit?"

Frank grunted his noncommittal assent and left it at that. *You're not even pointed in the right direction*, he thought, *and you're still useless.*

"I get that it's crap we're after, I'm alright with that. But even crap has to be good."

"You say? Not sure I follow. You should try working in a shop or a garage, that'll straighten your head right out."

"My head? I would if I could. In a flash."

Frank laughed, sounding less kind than he intended to. "You wouldn't last a morning, mate. Trust me. I've done it, and you've not got the bottle for honest graft any longer. It has to be the pop racket for you, I'm afraid."

"I don't appreciate your tone. I'm not that soft a cunt." It was true. Current status aside, none of it was handed to him on a salver. He'd worked hard to make it up the pop ladder, and how did a bit of factory work make his manager a better man? They were both enjoying the high life. He couldn't work out any further answer that didn't sound meager and foolish — grown men arguing over which of them worked harder. Feeling even more useless than when he'd arrived, Chaz got up and walked unsteadily out of the room without bothering to say goodbye.

Going Underground

TEATIME THURSDAY was no picnic at the Hammersmith tube station: ordinary people heading home from work or school, unhappiness baked into the week's grin-and-bear-it, one long day away from the weekend's promise of properly debilitating relief. Although technically the rush hour, trains were in no discernible rush to reach their destinations. A humid cloud of thick warmth enveloped the station, a motionless fug pierced by the sharp aroma of urine, a souvenir of the Chelsea supporters who filled the station after matches.

The waiting faces displayed varied mixtures of resignation and exhaustion; they might well have belonged to Wombles marooned in a desert. The only signs of life came from two uniformed fourth-formers, with a third standing uneasily off to the side, having an animated discussion about teachers and football and telly. Lined up neatly like soldiers several feet from the platform's edge, men in suits solemnly read the *Times*, neatly folded and held firmly at a well-practiced angle and distance. Two middle-aged ladies gossiped furtively, glancing about to check if they were being overheard. A hard-looking suede-head in braces and cuffed Wranglers, one scuffed and scratched boot planted on the wall, stared at the backs of their heads, the menace he hoped to exude undercut by the uncertainty of his knitted brow and weak chin.

Down in its subterranean core, London was dirty, crowded and still not washed clean of the residue of post-war. But the air, an ether heavy with soot, history and the imminence of precipitation, could not damp down the energy and excitement strewn throughout the vast city like shiny beads. The '60s had exploded in a riot of color and fun, a tidal wave of youth sweeping over the nation, pushing back the shoreline of venerated tradition and class privilege.

But the battle of Britain was not won overnight. Just ask the mods and rockers who did battle in Brighton about the great cultural changes they wrought. No, the flag continued to fly; the monarchy stood steadfast and unmoved even as Twiggy, hippies, CND, Carnaby Street and the Beatles all filed in. When the '70s arrived, just like clockwork, a turn of the calendar page paradoxically assured constancy rather than change. Visitors from America, Asia and the Continent were still able to immerse themselves in the theme park Britain of their travel brochures and Terry-Thomas films. But while the surface stayed calm, a generation of disconnected youth peeled off and swam an alternate route just below the surface like sharks.

Meantime, the agents of progress continued to beaver away. Free love had got to be a bore and peace was passé; anarchy and free gender were now on offer, paired with smart clothes, dreams of big money and expectations of a future careening closer, with wild imaginings of things to come in technology and communications.

Given the mechanics of underground travel, London commuters could do no better than be themselves. The daily work of living their lives, getting from here to there, was all this elderly transport system could support. The arrival of a bearded busker added another odious ingredient to the station's gloomy soup: he laid a hat on the floor and began a dolorous falsetto rendition of "Both Sides Now." Halfway through the song, like a jukebox given a hard shove, he switched to mangling "Like a Rolling Stone" at a brisk tempo. A tall man with a small head tried moving in time to the music, a flexible exclamation point jostling those nearby into unwilling acknowledgment of his existence. One older woman moved away, her scowl at being inconvenienced complicated by a look of annoyance and amazement how anyone could dare be so forward in public. A little further down the platform, leaning against a movie poster, a black man shook his dreadlocks and chuckled at the tableau.

Two verses in, having just sung "the misery stamp makes you real size," the busker changed his mind (or perhaps ran out of lyrics he didn't know) and landed on "Fire and Rain." Stymied by the song's slower tempo, the dancer stopped. The grin vanished from his narrow face, replaced by a look of sheepish discomfort. He retreated from the subterranean spotlight just in time to avoid a scrawny and unkempt creature of indeterminate age striding awkwardly past him. The wretch's awkward gait was rather like a march, but with the shaky equilibrium of a person who might be burdened by swaying buckets of water. She lurched as she walked, but straightened, inexactly, each time in what looked like a constant battle to remain upright while unseen forces conspired to topple her.

She had on a long coat, cinched at the waist with ribbon. On one foot she wore a battered plimsoll with a hole that showed toe; on the other a gaudy red pump. The difference in heel heights contributed to her unsteady gait. Her head, carried at a tilt counter to the angle of her body, was topped by a cheap wig, worn askew. As she paraded up and down the platform, she wielded the remnants of a discarded brolly as either a cane or a sword, and hissed a shrill word or two of invective — seemingly chosen at random from a vocabulary assembled especially for this purpose — as she rushed at each succeeding figure in her sights.

"Die!"
"Rot!"
"Fuck!"
"Die!"
"Idiot!"
"Out of my way!"
"Ratface!"
"Waste of space"
"Arsehole!"
"Rot and die, imbecile!"
"Die!"
"Bastard!"
"I don't care if you live!"
"Die!"
"Stupid git!"
"Out of my way!"
"Pillock!"
"MOVE!!!"
"Out of the road, hippie berko!"
"Die! Die Die!!"
"Push off, fucker"

She stopped to stare at a man in shiny trousers, mismatched socks and a frilly shirt, then came out with it: "You must've dressed in the dark, my pretty..."
He flinched and offered a wan smile in defense of his courageous individuality.
She wheeled to face a City gent with juggy ears that propped up the rim of his

bowler. He stiffened and wagged a folded *Financial Times* at her as she took a step forward and narrowed her eyes, like an alligator readying an attack. Her cackle caromed off the tiled walls.

"Cocksucker"
"Dogs bollocks"
"Feeble-minded fucker"
"Minister of shit!"

The skinhead beheld the absurdity of the mismatched gladiators: extravagant lunacy versus buttoned-down propriety. "Fwoah, this looks like a right tussle. You tossers had best get your bets down now."

In a voice louder than he wished to employ, the gent querulously ventured an admonition. "I say, madam, I'll thank you to peddle your foul wares elsewhere. I've a good mind..." — one of those things proper people say when they realize a situation is beyond their control and could get a lot worse. The old bat didn't miss a beat. "I doubt it. Now sod off or I'll kick yer bleedin' teef in." As she had already resumed her march, that reached him over a departing shoulder. All the same, he shuddered and emitted a gasp. That reduced the skinhead to sputtering, and he nearly collapsed on the platform in a puddle of side-holding mirth. The Rasta was chortling as well. "Mary Poppins told you, grandpa. Wha've you gorra say for yourself now? Hahahahaha."

Blushing and ducking his head as if facing a hard rain, the man hurried out of the station, ready to ante for a taxi rather than endure any more humiliation. "I never..." was the best he could do for a parting shot. The skin put up two fingers at the retreating form and then turned it around for a victory sign in the direction of the wacko.

"Fuckin' brilliant. Fuckin' brilliant!" The guy with dreads clapped merrily.

"Ooh, I don't like the looks of 'er," said one of the gossips under her breath. "Don't look. She might come over here."

"I can't help it, can I?" Her friend made a disapproving face at what she beheld. "I wish the Tories would do something about the likes of 'er."

"What are they going to do? It's her wot needs to straighten out. She's already on the dole, I wager. The 'elp she needs..." She trailed off.

"It's not 'er wot needs 'elp, it's us. We need to be saved, not 'er." They both tittered. "Lock 'em up, I say. Take 'em away so's nice people aren't bovvered."

"Why, Catherine, what a mean thing to say. She's one of God's creatures, a poor unfortunate soul. She can't help it, the poor dear."

Catherine started ambling down the platform, anxiously glancing for signs of an arriving train to take them away from all this sordidness. With a last look over her shoulder, Cilla followed a few steps behind. "I hope the train comes soon, my feet hurt like the dickens."

"I wouldn't half mind a WC, neiver, if one were to suddenly appear, with a locked door and a clean sink."

That she would have liked. Otherwise, it didn't really matter if the train came or if it didn't. Life at home had reached a state where being there and not being there were just about equal on the scale of things. Albert was poorly, never the same since his work accident, and his black moods had seeped into the pea-colored walls like smoke. Changing the bulbs had done no good, Catherine was sure the rooms were darker now than the day the lady policeman called, summoning her to Finchley Memorial, where they'd brought Albert, bleeding and pale. He looked a fright, like a flounder on a cutting board, with wires and tubes everywhere, and nurses fussing about. That day the Underground had run like a charm, although she fretted the whole way that it might be worse than they said, and why didn't she take a taxi, like they suggested. Well, it cost a lot of money, that's why not, she thought. And who's to say there wouldn't have been traffic. No, Albert would understand, unless of course he was gone by the time she got there. But she got there, and he was "stable," they told her. He looked awful. They got him back on his feet in no time and sent him home a fortnight later. Good as new, they said.

But he wasn't. All the fight had gone out of him, like a telly with a bad valve showing nothing but a white dot in the centre. He was always a bit of a sad arse, but they'd had fun in the early days, just after the war. Dancing, drinking a bit, a right laugh on paydays. Now he was the hopeless victim of the bad hand work had dealt him (and a piss poor showing by his union, whose support vaporized at the first intimation of operator error. Oh, there had been operator error, alright, but not by him.) The pension was small enough to be a source of anger, not aid, and he decided that he was no longer equal to the challenge of working. So he sat at home, sulking and stewing, making his injuries out to be worse than they were, limping and coughing and complaining. And loading it all on Catherine.

Right after it happened, she was Florence bloody Nightingale, strong and loving, drawing on a lode of kindness nearly two decades of marriage had all but mined away, doing what needed to be done and not minding. But as the months wore on, she wasn't as strong, or as good, as she thought she was, or needed to be, and the unfairness of it all caught up to her. She couldn't go out, she couldn't have anyone over. Their son came now and again but then began staying away, making excuses and then not even bothering with that. And Albert showed no gratitude, making her feel as if nothing she did was good enough to overcome the hurt he had endured. She started to believe it, too.

At first it was conscious, a keep-the-peace effort to settle him down, to not be the object of his bitterness. They shared the misery, and she wanted it that way, not have him be a fountain that spewed bile at her. It was easier to act as if the accident had happened to both of them, and in a way it had. But in time she lost track and came around to his way was of thinking. As the accusations and imprecations she knew to be not true became routine, her resistance to them, a private reassurance of rightness she wrapped herself in each time, like a mac in the storm, wore away. She lost the ability to distinguish between the lies — well, they weren't lies, exactly, more like beliefs she didn't quite share — and her own ideas, which no longer felt very true, either. She'd been saying what he needed to hear for so long that it was impossible to say, or think, anything else. It was like school. Sometimes after she had closed her eyes to fall asleep, she prayed Albert wouldn't need her for anything else.

"I dunno," said Cilla. "All this. You work, you cope, you suffer, right, and then on top of that all they tell you to try and be happy. To do something nice for yourself. I tell you, that's a lot of responsibility. How should I know when it's time to give and when it's time to get?"

"What?" Catherine wasn't listening to the conversation, if they'd been having one, or wasn't expecting its resumption, if that's what it was. "What's that, luv?" The arriving train prevented a repeat, and they boarded silently, pushing past a mother with one on her arm and another clutching her skirt. She looked at the crowds and opted to wait for the next.

A new group of boys came down the stairs and stopped by a vending machine, where they proceeded to have more or less the same conversation as their predecessors. Fans whirred loudly, stirring the smells and the grime with noisy inefficiency.

"Mary Poppins" turned her accusatory tirade to each arriving rider. From time to time she paused to lean over the edge of the platform and look down the tracks, as if it mattered to her whether a train was coming.

"Ladies and gentlemen, may I have your attention please." The speaker was a uniformed clerk, who must have been selected for this chore in appreciation of his booming voice, flanked by a pair of Her Majesty's minions in riot gear, kitted out with rounded plastic face guards and carrying automatic weapons.

"We ask that you remain calm. The Met are investigating a report of — now, again, I urge calm — of a bomb in the station. The official advice for now is that you all remain where you are. The investigation is concentrated on the entry-way to the station, not the platform or the tracks. It has been deemed safer for you to stay where you are rather than for you to exit the station at this time." As he spoke, the riot police shifted their positions, replacing polite advice with armed implacability. Passengers buzzed with animated conversation for a few minutes, then settled into a tense silence. As trains whizzed through without stopping in both directions, travelers moved to what they imagined were the safest parts of the platform, mostly against walls. Only the loony remained in motion, jittering up and down in her purposeless march.

The all-clear was announced after a while, with no explanation of what might have happened or any assurance that it yet wouldn't. Still, the next three trains rumbled through without slowing. With that, most of the passengers opted to take their chances aboveground. New arrivals were turned back by the uneasy faces and brusque warnings of those exiting. Only a few stayed put. A labourer in overalls leaned out over the track, searching for a light in the tunnel. There was a shuffling pensioner; Mary Poppins, still marching and snarling like a rabid dog surrounded by tormentors, a plump Asian woman holding the hands of two small girls and a tall man with stringy hair half-covered by a blue watch cap, who regarded them all from his position next to a bin.

It's fuckin' 'ard to be out 'ere in the world. People don't act right, make no bloody sense to me. Can't walk, can't hear theyselves, don't know the space they take, the shite they say. Mess it up for the rest of us, they do. Greedy, stupid bastards.

He scrutinized humanity, at least the bits of it he encountered on the streets, in parks, on the Underground and in his imagination, and found it all so deficient, so immoral and decaying, so far from the golden rules he'd learned as the son of a pastor in the Midlands, that it made daily life for him a torrent and torment of disgust. Worse than that, however, he judged himself against what he saw, and hated himself as well.

It's not me fault, no. The bastards done this to me, they done. But I should ha' been ready for their bollocks, and I wasn't. I let this happen. They wuz countin' on me to save 'em and I just let it happen. I'm weak. Stupid stupid stu... Not smart enough to know how to do wha' I knows needs doin'.

The man might have been anywhere between thirty and sixty. Between his beetled brow, sallow cheeks, ratty beard and stooped frame, he suggested a latter-day Fagin, save for the squat, porcine nose in place of the requisite Semitic beak of racist caricature.

It's like an ant farm down 'ere. Bugs climb over each other to get where they fink they need to be. I'll get that sorted. I'll scoop out those greedy ants, slow down the ones in an 'urry and pitch 'em straight in the Thames, just leave the ones wot can take their time and get along wiv the rest of us.

He thought of the woman who'd given him the sack, a right cunt married to the boss's son. He always suspected she shorted him in on his wages and he was certain that his final pay packet was thin.

"Fuckin' bint got my fuckin' money! Fuckin' money. Fuckin' monkey. Funky monkey."

The rhyme, spoken aloud, summoned a thin smile from its author, while the thought of money made him reach a hand inside his pants, a quick check that the few readies he had were still safe and sound.

"Mingy stingy, 'at's me."

Mary Poppins stopped a few feet away and cocked her head, parroting "mingy stingy" in a rising, piercing voice. The noise attracted the Asian woman's attention as the man clawed at an itch on his leg, and the woman drew a hand over her mouth at the sight of what she worried might be a solitary sex act.

"Oh my." She stepped in front of her children to shield their eyes as Mary Poppins' broken record started up again:

"Rot and die, imbecile!"
"I don't care if you live!"
"Idiot!"
"Die!"

The man stared back, surprised at being the centre of attention. He said nothing as his face hardened with anger.

"Stupid cow stupid kids....too many. Who told you t'ave 'em. Don't need the brats they just eat and make more. I'll fix it. Very easily done, pick one. Very easily done, pick one. Very easily done, pick one."

Mary circled toward him and continued her rant. A rumble signaled the arrival of a train. The man silently watched it enter the station for a moment, then strode quickly toward the woman and her children, hunched over, his hands reaching down, like a goalie preparing to block a low kick.

"Very easily done, Highway 61, pick one. Easily done, pick one. Easily done, pick one," he screamed.

In a flash, the man swept one of the little girls onto the tracks, into the path of the train. Brakes squealed; people screamed. Without so much as a glance at the carnage, he ran up the stairs.

Rehearsal for Retirement

CHAZ BONAPART strode purposefully into his upstairs music room — which Psi the Clock, the only member of his entourage to have ever set foot in it, called "the wanker's wardrobe," although it was a full eight meters square — and stopped in front of the floor-to-ceiling ballet mirror. Usually, he didn't enter the room in anything other than the latest bespoke plumage, but this morning (which was, by conventional chronology, late afternoon), he had on Black Watch pyjamas from M&S. His long locks evinced a similar lack of effort: roughly collected and pulled back with a band to a nesty effect. So instead of a rock god in full mufti, Chaz was mildly shocked to see a reflection of Arthur Trundle in all his rumpled ordinariness.

He had been feeling decidedly less Chaz-like of late, the potholes of his soul having swallowed, to a degree, the baubles of his outward excellence. While he was perfectly capable of acting the part, he wasn't quite seeing things, or enjoying things, as fully as a man in Chaz's position ought to. Isolation went with the territory — if there were too much room at the top, it wouldn't be such a desirable district — but there were moments of doubt and indecision when it was terrifying to feel alone. Despite the luxurious circumstances in which he traveled and the deference and esteem he enjoyed (all of which he accepted as his due), he had, with increasing frequency, felt small, without vision or purpose. He had been spending a fair bit of time on his own, both by design and circumstance, and solitude turned him brooding and obsessive. And not in a good way. "Get out of your head" was a rallying cry of drug-takers in the '60s, but psychedelics never suited him; trips turned him more deeply inward rather than further out. After a few disastrous experiences he'd sworn off drugs for good. Drink suited him; it just dulled the senses and helped him sleep.

In his down moods, Chaz felt like a hungry person staring at a menu and not seeing a single dish he could get the taste of in his mouth enough to imagine eating. And while he could simply march into the proverbial kitchen and order up whatever *did* strike his fancy, he came up empty there as well. That was the worst of it — not knowing what would please him, what would fill the void of infinite options. Others knew what they wanted (or believed they did). There wasn't anything he couldn't have, but that only made it harder. Half the time, he couldn't tell if he was hungry or just reckoned he ought to be.

Alone at home, he wished he were on tour. There was fuck all to do on the road except follow orders and do whatever was on the schedule. It was all arranged down to the smallest details and felt like fate — everything was worked out well in advance and revealed to him day by day. He had no duty other than to turn up and perform, whether that meant onstage at a gig, a radio station for a friendly natter, a charity bash of some sort, a party or a record company meeting. It was the easiest job in the world.

Once, after the end of a European tour — nine nations in a mad midwinter fortnight's dash — he'd asked the efficiently competent road manager to stay on the books and look after day-to-day things at home, an arrangement that sounded good but didn't work. Imposing structure on a life without having a clear purpose in mind — like getting from Antwerp to Barcelona in sixteen hours, renting a Bosendorfer grand piano (and having it tuned and covered in a champagne-resistant temporary finish to mollify Lloyds), arranging backstage access for a famous bullfighter and his teenaged boyfriend — turned Chaz's days into an absurdly over-scheduled farce, a printed itinerary that included meals, toilette, calisthenics and an hour of "private time" offering such options as (a) reading (b) recreation (c) romance (d) meditation (e) self-examination. With no compelling obligations like (f) rock out in front of ten-thousand screaming punters and collect a big cheque, Chaz found no reason to bother with any of it, and within a week made Frank give the fellow the push, not just from the off-road interval but for good.

Forward motion was good, Chaz knew, but the mechanics of his career didn't matter to him any longer. That battle had been won, and all that lay ahead was inevitable failure. But even that didn't truly alarm him. No, what kept Chaz up all night was much more personal than stardom, it was progress writ small. He missed the feeling of creating, of pulling a catchy song out of the mysterious ether of his mind and having it become a great and glorious piece of British culture. Still, it was less that sublime moment of feeling the pieces of a song fit together so that it flowed sweet and pure, like honey off a spoon. Chaz had no desire to relinquish the privilege and power he'd earned, but he had worked out that it might be preventing him from feeling good about himself.

Growing up poor in a place that scarcely figured in the contemporary culture, Arthur — encouraged by his resourceful mum against the protests of his bitter, pragmatic father — was always making stuff, using castoffs to fashion toys of his own design, working science experiments to learn more than school could offer, building tiny armies out of whatever was to hand to stage intricate wars that proceeded according to the checkerboard linoleum on his bedroom floor. The pleasure he got from giving his imagination form was what lead him to songwriting and performing in the first place, but somewhere along the way the opportunity to create had turned into a chore, one complicated by factors that he couldn't bear to think about.

Psi the Clock wasn't due for a bit, so Chaz rang down for a pot of tea. He stared down at the cold Italian marble on which his bare feet stood and had a flash of nostalgia. He picked a gorgeous old Martin D-28 off the wall and lowered himself into a fading and fraying semisphere of canvas that put your arse a few inches above the floor and required assistance to rise from. He strummed a G, then an A#, and wondered idly what day this was.

Get Back

THE PHONE rang for the what — fourth? fifth? time. Lying flat on her back on the rug, her eyes closed, Amanda winced at the pain in her gut. She let the empty gin bottle in her hand roll away on the carpeted floor and fingered the silver bracelet she had gotten herself as an eighteenth birthday treat, inscribed with an old song lyric — "Don't question why she needs to be so free." Words to live by, but so rarely respected.

Time had gotten away from her. She'd rung Mr Guy the previous morning, but he was out. Bloody liar. Now he could bloody well wait to speak with her. Until she was ready to speak with him. And, yes, that moment might have arrived, but it would still have to wait until her mouth could be made to speak and her eyes open enough to locate the telephone. Her tongue was thick and gauzy, her lips felt like the bloody Sahara. As it rang on and on, she rose and steadied herself enough to run a glass of water from the sink. Well, it was a start.

The next time it rang she was, more or less, ready to face her fate. She imagined how happy he would be to hear her good news. Releasing a deep breath as she lifted the receiver, she said hello and returned herself to the floor in a semi-recline against a pillow.

"Iz zat Amanda?" It was Laurence, Mr Guy's ridiculous French secretary. He said her name as if everything but the final "a" was of no significance. She made a noise. He snorted quietly and said, "Pleez hold for Meezter Ghi," which he alone rhymed with "key."

During the long pause that followed, Amanda put on and removed a pair of sunglasses (twice) and realized that her mouth was hanging open. She closed it. She sat up, switched the receiver to her left hand, found her way up and down into a soft chair, stood up, then sat down again. When Frank came on the line, she jumped up as if her bottom had been bitten.

He sounded like he was clicking onto an intercom. "Yes, what is it?" Even though he spoke slowly, the bluntness of his question disarmed her. She was expecting something more along the lines of "Have you got good news for me?" The speech she had prepared in her head proceeded from there. She would smartly announce, "As a matter of fact, Mr Guy, I do." And he would say something like, "Ah, lovely. Well done. We'll see you in the morning. And let me personally apologize for underestimating you, over-reacting and generally treating you in a manner you don't deserve." Things would be smoothed over, and peace would return to Amanda's little corner of Chaz's kingdom.

This, however, was *not* that conversation. He was abrupt and unfriendly; her words came tumbling out with none of the planned jollity. With not a single reassuring word about her future, he snapped, "Come by Monday afternoon, we'll discuss it" and rang off. A few minutes later, Laurence rang back, fixing a time and confirming her planned attendance so that he could inscribe it in Mr Ghi's "ah-poi-a-mahn buuuke."

THE MEETING, which Laurence rang about late Friday to move to early Tuesday, began with the same disagreeable tone. Rather than offer her a seat, Frank left her standing like an errant schoolgirl. He seemed less interested in anything she had to say than in making her feel crap about it. When she was finally asked to produce the marketing memo (which, to her horror, had mysteriously acquired what appeared to be a curry stain), he stared at it for a full two minutes while she stood mute, then announced blandly that she was welcome to return to work, and that her priority would be seeing to it that the launch was organized sharpish and go off without a hitch. As it was made quite clear that her continued employment rested in no small part thereon, she decided against asking about restoring her pay for the days of her sacking or suspension or whatever it had been.

"Now, before you go, I have another matter to take up with you. Sit." She settled on the settee and put her hands on her knees. She hadn't given the short skirt much thought when she dressed, but anxiety was indiscriminate, and not showing too much thigh was one of those maternal admonitions she'd never completely erased. He put his hands together as if in prayer, but he was staring directly at her. "Right. There's a matter I need to take up with you, and it's a bit...sensitive. I need your word that it will remain strictly between us."

Prospective topics flared in her imagination. An illegitimate child? A drug bust? A new record deal in America? As she waited, a pool of calm settled in her chest. Anything shared in confidence was sure to have value, and she was exactly the sort of calculating strategist who would immediately tick that box.

"Of course." She offered a sweet smile of obedient curiosity. All of the previous irritation was set aside. She was ready to play, whatever the game might be.

"Right. Here's the thing. It has to do with Chaz's songwriting process. He's been, well, you see, dragging his creative heels a bit of late. I need to get him back on track, as it were." It was unlike Mr Guy to faff about, and her sense of their relationship adjusted accordingly. "I've been looking for a way to, erm, contribute to his efforts, to get things moving along a bit better."

Amanda had never considered Chaz's "songwriting process," or even whether he even had one. Didn't he just bang out some rubbish, sling it down between swigs of champagne in a recording studio and then watch as the punters lapped it up, a saucer of milk for the kitties? As it were. "I see. How very astute of you. So how can I be of service?"

"What I think he needs is some outside stimulation."

Amanda hoped her face didn't reveal the horrors that implied. If he was going *there*, she'd soon be gone. She had no intention of shagging that old fart, no matter what it might mean for her overdraft. She held her breath, only to have Frank's pitch take an even deeper dive toward awful.

"I'm...wondering if you know any, uh, young people...Chaz's target audience, as it were. Obviously, we can't simply put him in a room with them for a chat, but I'd like to work out a way for him to get some idea what they're into. I'm betting that if he were to gain a better sense of who he was writing songs for, his lyrics would mean more to them and then he'd feel better — and more confidently productive — about it."

Amanda was enormously relieved that he wasn't asking her to whore or pimp, but this sounded no less ill-advised and probably about as useless. Plus it was well outside her realm. She had no qualifying relatives and certainly didn't hang out with any children. Then a light switched on. She remembered the little ruffian who took her bag. She fit the bill. As her inner calm returned, she flashed a reassuring smile. This would be a piece of piss. "I see. I'll do what I can," she said, conveying nothing more than acquiescence.

"Brilliant. Just give it a little thought, if you would. We'll meet again and sort out the details. Perhaps you can do a little outreach, something discreet via the fan club or a pop paper, that sort of thing. Just so long as neither Chaz nor the press gets wind of it, right? That would be a mess, so it can't happen. Do we understand each other?"

Amanda said she could see how that would be awkward, and assured Frank she would give it a good think. She was getting ready to leave for the second time when Chaz entered, resplendent in a shiny blue silk suit over a purple tank top, his face hidden by oversized round shades and a floppy black velvet hat that would have given Leonardo DaVinci sartorial pause. His hands swung loosely at his sides as he sashayed; a jivey hitch in his stride added a rhythmic shuffle to the promenade.

"Allo, luv, how ya keeping?" There was no telling who this was addressed to. He said it to the air en route to the bar, where he sought to fix himself a Pernod and Gilbey's on the rocks with the comical ineptitude of a *Benny Hill* skit. Amanda didn't know whether to excuse herself, fix the drink herself or sit mutely and try not to gape. Mr Guy offered no clues.

Frank, amused at Chaz's efforts, waited silently until he stopped — "finished" would be an inaccurate depiction of the end of the affair — making the drink. "Chaz, I've some news. We're going ahead with the launch of 'Prime Number' as planned. Miss Charles here has recovered her carry-all, including the missing marketing memo, and so we are back on track. What's more, she'll be staying on with the organization a while longer."

If Chaz had any idea what Frank was on about, or what Amanda's recent history had been, he did not let on. He sipped his drink — which tasted not at all as he had imagined — and waited for Frank to say something that actually concerned him. "That's nice. Good day, all?"

Amanda didn't wait to be acknowledged or dismissed. She got up and left, closing the door silently behind her.

Way Out

"OOH, I'M EVER so worried about the Duke of Windsor; I hear he's very poorly," said Mrs. Aldergate, paying no mind to the clerk waiting impatiently for her to put her purchases on the shelf by the till. Mrs Aldergate was, in fact, turned around to face Mrs Tilley, standing behind her in the queue. A row of women of similar age and demeanor, plus one lanky lad, were clearly stood behind her, but their presence seemed of no greater concern to her than the clerk's mounting impatience.

"Ma'am?"

Mrs Tilley frowned. "He should never have taken up with that woman."

"Excuse me, ma'am, would you care to..."

"I hear the Queen is going to Paris to look in on him next week. What a lovely woman she is, so kind, so thoughtful."

"Ma'am!"

Mrs Aldergate regarded the clerk with a loud sniff, as if both her dignity and her qualifications were being called into question, which — if paying for one's purchases in a timely fashion so as not to inconvenience others was essential to the role — in fact they were. She scowled, seeking her friend's sympathy at the beastly treatment, before setting about unloading her trolley.

She continued the conversation over her shoulder, raising the volume of her voice to where virtually everyone in the store could hear. "Nothing's gone right for that man since he married...that woman." So it was for many of her age: two calm and steady decades of Elizabeth as queen had done nothing to quell the shock and disapproval at her uncle's decision to give up his throne for an American divorcée. It remained an enigmatic thorn in their patriotic side, a tale that, in one view, was as romantic as any 19th century novel — enormous personal sacrifice for unlikely love — but in another, the most extraordinary example of feckless male foolishness in 20th century England. Bloody religious

69

wars, destructive labour actions, post-war deprivation: these were all common aspects of life, regrettable but understandable. But Mrs Simpson and the King? The logic of that remained a complete mystery, one which he would soon take to the grave.

"Ooh, I meant to tell you," Mrs Tilley said once they were finally outside, parked with their trolleys in the middle of the walk. "I saw the most 'orrible thing the other morning. I was on the Tube, going to my sister's house, when some 'orrible beggar attacked a lady at Hammersmith."

"Ooh, that's 'orrible. Was she hurt?"

"From what I could see, she really cracked her egg — blood everywhere, she was screaming bloody murder. I nearly fainted, I tell you. 'Orrible, it was. She really needed help, the poor cow, but I ran right up the stairs and took the bus."

"I don't blame ya. I wouldn't get involved, meself. Best get out while you can."

"No, you're absolutely right. Took me all morning. It was an 'orrible ride, just 'orrible."

"RIGHT THEN, Miss, tell me what 'appened." I was in a room somewhere in the bowels of the Hammersmith tube station with an old bobby who smelled of piss and beer. He didn't seem any keener to be there than I was. But his tone was gentle, which put me at ease. A little. "Take your time."

I brushed the hair out of my eyes and drew a breath. "I had just paid my fare and was going down the stairs. A man charged past me."

"Can you describe 'im?"

"No, not really. Tall. Scraggly hair. He had on a light mac. Your average wild-eyed loony, I reckon."

"You have experience with people like that?"

"No, not personally. I watch telly is all."

"Alright, go on."

"I saw him slam into a woman on the stairs. It didn't look like an accident. He

70

kind of veered to the side, it didn't look like he slipped or anything. He might have shoved her, I dunno."

"Did 'e say anything? Do you think 'e knew 'er?"

"I didn't hear him say anything. She let out a scream as she fell."

"Right. And then what 'appened?"

"I told you. She fell. Down the stairs, arse over elbow. She landed on the bottom, all twisted-up, like. There was a lot of blood." Just thinking about it made my stomach turn over.

"And what did the man do?"

"No idea. He disappeared up the stairs."

"Right. And what did you do?"

What did I do? Bugger all is what I did. I flashed on my Mum, face your fears and all that bollocks, and I couldn't do anything. I felt like a complete zero. Another thing to make me think of my Mum and how I let her die, another lame loser triumph I would carry around for the rest of my days.

I hadn't said any of those things out loud. I don't always say what's on my mind. I don't mean I can keep everything to myself, I can't, but I can't always keep straight if I've really said something or just thought about saying it, so I'm not always certain if people know things or not. It gets confusing, and I get looks. From teachers, mainly. But also from Dad. It makes me think I'm daft, because I don't get why they've lost the plot. Turns out they don't always have the script.

"Nothing."

"Is there anything else you can tell me?"

"The woman was face down in a pool of blood. By her head. A couple of people behind her stopped to look but then walked around her and got on their way. I went up to try and find someone who could help."

That wasn't exactly true. Outside the station I spotted a jobsworth in a uniform and told him a woman was hurt down the stairs. He seemed about as inclined to help as sing me a tune, but the last I saw of him he was headed down the stairs. I don't know what happened after that.

"I see. Very well."

"How's the lady getting on?"

"I reckon she'll be alright. The skin on yer 'ead bleeds a lot, but it isn't as serious as it looks. I was 'eadbutted in a pub once and survived. Lost a bucket of the red stuff and 'ad a blinding headache for a week." He chuckled as he closed the pad he'd been writing my pearls of rubbish in.

"You're a brave girl. Thanks for all yer help. We'll be in touch as our enquiries go along in the event we need to ask you anything else."

I didn't feel brave, and I wish he hadn't said that. I know what I am; fooling other people into thinking otherwise is no consolation. You can't fake courage, you either have it or you ain't. On the way home I kept thinking of Mum. She must have wished I wasn't going to become who I am.

Generation Landslide

LONDON IN 1972 was a city of tribes. In the tradition set a decade earlier by the mods and rockers, and then by the hippies and straights, each faction of England's youth nation had its own uniform, a cloak of unanimity used to declare individuality. Group think, as it long had been, came disguised as cultural isolation. Glam kids had their platforms and lurex, makeup and hair; hippies favored long unkempt hair and loon pants, tie-dye shirts and Edgar Broughton Band badges. Skins sported suede-length (or less) hair, Ben Sherman shirts, braces, carefully cuffed Wranglers and oxblood Doc Martens.

Everyone loved football — pop stars like Rod Stewart and the Rollers actively connected themselves and their fame to the sport, selling scarves to wave at matches and posing on the pitch with their teams — but none as much as the skins. Many of them were in the firms, those rabid supporters who took team loyalty to an extreme and frequently engaged in post-match brawls that had no point other than the macho release of energy, sweat and blood. To be a proper bovver boy, you had to go looking for bovver. They had their own match of the day, and they were always in the scrimmage. Gangs strode through the city, selecting targets based on prejudice, imagined offence or nothing more than opportunity. Those unlucky enough to encounter a bunch of lads out for trouble were likely to be left bleeding, with bruises anywhere a boot could be directed. The intent was not fatal — it was rare that anyone died from being duffed up — and the purpose never clear, except, of course, to immigrants and their British-born children subjected to the vicious urban sport known as Paki-bashing. The unprovoked violence was widespread but concentrated in certain London districts and not occurring so frequently as to be acted upon as a serious public menace. Until one was victimized, it was simply headlines in the press.

A FEW MINUTES past eight on the morning of 31 May, the wooden door of Wormwood Scrubs' inner gate creaked and discharged Desmond "Death"

Fitzsimmons, squinting in the morning sun as he passed between the prison's twin towers, regarded silently, perhaps unhappily, by the bas-reliefs of reformers Elizabeth Fry and John Howard. Folded in his back pocket, along with two tenners, Death proudly carried a formal apology from the Met. In roundabout legal language, it admitted that that he'd been fitted up on the word of a grass who'd lie about the day of the week and later confessed to the GBH Death had been sent down for. After being cajoled, threatened and finally all but begged, Fitzsimmons had agreed to keep shtum in exchange for the termination of two other inquiries into his activities.

Given his past stays at Her Majesty's pleasure, the authorities took weeks to accept that he might actually be innocent this time. In fact, he'd only been free for a few days when he was nicked, having done sixty days for beating the piss out of a student with a spanner over what proved to be a misheard remark in Trafalgar Square. The boy, as it happened, was the deaf nephew of the Indian ambassador, who threatened a diplomatic eruption unless the perpetrator was properly seen to by the CPS. It was an enormous embarrassment all around, and Death had been packed off in short order. The filth saw to it that he had it rough, and in turn he made it hard for them. So when he was hauled back to the Scrubs after barely seventy-two hours of freedom, presumption of his guilt was hard to resist. His rampant antagonism, quick temper and instinctive resistance to anyone in a uniform or a position of authority further impaired the process of clearing his name. But now that it was all sorted he was delivered on this bright morning, unshaven and undaunted, back into the bosom of his tribe.

Seeing his mates across the road who had turned up to welcome him out, he raised his tattooed arms high as he strode toward their cheers and bellowed "Invincible!" Amid the hugs and greetings, they had a right laugh about his letter and his curly ginger hair, which had grown well past its customary length at the insistence of his jailers who, imagining some sort of inverse Solomon effect, had refused to allow a barber to return him to his preferred state of tonsorial abbreviation. (None of his friends knew anything about Fitzsimmons' teen years spent in Glasgow as a Beatles-loving public school boy with collar-brushing curls. It was enough they knew he'd once worked as a junior cleaner on the Piccadilly Line.)

They crossed the cemetery to the Masons Arms on the Harrow Road, where more mates were waiting to get him pissed, ask how it had been inside and tell him about the brilliant bovver they'd had in his absence. Talking over one another, they excitedly shared their tales of mayhem. Maybe none of them would have said it in quite this way, but they knew no greater exhilaration than beating a man senseless in a knockdown brawl decided simply by strength, endurance and guts. That's the top of the animal chain, and any hard cunt can get there if he's fully prepared to inflict — and absorb — pain.

Death proudly displayed his new prison tattoo: off-centre between a small, precise Union Jack and his first one ("None Stronger") was a roughly drawn fist (which unfortunately resembled a sad clown's face). Wisely, they all said how much they admired it.

By mid-afternoon, the money Death had been given was nearly gone. He was well and truly bladdered and issued the inevitable call for a walkabout. They all knew what that meant, and none (least of all Death himself) bothered to consider that he might well land back in nick before the night was out. Live to fight, fight to live, that was their motto. As the hardiest handful of them poured out of the pub into the summer night, Death felt truly alive for the first time in weeks, and he would gladly stoke that marvel at the expense of any unlucky sod who crossed his path.

A few fucked off home, but Death spotted a battered Vespa and teased Mooney, his best mate, about riding with him. "C'mon, luv, hop on and do a little cuddle, what d'ya say?" But Mooney begged off, so Death liberated the scooter and set off on his own down the Westway, headed for Soho, where the day's excitement and the day's drinking caught up with him. As a light rain began to fall, he tucked into a Berwick Street doorway and fell asleep.

Laila Alive!

THE SHOPS OF Soho were brilliant. I went from window to window, reading Italian restaurant menus and wondering about the dirty business people got up to in the neon-pulsing sex shops. I browsed the racks at a news agent, looking for mentions of Chaz Bonapart that might tell me something about Amanda's boss. I bought a kebab through a window and wolfed it down as the shadows got longer.

On Wardour Street, spectacularly dressed groovers stood queued under a sign that said "Marquee." Colorful leather boots, shiny trousers with sewn-on stars, feather boas, velvet jackets cut tight. I asked a girl in gangster gear what was on and she said they were seeing a new group called Rocksy Music. I crossed the street so I could eye the scene.

Twilight led me to consider the explanation of my daylong whereabouts that would be needed upon my arrival home. Really, though, I was none too worried. So long as I turned up with ten fingers and ten toes, unpursued by police or a ponce, with my maidenhood intact, really, what did it matter where I'd been or what I'd gotten up to? And if it was going to be a problem to Dad, so what? Life was the endless sky above, and stray concerns about how any of that could matter to anyone else didn't feel like enough ballast to pull me back to Earth.

My headfloat was interrupted by a cackling laugh I quickly tracked to a hard-looking bloke in a blue flight jacket standing apart from the queue, grinning and pointing, tossing coins at the dandies. Other than the unlucky few who winced at the impact, the rest were doing their awkward best to pretend nothing was amiss.

After a minute, he pivoted and pointed across the road, sort of at me but I couldn't be certain. He waved an arm grandly. "Look at the bleeding monkeys, will ya? All dressed up for the circus!" He turned back. "'Ere, where's your dago organ grinder, monkeys?" He clipped the ear of a boy in a yellow suit with a coin and creased up at the reaction, pounding a fist on his hip to punctuate his mirth. Those nearest to him backed away as much as the narrow sidewalk would allow, glancing furtively, whispering behind their hands. There was loads of them and just one of him, but he had these fey poseurs too scared to speak up. It must be a blast to have people fear you.

"'Ere, you, lassie. Wha' you lookin' at?" All alone at the kerb, I was now certain of his gaze. He drew closer in a rolling swagger, as if his pants were chafing or his bollocks were too large to fit between his legs. I could feel the blood drain as I shifted from observer to object. In a sidelong snap, just as his imposing figure filled my frame, I saw the queue shuffle into the club, the gaily dressed peacocks leaving their big city fears to dissipate into the musky night air as they reached the sanctuary of whatever lay inside.

The world went still and quiet, as if a spotlight had fixed on me. A sour taste crept into my mouth; it was hard to draw breath. My legs went wobbly. "Nothing," was all I could manage. In a few steps he was on me, clenching my wrist firmly in a large hand. Up close, I could see him clearly in the streetlight. He was a right piece of work. Hard and scarred, with eyes that did whatever the opposite of twinkle was. Caught in a muscle-freezing panic, I looked in vain for help but saw only turned backs. I thought of crying out but guessed that would only anger him.

He reeked of sweat and booze and looked like a pirate: scarred, scaly, snarly, loud. He flashed a crooked collection of rotten teeth and laughed — a sad, faraway noise that did bugger all to reassure me that this wasn't going to end badly. He looked me straight in the face but betrayed no expression; I could only imagine the fear showing in mine. His grip wasn't cruel, and I didn't bother pretending to struggle.

"I'm Death, yeah? The last thing you'll ever see. You'll do what I say or you won't live to see the sun rise in the morning." He laughed, but I was still terrified.

"Oh, for fuck's sake, don't wet yourself, girly." (It was probably too late for that. I didn't dare look down, but I reckoned he had already scared the piss out of me.) "I'm not gonna hurt you. Just windin' them up. You don't look like one of those pricks. I fuckin' hate those poofs." He either didn't notice or care that no one was looking at us. Maybe, like the objects of his derision, he always considered himself worthy of attention. He definitely had mine.

"I just got out of nick and I need a bit o' fun." I prayed it wasn't going to be anything dirty. He pulled me roughly across the road, stopping traffic, to the club door. "Let's have a look at what these cunts get up to when they reckon no one from the real world is there to see."

There was no discussion of a membership fee or whether I was old enough for admittance; Death simply leaned in and glared at the bloke by the till and that sufficed. I said nothing. I presumed my chances of survival were better inside with loads of people than alone on the street with this monster.

Those who'd seen him outside widened their eyes and swiftly parted to let him pass; those who didn't move were thrust aside as we headed to the bar, my feet doing their best not to get tangled. The lights were on, so that helped.

"What're you having? I'll stand you a round, little thing." He grinned and let go of my arm. I debated whether that signaled the end of his interest in me or a test that I needed to pass. I guessed the latter and stayed put.

"Cider, please." Having managed that, I registered the low ceiling and dark walls, the heat, humidity and rotten smell. The floor was full, and the stage, what I could see of it, was aflurry with blokes moving sound gear. I relaxed a little, at least to the point where I didn't expect to die in the next two minutes.

"'Ere, gi's two ciders then, sharpish. No larkin' about, boyo." Before the man could finish drawing the pints, the lights went off and the crowd cheered. I turned, thoughtlessly, to the stage, which was filling with the wildest collection of people I'd ever seen: a riot of quiffs and feathers, animal skins, shiny Teddy Boy costumes and space-age gear. I gaped, baffled and riveted, before coming to my senses. Glancing over to check that Death was not looking at me, I thought I could see the barman's face weighing the wisdom of requesting payment. Seizing the opportunity, I pushed headlong into the throng, aiming for the entrance, half-expecting to be grabbed from behind.

Then the music started, and the urgency of dashing out flew away. Excitement lit up the room; the sonic frenzy froze me in place. "*Make me a deal...*" I had to hear more. "*Teenage rebel of the week.*" Definitely not leaving just yet.

I don't think my fear of Death (or death, for that matter) was fully alleviated at that moment, but the adrenaline rushing through me pushed it away. The thrill of it all — what I was seeing, hearing and feeling — was a lot more compelling. (Was this facing my fears or just a terrible miscalculation of the risk? Couldn't say.) I squeezed against a wall between two tall lads in fur coats and kept an eye out for Death, who was raising a glass at the bar.

A poster on the wall by my head identified the evening's bands as Roxy Music and UFO. I didn't know which one this was — either name seemed equally likely to fit what I was witnessing. Getting my courage up (but making sure to stay as far from the bar as I could), calculating that a trip to the loo could be suicidal, I slid between people to get closer to the stage. Up close, I had to admire the outfits and the crazy makeup that made everyone look like a movie star. I looked down at what I had on and thought I should maybe make an effort. I didn't want to be one of this lot but seeing how much better people could make themselves look made me think I might do the same. What if I didn't have to be a total prat my whole life? I wondered what lipstick and eyeshadow might do for me.

A riot of elements — horns, guitars, squonking plinks and bonks, dapper singing, animal noises, drums — were all going at once. I'd seen a symphony orchestra once, and this was a lot less focused. The music was so loud that I only caught bits and pieces of what the bloke banging the piano was singing. With black hair slicked back, a shiny shirt and leather trousers, he waggled his arse like a dog shaking off a bath. He kind of warbled, like one of those real old guys on the records my gran used to play. At one point, they counted off a sequence of numbers that sounded very scientific (and made me think about that Chaz song — maths in the air?). The guitar player's glasses made him look like a big fly, but he played like a demon. Oddest of all was this blonde bloke (leastways I think it was a bloke) wearing angel wings and makeup who was stood facing a pile of wired-up gizmos and tape recorders off to the side.

I had no idea what any of this was, but surrendering to it made me feel more excited and alive than I'd ever been. If this was where pop music was headed, I couldn't see how my generation would be prepared to follow. But I knew I was.

The show ended, and it felt like the sun had set on a bright summer day.

Things had been all colorful and alive one minute, and then silent and grey the next. Made me sad, it did. The audience, which had pushed forward with frightening fervor, dispersed to the bar and the exit. Maybe this was like the up and the down of drug-taking. Possibilities swirled: was it like this every night at the Marquee? Were there dozens of other bands as good as this? I looked at the departing faces to search for answers, but it didn't feel right to talk to any of them. This was theirs. I was just a keen tourist.

I looked to see if Death was still lurking about, but I couldn't see him, or a commotion that would mark his presence. With escape both desirable and possible, I hurried to the street, grabbing the club schedule on my way out.

The layout of Soho has always been a bit of a puzzle to me, but I have a fair sense of direction and reckoned I could find my way to Oxford Circus. The air was warm in the dark, with a thickness that promised rain. Wardour Street led to Broadwick and then to Berwick. As I neared the corner of D'Arblay, a sign I could barely make out in the weak light, I heard a dog barking. I wouldn't have paid it any mind, but the sound was strangled, pitiful; I'm no do-gooder but I guessed the animal was hurt and in need of help.

The road was too dark to make anything out clearly, but then a turning motor provided a flash of illumination. A man had a knee planted on a dog's back, lashing it with a belt. It took a moment to work out what I was seeing, but when the penny dropped I cried out in shock. The man turned and looked. It was Death in a doorway. I'd gotten away only to find him again.

I must have let out a noise. He turned to squint at me. Raising his voice over the dog's strangled baying, he yelled, "Fuck off, this has nowt to do with ya." I wasn't certain if that was true or not, but I stayed put. "He fucking pissed on me," he shouted, as if arguing his case for justified brutality before an invisible street court. I froze as he resumed his vicious business.

Suddenly, all the loose ends of my psyche connected — dead mother, dead space dog, killer motorcycle, cruelty, terror, courage, shame, resentment. It was surely not a conscious thought, and I don't even remember making a decision about what I was going to do or how I was going to do it. All I felt was energy and anger, formed as blinding white light that obliterated the details of my vision. I put my head down and ran at him like a torpedo, nailing him

80

square on the head with my shoulder. He fell backward, and the dog scrambled up, bleeding and baying, its eyes wild. Screaming words I didn't know were in my vocabulary with seemingly inexhaustible breath, I kicked Death with instinctive, random savagery wherever I could see a spot.

He looked to be a solid brawler, but I don't suppose such a hard bloke ever expected to be set upon by a girl. Boozy battles with slags from time to time? No doubt there'd been those, but I'd bet this was different. And to his disadvantage he was currently on the ground. For a moment he was amused and made no effort to rise, but drink must have slowed his reflexes, and it took him a few beats to realize the battle to which he was now joined. Maybe he didn't expect I could do much damage. As he tried to get back up on his feet, ready to flatten me, the dog grabbed ahold of his Levis in his mouth and pulled him back down, waving its bloody head like an insane pinball flipper before dashing back to a safe remove to lick its wounds.

The dog barked — at me, I thought — so I guessed it was my turn. I ran up and put the boot in, kicking Death right between the legs. He howled, and the dog took it as his cue, running past me to clamp his jaws on the same spot. Death screamed and flopped about like a fish out of water. I saw the "None Stronger" tattoo on his bare arm and was about to laugh when I thought better than hanging about. I legged it down Poland Street, running until my lungs were ready to burst. I found a doorway and ducked in to rest. I'd sweated straight through my shirt and smelled like a fishmonger's skip in the summertime.

Riding home, I thought about what had happened and decided that the secret, the thing I'd never done before, was I'd acted without thinking. Don't give it a first thought, much less a second one. Weighing the risks, judging the benefits, considering the angles, those were all stupid excuses for inaction and a recipe for certain failure. Just fucking do it. Just fucking do it and they'll never see you coming. Just fucking do it and then get the bloody hell out of there. That's how to beat the odds. Logic is for losers. That surge of unfamiliar confidence felt like a way to deal when things got bad. I decided I would try and cling to that rule as long as I could. As the Underground rumbled along, I sensed that I had grown up. Not that I planned to go around assaulting skins, but I had gone against every bit of sense I'd been taught and always carried with me and that felt momentous. Maybe I'd finally done Mum proud. She would understand.

81

After all, she had me, and parenthood can't be a decision you weigh too carefully, right? Or you'd never do it. Nearing home, I walked taller and tried on the feeling that I was the sort of girl who faced her fears. I dug that. It was like having a shield, even though it was entirely internal. I could act on impulse and do the right thing. I could only imagine the sort of trouble this might lead me into — I had not properly weighed the beating I might have got had the hound not pitched in — then dismissed that as the kind of fretting that would have stymied the old me into doing nothing. The new me, at least I hoped, would do what was needed without worrying the risks. We'll see how that goes.

Ploughman's Lunch

THE WHEY INN stood next to a petrol station off the M1 outside of Stafford. Chaz's crew, tucked in for a late lunch, were immune to the awfulness of motorway dining. So long as they could save a few bob from their meager per diems, the quality of food or service was of little concern to them.

The drive back to London had been delayed — first by a labour action that held them up loading out of the Manchester Apollo, then by a blinding rain and, adding deflation to defeat, a flat tire that left the equipment van parked in, of all places, a churchyard. After explaining the situation to the vicar, it had taken hours to get the gear inside without a good soaking. Then changing the tire, then loading the whole lot back on. And so the morning had sloped into the shank of the evening. It was coming up on nine o'clock, and the road crew was wet, knackered and ravenous.

The clock's truth to the contrary, the lads were set on lunch, and so lunch it was. The short-tempered Irish waitress nearing the end of her shift was none too pleased to welcome this demanding, boisterous lot. She took their orders quickly and made herself scarce as soon as she'd brought the food.

"So fuckin Cheese couldn't fuckin be arsed to do a fuckin encore, could he. He fuckin well knew the punters'd go fuckin mad and still he fuckin didn't." A fist pounded the table, rattling cutlery. "Left us to fuckin clean up his fuckin mess, didn't he. As ever it was. Fuck."

A middle-aged woman sipping tea at a table nearby blanched and fidgeted, eying the source of this profanity with concern.

Fuckin Phil. A portly Midlander with long, stringy hair he rarely washed, Phil invariably, regardless of the weather, wore a tattered denim jacket and knee-high red boots embroidered with green dragons. If he looked more like a gay biker than a hard rock roadie, it was not his distinctive appearance that people remembered. What made the man a legend and occasionally earned him mentions in articles about those he served was his inability to utter more than a half-dozen words in a row without inserting his cherished expletive. The rest of the crew had long since stopped noticing, but his constant public display of filthy English invariably jarred sensibilities among the more decorous. (The funniest episode, and the one that occupied a substantial chunk of an otherwise dull article about a lame blues-metal trio from Aberdeen in the *NME*, occurred in a train station, when a group of parish priests attempted to save his blasphemous soul — while covering their ears to protect theirs.)

Phil's newish variant on Chaz's name still elicited a few smiles. Gerry, a lighting guy who had recently come on board after being sacked by Black Sabbath and was finding this gig far more agreeable, was as yet unfamiliar with the tenor of Phil's syntax, and mistook the profanity for anger. "'Ere, mate, no need to get all wound up. If I was you, I'd be keeping my frustrations to myself. After all, isn't it Chaz wot pays your — *our* — wages?"

Spatch, whose undeclared role in the road crew was to translate to the outside world, to fill in the gaps left by longstanding camaraderie and close-knit knowledge, thought to explain the special world of Fuckin Phil, but decided not to bother. His sausage was going cold in a pool of HP sauce. It wouldn't have helped. Phil was going to be Phil whether this git understood him or not.

"Oh, you fuckin would you? Then you're a fuckin fool, Gazza. If you fuckin knew what you was fuckin on about you might fuckin know I haven't had a fuckin rise in two fuckin years."

Gerry let it go with a shrug, and shook more vinegar on his chips, splashing a bit into his eye on the upswing. Spatch noticed and laughed. The tea-drinker put some coins on the table and slipped out the door.

"Look at that fuckin weeble weeblin out of the fuckin place. Fuckin hilarious."

Filled stomachs brightened their mood a bit. They had a long ride ahead of them and were in no hurry to get to it. There was no gig on the docket, just put the gear back in lockup and wait for a call. They ordered teas and coffees, and told each other familiar fables, repeated old complaints and speculated worthlessly about the future.

"Hey, gi's a beer, would you, luv," said Spatch, grabbing the waitress's bare leg like a guitar neck. She was not amused. But the humor of the situation was not lost on Phil, whose delight spilled out in a torrent of profanity. The others joined in, and for a minute it seemed as if mayhem was the likely next result. The waitress gave Spatch a friendly poke in the ribs and a broad smile, which was all it took to turn the threat of violence into good-natured foolishness.

"You could have lost an 'and there, Des." In reply, Spatch — whose name wasn't Des (neither was it Spatch, but once he'd acquired the latter, the former became an inevitability; no one on the crew had any idea what name he'd been born with) — grinned widely, showing the space where his front teeth used to be. Lippy, the lone American in the crew, hailed from San Francisco, where he had supposedly been Bill Graham's right-hand man, said something everyone ignored. No one knew his given name; on his first day, Phil took one look at his damaged face and called him Lippy and that was that.

More than a few people had compared Psi the Clock to Charlie Watts, not as a musician, but as the one member of an entourage who could remain outside the craziness without putting any sort of a damper on it. Psi was, in a word, cool. He spoke little, but what he did say was generally worth hearing. Despite the drastic difference in comfort it afforded, Chaz's longtime drummer preferred the company of the crew and travelled in the van more often than with his fellow musicians. And they enjoyed his taciturn company, as a sort of silent pasha of mature wisdom and unflappable cool.

Although an outsider would not have been able to discern it, Psi was friendlier and more forthcoming with the yobbos who humped the gear than with the coddled babies who made a good crust using it. To those he didn't rate, he was as inexpressive as a road dog could be. (Except behind the kit, where he expressed himself ably, loudly and indefatigably.) The guitarist told him what to play, the road manager told him where and when to turn up, his accountant told him how much he had in the bank and his father-in-law advised him on profitably investing it, which he had done to no small success. His girlfriend Abby told him when to shag. He never argued, disputed or demurred, never turned up late, drunk or too knackered to play, never sped up and always put the seat down, so the amount of friction his quiet caused was minimal. And he never complained about anything, leastways not to anyone in the band.

"Hey Psi, ya fink Cheese will go full fuckin monty into girlyboy glam? Might've

85

helped in the fuckin Blue Balls Dog days, right? Start wearing fuckin boa constrictors and fuckin platform boots and fuckin lipstick? Might fuckin help put him back on the fuckin top, ya fink?" It was habitual for roadies to ask Psi questions they knew he'd never answer. It was rather like praying. Over the years, it had developed into a reassuring ritual, and Phil had already turned to his left to ask the same question of Spatch. "Dunno, but it might be good for business," he said softly. He got up and went to the loo.

Lippy started a story about the time Arthur Brown nearly set the Avalon on fire with his flaming headdress but trailed off when he realized no one was listening to him; Phil, as usual, had the floor, recalling how he found three (fuckin) girls in Chaz's (fuckin) bathroom backstage at the Glasgow (fuckin) Apollo and told them he was Paul (fuckin) McCartney, which was good for a (fuckin) shag and an offer to (fuckin) autograph the largest (fuckin) pair of bristols he'd ever seen, only he didn't (fuckin) have a biro, and didn't (fuckin) know how to spell (fuckin) McCartney! The lads fell about at that. They paid the bill and got back in the van. Psi the Clock, who no one had seen leave, was already asleep in his seat.

The Big Lig

TOP OF THE POPS ended, and I went upstairs to change. I wasn't sure what I'd seen (what in hell was the point of Pan's People, other than perhaps to get dirty dads to lurk about and watch the programme from doorways?) and I still didn't feel prepared for what I was about to attempt, but at least now I'd seen and heard the world premiere of "Prime Number" and had an idea of how it sounded. And how Chaz looked performing, which did have a certain flair. My imaginings of the song were wildly off the mark, but the words on the record weren't a patch on what I'd come up with. Turned out the song had bugger all to do with maths, so the title — which made up most of the chorus — didn't make much sense. Dad watched it along with me and he was (no surprise) downright derisive. He hated the show and all of it on principle. He was a bit drunk, which amplified the sourness of his mood. "Poofs... ponces... shysters... imbeciles..." I sometimes wonder if he was ever really a kid.

I'd been planning for days so I avoided the usual faffing about and got myself ready in short order. Inside of a half-hour, I bounded back down and came into the front room. He had switched the channel to a football match and seemed altogether more at peace with the world, as sweaty men knocked each other senseless in pursuit of a ball. Got it. I emptied the ashtray and thought for the hundredth time that he was going to kill us both, smoking and drinking in that blasted comfy chair, the second Great Fire of London just waiting to be ignited by Cliff Russell of East Acton.

He looked near to nodding off. I felt one of those now-or-never surges and gave it a go. "I'm going out, Dad...to the pictures with some mates." I should have left off that last bit. The first half wasn't suspicious sounding, but the second pushed it, testing his powers of blithe acceptance. I'd been to a couple of pictures with "mates" in my day, but it was by no means a routine activity, or one that I could likely accomplish without a more visible expenditure of social effort. I didn't have a lot of mates, so the idea that, out of a dark blue sky, I could round some up to go out on a school night should have raised a bunch of different alarms in the paternal cranium, but this time it passed without notice or comment. He didn't even look up. A right Englishman, he is. Football trumps all, even flesh and blood. I thought I might escape in silence, but first I let out a noisy sneeze. *Hachoo!*

My annual spring cold had blossomed: three days of snot invariably followed by three (sometimes four) days of coughing and then finished off with chapped lips and a red nose. Lovely. I've been reliving this particular horrorshow all my life, once a year, just around this time. I should put it on my calendar. Dad always has the same, usually a week or two later, and blames me for it in a good-natured sort of way. Honest though, it's one of the few father-daughter things we share.

He looked over. "Got a cold, luv?" I was surprised he'd registered it and suddenly worried that he might quash my going-out plans by ordering sick-bed confinement.

"I'll be alright, Dad. Just a sneeze." I went in the kitchen for a tissue. I blew my nose and opened it to check the results — a foul habit, I know, but at least I don't carry a rag in my pocket like some of the boys at school. It gave me the shakes to imagine their mums washing them. Maybe they just bin them and buy new ones each time. There's a growth industry to consider when the time comes. Me, I prefer paper. I jammed a bunch in my pocket.

"Need a few bob?" For a government-funded layabout, he still had a streak of parental consideration that melted my insides a little. I considered taking advantage here, but first I had to sneeze again. I covered my face and made a ridiculous noise into my palm. I felt guilty enough already for lying; taking his dole money to aid in my scheme would only make it worse. We might need to buy food or something. Still, I paused by the door and gave it a think before going on my way. I must be a more terrible person than I even imagined.

The cool outside air hit me; I shuddered with a sudden chill. Never fails. But it was too late to stop now. I wasn't gonna spend the night in my pyjamas with a cuppa and a runny nose. No sir, not tonight.

Having escaped into the world, the rest of my plan wasn't intricate, more of a turn-up-and-see-what-happens on the hunch that it would be fun to use my insider information to catch a whiff of rock star royalty on parade. I rather thought that if I saw Amanda she might get me in to make up for how horrid she'd been and to show how grateful she was. It was all terribly exciting.

I'd put myself to and some to look like I belonged. Probably didn't do the greatest job, but it was the best I could manage without a mum or a big sister to guide me through the girl stuff. Lacking the dosh for posh, I went with the obvious: underneath the jumper I had to wear to escape the house (and stowed behind the bush outside the door so I could safely re-enter it later) I had scissored off the collar and sleeves of an old black T and safety-pinned the bottom of it inside my skirt so the scoop pulled nearly down to my navel. That meant going without a bra. I took a glance down and saw that there wasn't much being hid, and I prayed to Minerva that it didn't rain.

I had more hardware in my bag and stopped in a Basil Street doorway to pin up my school skirt so it came up almost to my knickers. Then I applied tons of mascara and bright red lipstick that I had swiped for this very purpose. I felt quite shit by this point and discovered the challenge of managing a snotty nose with a face full of paint. Wherever this dare-to-be-sexy came from, I'm just glad there was no mirror on the way, 'cause I reckon seeing myself tarted up like that would have knocked all the bottle out of me.

I'd done my homework and found that the party for Chaz that I wasn't invited to was in a hotel off Sloane Square at a posh restaurant called the Rib Room. (They were dead snooty when I rang to find out where it was.) I stood across Cadogan Place, watching as limousines pulled up, chucked out their glamorous passengers and drove away. I could see their faces clearly as they posed for the photographers mobbed around the entrance but didn't recognize any of them, a failing grade on my competence as a teenager. Any of the kids at school could have named them as easily as if they were wearing numbered jerseys.

"Hullo, hen. Waiting for an autograph? You'll need tae try a wee bit harder...Ah don't think any o' that lot is gonna cross th' road on yer account." The owner of this voice stepped back and appraised me in a creepy, old man way. He was awfully fit, though, in a not-creepy young man way. "Or mebbe they would."

I blushed; I'd forgotten how I was dressed. In my head, I was plain old Laila, never worth a second look. But that, it seemed, was not the message I was sending. He put out a hand and faked a little bit of a bow, which was funny.

"I'm Stephen. 'N' ye are?" I looked down. "Laila." I started an ironic curtsey before thinking better of it, given the immodest risks of gravity on my outfit. I awaited the inevitable remark on my name.

"Ye a muckle Chaz fan, then?"

I didn't know what that meant, but I didn't guess I was whatever it was. "Never heard him before today. Tonight. On telly."

He laughed and made a puzzled face. "That's an odd way to hear music, innit? Ye dinnae hae a record player?"

"We do, I do. But we don't have his records. I just needed to hear the new one, 'Prime Number'."

"And how come would that be? Heard about it fae the weans at schule?"

I felt like a girl on the street being interviewed by some Radio 1 berk. While it was taking real effort to understand and answer his questions, I was dead keen to continue the conversation.

"No, the thing is....it's more complicated... Someone I met works...for him..." I stopped as I realized I was rubbing one foot against the back of the other leg. I have no idea why I was doing it, but it hurt and must have looked ridiculous. Wasn't that one of those things girls in movies did when they liked a boy? "She left her bag on the Tube..."

"Wait, you're th' wee yin wha nicked Amanda's bag?" He laughed lightly. "You don't look like a desperate ruffian tae me."

"I didn't take anything. I rescued it and brought it back to that ungrateful...." I stopped myself from saying a bad word. "And what's it to you, anyway?" I heard that line on TV in a crime show from America once, and liked the surly way it came out, like I was the one who might do GBH.

He laughed again, with eyebrows lifted this time. He was really fit. With large, even teeth, he was either the son of a dentist, or a new species of man that would soon put the dental profession out of business.

"I'm nae surprised. Our lassie innae the most thoughtful ingénue at the ball. If she was a box of chocolate, she'd scoff the lot herself."

90

I had never paid boys much mind, at least not in the make-you-feel-like-jelly way, but I was starting to get a sense of what that might feel like. If I was a total idiot, the word "dreamy" might have come to mind. He was like a male Amanda: ridiculously attractive and perfectly dressed, with girlish dimples, an exotic accent and that appalling American assurance that was a key to a successful life in new England. I wondered why he was bothering with me, other than that he was a lad and I was dressed like a slut. And was the only other person standing across from what was clearly the evening's coolest event in London. Perhaps he liked having someone to feel smarter than.

He glanced toward the restaurant, the front of which was now hidden behind a shapeless crowd of shapely women and sharp-dressed men. "Looks like we're th' only ones without invitations tae this lig. What say we gie it a go?" He flashed a big smile, and I smiled back at the weirdness of it all.

My girl bits were in a state of alertness I'd never felt before — full and fleshed out, like I might need a pee, but warm and melty like I was sitting in a pudding fresh from the oven. When he turned away to light a fag, I gave a little wriggle in case my smalls had bunched up and was surprised by the pleasurable tingle that resulted. It felt like an itch that scratched itself. Otherwise, I didn't move. Part of my body might be screaming bloody murder, but the part of my brain that hadn't chucked it all in was still worried about what I might be getting myself into with a complete stranger. I felt woozy, but that was probably my cold. He looked puzzled, so I spoke up in as confident a voice as I could manage. "How do you know who I am?"

"Aye," he chuckled, as if he'd just remembered something. "We used tae go out, Amanda and me, but she gave me the push. Water under the bridge, ah suppose. But now we're mates, of a sort. She mentioned the business with the bag th' other day. I'm feart she was rather unkind about yer part in the mess, but I'd nae be shocked if her telling o' th' story was less than reliable."

"So that's why you don't have an invitation?" Inexplicably, indignation on his behalf had welled up in me. What a cow.

"Ah probably shouldn't hae come, but ah hae dane, sae sod it. If ah can blag my way in, there's probably a good meal tae be had and some fine dram. And ah like being where th' smart set goes. Good for business."

"What business is that?"

"Locks. Ah work at a hairdressers."

"Are you Welsh?"

"I'm fae Glasgow, well, a suburb of Glasgow."

"So, you're Scottish. Sorry. I'm crap with accents."

"Dinna trouble yirsel about it, lassie."

"Are you good at this?" I pointed across at the restaurant, wondering how he planned on getting us inside. It was a stupid question, but his self-assurance implied a well-practiced skill. As I said it, I realized he probably hadn't a clue what I was referring to.

"Dunno. Ne'er tried it afore. Let me hae a blether with th' laddie at th' door."

I laughed at the cheek without understanding the word, but it was starting to matter a lot to me that he be able to accomplish this feat. Even more than my desire to get inside and make Amanda mad, I wanted to be able to receive the kindness of this fit boy.

He grabbed my hand and all but pulled me into the road, where we missed being hit by a taxi and motorbike. (I thought of Dad. That just wouldn't do.) With no evident awareness that death could arrive at any second, Stephen gave me a reassuring smile when we got to the front door of the Rib Room.

Marching over to a guy in a dull black suit, with a clipboard and a plastic card hanging over his silver tie, he leaned in close to speak in his ear, grasping the man's elbow. The man frowned and pulled back, but Stephen pushed in again, a broad smile on his face. Then, like a balky lock finally giving way to a key, the man smiled back, and proffered a green badge with "711" in white. Stephen came over and pressed it in my hand.

"Sorry, but ah could only sort one." My face fell, and he saw it. "Ye take it."

"Really?" I was asking myself as much as him, but it came out more grateful than dubious. "What about you? That's not fair."

"Not to worry. I've been tae a load o' these, 'n' if you've been tae one knees up, you've been tae 'em all. You'll surely hae more fun than ah would. I'll gae

92

home, spare myself th' hangover. Honest, I'm nae bothered. Ah bet you'll hae a brilliant time." He pinned the badge on me carefully, avoiding both injury and affront. A gentleman an' all.

"You're all set. Gae on in. Just behave yerself." He winked and I blushed. "Dae me a favour, wid ye? Gie Amanda a message fae me. Tell her..."

I missed what he said to tell her, distracted as I was by the roar that greeted the arrival of Chaz Bonapart, stepping out of a white Bentley, resplendent in a bright green morning coat. Flashbulbs went off as he stood on the sidewalk, grinning and waving. The noise died down as he strolled into the restaurant. I turned back to have him repeat the message for Amanda, but he was gone.

I took a deep breath and marched up to the door with as much I-belong-here bottle as I could muster. The bloke Stephen had spoken to spotted the badge I had on and waved me in without a second look. For once, I had the golden ticket and I was entering the magic kingdom.

The crush of amazingly dressed people inside the Rib Room must have used up all the air in the restaurant; within minutes, I felt winded and dozy. Meanwhile, "Prime Number" was being played loud enough to push through the stuffing in my ears that worsened with each muffled sneeze. There was no sign of Chaz, but I spotted — and, to my surprise, recognized — two of the blokes who'd been on TV with him. The one that played guitar had a silly little mustache and a massive bleached blond quiff. A pair of shiny gold platform boots made him a tower, easily the tallest person in the place. The other, I think the bassist, was got up as a jockey, with jodhpurs, crop and a black beanie — a right prat. I turned away and saw there was a gap in the crowd at the bar.

I'd never had a proper drink, and wasn't sure why I would want one, but a rush of unsupervised teen courage pushed me forward. I got between two geezers in suits and, when the barman's glance lit on me, asked for a cider. I'd had apple juice before, so how different could it be? And it would probably be the cheapest drink in the place.

"Don't have any, luv. Fancy something sweet, do you?" I nodded. After another chorus of "Prime number, prime number / Pick one, don't be dumber," a large glass filled with ice cubes and a dark red liquid was placed in front of me. I took a sip and coughed.

The men I was fit between took no notice of me. I wasn't sure if I was supposed to move on, hold my spot or simply vanish, but it seemed safest to stay put, so I did, taking a step back, keeping my head down, staring at the glass in front of me, admiring the cork mat on which it stood. The record had reached a quiet part when one said, "He's fuckin' lost it, hasn't he?"

"Absolutely. This one's even naffer than the last one. What self-respecting punter is going to give a toss about this rubbish?"

"I've got to file twenty inches about it tomorrow, and I can tell you now it won't be a rave. But the truth is I like the geezer. He can do better."

"Christ, I can do better." They both laughed. I fought back a smile.

"So, d'ya reckon it's on us to put him straight?"

"Someone's got to. If you set his pants on fire, I bet it brings your standing up at the paper. You don't want to be a compliant lackey all your life, Max." He tipped his glass at the other bloke. I tried to pretend that I was not listening.

"Maybe a call to Bugger is in order." I wondered what that could possibly mean. I know what buggery is, sort of, but who ring for an arsing?

"Perhaps. But it won't be me what makes it. Frank scares the piss out of me."

"You reckon that talk about Chaz being married to some old bird is true? We keep running it in Teazers. It could be one of those rumors so perfect that, true or false, it won't fade away." Without a signal, they both banged their hands smartly on the bar in a bump-ba-ba-bump bump-bump rhythm. It was like some secret code.

"Have you heard the new Sweet single?"

"Oh, yeah. 'Little Willy.' What cheek! Think they'll slip that one past the uptight bastards at Radio One?"

"Well, it's not so obvious that your mum'd know."

"The little girls — and the boys — will understand. Bet it's a huge hit."

"Slang. The secret language of the working class."

"Truly said. Like 'Louie Louie.'"

"'Mother's Little Helper.'"

"Right. The old farts won't suss it but the kids will know it's well out of order and wet themselves listening."

"You reckon Bri's a bender?"

"Connolly? Get the fuck. I was out with them for a week and they go through girls like lager turns to piss. Those lads are pure pussy hounds, I can assure you. All those glam bands, the effeminate thing is just a fuckin' pose, the glitter, the makeup, the fancy dress."

"What a shame. My nan saw them on the telly and thought they looked like sweet boys." They both laughed at the pun.

"I should write about how girls' clothes make the modern man."

"Strange times in the rock biz, to be sure. No one wants to be who they are anymore."

"And why should they? I don't care if the bands are queer or just playing at it. It all comes down to the songs."

"Someone should remind his nibs of that." He tipped his pint in Chaz's direction. They finished their drinks and pushed off.

A tickle in my throat set off a fit of coughing. I covered my face and tried to keep the racket down. The bloke behind the bar turned up out of nowhere and pushed a small glass of something brown at me.

"'Ere luv, this'll do ya good. Drink it down in a go." I did, and it felt like boiling tea, only it wasn't hot. Tears welled up and I felt like I might hack up a hairball. He watched my distress with silent concern. I thought a glass of water would help, but I couldn't make the word come out. I swallowed a couple of times and suddenly felt nearly right as rain. Well, right as rain going sideways — my head was on a slow turntable spinning around the room — but my cold had fled. He put a finger to the side of his forehead and gave me a secret salute. I did it back to him and smiled. Oh shit, how much was this going to cost? He must have seen the anxiety on my face. "It's a lig, darling. Drinks are on the house."

Feeling a bit more courageous, I turned to mingle with the beautiful people. I hadn't got more than five steps when I came face to face with Amanda, who was in full glitter mufti. I couldn't tell if she was fabulous or ridiculous. Maybe both. We stared in each other's eyes for a split second; I was trying to think of what to say when she grabbed my shoulder and pulled me in close.

"How the fuck did you get in?" She smelled like a freshly mowed lawn, with a hint of mint. I reached down and pushed the badge pinned to my shirt up toward her, which had the unintended effect of providing a clear view of my bits to a bloke behind her. I held it high until Amanda saw, then released it, and hurriedly patted myself back into a semblance of decency.

"I know you're not on the list, so you must have stolen that from someone. You are absolutely shameless, you little thief."

I pulled back and put both hands on my hip, leaning forward from the waist. "A fellow named Stephen got it for me. He said he's a friend of yours."

That got a rise. Her face crumpled for an instant and I could see the fight leave her. She gave me an appraising look. "He did? Where did you meet him?"

"Outside. He chatted me up and worked it so I could get in."

"Oh, so now you're trying to pinch my boyfriend as well as my bag. And sneaking into private events where you don't belong. Aren't you a little young to have knockers to wave about?" She looked down and batted lightly at one of them. Since when do girls you barely know touch your bits? I was speechless but tried not to look freaked out. "That's fucking lovely, it is. You're quite the brazen little shit, you are."

I froze. Grownups didn't often speak to me this way. Classmates, sure, in fun, but coming from Miss Hoity Toity, it stung. I stammered out "no" a couple of times, but she was already gone into the crowd.

A few seconds later, she reappeared. "But I didn't see Stephen come in." Her eyes darted about as she worked her memory banks and came up vague. "He wasn't on my list."

"Perhaps you'd best see to that, then," I said, trying out what it felt to be a brazen little shit.

She began to walk away, but pivoted and strode back, like one of those girls in a *Miss Britain* contest. I would have to say she had both poise and pride. She carried herself tall, with her shoulders back and her chin up; remembering both an image and an admonition, I had a strong ache for Mum.

"Come with me," she all but hissed. She grabbed me by the elbow and pulled me through a glass door with the word "Femmes" and a painting of a ballerina. If this was a rich people's toilet, I can only imagine their houses. Everything was gold or marble. There were no bad smells or water stains; I couldn't imagine a surgery so clean. The lighting was soft but brilliant.

With a finger to her lips, she waited for the one occupant to finish and leave. She stood me against the door, so anyone coming in would knock me flat. I don't know why I went along, but then (not that I quite knew it at the time) I was learning what it felt like to be pissed. My head felt fuzzy, with an extra-cottony feel in my ears and a disconcerting lack of stability.

"Look here, I don't like you and I certainly don't trust you. But you need to do something for me." I gave her a scrunched-up face meant to convey all the confusion and displeasure I could manage.

"You know I work for Chaz, right? Well, for his manager, really. We've got a plan for assessing the creative vision of his target audience, see, and I'm the one to get it for him. I was supposed to be getting this sorted but...well, I'm not done working out the details, but you're here, and that gives me an idea. We've got a meet tomorrow, and now I can tell him I've done my bit. All shtum, understand? Not a word to anyone, not the papers, not your mum, not your schoolmates."

I burst out laughing. She shot back a look of monumental disgust that dissolved into a plea. "No, look, you just need to do this. It's simple. No big deal. Just tell me what you and your little mates at school are into, a report from the front, let's call it, and I'll do the rest. You do have mates, don't you?" She took a deep breath. "I can probably get you a few bob for your troubles, if that's what it will take to get you off your arse to do this for me."

I felt a push at my back and stepped away to let the door open. Two women came in, holding each other up. They pushed by us, oblivious, and made for the sink, where they proceeded to spoon powder up their noses. This was the real world, a place where glamorous people took hard drugs in WCs. The sight distracted me, but as I came back to attention, it struck me that the giddiness of drink had evaporated, leaving behind a vision of wicked opportunity, like rubbing your eyes and then spotting a fiver left in the street. A way to stomp on the seesaw and make it rise.

I fixed Amanda with as serious a stare as I could manage and thought of another thing on Mum's list: *Pull the plaster*. I thought the lesson in that was supposed to be about getting the bad stuff done quickly, trading seconds of agony for a needlessly extended bout of discomfort and anxiety. But in the loo, with my head in the fog and my body taking charge of things, I translated it as "do what you want and do it now." I couldn't say if I even wanted what I was about to demand, but I did want to prove something, at least to myself. In the instant, it felt momentous.

"Alright, I'll do it. Whatever it is. But I don't want your money." An evil thought had occurred to me. I wanted to punish her for being a shit and I wanted physical contact with a gorgeous creature and I wanted to feel like I was a person who could get what she wanted just because she wanted it.

"I want you to kiss me. On the mouth." I pointed, just in case my words weren't clear enough. In my mind's eye, I stood back and, in a way that I can't quite explain, admired myself, feeling awe for my boldness. I probably blushed, but who's to say — the mirror was behind me. A knot formed in my stomach.

She put a hand on her slim waist and tipped her head to the side, as if she hadn't quite understood. Her face registered anger, shock, then anger again. It was funny to watch, and I hadn't given any real thought to her acceding. It just felt like a thing to say. She shrugged, looked heavenward for an instant, and grabbed my face roughly in her hands.

Her mouth was warm and soft, and I felt a surge of power shoot through me, a bolt from my face to my fanny. An unfamiliar motor inside switched on, and — to my consternation — seemed to have sprung a bit of a leak. Fortunately, we were in the loo. I excused myself and cleaned up a bit, then followed her back out to the party, where a waiter put a drink in my hand. That's the last thing I recall about the night.

TIRED AND ALONE, Chaz was sat at a large round table in the back of the restaurant, his privacy guarded by a massive bloke whose baleful countenance scared off everyone but Frank, who chatted with Chaz for a few moments and then got up to work the room. A waiter pushing a carving cart laden with joints of meat, knives and sauce cautiously approached. With a nod, Chaz granted him access and did a curious scan of the spread, but then raised a hand and waved him away. A bottle of champagne, open but untouched, sat in a silver ice bucket behind him.

The record had played a half-dozen times, and he'd heard it enough. The "Prime Number" sessions had been a drag. His faith in the song, a relic which had been rejected, forgotten, found, dusted off and given enough of an overhaul to be adequate, did not grow as it took form on tape; by the third day of work, he loathed it. In the playback it sounded like him, like the records that had first set him on the road to fame, but it also felt foreign, irrelevant. Maybe it was just the sound. The style was fucked out of date, he ruminated, as he sat, silent and isolated, while the soirée swirled and surged in plain view. It sounded as if he was singing someone else's music. He didn't believe in the song. But that made no sense: he'd written the damn thing, and it was the best item in the cupboard when Frank insisted that he needed to go in the studio and bang out a new 45 in time for a scheduled summer tour.

"Right, I've had my fill." Chaz said these words under his breath, to no one in particular, patting his knees to finalize the sense of purpose that would carry him up and out of all this. He wasn't drunk, he was just bored. Bored with everything. Bored with the people, the game, the hamster wheel, all of it. Bored at the sound of his own voice, his own music. The public's needs oppressed him; so did his own. Lately, being the centre of attention wasn't always a pleasurable sensation. It felt like sleepwalking. Your body had to turn up, that was easy enough, but your mind and soul, ego, joy and curiosity — they could all decline to attend, leaving the skin and bones to do their duty alone. Some of the musicians Chaz knew skipped all of it when it suited them. While their souls cruised on some other plane, their corporeal beings missed shows, turned up too pissed to stand, too drugged to speak. Even when the chips were down, they still opted to roll the dice and, when they lost, left others to cover for them.

He managed a forced, flashed smile for an alert photographer and brushed passed his bodyguard, whose usually implacable face flashed concern as he looked to Frank, several tables away, for direction. In reply, Frank gave a side-to-side shake of his head and made a patting motion in the air. The stand-down signal finished with a small smile. Thus relieved of his responsibilities for the night, the heavy sloped off to the bar.

Chaz quickly disappeared around the corner onto Sloane Street. The fans gathered across the street saw his departure, and a few followed him at a respectful distance. Walking briskly, Chaz reached Hans Crescent in minutes. He stopped at the top of the left stair of the two attached red brick mansions he owned and turned to regard his (literal) followers, a small clutch of scruffy teens with backpacks and record albums sandwiched under their arms. As they stared up at him, unsure of their role and rights, his heart was briefly pierced by the realization that in some way they depended on him. How sad, he thought.

No. 10, which Chaz called the Tally Ho after *The Prisoner*, was his London abode, a way to sink, protect and enjoy the fiscal benefits of stardom. He'd been obliged to also purchase No. 12, which was attached and shared a stair to the two identical doors. Perhaps it was a hasty, foolish move (his friends were undivided in their conviction about that) but it served the purpose at the time and he'd grown to enjoy it as an oasis in the heart of the city.

FRANK ROLLED OVER and buried his face in the pillow. Ignoring the sounds of Joe showering — an off-key aria from *Pagliacci* competing with the arrhythmic clanging of old pipes — he recapped the evening in his head. The drummer from Slade showed up, plus a couple of producers keen to work with Chaz and a few other minor luminaries. The weeklies supplied the usual liggers to prop up the bar and talk to themselves. No sign of John Peel, but it would have been surprising had he turned up; he was rarely seen outside his radio studio. The five invited fan-clubbers were suitably chuffed but behaved themselves and did nothing to put Chaz's nose out of joint. Chaz appeared to have a good time: he stayed nearly thirty minutes. Frank didn't expect there'd be much cause for him to complain, but you never know. Anything could have got in that head of his.

All in all, things at the Rib Room had gone as well as expected. That didn't guarantee anything, of course. The results would be in the charts, and that element did concern him a bit. With the seasoned instincts of a tout who knows his nags, Frank could sense a potential problem.

"This one isn't happening," he said to Joe over coffee. "I could hear it in the room. Sometimes there's electricity in the air, and sometimes it's like you're swimming in soup. This one definitely called for a spoon."

"Sorry I wasn't there for you."

"Not to worry. It's just work, not real life."

"Did you have to see Chaz home yourself or was his driver sober enough to convey him this time?"

"Neither, as it happens. He left on foot. Robert had the night off. I expect he spent the night on Hans Crescent. I had that in mind when I booked the Rib Room — just up the road from his gaff."

"With?"

"I have no idea. With all I do for that man, worrying about his sex life is simply more than I can bear."

Joe smiled and patted his hand affectionately. "And I, for one, am glad for that."

Frank didn't say anything. He was already on to other matters. Joe was his rock, and that was the main thing.

"You should bell him later and see what he's got up to."

"I'll do that. I'm off for a bath."

"Alright, luv. I've got to go into town for a few things. See you for dinner then."

The water was hot and stung, but that was how Frank liked it. He strategized as he smoked and soaked. The future depended on getting Chaz to relocate himself, from the world he knew and presumably loved, to one he could scarcely discern and would never enjoy. He would need to hand himself over to the imagination of millions who inhabited a world so vivid and easy that they

could each believe they alone had dreamed it up. That was the real trick to it —
creating and satisfying a desire all in one go.

Frank well knew that Chaz had the look and the sound, the charisma and
confidence to push forward. What he lacked was a dream to flog that kids
would buy. He couldn't pretend to be a carefree yobbo or a mystical hippie, a
wideboy party-starter or a pun-spewing wisearse in the Edward Lear mold.

No, Frank told himself, what he needs is the mind of a modern teenager.

English Thighs

MY EYES OPENED to a room they didn't recognize. It took half a second to reach the awful conclusion that unfamiliarity meant I wasn't home, and with it came a tidal wave of dread of what that might entail. As a bonus, my head was clogged and hurt. The brightness pouring in through the thin shades made it clear that night, having long ago fallen, had gotten itself back up and moved on to wait out the day.

In the second chapter of My Idiotic Realizations, I discovered that I was cold, despite a blanket and the radiant spring sun. Sliding a hand under the sheet led to another surprise: I was starkers. I'd never slept without pyjamas before, and nothing in my accessible memory could supply any explanation of why I had chosen to do so now. Or of where I was. The pinball in my head caromed between considering the advisability of getting out of bed, the fear of staying in it, the mystery of where I was, concerns of how I might have got here and how badly I needed to pee. I instinctively clapped a hand over my crotch and sent a warm shudder down my legs.

Now I may be young, but I'm not stupid. I knew full well what it likely means when a young girl wakes up naked in a strange bed with no memory of the pre-sleeping bits. But, surprise surprise, this did not freak me out. At least not yet. I might have been in shock, or just not fully grasping the seriousness of the situation. Good sense would have to wait for a clear head.

My clothes were nowhere to be seen, but there was a terry robe draped over the back of a chair, so after concluding a wobbly visit to the loo, which was just off the room and posh as all get out, I put that on and had a look around. The room was large and swank, with a box of tissues in a gold-colored box. I was blowing my nose (worsening the cotton wool feeling in my ears) when there was a knock on the door.

"Pardon me, are you awake? May I come in?" It was a woman's voice. At least I wasn't being held captive by pirates. I grunted in reply pulled myself up in the bed, covers to my chin. In she came, a lady about the age my mother would have been, only dressed more like my dad. Pants and shirt, short hair, no makeup. Plain, I'd guess you'd say, although her eyes were twinkly. Her skin was soft and smooth. She looked kind and a bit sad. On telly she would have been the quiet librarian left on a shelf who had just been informed that her services were no longer required.

"Hello, my dear, are you feeling alright? There's some paracetamol and water on the nightstand if you need them. I see you found the robe. I'm sorry, but I didn't get your name."

"Laila Russell. Where am I?"

"Oh, frightfully sorry, you must be quite... You're in my house. Well, Chaz Bonapart owns it, but my son and I live here. My name is Willette Poole. Are you a, err, friend of his?"

A strange turn, but at least the dots were starting to connect. "No, I've never met him. But I was at a party last night for him. What's that got to do with...?" I motioned around me and swallowed hard. "Did he...?"

She laughed, but not the kind of laugh you do when something's funny. "Lord, no. I'm sure you're...as pure as you were when you arrived. But you do look a bit pale. A girl who works for him brought you round in a taxi, from the event, which was nearby, or so I gather. It was after eleven and you were well and truly pissed. She wasn't very polite, I must say. Said you'd passed out and she didn't know where you lived, so she brought you here."

"Oh." This was a lot to take in.

"Anyway, I did the merciful thing and put you to bed. How do you feel, dear? I expect your parents must be awfully concerned about you — would you like to ring someone and tell them you're alright?"

I did a quick inventory — head, chest, stomach, etcetera — and none of it felt quite right. But I did want to be on my way, so I made the best of it. "I expect I'll live," I said with a wan smile.

"That's good." I liked how she said that, like it actually mattered to her.

"I need to ring my dad."

104

"Help yourself to the phone. It's on the nightstand. Need anything else?"

I wasn't quite ready to face that music. "My clothes?"

"I'm afraid the skirt needed a wash, and that that shirt of yours was a right mess, all tattered and held together by pins. Not what a young lady should be seen in. I put it in the bin, sorry. I'll find you a frock."

After some scenario cobbling and strategizing, I rang home and, with a bit of fiction in the details, attempted to explain a series of events that I couldn't quite account for myself. Naturally I didn't mention that I'd got pissed. I apologized repeatedly for worrying him and promised never to stay out all night again. Dad was, in turn, furious, concerned and relieved. He offered to come and get me, but when I asked Willette, who I guessed was some sort of maid or secretary to his nibs, for the address, she assured me that he I would be driven home after breakfast. She fed me at a large table with her son William, who was in his first term at Newcastle University. He was an odd duck, wearing these headphone-type things, only bigger, with no wires or anything. I tried to chat him up, but the knob wasn't having any of it. His mum finally explained that he was acutely sensitive to noise and wore airport gear as protection. He wasn't at the table long. If I was him I'd be wanting to know who I was and how I came to be dining in his house without so much as an introduction. Perhaps he was used to his mum taking in strays.

Outside, Willette pointed to the biggest, grandest motor I'd ever seen. I gave her a hug goodbye, and she seemed to like it as much as I did. When the chauffeur opened the door for me I was surprised to find William already inside. The driver asked me, politely, where we were going.

It was weird talking to someone wearing gear meant to keep sounds out, but William was a bit friendlier this time. I don't recall much of what was said, but when we arrived he didn't seem too impressed by the looks of the Russell residence. Balls to that. I said goodbye and thanks and he shrugged in return. I guess when you're accustomed to being carted around in the lap of luxury the common people and their two-up-two-downs don't amount to very much.

Seconds of Pleasure

WITH STILL a few years to go in his twenties, at a time of heady indifference to both risk and responsibility, Stephen Dowery had already lost interest in sex. The problem, if he had bothered to think of it as such, wasn't physical. British youth, finally freed of ancestral inhibitions, had rethought the stiff upper lip and found far more lubricious purposes for their mouths. Starting at what many would deem a ridiculously precocious age, he had joined in heartily, frequently and enthusiastically. A deadly potion of good looks, confidence and indifference made him irresistible to a certain type of girl, and many of them had gladly shared a bed (or a compartment, cupboard, stall or, once, a Tube carriage) with him. Scotland, London, school, work — it was all his forest, and he cut down what he wanted with little or no resistance.

What he had found, he told himself, was that, beyond the unique topography of each example of the female form, sexual pleasure was too contingent on his sensibilities, and after getting a leg over with a couple of dozen bints, he couldn't discern anything to make each one special. Pulling was a diverting challenge until his high success rate took the sport out of it. And once he'd gotten the hang of it, bringing girls (other than Amanda) off became routine, a careful appraisal and a custom adjustment of technique. Women, an unsolvable mystery to so many men, were child's play to him.

More flesh, less flesh, more hair, less hair, tight, loose, wild, quiet — basically, girls were all the same to him. His enjoyment of the act had more to do with his state of mind and his degree of sobriety than the efforts, physique or engagement of a transient partner. The mysteries of life (well, sex), which first seized his imagination as a boy when he accidentally glimpsed an elder sister entering the shower, had been solved by abundant experience. While there may have been countless questions on the subject still to be answered for others of his generation, he had graduated with honors and had no further curiosity. That left him with a clear view of the shortcomings, disappointments and imperfections — in the girls, in himself, in everything.

What he liked was the feeling of getting on with a woman as she opened up to him. It was all social and emotional until, of course, it became literal, at which point the interest in it drained from him like water down a spout. He could occasionally marry an emotional climax to the physical one; more often, he was done with that part of it before the act was under way.

The women didn't care. He had enough natural charm and artificial grace to chuck them out without offence, and if he didn't call again, well, the sexual revolution cut both ways, didn't it? As word spread of his competence at, and dedication to, making women climax, he gained a decisive competitive advantage over his peers, who invariably finished first and did a bunk or fell asleep. Easy as it was for him to feel disgust with them, fed by the litany of appreciative comparisons and tales of incompetence and inconsideration shared by his satisfied partners, the temptation to smugness was tempered by his devaluation of the skills he possessed. Stephen saw himself as a fixit man, able to pry a shuddering spasm out of those who had no clue how to get it from other men. He pitied the girls: they had no clue to help the boys or themselves. They lay there, still as corpses awaiting life, or flailed about like an electrified fish, pursed their lips as if they were about to be sick or screamed like football yobs.

Lacking the supreme concern with his own experience which caused so many of his generation to make a quick and useless mess of the sex act, Stephen was able to make each girl in bed feel special, which he knew was a more powerful tool than size, thrust or endurance. While friends had suggested he could make his way as a lothario, he wouldn't entertain the thought. All the same, sex to him remained a task, like cooking a meal. Depictions of the spiritual exaltation of physical congress in stories made him laugh.

Shagging was never his motivation for being with Amanda. They were friends, which was a highly unlikely male-female relationship for both, and that kept him involved deeper and longer than if she'd just been one of his ordinary girlfriends. He liked being with her better when her clothes were on rather than off, in no small part because she was a perfect dresser and it was dead good to be seen with her. She had a face that turned heads, but style was what made her special. It was her art, her creative expression, the thing she was best at. In bed, she was lazy and blasé; she fucked without enthusiasm or imagination.

Other girls with her looks and arrogance were far more selfish; she didn't put much effort into it. She never lost control, and she never came.

Early in their relationship, which began when she accompanied a friend to the salon where he worked, he assumed some failing on his part and applied himself to the task, but quickly concluded that either she didn't care enough to orgasm or simply didn't want to, and stopped considering it his problem. Their desultory sex charade continued, satisfactory to neither except as the sporadic discharge of a socio-cultural duty. Her attitude about food was equally diffident and detached. Her job got her into the best places in London, but their culinary achievements were all lost on her. "Yah, it was a bit of all right. I had something French that I didn't care for. The coffee was good, I think."

She did like gin, but drinking didn't so much loosen her up as unravel her. She was useless after too many: sloppy, confused, emotionally unpredictable (and not in a potentially amusing anything goes sort of way). Once she had more than a couple in her, the good part of the evening was over, and trouble could be on the way.

Once, visiting his mate Blake's house for a mostly liquid dinner, she'd gotten so obnoxious that he'd gone outside, taken acid and had a few smokes, and returned to find her methodically smashing his gran's dishes into the kitchen sink, complaining bitterly about their "hideous pattern." He hauled her out of there, promising to make good on the damages, got her in a taxi, shagged her at home and went to work without so much as a shower or a kip. That was when he realized it was over. She wasn't enough fun to bother with, and the line between her poles — chilly indifference and crazy antagonism — was awfully wearing. She pretended not to care when he sent her packing but turned out to be difficult to shake. For all her haughtiness and inconsideration, she could take a lot of abuse, doling it back in amplified measure. After a few fraught and occasionally ugly months, they reached an arch accommodation of sorts and became even better friends, immune enough to each other's charms to share gossip, news and secrets without sparking jealousy or resentment. It was a new experience for both but served them equally well.

Work was easy. He washed hair, swept up, did the odd cut and kept accounts at the absurdly named Hammersickle Blowtorch Salon in Bayswater. The pay was decent, the work undemanding and the female pickings prime. The only downside was the endless flirting a good-looking young man was obliged to endure from the great washed. They often got carried away when their heads were in his hands. ("Now, now, calm down," was his routine reply, delivered with a grin. "It's a wash, luv, nae a shag.") He left bang on at five every day, whether or not there was work left to be done, and spent his evenings with girls or mates who valued his drug-selling sideline. He made twice as much moving speed, acid and hash than he did from honest graft, but the two-toned aspect of his existence kept things right where he wanted them to be, shifting from side to side in the middle, never getting too routine or too crazy.

Throw Me a Line

THE MOOD in Frank's office was tense. *Music Week* was on the desk, open to the singles chart, which was noticeably free of any reference to "Prime Number." The sort to face facts and not pretend things were otherwise, Frank saw there was a problem and had resolved that his star's salvation rested on one real girl, not guesses about millions of them. And he knew with equally certainty that this was hardly the moment to share that insight.

"It must be a mistake," Chaz said. "It's got to be in there somewhere." Frank thought he heard a trace of pleading, an undercurrent of weakness in the tsunami of indignation. Chaz had every right to feel a sense of entitlement about the charts, which had embraced him as reliably as an infant returned to its mother's breast, so the shock of rejection was absolutely understandable. But there it was, and no amount of whingeing was going to bring the satisfaction every fibre of his psyche demanded.

"'Fraid not, mate. I've already been on to them, and Turrington swears he's had the store reports checked twice. Not enough sales to qualify." Frank took pains not to personalize the failure, but to keep it abstract, as if it were the vinyl itself that had been too scrawny, too lacking in faith and hope, to thrive in the world.

"*Qualify?* That's a joke. He's having you on." Chaz snatched up the magazine, and squinting at the type, read off titles with exaggerated scorn. "Hurricane Smith? Chakawhatsis? Vicky *fucking* Leandros? I've never heard of these cunts, and *they're* on the bleeding charts? Where the hell am I?"

Frank stared at him kindly, as a parent might regard a child left off the invitation list for a birthday party. "Chaz, you're better than this. You've always had a kind word for your fellow artists."

"Sorry?" Frank knew Chaz was too sensitive about his hearing for it to be a topic that could be discussed but it would be hard to keep under wraps forever. *That* would be rich — "Rocker Can't Hear His Own Music." "Deaf as a Rock." The thought of a device of some sort was, naturally, unthinkable. Still, Frank had got Joe to ring a Harley Street ear quack under an assumed name and pretend that he had a hearing problem so that he could at least suss out the options. The technology had come a long way since the days of ear trumpets, and the gizmos would surely be even better — smaller, less visible, more controllable and with better fidelity — when the time came.

"Sorry?"

"I said you've always been nice to other stars."

"Nice, yeah, but then I've never had to look up the ladder at their arses before. It's not a pretty sight, let me tell you. Chicory bleeding Tip, yeah?"

The failure of "Prime Number" was being portrayed by CBS as a stroke of bad luck, a brief interruption in the parade of commercial triumph that was Chaz Bonapart's fixed station in life. But Chaz himself sensed that something profound had happened, that the plinth on which he had built the majesty of his stardom was crumbling. Frank was well ahead of him on that score.

"It's a mystery to me as well, mate."

Chaz sneezed several times.

"Oh, my." Frank handed him a silk handkerchief. His brow furrowed and his mouth tightened as he turned away, politely, so that Chaz could blow his nose.

"I knew something was wrong when I got up this morning."

"What do you reckon?"

"What?"

"Why are you sneezing?"

"Why do you think? I'm coming down with the grippe, which..."

Frank knew the schedule and was well aware what it would mean to the impending U.S. tour if Chaz fell ill for more than a day or three. "Why don't you go home and get into bed with a nice cuppa and I'll pop round in the morning to continue this."

"My ears are completely stuffed. I can't hear a word you're saying. Like coming down in a plane. I'm going home, but first you need to tell me exactly how

111

you're going to fix this mess you've made. I don't care if I'm sick, I want my damn hit record, and I want it now." With that, Chaz unleashed a veritable symphony of sneezes, coughs and sniffles. Once that was done, he continued, in a resigned voice, hoarse and tentative.

"If I wasn't already worried about losing my touch, I could brush this off and find someone to blame. Soho Square. The Beeb. You. But the charts and the pen-pushers are only confirming what I already suspect." He ended with a sigh, the sound of his confidence escaping.

Chaz so rarely lifted the veil of vanity and bluster to admit vulnerability that Frank felt a profound responsibility, akin to what heart surgeons must undergo while holding that pulsing muscle of life in their hands. Or when priests hear confession. It was the only part of their relationship he didn't control.

Frank took a deep breath, recognizing his obligation — like a deep-sea diver whose partner's air tank has run out — to get Chaz safely back to the surface. Psychology wasn't in his blood, but it was in his portfolio, and this wasn't the first time he'd mucked in to rescue a dying ego. He took a last gulp of whiskey and launched his rescue mission.

"I understand you're a bit rattled, but the solution, mate, is not to declare a loss and withdraw from the pitch. It's nothing serious, and there's nothing wrong with you. You put the wrong foot forward this time, that's all. The shot went wide. Next time will be different, you'll see."

Chaz said nothing, which was not a good sign. Frank took it to mean he was sinking deeper into his own thoughts, which would only increase the difficulty of bringing him back.

"Chaz?"

Chaz got out of his chair and walked to the window, striking a pose of artistic vision and profundity. Frank recalled an idea he'd had, of putting Chaz in a gothic horror picture, one like *Dr Jekyll and Sister Hyde*, not one of those cheesy vampire nasties, and flog it to the parents of record-buyers, so that they, too, might come to appreciate Chaz's talents. That would be a strong approach, he thought, to turn whole families into Chazzies. He could envision whole Chaz-themed holiday camps, a bit like Pete Townshend had conjured up for *Tommy*, only without the spiritual piffle, the pinball or the Helen Keller business. He also had a thought about putting him in as the star of a movie about rock stardom. That'd suit him down to the ground.

"I don't know if I know how to speak to them any longer." Frank made a mental note to add "Don't Know If I Know" to the list of possible song titles he kept and subtly slid into conversations when Chaz was in writing mode.

"Oh, please. Of course you do. You've been doing this a long time" — he glanced over to see if this would be taken as an unwelcome reminder of Chaz's chronological reality but couldn't read the fleeting reaction — "and no one's had more success at connecting with an audience than you. Not Mick, not Rod, not Bowie. You've got the proverbial finger on the pulse..."

Chaz put the rag to his face and sneezed again. "What? Never mind. I'm usually good about this stuff. That cunt at *Sounds*, when he slagged off my last album, I couldn't be arsed."

Frank laughed. "No disrespect, mate, but you could be and you were — angry enough to send a bag of fresh horse manure to Benwell Road."

"I *didn't*," Chaz replied indignantly, knowing full well, as Frank did, that the framed delivery receipt to Spotlight House hung in an upstairs loo of his mansion. Frank fixed him with a comical frown, and they both dissolved in laughter, followed by more sneezing and hacking. Frank got up and poured them both fresh drinks. "You'll be alright, mate."

Chaz's voice was scarcely a whisper. "No, mate, I'm worried this time. Honestly, I wouldn't be bothered by a flopper if I didn't already suspect that my best days are behind me. I know it wasn't one of me best, but I'm not sure. Maybe I've lost the plot for good." He sneezed three times in a row, and mopped his brow, which was damp.

Frank calculated the wisdom of a flip reply and rejected it. His immediate concern was the prospect of postponing the start of a tour. Joe thought Chaz should tour Britain as soon as the record was in the shops, but he'd decided to wait and let it catch on first to bring fans out to the shows, and now he was regretting that gamble, since the failure of one would limit the prospects of the other. But that didn't relieve Chaz of his contractual obligations.

"Not good, mate. This doesn't seem very good at all. You've got a tour to do."

"Can't you at least *feign* optimism? Do you think I'm really that sick?"

"I suspect you are. Your eyes are red and you sound like Noddy. I'm going to ring Dr. Ballence. And while you're resting up, I'll see if I can't find you a sure-fire hit song to record. Just this once we'll save you the bother and get someone else to do the work. We can buy it off 'em and no one will ever know." Frank knew the line he was crossing here, but he was feeling a bit panicky, and it would have to happen at some point. He tried to gauge a reaction but saw nothing useful in Chaz's illness-clouded visage.

Frank clicked a button on his desk and his assistant appeared. With a nod and a word, he conveyed his instructions. In a flash, his driver, Robert, turned up to get Chaz home and tucked in. Then Frank got on to the booking agency to tell them they'd best get to work rescheduling the first week of dates in the States.

Mend Your Manors

CHAZ WAS utter rubbish at being ill, no better than an irritable infant, mad at everyone for his misery. There was little for him to do or say, until he recovered from what Dr. Ballence almost gleefully declared "one of the worst cases of strep throat" he'd seen in thirty years of practice.

"Delighted to hear that you're impressed," said Frank dryly. Dr. B was a valued resource, but his exorbitant fees did not include any allotment for empathy. Popular among the London rock mob, the man about whom John Lennon had written "Dr. Robert" was a crusty old Manc with cold hands and a bushy beard. He could always be relied on for discretion, as well as flexibility when it came to prescribing drugs that might not be strictly called for, medically speaking.

So, singing was out. So were girls, the public, travel and pretty much every other diversion that might have helped Chaz pass the time. It didn't take long for his patience to overcome his incapacity, and after several irritable days of bed rest and top-notch nursing care, he escaped home confinement and took to dropping by Frank's office, much to the consternation of staff. There was no pleasure in being able to trace the provenance of one's influenza to a pop star; no one down the pub would be favorably disposed to the acquisition of a contagious disease, no matter who passed it along. Frank attempted to persuade Chaz that the germs had been delivered to him, as if by divine summons, to show human frailty; a humbling reminder that no one was immune from illness, not even the idol of millions. On a whim, he floated the idea of Chaz funding a hospital wing somewhere, but that got nowhere.

With the high probability of contagion, Frank warned Joe of Chaz's condition and arranged for Ballence to give them both prophylactic vitamin shots. The shots cost twenty quid each and contained God knows what. But it was a good job they got them, as neither took ill.

After a week, if not in full fettle, Chaz was at least fever-free and reasonably clear-headed. With the rescheduled tour looming, Frank decided it was time to do something. After a few gentle soundings of the state of Chaz's ego and outlook, he saw that the window of opportunity was open. As soon as Chaz strolled in for their regular chinwag, his hangdog look promising another long after-noon of sighing and complaining, Frank leaped up, threw an arm around his shoulders, and said, "Let's go for a drive."

Chaz frowned and thought for a moment. "We'll take mine, yeah?" Frank ignored that; his car was already idling outside.

Chaz paused briefly by the rear door, pointedly feigning the expectant look of a toff waiting for it to be opened. Frank rolled his eyes heavenward, like a well-rehearsed vaudevillian, opened it, and then slid in, leaving Chaz to sputter on the pavement before joining him. They'd played this game many times, a wry touchstone in a relationship that had grown both more complicated and simpler in the years they'd been together. Frank didn't mind bending his will now and again so long as he could enjoy the ego-salvaging privilege of jokey disrespect, while Chaz retained at least the semblance of the *droit du seigneur* entitlements of his position. Both men veiled their roles in this charade in face-saving irony, and each felt himself the better man for not making an issue of it.

As they set off, Frank began with a diversion. "I get that songs aren't coming to you so easily at the moment. I'm sure that'll change. But tell me, just so I know where we're trying to go and all, what do you want to accomplish? Not the easy stuff, that's just a matter of ringing the accountant and having a cheque cut, I mean the big idea. What's your big idea, Chaz? Your really *grand* idea?"

Frank didn't expect an answer; in fact, he was counting on there being none. His idea was to send Chaz ambling down a dead-end street so he would be grateful for the offer of a way back. Bait-and-switch mind games, worry-and-save, they were all tools of the trade. He was surprised when Chaz didn't just shrug it off like an ill-fitting jacket and instead mustered a serious reply. "Success is lovely and all, but what does it prove? It doesn't mean that you're talented or the work you're doing is good. Just that sods will buy it. They sell loads of HP Sauce, right, but does the bloke who mixes it up feel any great satisfaction about what he's doing? I'm not even sure records are as significant as that. Certainly not the rubbish I strive to polish for the sweet teeth of children too thick to know what they could be feasting on."

Frank held his breath; this was an uncharted sea, and not at all what he had counted on as a comeback.

"I need to get back on solid ground. I want to know for sure who I am and what I am capable of doing. I need a purpose, something to believe in. It's so easy to let other people tell you who you are — charts, TV presenters, *Melody Maker* scribblers. I need to believe in myself. I guess for some people it's down to God and that church bollocks. I'd rather be certain who and what I am and not count on other people who might taketh as soon as giveth, right?"

This was a new side of Chaz, and it left Frank at a loss for words. "Do you agree with me? Because I'm not sure *I* agree with me."

Frank needed time to wrap his head around all of this. He opted for a joke. "Is that some zen thing, like the Maharishi?"

"No, you tit. I just can't see the point of getting and spending without some reason for it all. And I can't find it in me to keep doing all of this unless I know why. And who I am. If that means forgoing some easy pleasures up front, well, I can do that."

"Awful, that sounds. Like saving yourself for Christ. Why bother living if you don't have any fun? Sounds like you're taking lifestyle advice from Simon and Garfinkle."

The title of a song Pete Townshend's music publisher had sent over came into Frank's head. "Faith in Something Bigger." Chaz seemed to be looking for faith in something smaller. He pretended to be lost in thought. "I might have an idea how to get the creative wick back to full flame. As it were."

Chaz made a small noise in assent, a sign of interest. Frank could sense the need, the childlike hopefulness at the heart, but rarely on the surface, of their professional relationship. Frank touched the bird on his neck and cleared his throat. "I reckon we" — it was crucial to keep Chaz from feeling like anything would be expected just of *him* — "need to reconnect you to your audience, to make you feel their love and them yours. Perhaps if we can identify" (the word sounded wrong even as it formed in his mouth) "what you and the Chazzies have in common. Other, of course, than both being in love with you."

Chaz replied as sharply as he might were he punctuating the words with a jabbing finger. "You know, mate, you could show a little more respect. If I didn't have the ego to carry it off, you'd have sold bugger all to those little snots. When I stop buying your bullshit, so will they, so tread lightly, my son."

They were stopped at a light. Frank smirked and took a beat to recalculate and reset the seriousness of the natter. "Here's the thing, mate. We see the challenges facing us differently, of course we do. Yours is far greater than mine, I understand that. And I am ready to help you in any way I can. Here's a thought. I've been contemplating —"

"Your bleeding bellybutton, no doubt..."

"— other ways we might regain chart momentum. *Your* momentum."

"Pretend that I'm listening." If Frank hadn't known the ins and outs of Chaz's personality, he might have been discouraged, but having stepped over the details of Chaz's new anxieties, this was now moving more or less in the direction he wished it to.

"Right. So, like I told you, I'm going to get you a song you can record to clear the decks. I've not done it yet, but it's in the works, and I'm sure you'll be happy with the results." Chaz looked stricken but didn't object. Frank pressed on. "We'll do it all backroom hush-hush, we'll put your name on it. That will buy us some time for you to recharge and write your next hit." Frank scrutinized Chaz for signs of total mutiny or lack of attention. Finding neither, he pushed on.

"I think we can agree that your songs come from some unknown place deep inside your subconscious." He waited for the flattery to sink in. Some of the songs which regularly caused punter palpitations had started with a phrase from the telly or a melody Chaz picked up from an old record. His genius, such as it was, came from using these borrowed bits to make music that sounded — and, more importantly, felt — uniquely his. But that approach wasn't working any longer, at least not reliably, and they both knew it. There were new sounds, new styles, new values in the marketplace, in the culture, and that put Chaz at the risk of becoming a relic. Not a nostalgia panto like Sha Na Na, or even traditionalist blues rockers like the Pie, who were still doing good business. But their audience didn't need change, they liked the old stuff. Chaz was competing in the speed lane, where gears shifted weekly. Keep up or get run over, that was the rule, and his windscreen was becoming seriously fogged.

Frank did a quick mental recap of the short meeting he'd had with Amanda, who assured him she'd have no trouble convening an "expert board" of young punters to do secret reconnaissance for him. He didn't have much faith in her, but he did have confidence in his ability to bully her into getting the job done. He saw the fork in the road leading to Chaz's future and took it.

"I think we might benefit from a little research. Get a fix on what's become of Britain's teenagers, where they're at, what they care about, how they see the world. Things are changing. It's a long way from the stage to the stalls, from studio to bedsit. We need to bridge those gaps. We work out who your fans are, and who else could follow them in the royal pursuit of Chazness, and I wager you'll be inspired to create music that joins, rather than separates, you to them. You *and* them."

"Hold on, mate. Let me get this right. You want me to make music by asking cunts who no longer buy my records what they want to hear? Like I'm some bloody soap powder testing out a new box design or ad slogan?" He was raging now, spittle flecks punctuating his anger. "That's the biggest load of shite you've ever shot out of your bum. P'rhaps you'd like to me pop round the fan clubbers' gaffs and take requests so I can do them up special? I can hear the radio advert now: *Chaz Bonapart — bespoke pop songs for any occasion.*"

That was, of course, roughly, what Frank was suggesting, but on a grand scale. Only he couldn't put it that way, since — predictably — Chaz was aghast at the very thought of doing anything quite so logical, even to his likely benefit. This was all part of the plan. To slide an idea under his door then whisk it away so Chaz would come back to look for it on his own.

"No, of course not." Chaz's face had gone all red, but Frank had the calm assurance of a poker player holding an unbeatable hand.

"What do you reckon, I should title my next album *Money, Sex and Football*?"

"You know who Doc Pomus is, right?"

Chaz nodded. "The cripple who wrote hits for Elvis Presley?"

"That's the one. Well, he may be a genius, but he didn't do it alone. There's this younger bloke called Mort something who he worked with."

"What kind of name is Mort? Co-written by Death?"

"No, it's some Jewish thing. Never mind. I read that Pomus first met this Mort character as a lad and paid him to sit and listen as he wrote songs, tell him what he liked and what he didn't."

"I'm not having that."

"Chaz, think about it. If the kid has ears, it saves all the waiting and tells you how a song might go down without the bother and risk of making a record."

"My very own Mary Whitehouse."

"I don't see it as censorship. It would be like trying out a new song you've written for your missus, only he or she will tell you the truth."

Chaz hadn't considered the possibility of Mort being a girl. But still it sounded like a gross intrusion and insult to his talent. Jagger wouldn't do anything like that, he was certain.

He fixed Frank with a distant look. "Right. I see."

It was hardly agreement, but better than flat-out rejection. But it wasn't even the idea Frank had to sell him on. "You told me that you've been abandoning songs like left-handed sketches for months. You said you're a little lost in space. You need a confidence builder. I'm not saying we place an advert in the back of *Melody Maker* asking kids what you should write songs about. All I'm suggesting is we — *you* — give a little listen to the audience, find out what they're thinking about, and see if that might be of some help to you. Nothing ventured, all that. No obligation on your part." It was to Frank's advantage that he understood how rejecting an idea in one form was just a prelude to selling it back in a different package.

"That would be hilarious. 'Superstar requires young person to explain the world of punters to him for songwriting purposes. No brains required. Post your CV to Chaz Bonapart...' Ha, brilliant. That would be the end of me. And you."

"Not at all what I meant. You're just being silly. More like this Mort fellow, but

I've got an idea how to go about it without the needless discomfort of having some teenaged berk watch you make magic. This is how I see it, mate. You spend some time making up a list —"

"Like a shopping list? You'd best ring up your man, if that's what you need."

Frank pressed on. He knew the rhythm. "— of the things that are most important to you. In your life. Real things, big things. And I don't just mean possessions. I mean ideas, beliefs, people, dreams, opinions, values. The heavy stuff." Frank knew he was repeating back to Chaz things he'd just said. That was part of the technique. To make the client feel understood, heard. "Don't think of songs you've written, or birds you've banged. Really dig down and make a list that gets to the heart of Bonapartitude. What bits go into the totality of you-ness. Then, we'll figure some way to get the same sort of list from the youth of Britain. No connection between the two efforts, but we get to compare the results."

"So you *do* mean to place an advert in the *MM*? You bastard!"

"Of *course* not. There are many ways to go about such a project without being an absolute nit. Let me sort it out and get back to you."

Frank already had it sorted. But Chaz had to believe he was part of the process, not just a hapless cog in it. For a consummate manipulator, it would have been unthinkable to recommend a course of action without already having a way to effect it and a half-dozen ways to steer it back on the track from wherever Chaz might attempt to divert it. All of it was set out in his head like a logic chart...if this, then that, then if that then this...

He dropped Chaz back at Hans Crescent and then drove home. After a bath, he rang Amanda to tell her that the secret project was a go.

Mouldy Old Dough

SCHOOL WAS down to a few review sessions and then final exams before total release. I could handle it all in a tick. Otherwise I was just faffing about, doing a bit of this and that while pretending not to have heard Dad's advice that I should give wage slavery a go. I couldn't see my way clear to that, especially as I'd found a new hobby, one that kept me well occupied at no cost whatsoever. It didn't take me long to learn what happened when I scratched the itch I got from thinking about kissing Amanda or dreaming of Stephen. What a treat! I don't know if I was any good at wanking, but even at my novice level the results were quite satisfactory. (Having watched the Japan Olympics a few months back, I couldn't help imagining stern-faced judges waving low numbers and throwing down the occasional flag for loutish behaviour on my part.) Which got me wondering how a bloke could be useful. All the fun was sort of around the inside of the outside. I didn't see how there'd be much more fun to have some git's percy jammed all the way up in there. It's not like I get off on using tampons.

I did it in bed a lot, but my favourite place was in the shower, where I gained real appreciation for whoever invented the nozzle head thingy. My fanny must have been the cleanest in London, since it got an extra-long washing every day. I read somewhere that people make a lot of noise when you do sex, but I didn't want to worry Dad, so I made sure to keep my mouth shut. I was concerned there might be a spike in the water bill and had promised myself to come up with a tale to explain the sudden surge of long showers as I explored ways to use that lovely strong spray.

I went to Acton Memorial to see what I could learn, but all the library had was some ancient books written by priests about the risks of self-abuse. A lady in a baggy jumper and a boy's haircut came over with an armful of books and asked what I was looking for. (I couldn't work out if she was a librarian or just a random meddler.) She said a bookstore in Camden Town might have more, as she put it, up-to-date literature. She wrote the name on the back of a leaflet for the Campaign for Homosexual Equality. As little as I cared for the idea of trekking all over London, I did want some assurance that I wasn't doing myself any harm, so I got on the Tube and found the store. They had a pamphlet on import from America called *Women and Their Bodies (a course)*. That set me back two quid. I didn't dare take it out of the bag until I got home and locked my bedroom door, and then I had to grapple with all this political bollocks, not to mention science words like Bartholin's and gonorrhea and epithelial, and skip the chapter on childbirth (virgin birth being a one-off, assumed), I found some bits that were definitely useful. The section about wanking never used that word, but it did help me understand and relax about what I was doing. In fact, I learned a thing or three, although I could not bring myself to follow the advice to "Take a mirror and examine yourself."

I DIDN'T NEED much to get going, just a quick think back to the night of the party, to Stephen's dimples and Amanda's mouth. In a way, though, I knew neither was the point. I wasn't pining, just enjoying the physical attraction.

Still, my stomach did a flip when I answered the phone on a Tuesday evening to hear the voice of Miss Amanda Charles, all peaches and cream. I'd been thinking about it, wondering what she meant about me helping Chaz. Maybe the kiss freaked her out and so she'd dropped the idea and me. Or she'd just left it behind, like her bag on the Tube.

We talked rubbish for a few minutes before she finally got around to the point, which — after another speech about how this was all hush-hush and super-secret — was to ask me again if I kept a diary. I said I didn't. (That's not quite true. I have done at times. I give it a go for a couple of days and then get sick of what I've put down and stop it. I've never been too sharp with remembering things — the more that goes in my head, the more goes out — so the idea of writing it down always made sense. Until I didn't remember to do it.)

"And even if I did, why would that be of any interest to Chaz? Or you?"

"Shhh. I can't tell you. But if you don't, you don't."

"Do *you*? Keep a diary?" The line went silent for a bit and then said, very softly, "I do, but you can't tell anyone."

I did one of those stare-at-the-phone things, finding her secrecy more than a little odd. It's not like I had any clue what might be in it. "Planning to sell it to the *News of the World* for a pop world exposé?"

"What would make you say that?" Agitation animated her voice. "It's not like I've ever done anything sordid."

I lowered my voice in case Dad was in hearing range. "Well...you did kiss a girl."

"Fuck off. Everyone plays at being queer nowadays — it's fashionable. Doesn't mean anything. American women get those beehive haircuts, doesn't make them bees, now does it? Anyway, this is your lucky day. Chaz's manager wants to meet you." Before I could ask what about, she said, "He's got a suite at the Connaught. In Mayfair. Room 619. Half three tomorrow. Don't be late. Code name Enigma." And with that the line went dead. I wrote the information on the pad by the phone and then pulled off the top five sheets so there wouldn't be a telltale dent Dad might find. (I read that in a mystery, that was how they copped on to a blackmailer, by discovering impressions of a name on his note.)

THE NEXT DAY, I woke up early with a stray thought about shoes. Platform shoes. I had a little dosh saved in a jar and I suddenly found myself needing to spend it on footwear of a sort I'd never previously imagined wearing.

I set off for the King's Road right after breakfast and soon emerged from a shop fifteen quid lighter in the pocket but four inches taller, raised aloft on a smashing pair of cherry red patent leather platforms with yellow soles and green laces. My feet looked like spit-shined apples, but I felt like brilliant. Some of those magazines I used to read made it out that shopping could improve one's self-esteem, but this was the first time I ever believed it. Gazing down at the world, I felt smarter, cooler, sexier. And taller. Definitely taller. Dad was going to have my arse on a plate. On the way home, I stopped and bought a cheap gym bag to put the new shoes in. That was the end of my readies. I hoped there was more to come.

The stylish shoes were killing my feet, and I still had a couple of hours to kill. I looked in to the Chelsea Drugstore, wandering the shops, soaking up the atmosphere and listening to the music playing. I'd never set foot inside before, and it took a while to find the record shop in the basement. 50p for a single was alright, but I couldn't imagine how punters were able to keep up with it all — the albums, the fashion, the posters, the glossy magazines and whatever else they scarfed up in their manic need to worship at the altar of rock and roll. Or whatever it was. My participation was strictly as an observer — I didn't need to own any of this rubbish.

As I tottered about, picking up records and looking at them, a shaggy boy came over and asked if I needed help. The platforms made me taller than him, and maybe a little more confident than I usually am. So, while I didn't have an answer for that, I didn't just shrug and walk off. We ended up talking. I expected he'd tell me to sod off when it was clear that I wasn't going to buy anything, but the shop was nearly empty and he seemed up for a natter. A record came on — an oompah marching throb with some berk groaning out a few words. I made a face and asked him what that horrible noise was.

He laughed. "Oh yeah, that's Lieutenant Pigeon. 'Mouldy Old Dough.' It did fuck all — pardon my English — when it first came out but then it caught on in Belgium so it's only a matter of time before it gets another push here."

In a burst of what I hoped was cleverness, I blurted out, "I think Lieutenant Pigeon belongs in an oven more than on the radio."

He laughed again and said (much to my relief), "Absolutely. It's a novelty number by some studio hacks. My boss insists on keeping it in heavy rotation. She says we're going to shift them by the boxload. I don't hear it. Who would shell out for this crud?"

"Who *do* you like? What's your name? And where are you from?" My thoughts were spilling out on top of each other.

Without a word he went and got a single, slid it from the paper sleeve and put it on the fanciest Dansette I'd ever seen, a glowing space-age stack of gear, and gave the volume knob a firm turn. "Listen to this. It's coming out next month, and I simply can't stand how amazing it is." The sound of a guitar, the greatest guitar I'd ever heard (my knowledge was admittedly skimpy, but still) came stabbing out of the speakers. He saw the grin on my face and pointed to the sleeve. "Mott the Hoople," he shouted. "'All the Young Dudes'."

I couldn't hear him clearly, but it appeared to match the scrawl on the paper, so I went with that. Then he added something about Bowie that I couldn't make out. I smiled but put up a hand to quiet him. I wanted to hear this, not try to work out what he was shouting. I was transported to a place that I might have imagined in my dreams but knew it was where I'd always wanted to be. I can't explain it, it was the most amazing feeling. I was nearly breathless. Shaggy boy appeared to be enjoying my reaction almost as much as I was, which was weird but nice. It ended with the singer urging his fantasy fans to come right down front; I almost felt like I was there. My feet were ready to move. I wanted more, but I had no words.

He laughed. "Right? A real winner, yeah? They've been around for a while, but never sounded like this until they met Bowie. He wrote and produced the single and I think it's just what they needed." His head was going up and down like a seesaw. "They used to be Dylanesque rockers, now they've gone glam. Isn't it awesome?"

He plucked the single off the record player, forefinger under the centre, thumb on the edge, and held it out to me. I didn't dare touch it, so I just stared down at the plastic as if there were secrets to be learned from regarding the grooves.

"Chaz Bonapart was almost their singer, but they got this curly haired guy with shades instead."

I gulped hard, feeling a bit exposed in my surprise, but didn't say anything about the meeting with his manager. "Oh yeah? Cool."

He slid the record back in its sleeve and laid it aside. "It's not even out yet — we got a couple of advance copies."

"I love it. Play it again."

He obliged while rabbiting on about other glam bands: Slade, Sweet, Sparks, T. Rex, Bowie, Elton, Alice somebody. I did a lot of enthusiastic nodding without taking it all in. If he was making it all up on the spot, I didn't care. I was enthralled. If none of it was true, it should be. I wanted it to be. It all sounded so exciting, I couldn't wait to hear more.

"New York." I gave him a quizzical frown.

"You asked where I was from. The Bronx. That's a borough in New York. City."

"Oh." I don't know why I wanted to know that.

A short woman came over and said a few words to him. He might have rolled his eyes while she was talking, but I wasn't sure. When she walked away, he mouthed "my boss." I figured our hang was over, but I wanted to convey how much I enjoyed it. I reached out a hand and said "Laila."

He replied "Bryan," but instead of shaking my hand he slipped a small paper sac into it, with a friendly frown and a slight nod. "Come by anytime except Saturdays — that's when the tourists swarm in and it's too mad to talk."

I thanked him, promised I'd be back and sloped off with a smile on my face. Once I rounded the corner, I looked in the bag and found the record he'd played and a Marc Bolan badge. Grinning like an idiot, I pinned it on and felt like a million pounds.

WIRES GROANED as the lift rose imperceptibly, finally arriving on the second floor of the Connaught with a judder. I went through the fire doors and was clonking down the corridor when I realized the room numbers were going the wrong way. I doubled back and finally came face to face with a gold-trimmed door marked 619. I paused. While I didn't expect to be set upon by a gang of sex pervs poised to ship me off to do unspeakable things in Madagascar, I really had no idea what fate awaited me inside. Taking a deep breath, with a quick look down at my fab new shoes for reassurance, I knocked gently. That got no response, so I did it again, harder.

Amanda opened the door, wearing a cream-colored jumpsuit, very Emma Peel but for the black feather boa hanging down and a ribbed cap. I was dead impressed, but she was all business.

"Look, this is serious, so pay attention. Fr...Mr Guy will explain, and you'll do as you're told. Got it, yeah?" In fact, I hadn't got anything, except a ferocious reminder of my crush on her. She was smashing and I wanted...I didn't know what I wanted, but I wanted something off her.

She leaned in and whispered in my ear; in the excitement, I barely heard what she said. "Two things to be aware of. He's not as mean as he looks and it's not so much that he's short-tempered as he has no patience whatsoever. Choose wisely and make your words count." She straightened up. "Now follow me."

Anywhere, I thought. We went down a short passage into an enormous room. There were tables piled high with colorful food and more furniture than Dad and had in the whole house. In the centre of it all, on a throne of some sort, sat a hard-looking bald bloke in a black suit. He stood up as I walked toward him, propelled by a not unpleasant shove in the small of my back from Amanda.

He stood up and offered a hand. "Hullo, you must be Laila, is that right? My name is Mr Guy. I look after Chaz Bonapart. I'm sorry we didn't have the chance meet at the little knees up the other week. I'm glad you were able to attend. Did you have a good time? Quite a mad scene, wasn't it?"

He looked like a movie gangster, but his manner was gentle and polite, so instead of being scared, I felt at ease. I guessed he'd been detained on occasion, but the scene didn't feel heavy so what it didn't matter. After all, this was the superstar music business, not some shady underworld lair. I sank softly into an enormous chair he directed me towards. He smiled. "Fancy a drink?"

Amanda put up a hand, as if to deflect the comment out of my hearing. "I don't believe she's old enough for that, Frank. A Coca-Cola or a cuppa?" They both looked to me, perhaps expecting to find my age inscribed on my forehead, like a sell-by date in Tesco.

That felt like a cue for me to speak, which I hadn't done any of since entering the room. "Sure, Coke please." Oddly, my request didn't cause anything to occur. I didn't give a toss about the bleeding soda, but I was keen on seeing the wheels on the machine turn, to see the drinks offer result in something liquid going in a glass. I was thinking I'd've gone to get it myself if I'd had any idea where it might be when a double-door at the other end of the room opened and a butler entered; within seconds, lacking any audible instructions or bottle openings, a tall, fizzy glass on what must have been a genuine silver platter was set down on a table near me. I could have pissed myself. So it wasn't just something people said, or a luxury reserved solely for the Queen. Before I had time to feel the cold in the glass much less put it to my lips, the butler vanished. I took a sip and wondered if there was one kind for rich people and another for the rest of us — this was better than anything I'd ever tasted.

Another me might have found this all posh bollocks incredibly nerve-wracking, but instead I watched it all play out like a movie and found it entertaining, in a why-the-hell-not sort of way. What's the worst that could happen, I thought, and not for the last time.

Mr Guy leaned forward and smiled a little, but it wasn't one of those looks that makes you feel better, it was the kind nurses use when they're pretending demerara can mask nasty-tasting medicine. Adults, they're all the same.

"Are you a big music fan? Of particular groups? Perhaps you'd care to name some of your favourite records. Or tell us about concerts you've been to."

I shot a glance at Amanda; it felt like a setup; if this pop quiz was the entry fee, I was unprepared and about to be sent home. Then I surprised myself by realizing I had a ready answer. "I caught Roxy Music recently and was pretty keen on them. Quite the spectacle and a far sight better than that horrid Lieutenant Pigeon record." I screwed on a pleasant face to show that I wasn't freaked out. Which, truth be told, I wasn't. This all seemed a bit daft, and I didn't care what happened one way or the other. It can't be like this when you go for a job at Boots, can it?

"I daresay!" He looked over at Amanda, confused but perhaps pleased. "Roxy Music, indeed." She didn't respond. Mr Guy's discomfort counteracted my own. I let out a breath, cocked my head at him and said, "Look, I don't give a toss. I don't know much about rock and roll. Why don't you just tell me whatever it is I'm here to be told and then I'll be off. A'right?"

Mr Guy laughed. "Oh, I like this one, I do. Good job, Amanda." He turned back to me. "Let me explain why I asked to meet you." I put the glass down.

"Chaz, as you know, or don't, is the biggest pop star in Britain. Has been for yonks. I guess you don't care but, trust me, millions of you have got his picture on their bedroom walls."

"*I* haven't." He was still smiling, so I guessed that my suddenly surly act was at least keeping me on the pitch, if not scoring any goals. I watched his eyes as he glanced again at Amanda, who was looking elsewhere.

"Chaz is the idol of British youth, and yet he feels less in touch with them — you — than he would like to be. He finds himself unhappily out of synch with the collective subconscious of Britain's spotty generation. He needs to know what you're getting up to. We need to refocus him, reconnect him to the spirit of the times." I had no idea what he was on about.

"Sorry, what?"

Amanda could sense her future fading. Mr Guy demanded quick solutions to problems, and those who couldn't deliver were useless to him. She also knew he suspected she was a conniving tart who would say or do anything to get by. It was up to her to find real significance in this before it all collapsed on her.

"Chaz, of course, has the talent, he just — for the moment — lacks focus. He's got plenty of songs to write, he's just not sure what kinds of songs he should concentrate on writing. Subject matter and that. He's a bit...isolated...y'know, room at the top and all, and it's become difficult for him to maintain the deep and meaningful connection he's always had with his fans." She looked hopefully at Mr Guy, who nodded with enthusiasm.

"The music audience nowadays are younger, and rather new to him. He hasn't had the opportunity for a proper introduction, as it were. At least not yet." She finished, and I still had no idea what I was doing here.

"Amanda tells me you're keen to get on board the good ship Bonapart. I want to make sure you understand what's at stake here. We'd like to enlist your aid in the area of creative conceptualization."

I wasn't alone in being baffled by that phrase. Amanda blinked as if a fly had taken a run at her and scrambled for a translation. "We thought you might be able to give us some ideas that we can pass along to help him get back on track." I gave them both my best what-the-fuck-are-you-on-about face.

"Well, Amanda is overstating the case a bit. Chaz doesn't need any assistance, certainly not, but it never hurts to — what do they say in the States? — cover all your bases, have a bit of insurance. Small matter, just trying to do what we can to ensure that the wheels keep turning smoothly." Now it was Amanda's turn to look perplexed. He was losing both of us at once. These are the people who handle stars? Not too impressive.

"Can you tell Frank what sort of things you feel are important to your, your…"

Frank must have liked this line of questioning. He jumped in to take it for himself. "Yes, Lara, what would you say 'turns' you on?"

Turns me on? I wasn't about to mention my hobby, so I made up some rubbish about learning and being kind to my friends, stuff I'd seen some plonker say on the *Miss Britain* programme. That didn't please them, and I got the distinct impression my brush with luxury was about to end. I scoffed the rest of the Coke, which was refilled in a flash.

Mr Guy stared at Amanda. "We need to introduce our young friend into Chaz's creative process. How shall we do that?" When she didn't reply — the blank look on her face made it obvious she had no ready answer — he turned back to me while still addressing her. "I suspect we don't yet know enough about our young friend. Or her about us. Miss Charles, your assignment is to find out more about Lara and then help me decide how to best put her to use. Or not."

She nodded, looking none too pleased.

"The sticky bit, you see, is that we absolutely cannot bring anything to Chaz that he doesn't think was his own idea. So we're doing this in secret. And I've come up with a way to do that."

Amanda was first to ask. "How do you propose to make that happen?"

"Enigma has a secret weapon — Psi the Clock. Chaz believes he's some kind of fucking mystical oracle because he never says anything. And he doesn't give a toss what happens so long as he's left to himself to hit those drums."

"I don't follow."

Frank stroked his chin, perhaps an effort to seem Gandalf wise. "I bet if Psi were to share the odd idea with Chaz now and again, without any discussion of money or credit, then the nature of the human ego will do its worst, and Chaz will manage to convince himself that it was his idea in the first place."

I squirmed in the chair and wagged my foot. "Can someone please tell me what you're asking me to do?"

Mr Guy spoke directly to Amanda. "Would you be so kind to spend some time together and move this forward? Thank you for coming. Forgive me, but I have another meeting about to begin."

Closing the door behind them, he worried that this might not work out as he needed it to. The message was not getting through. But he wasn't ready to let the scheme go down the plughole. He was amused by the girl — she seemed unfazed and didn't seem the sort of pliable poseur Chaz would take to bed. He saw her as the anti-Amanda, armed and doomed, in equal measure, by a lack of guile. He suspected she had potential, but it would have to be squeezed out of her. And Amanda would have to be the one doing the squeezing.

I FOLLOWED AMANDA into an adjacent room with the biggest bed I've ever seen. She closed the door and dropped her voice low, which sounded exciting. "I think I see what our problem is."

"We have a problem?"

"Sit down. No, there. They — well, we — need you to help Chaz understand who his audience is and what they're thinking about so he can write songs that will matter to them. Things they'll care about. Enigma. I thought you might be a good representative of the punters of Britain. An avatar, I believe they call it."

"I don't even know what that is. What am I supposed to do to help a rock star?"

"Well, that's rather the point, isn't it? Your generation knows fuck all about anything, but the records you buy have to be about *something*, no? We just need to work out what that something is. So Chaz can write songs about it."

"I don't buy a lot of records."

"You will now. I'll set you up with an account at one of the shops and you can just go there and pick up whatever you want and put it on our tab."

"Really?" That sounded pretty cool, even if records were not what I fancy. But I liked the sound of privilege. And I felt the same surge of strength I had in the loo at the party. This wasn't home, it wasn't school, and it wasn't prison, so they couldn't make me do anything, could they, unless I agreed? Once I knew what they wanted of me, I could decide what I would ask for doing it.

"Can it be at the Chelsea Drugstore on the King's Road?" I felt a bit clever for knowing that, and even more so for thinking of it at this exact moment. It was a pleasure to see the surprise that crossed her face.

"Yes, I can arrange that. I'll get you a letter of introduction you can take there. In the meantime, I'll organize some of the current hits and have them sent round so you can get yourself orientated." She pushed a pad at me. "Write down your address, will you? I trust you live somewhere...in London?" How do people get it in their heads that they're so much better than other people?

"Yes, East Acton. I might need a record player as well."

"I see. I'll get you one." I couldn't decide if she was exasperated or impressed by my negotiating skill.

"Cool. What do I have to do for you?" I was already feeling better about all of this. "Mr Guy said you need to get to know me better."

"Yes, well. Forget that. You need to tell us what you and your little friends are obsessed with. If you can see how any of them could be the subject of songs, all the better. I'm not sure how Mr Guy is going to convey your ideas to Chaz but he'll work it out. You come up with topics and I'll take it from there."

All this double-talk was giving me a headache. "I don't think my friends have any obsessions." (Wait, do I have friends?) "And if they do, it's about stupid things like spots and boys and grades and pop stars."

"That won't do." We sat in silence. She stared into space; I stared at the backs of my hands.

"Right. Have you ever been in love?"

"No. I'm fifteen."

"Sex?" Now I was well and truly confused. Was she offering? Demanding? Warning? I considered all the ways that question — if indeed that's what it was — could be taken.

"Does wanking count?" She laughed, but not in a nice way. "Of course it does. But there's a bit more to it than you and your hairbrush. Trust me." She suddenly seemed like a friend or a big sister.

133

As I considered the pleasurable value a pink plastic implement might offer, Amanda said, "I haven't thought enough about the inner workings of Enigma. I've got to, oh, bugger..." In quick order, she worked herself into — and out of — a state of agitation that did awful things to the perfection of her face.

"Right." She grabbed my arm and pulled me back into the other room, where Mr Guy was talking to a tall bloke with a ginger mustache, white ponytail, bright blue satin jacket, tight Levis and cowboy boots with silver studs tracing out the word "ROLL" on the one I could see. Amanda looked as bemused as I felt but Mr Guy didn't seem upset by our return.

"Lara, I'm glad you came back. This is Howard Moore. He's come over to produce Chaz's next album. Howard, this is Amanda's little friend." The bloke opened his mouth in what I took to be a smile and revealed two rows of huge teeth, even and polished to ivory perfection. I'd never seen such a thing before and probably stared a little longer than Mum would have deemed polite.

"Well, bonjour y'all. I'm chafed to make your acquaintance, little lassie. Tootle pop and all that. I sure hope to be seeing more of your bonnet around these parts." I had no idea how to reply. Fortunately, I didn't need to. It was clear that everyone in the room thought him a right pillock, which made the effort to be genial and polite feel like an episode of *Mission: Impossible*. The shaggy boy in the shop had been cool, but this was old John Wayne America in the coarse, outsized flesh, reeking of privilege, ignorance and misplaced self-confidence. A lot of things about the world suddenly made sense to me.

"Hey there, Mandy, how's it hanging?" I marveled that she was able to manage a grimace and a smile in one facial maneuver. Her reply, in a honeyed voice that concealed the scorn, was as polite as a visitor to the palace. "Split right down the middle, as ever. Thank you for asking. I'm very well, thank you, kind sir." I half-expected her to curtsy.

He didn't take any notice. "I love how you limeys talk. Just like King Arthur and his wife, Lady Godiver."

I should have kept my mouth shut. "I believe you mean Guinevere, not Godiva. Couple of centuries apart." I know how rude stroppiness is, but I couldn't help being a smartarse. Mr Guy glared at me, but then I did see the corners of his mouth curl up a bit.

134

"No, that can't be. And what the hell do you know about it anyhow? You're just a little girl."

Mr Guy smiled pleasantly at him but shook his head in dissent. "No, sorry, she's right."

The American wrapped his face in huge hands and then guffawed. I don't think I've ever heard anyone guffaw before — I saw the word in a book — but he did what I guessed was a perfect rendition.

"Goddamn, I must be just plain dumb." He continued to laugh, a huge, wall-shaking roar that no one else in the room shared. Awkward? Why, yes. Funny? If what he said was meant as a joke, he alone found it clever.

Mr Guy said something quietly to Amanda, who exited. I hesitated and then started toward the door but stopped when the overgrown berk spoke again. "When we get in the studio, I want this one there, as a good luck charm. She can be a dogsboy or something, fetch the drugs or whatever."

"We'll see," said Mr Guy with a frown. "She's not exactly in my employ. She's a temp, like, that we're possibly going to engage for a small task."

"You should put her on the payroll. Charge it to Chaz's account and let the label pay for it."

"I'll think about it, Howard, before the sessions start. Promise." He flashed me a smile that was either friendly or pitying. I didn't like the sound of this one bit, but I was weirdly excited that I mattered to these people. Maybe not a lot, but it was a new feeling.

Outside, the wind blew hard in my face, but I kept my eyes wide to take in the bright blue sky, a herd of soft clouds going nowhere. I felt elated, happier to be alive than I could recall. I didn't know where the feeling came from — this was England, after all, but I had seen good weather before. I gave it a think but couldn't reckon why. I was still me, school was still going to be school and Dad was still Sad Dad. But everything was different.

Liquorice Allsorts

I WAS IN my room trying to read *The Diary of Anne Frank,* but I kept reaching the end of paragraphs without any idea what I had just read. My life was going much the same, and I'd been feeling sorry for myself. And feeling ridiculous for that. Anne had to hide in a Dutch attic for years to keep from being murdered and here I was unable to even follow what she had written. It got me thinking.

She'd be a few years older than Mum now, but what a different world it had been. War and death at every turn, mortal terror like I could never imagine. If Anne had been swept away from all that and set up in a London flat, would she have grown up ordinary like everyone else? Everyone Dad's age talks about the Blitz. They were scared of the bombs and saw the destruction but didn't really expect to die. England, in its own damaged, defensive way, had it sorted. I remember him telling me about keeping the lights off, spending nights in Tube stations where the walls shook and plaster got in your mouth and your hair. I don't know any of that, and I'm glad for it. We're different now. My generation had a clean start, nothing to worry about except the Russians and the Yanks blowing each other up with nuclear bombs. Not exactly comforting, but I didn't let it keep me awake at night.

At the alarming sound of a loud knock, I went down and opened the door to find a geezer in a motorcycle helmet and a package under his arm. A large box with a handle stood by his boots.

"Are you Laila Russell?" He thrust a clipboard and a biro at me. I nodded, wrote my name on the paper and handed it back to him. Maybe I was supposed to give him a shilling. I reached for the box, swung it inside, turned back and put my hands out for the package. I went inside and kicked the door closed.

I unwrapped the big one first: a brand-new Dansette that must have cost a packet. Cor! The smaller one had a note from Mr Guy.

> Give these a listen and see what they make you think of. Cheers.
> –FCG.

"These" were 7-inch singles, maybe a dozen of them, wrapped up in tissue like a birthday present. I binned the paper and laid them out on the table. We never had many records in the house, just a small collection of LPs and singles by Dave Clark, Donovan and Elvis Presley. The most recent thing there is *Hunky Dory*, which he claims was sold to him on false pretense and is always threatening to bring it back to HMV because it didn't all sound like "Changes" and because "Song for Bob Dylan" didn't strike him as a song Bob Dylan would have enjoyed receiving. I wondered if these new lot was mine to keep.

We'd had a record player for a long time before I knew we did. Dad must have shoved it in the cupboard after Mum died; I guess hearing songs they both knew made him sad. A year or two back, he pulled down an old Steepletone and put it on the table in the front room. I never paid it much mind. Dusty as rot, it is. Rather than stir up questions I wasn't ready to answer, I hid the new one behind my bed. I hoped the old one worked.

After giving the records a long look (disappointingly, no Roxy Music), I began to do as Mr Guy asked. I turned on the player to warm up and grabbed half of them. I was about to stick them on the bindle or spindle (or whatever the thing in the middle is called) when it occurred to me I should probably take notes, so I got a pad and a biro from my room and wrote down their names. Then I put them on and got to work.

T. Rex - Metal Guru

Good one, this. Marc Bolan, like on the badge. Kids at school totally rate him. Sexy, right? Crazy but <u>fun</u> X3, lunatic lyrics make no sense. The other side is called Thunderwing. Silly. Like a foreign language, or babytalk. But the rhyme tickled me, making fun use of that phrase of the day.

Elton John - Rocket Man

Piano and singing – tells a story, but not one I care about – astronauts???? – astro-dogs? (I have to tell dad...maybe he'll think it's about me) but ok. sounds like he knows what he's doing. Don't fancy his singing much. Goes on a bit doesn't it.........................

<u>Donny Osmond - Puppy Love</u>

This pillock looks younger than me. Awful rubbish. Had to take it <u>off</u> halfway through.. Horrible twee bollocks. In the bin, whoever you are.

<u>Chicory Tip - Son of My Father</u>

Bouncy, ok, funny squibbly noises...be just like yore dad...plastic vac pack ... what are alibi signs? This record is not as clever as they probably think it is...better than calling it <u>a song about me</u>. (I was my mum's daughter...)

<u>Gilbert O'Sullivan - Alone Again (Natureally)</u>

Oh lovely. a bloke singing about topping himself and talking to God with drippy strings. By the end his mum and dad are both dead. Now <u>I'm</u> depressed. Who needs to hear this garbage? But then being alone is something a lot of kids can feel.

<u>Slade - Coz I Luv You</u>

Singer needs to get over that sore throat. It sounds painful! I get that it's a gimmick, the speeling (haha), but isn't a bit obvius? S'coz I wuv u. I've seen pix of 'em in the papers, they wear crazy clobber. And have weird hair. Violin is weird in rock, innit?

I took the first stack off and got myself a glass of milk and some McVitie's. I also fished out the single the boy in the shop gave me. I wanted to check if I still liked it as much. I did, and played it three times, trying to understand all the words.

I fitted another batch onto the spindle. I was completely unclear what I was supposed to be getting out of all this, but it wasn't such a bad way to spend an afternoon.

<u>Jonathan King – Flirt</u>

Grown up but more of same rubbish — lalalalalalalala / pleasin pleasin pleasin / hurt-flirt. bounces like a superball.

<u>Bowie – Starman</u>

A lot of space in pop these days, no? — sort of the same song as Mr John..? moon landings must be the thing this year. Message to Dave — try coming back to earth, okay? (Note to myself: maybe I should start telling people I'm named after a space dog. I could be cool for a change!)

<u>Wings - Mary Had a Little Lamb</u>

More twee spittle. Who buys this junk? Earth to Paul McCartney — piss off! David Cassidy - Could it,.. & Cherish Love the hair, hate the record. He's too cute to be such a terrible singer. Opera? warbly man-ness. Ick.

There were more, but I just couldn't go on. There was no rhyme or reason, and if this was what we — kids — wanted to hear, I'd have to confess to being a generation traitor. How could you like one song that made your ears bleed *and* another that came baked in a sugar pie?

I went back to see how Anne was making out.

AMANDA RANG the next morning, confirming the delivery and asking for a detailed report. Christ, school was out, and this already felt like homework. I read her what I'd jotted down and heard a couple of muted chuckles.

When I finished, she said, "Now, can you work out how to turn that into ideas Chaz can use?" Fuck if I know, and I said as much. Listening to records was one thing, sussing how it could help a pop star with whatever problems he was having quite another.

I heard a sigh, a nervous laugh and a pause. "OK, here's what you need to do. Start by making a list of the things that are important to you and your mates at school. Got that? Bring it by the office next week. And the sooner the better."

I was about to remind her that school is done for the year, but she rang off. I can't say I liked being bossed around. The assignment still didn't make sense — either what she wanted from me, or how I was supposed to get it — but I did like the sense of being a person people wanted, even needed, things from. I was being counted on, at least in some small way. For an otherwise useless teen wanker, a role in something bigger was quite a change from being universally ignored. Or serving as a living souvenir of the dead.

I needed to know more about how people wrote songs, so I stopped in to the British Museum Reading Room and got out microfilm of a pamphlet called *Writing Popular Music: A Basic Course* by one Rupert Stilton, who evidently wrote a few "chestnuts" in his day, whenever that was. I hoped he could tell me what it was all about.

P opular songwriting is a wide and frightening chasm to undertake crossing. Although the rules make it deceptively simple to attempt, it's nearly impossible to tell when you've succeeded (unless one gets so far as commercial affirmation). And you never know if you've gotten where you wanted to be since you can never truly know where that is. Ready to begin?

To construct a winning object from an infinity of options, using flavorless and routine blocks and a formal blueprint that can be revised only at great peril to common appeal, and shadowed by the looming dangers of unconscious derivation, repetition, redundancy, cliché, triteness, plagiarism and, below all, mediocrity, the songwriter must be music's architect of fantasy, using elementary tools to erect a monument that is both familiar yet original, functional but stylish, audacious yet economical. And it has to matter — profoundly — to an audience that cannot be counted on to possess education, knowledge or wit, without resorting to the benefit of footnotes, explanation or illustration. One has between one hundred and two hundred words with which to create a world that can help people understand how to live. You are shaping minds; do not think of it as a fanciful task.

How to begin? Pick a word: any word will do. But what you spin out from that word will separate worthlessness from gold. Only a particular collection of subsequent words will merit value; everything else must be discarded, with ruthless self-awareness of the intangible ephemera of superlative quality. One must connect with what the audience already feels and senses, but in a way that makes them think anew of their world, their lives.

The words need not follow any evident scheme, but they must be rich with meaning to many, either by presenting old ideas in new ways, or new ideas in any way. But do not lead your audience with obscurity or controversy. You are creating a prism that can be viewed from many directions and reflect each listener's individualism from within. Cleverness can be an asset or an insurmountable hindrance to comprehension and positive regard. Subject matter is the entirety of existence, multiplied by the possibilities of imagination. When it works, a song can adjust the public's understanding of itself, alter the language and join the vocabulary of modern culture. Far more likely, it will pass unnoticed.

The process of songwriting is fraught with potholes. You will feel yourself part of a machine that continues running without variation or evident purpose. You will despair of sifting the dirt, hauling countless buckets of sand and water from the seashore. The possibility that any of this will somehow turn to glass retreats out of sight, over the horizon. And then, without warning, at a point when the work you have invested seems to have achieved nothing but lumps of intransigent clay, out will pop a fully formed and polished gem. You will have a lyric that literally sings. You will have to balance the elation of achievement with the misery of knowing how crude and irrational a process was required to arrive there. Art is randomly made; be warned that you may never quite control the effort, even when it is your own. Your role is to conduct your creative subconscious down pleasing pathways. Blame it on the Creator if you must, but I do not believe that He is at the source of our songwriting. (For evidence, consider that even heathens have music.) No, we are all orang-outans, hammering away randomly on our typewriters, waiting for good fortune and happenstance to emerge magically from our native intelligence and musical spirit, to deliver a lucky collusion of ideas that will be recognized as great songwriting. We have the great advantage over the apes of being able to appraise the merits of our blind stumblings, but, by God, I can assure you that stumblings they are.

Melody, of course, is a whole different matter...

Christ, this made it look hopeless. And I was feeling a bit dizzy from watching the words zoom by. It was nice that musty old books could be read without breathing in the must, but reading moving pictures was no treat. I unspooled the film and handed it in. But my gears kept turning; I couldn't stop thinking about the idea of song ideas. The first words to pop into my head were "Baby baby baby...what's your problem....why don't you love me...why don't" — and then realized I couldn't think of a rhyme with "problem." I stared off into space for a while and started to see why rock stars take drugs — there was nothing to be plucked from the air where I sat. I moved to another chair and gave it another ten fruitless minutes, then home for a wank. That I could manage.

FRANK CHECKED his watch as he lifted the phone. It was going on two. After some prodding, Amanda had admitted that the list-making by her young charge was not yet under way. He made it clear that she needed to pull her thumb out, but that didn't satisfy the needles of his impatience, so he was moving ahead with another piece of the plan. With Chaz at the manor, he was likely to be awake at this hour, but would not yet have fully faced the day. Just as needed. Frank kept it short and to the point, aiming to get in and out of the conversation before its import could fully sink in.

"Hullo, mate. How ya keeping? Good. I'll be quick. I've given it some thought, and despite my initial reluctance to your suggestion, I think you might be on to something." Frank waited to confirm that his flattering fiction would pass unremarked upon. He could envision Chaz smiling with smug pleasure while failing to recall what it was he'd done to make Frank see things his way.

"Good for you. About bloody time." Frank smiled to himself.

"Remember our thought of getting in publishing demos in search of a song you want to do? I have a better idea." It didn't matter that he was reintroducing an idea Chaz had already more or less rejected. Stars were not rational people, and dealing with them could seem very odd, indeed. "I reckon it would be faster, easier and cheaper to just find out what punters are into these days, a little market research as it were, and let you work your musical alchemy."

"Hmph." That was one hurdle surmounted.

"D'ya reckon William is your man?"

"William?"

"Your son, man. He's a teenager, right?"

"Oh, I reckon so, maybe. Not sure. Time flicks by. He's at school up north somewhere, no? I'll get the number — you could ring and ask." Chaz yawned loudly. "What's this about again?"

"Your clever suggestion that we take a peek into the psyche of today's punters. I thought your William might be just the ticket."

"*That* boffin? I doubt he has a fucking clue. He's half-deaf, or leastways he makes out like he is. Between those grotesque ear boxes he wears and the books he's always buried in, I don't know where his head might be at. Good on him that he's paying attention to that uni bollocks I pay for, but I wish he'd show me and his mum a little more respect. No, that one's not got a clue. We'll have to come up with someone else."

Frank had Chaz where he needed him to be. Of course, William was as likely a candidate for this chore as Mary Whitehouse — in fact, he would be of substantially less use, since the national scold could be counted on to have exactly the opposite view of what kids would like — but he was just a way station on this ride. As Frank clenched his fist in victory his voice remained neutral, offering only a humble dose of ersatz disappointment. "Ah, yeah. Right. Erm, I see your point. That's a shame. Let me have a think and see if I can come up with someone else right for the job. I'll ring you back."

Meet the Man

AFTER TWO preparatory chats with Amanda in which she warned me to keep my mouth shut, nod politely and listen, I was collected in a car and brought to Mr Guy's office, where I found Amanda seated stiffly on a couch. Mr Guy was nowhere to be seen.

"Wait here." She went out for a moment and returned with Chaz Bonapart. Introductions made, she pointed to a chair and motioned for me to sit. When she began to speak; he silenced her with a hand raised in regal condescension.

He took his time in appraising me. I can't say I was dressed for the occasion, but I did have my shiny new boots on. My wardrobe is miles from rock star snuff. I felt a bit pathetic and resentful. Chaz's stare made me feel like I was being judged, and I doubted the appraisal was positive. As the silence ground on, a whole conversation took place in my head.

"You're staring at me."

"Yes, I suppose I am."

"Stop it. It's rude. Nobody likes being stared at. By strangers."

"*I* do. Quite a lot. Like being stared at. And I like staring as well."

"Obviously. But doesn't it make you feel creepy? Like there must be something wrong with you to make people scrutinize you so closely?"

"No, I rather like the attention. In my line of work, other than chart rankings, it's the only proof that one exists." He laughed, a girlish whinny that suited him not at all. And with it, I sensed an echo, sort of a hallucination of reality that took me out of the fantasy I'd been enacting. I realized this conversation had, in fact, taken place.

"The point, don't you see, is that you're you and I'm me. You're a smart girl?" I didn't know how to answer that, or even if it was a question at all. I looked at Amanda for help, but she was intently looking at Chaz. "If I write about my life,

144

that is to say, tell what truly happened to me, what got written about or talked about so that people *know* it actually did happen — then they'll know more about me than I do. I write songs from the gut, it's like it comes from inside me and outside me at the same time. Dunno where exactly. Or who. But I want my fans to feel as if I am."

"Sorry? What are you on about?" I expected this had something to do with what Amanda and Mr Guy had talked to me about, but I couldn't work out what. Or why I'd been asked to come hear this wanker rabbit on about his guts.

A moment passed as Chaz and Amanda looked uselessly at each other. "Chaz, you see, has a song that he's working on. It's a touching, sad, romantic number that will resonate with the youth of..." Chaz cut her off again. "I don't think 'resonate' is quite the word. More like 'rock,' I daresay."

Amanda pursed her lips for an instant, smoothed her skirt, and continued. "I believe what Chaz would like is for you to tell him something about how a young girl experiences heartache so that he can process it to give his song a frisson of relevance. And balance."

I had no idea what a "frisson of relevance" might sound like; evidently Chaz didn't either. He scowled at Amanda as if she had broken wind. I pointed at a slab of a guitar case stood against a wall and said, "Can I hear what you've got so far?" Chaz considered the question for a moment. "No, no, can't do that."

"I don't think that's appropriate," said Amanda quickly. "He's not asking you to fill in bits, just share some of your feelings. We're trying an experiment here."

"Quite. I'm breaking new ground here, the first star of my stature to do — what did Frank call it? — audience research. That's right. So that's where you come in. You're the audience, the target market, an anonymous nobody."

I looked anxiously at Amanda. "I think I should go home now." I didn't like the sound of being a target.

"No. Yes. Wait. That's not what I mean. Let me put it another way. You're not nobody, you're everybody. You're all of England's absurd adolescence sitting here, and you know exactly what you — and I mean all of you, from Brighton to Birmingham — want in a pop song. I mean you don't rightly know, because if you did, you'd write the bleeding things yourself. But that's not the point. You don't want to hear me singing about my life, Christ, I'm a decade older than you" — Amanda stifled a chuckle at the pretense — "with more money than your entire family will ever make, jetting off like the man who sold the world. But the secret to my success, if you must know, is that you just want to hear about yourselves, sung by a star you can idolize and imbue with your hopes and dreams, like a minor god descended from Mt. Olympia. I just need a little — let's call it 'insight' — so I can focus my attentions. And not just does-he-love-me Laura's-a-twat oh-bother-I've-got-a-spot! Things you care about without realizing that you do. That's the experiment being undertaken here. I'll pull it out of you, like a sword from a stone."

"How? I'm no songwriter."

"I see you as an animal in the wild, a butterfly. You do, I observe. You'll sort of be my peephole into the world in which you live in."

"Sounds dirty."

"Only if you are." Amanda coughed in an effort to detour Chaz from possibly embarrassing himself.

"But why me?" He looked to Amanda to explain it to me, but she demurred.

"There's millions of girls who would leap through a flaming ring of Kotex to be sat where you are. I've chosen you to contribute in a small, insignificant way to my art. You don't need to understand how that mysterious process works. It'll be for the good of England. Queen and country. My success is important to the nation. The thought is that, in a trivial sense, you can help find the missing link it needs to continue." I'd learned about missing links in science class, but those waddled on fins and breathed through their ears or something.

The look on Amanda's face could have been mistaken for a sudden bout of nausea, but she regained her composure in a flash and changed the subject. "Miss Russell will be compensated for her participation. Frank's orders." (It turned out Amanda made that up, but if Chaz could improvise, so could she.)

"Very well, but you won't be paid just for living your little life. You don't think that's worth a wage, do you?"

146

"Dunno. I expect we'll find out, won't we?"

Chaz glared at me, and Amanda made a sour face. I had clearly overstepped, but I wasn't bothered. None of this made any sense to me, and they'd probably forget all about it.

Amanda jumped in. "We will, of course, cover your expenses. Keep the receipts for anything you need to buy."

"Alright." (If I'm just to keep living my "little life," what would I possibly need to buy? Milk?)

Chaz glanced at Amanda and left the room. She pressed a button on the desk. After a brief but awkward silence, a uniformed bloke turned up, hat in hand. "Miss Russell is leaving. Please take her wherever she needs to go."

Editions of Me

AMANDA RANG daily to remind me that she was awaiting my lists with diminishing patience. My pleasure at hearing her voice was fading; she'd become just another nagging nuisance to me.

This felt just like school — an assignment that I didn't understand, couldn't (or wouldn't) grapple with, a looming misery that was preventing me from doing whatever else it was I needed or wanted to do. I wished it would go away and wondered how I got myself into this mess, although I knew quite well how, and I knew quite well why. For all the discomfort this was causing me, at the same time I still wanted to please her, to give her a reason to think well of me and maybe be nice to me. Or nicer than that.

I visited Mercer's and picked out a red leather diary embossed with the words "My Young Life." I made sure to get a receipt — my first expense account purchase. Then I went to Chelsea.

Bryan wasn't at the shop, so I showed a clerk my letter from Burgher — which described me as a "friend of the family" — and she wrote my name in a book, alongside a number. "Just tell whoever's at the till that you've got an account. Give them this number: 7-18."

Back home, I chucked the diary on my bed and lay down beside it, staring at the blank pages, smelling the newness for a long time. I scrunched up my face and chewed on my lower lip, but nothing came to mind except the idea of my so-called mates as mysterious creatures with bizarre habits and beliefs that were my job to decipher and document. I wrote that down: "decipher and document." And then I couldn't think of anything more for either category. I shut it and put it in my bag and went down to watch telly with Dad.

He had on a programme about that Margaret lady, the one what went to the darkest jungles of Africa to study the tribes there. I reckon that's what I was supposed to be doing, studying the tribe at East Acton Comprehensive — only it was like looking in a mirror. If they were prats, well, then, so was I. And if I found something admirable to share, that made me a bit of twat. This wasn't going to be easy.

I got bored and Dad fell asleep at the same time, so I went back upstairs to give it another go. What if I viewed it as a school assignment?

<u>Who Are the Children of England and What Are They on About?</u>

I wrote that down at the top of the page. Between bites on the biro, I tried making an outline, like we'd been taught.

Question: What is in the heads of kids such that they can be so swayed this way or that to elevate any bellend into a reigning pop star?

1) Public school girls, smugly tearing down their betters in whispered condescension, reassuring themselves of the wondrous lives of, at least imagined, yachts and foxes, of the privilege and position they were sure to enjoy provided they save themselves for a polite and pleasant lad from a good family.

2) Are they all trying to be themselves the same way or are they making sure they fit in?

3) Yobs queuing up to sign on. A stupid portion of their meager income might go to entertainment, but music would not be the priority, not when there were pubs and drug dealers to be patronized. They knew all the latest songs, a mysterious skill rooted in the same neurons that could effortlessly memorize football scores, bra sizes and dirty jokes, but they could never be arsed to buy records, at least not the ones that would make a difference in chart placings.

4) Swots who follow a band blindly so they can feel like somebody.

5) Trainspotters searching for that perfect specimen of an LP that once served as the soundtrack to their first snog, the one that almost led to an adolescent introduction to shagging — for 99p.

No help there. I chewed on the biro some more.

149

Top 10 things kids at school are into:

1. Boys (well, the girls)
2. Girls (the boys, except for Ian Watson, I reckon)
3. Sports
4. Telly, especially the Two Ronnies (what a load of silly buggers)
5. Clothes
6. Music
7. Film
8. Fitness
9. Reading (books and magazines)
10. Pets

After some reflection, I crossed out "Pets" and put in "Spots." Then replaced it with "World Peace," which sounded a bit more thoughtful.

Was that all we were? Could school really be that dull? The more I stared at it, looking to puff it up with cooler ideas, the shorter it got. I even tried making stuff up, but it was like sitting on the throne when you don't need to — I tried and tried, but nothing much came out. I put it away and went to sleep.

The next morning, I made another list — of the people I had crushes on. That didn't take any hard graft: Amanda, Stephen, Bryan. I tried putting them in order but couldn't make up my mind about that. I put a star next to the one I'd kissed. Just looking at the list made me feel a bit sexy. After breakfast, I went for a walk hoping it would clear (or, preferably, fill) my head. It didn't.

The next time Amanda rang to check on my progress, I told her I had "a bit of this, a bit of that" and asked for a few days more. She wasn't happy and got me to promise I'd have it "done" — whatever that meant under the circumstances — and delivered to her on Monday. I said I would, not sure that I could.

I SPENT FRIDAY NIGHT grappling further with the list, armed with the suspicion that this wasn't scientific research, it was more like a creative writing project. Not that it felt glamorous or exciting, but I had decided that if I was going to contribute in any small way to the pop trade, it was not going to be by suggesting that Chaz Bonapart select world peace or physical fitness as the

topic of his next single. I shuddered, imagining how awful that could be —
"Take deep breaths / Run in place / Exercise is a must / Now do ten more squat
thrusts!" But it seemed like I was getting better at dreaming stuff up. When I
rooted around the unexplored caves of my brain, I found them occupied for a
change. "Terry is a cow / I'll tell you how / I know / She hates my guts / I think
she's nuts." Again, it wasn't ready for sharing, but it felt like progress. Of a sort.

Bryan was working when I visited the shop Saturday morning. I didn't know if
he'd remember me, but he did, my name and all. That was really nice. We had
a natter about the pop racket. He told me the song playing was by T. Rex;
"boss," he said, and looked pleased when I meekly concurred. I told him about
my store account, explaining it as a gift from a well-off relative (not considering
the likelihood he would have seen the Burgher letter; if he had, he never said). I
went kind of blank when he asked me what records were on my shopping list;
I'd not given it any thought, and a shop full of choices was overwhelming. I told
him I had to narrow it down before hauling anything home. Dunno if he knew I
was bullshitting, but when he offered to pick some out for me that he reckoned
were worth hearing I said, "cool." I liked having him be my tour guide; I got a
kick out of his enthusiasm for all of it. I twiddled my thumbs, listening and
looking, while he scurried about the shop putting together a pile of albums,
which he took to the till and then handed to me proudly, like a cat with a
mouse in its mouth. I thanked him and promised to give them all a good listen
and not return until I had an idea of what I wanted to hear next. He made it
sound like I was welcome anytime, regardless, and I quite liked that.

Back home, I spread the LPs out on my bed, and spent a couple of hours
reading the liner notes, staring at the covers and trying to guess what they'd
sound like before putting them on. I realized after a while that I was just
avoiding stuff I needed to get on with, so I stood them in a tidy stack against
my bed (the side I don't get in and out of) and resumed list duty.

An hour later, I ripped out the page I'd been slaving over and started again, this
time determined to simply make it all up. I mean, who's going to check my
work and tell me I'm wrong, that I don't know anything about the youth of
Britain? I put Bryan in my head, and the songs he'd played me. That was too
distracting, so I unzipped my jeans and slid my hand down for a quick wank — I
mean really quick, I was done in two minutes flat — and promptly fell asleep. I

had a dream he was chatting me up, romantic like, and mentioned that his dad was dead rich and owned a whole chain of shops, and he got a big allowance and only worked in one when he felt like it for a laugh. I went down and got some sultanas, crisps and Ribena to fortify myself while listening to one of the discs Bryan had chosen for me, *Love It to Death* by an American group of blokes called (!) Alice Cooper.

ENIGMA ideas

1 Rockets
2 Love
3 Clothes
4 Cute boys
5 Drugs
6 Death
7 Record shops
8 Telegrams
9 School leaving
10 Sex

I liked where this was going. Did it make sense? Don't suppose so, not really. I hoped some of it was on the mark just by dumb luck, since I really had no way of gauging if I was on the right road or not. After thinking again, I scratched out the last two and folded it into an envelope. Eight would have to do.

1 Sex
2 Clothes
3 Drugs
4 Space travel
5 Cute boys
6 Dancing (or death?)
7 Money
8 Looks (makeup?) and love

On Monday, when I went to deliver it as promised, Laurence was alone in the office. He didn't even ask what it was, just pointed and watched me leave it on his desk with what I took to be either horror or disdain.

I got out of there as fast as I could and took myself to the pictures, to push down the disappointment I felt for having my small accomplishment greeted like a dog depositing a poo.

The Ruling Class starred Peter O'Toole as a rich nutter. I thought it might give me some insight into uppercrusters like Chaz, but other than confirming that they're all mad as hatters, I didn't learn anything from it. I did like the butler, though. Maybe that was worth keeping in mind.

As I chewed my last crisp in the foyer before heading home, four words popped into my head: yearning burning turning learning. I didn't know what, if anything, could be done with them, but I did think they went together nicely.

Grace of State

AT AN HOUR when she should have been beavering away at her desk, Amanda was a good distance away from it, in Soho, having lunch with a school friend. Graziela Schraeder may have looked the part of the glamorous girl's plump and plain confidante, but she was neither a pitiable frump nor a dutiful subordinate. She was haughty enough for the both of them, and found Amanda equal parts detestable and entertaining, a social yardstick with whom to compare notes and dish the dirt from time to time. Just who had the advantage in the relationship was neither clear nor constant.

While the one considered the other privileged to spend time with her, the other — who considered her job in the Italian consulate a lot more important than "functionary in the pop parade," as she had described Amanda's job to others — viewed their social compact as if it were a scripted programme arranged for her amusement and emotional nourishment. Although unblessed by fine looks or a svelte figure, Grace was the antithesis of a sad but cheerful slag. She had grown up sharp-tongued and vindictive, judgmental and intolerant. She laughed loudly and broadly; but rather than lift the spirits of those around her, her expressions of mirth could tamp the air in a room down to a joyless fug. Whatever the provocation, her outsized enthusiasm always sounded forced and phony, the flip side of an undertaker's painted-on sympathy. Amanda thought she was a hoot, but it had never occurred to her that Grace was not put on Earth to play a supporting role in her life or that, in fact, the exact opposite might be the case. As oblivious as she was to her own heedless insults and rampant insensitivity, Amanda was equally incapable of processing Grace's bellicose meanness as anything but an act, one which couldn't possibly be, with any sincerity, directed at her. They were quite a pair.

After a cursory glance, Grace put down the menu, observed the stress evident on Amanda's face, and dove right in.

"Disillusioned, are we? Not all cognac and limos, eh? There's real graft involved, yeah?"

154

"I'm not disillusioned," countered Amanda, with a trace of irritation. She generally spoke in a neutral approximation of a newsreader's voice, bereft of accent but not as forcefully enunciated; people found it easy to listen to her without quite realizing why.

She had put extra thought into her outfit today, and she felt good about it: a black dress and a mauve pillbox hat, which — except for the hot pink stockings and the clunky plastic shoes — would have suited Audrey Hepburn. "I never had any illusions to begin with. I was born without belief and I will go to my grave without it as well."

"Faith in not believing. I get it. Bravo. So then what's got you all wound up?"

"This little git, the one who stole my bag on the Tube. Frank has got this idiot notion about her being useful to Chaz and now my future rests on my making her so. We need her to do a job, and I'm expected to ensure that she does. She seems clever enough, and Christ she's got a mouth on her, but I didn't sign on for this. What do I know about teenagers?"

Grace laughed; it hadn't been that long ago they'd been knee deep in the world of notebooks, uniforms and teachers themselves. "What exactly is she supposed to be doing for you? *Your* job, you useless ninny?" The ensuing laugh contained both cruelty and affection, a seesaw of friend and enemy. Amanda winced. She had not mentioned how she nearly got the sack, which would paint her as vulnerable, careless and insecure, qualities she would sooner die than deliver, unforced, to Grace.

"I can't talk about it, but it's got to do with, dunno, let's call it market research." "Does that pitiful old fart think he can find out what kids want to hear so he can stop making flops, is that it? What a fucking larf." Amanda regretted saying anything. Was it so obvious?

"Look, you can't tell anyone about this."

"Sod off, you pitiful jobsworth. Who am I going to tell? The ambassador? Y'think he'd like to take it up with the Queen, p'rhaps? Ohhhhh yesssssss, mummmmm, it's a matter *mosttttt* grave!!! A *genuine* scandal!!!!"

Grace laughed again, then turned serious. "Really, now. I don't give a toss

155

about your job, your employer or any of that." The waiter brought a carafe of Chablis and filled their glasses.

"Good." The diatribe didn't ease Amanda's mind one jot, but it was something. Grace could be such a bitch. "You're just such a bitch, you know."

"Takes one to know one. You *know*? Look, princess, if you don't tell me what this is about, I can't be expected to save your bacon, now can I? What exactly are you supposed to have her do?"

Amanda had not intended to ask for help, but the offer was comforting. Grace could be domineering, but this was one time her confidence might be more useful than aggravating. And, so long as she could trust her discretion, what did she have to lose? She unfolded Laila's Top Eight list, which she had yet to show anyone at work, and slid it across the table.

Grace looked down and gave it a disapproving scowl that dissolved into a big smile. "I was *right*!" Then she burst out laughing, reading aloud the more risible selections as Amanda desperately tried to shush her. The triumph in Grace's tone was as irritating as shampoo in your eye. She leaned back and milked the moment. Not only did she have confirmation of what she had deduced without even a proper clue, it proved that Amanda's milieu was as tatty and fake as she always hoped it to be. Friends' competition could be fierce, and this was better than good. This was like finding another layer of chocolates under the plastic tray when you thought you had just eaten the last one.

"OK, so now you know. Take a bloody bow. Can you help me work out how to get her to do that? She's just a kid. How should she know what she would want to hear in a pop record, much less what a million shes would?" Amanda was close to pleading, leaving the superficial armor of *sangfroid* to those not genuinely frightened.

Grace stopped smiling and rubbed her forehead. "OK, this shouldn't be too difficult. What are hit songs usually about?"

In a flash, Amanda rejected "How the hell should I know?" as a reply and instead offered "love, romance, dreams, heartbreak, cheating, drugs, that sort of rubbish. Shagging."

"And how old is this belated fetus?"

"Fifteen or sixteen."

"And does she know anything about, y'know, life?"

"Life?"

"Don't be thick. Is she a virgin?"

"How the hell should I know? Weren't you at that age?"

"No, as it happens, but that's not the point, now is it?" Grace took the question as a sign of Amanda's blithe assumption that Grace had never been popular and added it to the mountain of grievances she'd been storing up for years.

She waved Laila's list like a soiled rag. "It would aid your cause if she had some, as it were, experience. Give her a more compelling idea about the nature of the beast. At least the beast with two backs." She roared at her own cleverness.

"Hmm," said Amanda. "Not sure I get what you're suggesting."

Grace rolled her eyes. "Christ, you're useless."

"What?"

"Find some oik to make a proper woman of her. Get her juices flowing. That's how you'll get your songs."

Amanda blushed. "Oh! Grace, Christ, I'm not a bleeding ponce. We don't need her to write songs, just to gi's an idea what Chaz should be writing songs *about*. And we surely don't need to get *his* juices flowing."

As she was saying that, Amanda could sense the oddly twisted logic in that suggestion. Grace's enthusiasm, meanwhile, was already well further along.

"Hey, you know what would even be better? Have someone give her one and then chuck her aside. She won't know the difference between her fanny and her heart, and so long as it's done properly — no grabby herbert in his motor, a proper shag in a bed with a fit lad — she'll mistake it for the love of a lifetime and Bob's your uncle. Songs will come pouring out of her like a nuclear reactor of chart sap. You'll all make out. If you tap the wounds efficiently, your employer will have the little girls of Britain eating out of the palm of his hand."

Amanda said nothing, but gears were turning in her head. Grace waited for her to return to the conversation. It took a while, but Amanda finally replied. "I suppose that could work."

"My kid brother's doing science at school and he brought home a what-do-you-call-it dish the other day, a glass thing with goo in it. You drop something germy on it and leave it for a few days and see what sprouts. Completely disgusting, it is. My gran almost died — she thought it was jam and was about to put it on toast when Daniel stopped her. It was so foul."

"And the point of this would be...?"

"Oh, sorry. Petri dish, that's it. Your girl is like one of them — add some boy germs and see what grows from them. Could be a bit foul for her, but if you can get her feeling rather than just moaning about what she doesn't yet know, you might fish an idea or three out of her battered heart."

"Hmm," said Amanda. A frown crossed her face. "But who would I get to supply the germs, and how would I smush them together?"

"Come on, Am. I can't do it all for you. You'll have to work that out yourself. I had the idea, but I'm no pimp. But I suggest you proceed with care, since your young charge might well be shy of sixteen. That could be delinquency of a minor. Or rape. And especially risky if she decides to get even with the boy who seduces and abandons her. Whatever you do, make sure she doesn't get knocked up in the process. That'd be the end of everything."

Amanda could dismiss such remote possibilities as she came to savor the value of a good idea, one that might solve her problems and then some. "So, a dose of romantic reality. Right. She feels the pangs of adolescent love and that would lead to songs that millions of other spotty dolts could relate to and buy."

"I confess, it all sounds very *Liaisons Dangereuses*..."

"Lazon what?"

"You know, the Jeanne Moreau movie about French people who fuck for sport and vengeance? Like on a dare?"

"Really?"

The sarcasm in Grace's voice was thick as oil. "Yeah, *exactly* like that. Only minus the, blackmail, aristocracy and French names. But, yeah, pretty much the same."

Amanda ignored the insulting tone. "I suppose that *could* work."

Grace handed back the list. "I don't know. My people only screw for love. Much more wholesome." Grace folded her napkin in front of her and pointed at the paper on the table. "The least you can do is pay the bill."

"Happy to." As she reached into her new bag for her wallet, Amanda's mind was already walking down the King's Road.

There was a boldness to the girl that Amanda recognized and, if she did not exactly admire, thought worth keeping in mind. Unlike her own resources of condescension and imperiousness, the girl's were primitive, possibly more powerful, a blur of unfocused need lacking any defined purpose. Perhaps that's just what the children of England were blindly awaiting. Innocence and courage, naïveté and calculation, all mixed up together and turned, somehow, into singable 7-inch missives delivered via radio. Rather like an adult stimulant packaged in sweet, chewy form.

Now it was her task to find the secret, the magic, the trick to make that happen. The thought that she might be on to something big, really big, made her as excited as she had been in a very long time.

If Grace had not put her finger on it, she had at least pointed at it, Amanda thought. Laila was a lump of warmed coal; all she needed was a hot enough spark to make her burn, to unleash the desperate need inside her. There was no direct path Amanda could envision from there to hit songs, but it felt like a promising start to the process, like turning the key in a motor before selecting a destination. She'd figure it out, and she wouldn't need Frank to tell her what to do this time.

159

Top of the Shops

I WAS DAYDREAMING about Bryan when Amanda rang; my lusty loyalty switched sides in a flash. She'd "reviewed" the list and thought it "interesting," her word. I expected her to be cross, but she wasn't. She stayed on the friendly side of cool as we chatted a bit. Then, in a stop-press shocker, she invited me to come shopping with her on Saturday.

On the Piccadilly line to Covent Garden, an advert set me to thinking about the three choices kids had with each other: getting along, misunderstanding everything or being lying little shits. I wrote down "lazy, mediocre, indignant," but then couldn't see how any of that could be of use in a song. But it was a step in the right direction, like doing a single cartwheel after a month of flopping sideways.

I put down some stuff from my dreams and made up a couple of lines about fancying a boy in fifth form. Then I changed it to a girl. If it was going to be Chaz singing, people would think he was a poof if it was about a boy.

A bright, clear day had me squinting in the light when I spotted her, faced away. I walked up close and shouted her name. She looked smashing in a deep blue shirt, black midi and yellow boots. When I told her that I was glad she had asked me along, she grasped my shoulder and gave it a little squeeze. I might have shuddered with delight. I forgot all about showing her any ideas I'd got on paper. And she didn't ask.

Fashion camp, Amanda called it. She asked me what I liked and insulted me repeatedly about my lack of taste but oohed with delight any time I tried on a shirt or skirt she thought suited me. I was lost somewhere between feeling like a little sister and something else entirely, which made my stomach flip every time she smiled. I knew she was smiling at the clothes and not me, but as I was in them, I allowed myself to bask a bit in it as well.

As we bounced in and out of places, she said, more than once, that she wanted to hear what I thought of the singles, but then kept changing the subject each time I fished out my diary and started reading her my notes. As I readied myself to sound smart and, dunno, professional like, she rabbited on about this and that. But the day was still brilliant, like a personal guided tour through exotic lands by an experienced trailblazer. She knew all the shops, all the staff, the names of all the designers. Amazing.

Nearing Carnaby Street, she sneered "the *worst*" with a laugh and turned down Little Marlborough Street instead. I stopped at a stall to look at trainers, but she pulled me away with rolled eyes. By and large, I was in a fog of how and who and why. But it didn't matter. I was having a blast, thoroughly enjoying the attention.

Regent Street, Savile Row, Oxford Street…then the Underground for a mad dash down the Kings Road, all in a blurry blaze of staring, grabbing, trying, scowling and dropping. The buying part didn't happen too often — more for her than me — but then I didn't have to pay for any of what we did settle on as it was all on Burgher's account, as she said more than once. I tried to find out more about Stephen from her, how she knew him, what he was into. I thought I was being subtle about it, but apparently not.

"Why, do you fancy him, you little slapper?"

I stammered out a denial which, if real life is anything like telly, only made my interest more obvious. Amanda snickered and stuck out a bit of pink tongue. "I think you need to be thinking more about songs and less about boys, right now. Especially boys who don't know you're alive." That seemed a little cruel, but it was likely true. I changed the subject, hoping to make my inquiry about Stephen just one in a series of harmless curiosities.

We crossed Fulham Road and were about to enter Fash-Uns. "So what's the deal with Chaz? What's he want with me?"

She looked around, like a spy in some James Bond picture, and gave me a stern look but said nothing. She grabbed my arm and frog-marched me to the back of the store, snatching a blouse off a rack on the way, and into a changing room. She pulled the curtain and backed me into a corner. Putting her face right up close to mine, she spoke in a whisper that I had to struggle to hear over the loud music playing in the shop.

161

"Forget what Mr Guy told you. The truth is, Chaz desperately needs help writing songs punters will pay money to hear, but either he doesn't know it or can't admit that he does. We — *I* — need you to sort that out for him."

As she was talking, I noticed a bit of tree fluff had blown onto her front. Giddy from the day, and buzzed by the intimacy of her voice, I had another courage seizure and reached out to brush it off, right across a nipple. I'd never touched a girl's chest before. She looked down at my hand and then gave me a look that said I'd best not do it again.

It took me a few breaths to resume. "How would *I* know what they want to hear? Frank asked me what I was into…"

"Show me what else you've got. There must be more than those eight things you gave me."

I handed her my notebook, turned to the latest page. She read aloud. "'Lazy, mediocre, indignant'… Yeah, that's sure to set the charts on fire. Maybe the charts on Mars. Puh-leeze. You might have something here with the girl, but it's barely a thought. And a common one at that. Maybe we could make her a lad and see who's paying attention."

As she had on the phone, her tone was more eager than angry. "Remember what Frank said about cause and effect? That goes double. Look, this is not really about things, or songs, or any of that. It's about marketing. Do you know what that is?"

"Going to Tesco's for milk and eggs, that sort of thing?"

"No, you silly bunny, not that."

I gasped. "Wait, why did you call me 'bunny'?"

"I've no idea, just came out that way. Why? Have you got a rabbit at home?"

I didn't want to get into it, so I changed back to the subject at hand. "How am I supposed to know what kinds of songs he should be writing? Isn't he the big pop star? This is pretty funny. I'm nobody."

"You're not making this easy. You should be excited about the opportunity."

I shrugged, not knowing what else to say or do.

"For fuck's sake, no one's asking you to shag the old tosser." I pulled a face and she smiled. "Anyway, you're not his type." Which, she considered, is probably why Frank went along with this scheme. The last thing he needed was for the press to get snaps of another underage girl who'd been to bed with Chaz. That would be the end of all of them.

ON HER WAY HOME, Amanda thought more about the awful thing Grace had suggested. It seemed less awful. And a lot more practical. As she understood it, shock therapy can yield surprising results — and that was exactly what the boss ordered. At the very least, assuming Laila was not equal to the task of coming up with lyrics for a surefire smash (how could she be?), Amanda could keep her ears open and her pen ready for useful scraps from the inevitable torrent of tears on her shoulder. She shuddered at the very thought.

By the time the District Line pulled out of West Brompton, she'd decided that Stephen was her only hope to turn a naïve girl into a pop savant. He wasn't home when she rang, nor again a few hours later. The next afternoon, she found him in the Ruddy Pirate, having a bash at snooker with his mate Blake. She hung in the shadows until they finished and repaired to a table in the back.

Although patience was not among Amanda's virtues, under the circumstances, she understood that waiting was essential. That git would have to be dispensed with before she could get down to business; if she provoked their amusement, the two of them would go at her like hungry dogs at a steak.

"Here's the thing," Blake was saying as she sat down, unacknowledged. "The thing is, with a girl, all of her is involved in the, erm, act: tits, face, stomach, legs, arms, arse, neck, minge, clit, the lot. When you're in the trenches, right, you want to lick or bite or kiss or squeeze or suck all of it at once. Unless she's an utter cow, right, you're dealing with 360 degrees of fuck. You need more hands, right? And more tongues. You can't take it all in at once, so it's a blur, a veritable tsunami of pleasure. But for her, right, you're essentially just a cock, hands and a mouth. Once you're up in it, she focuses everything on the comings and goings in her minge and sod the rest. Her eyes are closed, her mind is focused and you're just a flesh pole doing its best to stay cocked and loaded. Pun intended."

163

"Ah suppose you're right. What's yer point?" In the face of Blake's enthusiasm, Stephen sounded dead bored. For all the ambivalent effort Stephen invested in its pursuit, sex itself was not something he expended a lot of thought on. Blake, on the other hand — in indirect proportion to his actual participation — contemplated little else and had evolved intricate theories on the subject.

Amanda strategized as she bided her time. She needed to charm Stephen into doing her business, but she would need to go about it subtly. There was only so much restraint she could manage when it came to disguising hurt feelings or need. The lack of a poker face served her poorly in shops and school; at work, however, transparency was the perfect calling card for a woman who lacked compunction about blowing people off or seeking outrageous favours.

"Drinks, boys?" She knew she'd be wise to buy her way into this session.

"McEwans, ta." Stephen pretended not to notice her. It was a game they'd played before.

"Mine's a Guinness, please." After Amanda went to the bar, Blake pointed to the table. "Here, gi's one of those, would you?" Stephen passed the packet over. "Winstons, eh? Why not Churchills, eh? You trying to pass for a Yank?"

"Funny." The feigned indifference hid a regular weekly visit to a tobacconist in the City who specialized in imports. They cost a packet, too. Blake lit it and took a long drag. "Good, this. Well done, mate."

Stephen had never been impressed by the taste one way or the other. He just thought smoking an exotic brand set him apart, and that was enough. Amanda couldn't stand the smell, which was a bit of an added benefit. She returned with the drinks and set them down, spilling a bit in the process.

"Bloody hell, Blakey. Has he got you hooked on these foul things as well?" She dug in her bag and fished out a Silk Cut, which she pointed at his mouth. "Wouldn't you rather a proper smoke?"

After what felt like a long afternoon — long enough for several visits to the bog — Blake finally pushed off; Stephen looked ready to leave as well, but Amanda convinced him to stay with the promise of more drinks. Once settled back in, she circled the subject like a matador, drawing Stephen into the story without revealing precisely the role or significance Laila had in Chaz's — and her —

164

world. She started off describing Laila as her new friend, wondering if he remembered the girl he'd gotten into the "Prime Number" lig. He didn't (or leastways claimed not to). She intimated that, besides Laila's likability, there was maybe a work-related reason for her extending herself to be nice to the child. She knew Stephen thought of her as a cynical manipulator, so playing into that image worked to her advantage.

As she parceled out the setup in measured doses, she was horrified to discover that his mind, carried off by drink, was clearly elsewhere. "Th' strangest thing happened tae me a week Sunday. I had a kip in Highgate…"

She would have to indulge this digression before reeling the conversation back in the direction it needed to go. "The cemetery?"

"Aye, th' cemetery. Th' new half."

"What in God's name were you doing there?"

"Perhaps I've nae mentioned this afore, but ah often gang there tae think."

"No, you've never mentioned it. Sounds ghastly. I understand why you wouldn't think to tell anyone."

"Actually, I dinnae. I was rat-arsed and wandered in for a moonlight pish. I sat down tae clear my head; I must hae nodded off."

"Lovely. Stephen, is there a point to this story?" Her face was a cross of exasperation and mild amusement. That having been his goal in telling this silly fib, he felt a spoonful of satisfaction.

"Why, aye, indeed there is. Ah woke up an hour after, 'n' ah wis a good distance fae where I'd bin when ah sat down, 'n' my shoes were on th' wrong feet."

"So, Martians came and diddled you while you dozed, did they? Did you check for missing organs?"

He laughed dryly. She joined him, hoping to firmly end this detour and resume her angling.

"So, I took her shopping —"

"Who?"

"The girl from the lig, the one you don't recall. Anyway, she didn't fit any of the dresses I picked out for her. She's got these...big..." Amanda rolled her eyes but didn't elaborate. "You should have seen her — she barely knew which arm went in which sleeve."

"You're nae pure that shallow, are ye? Aye, o' course ye are. Ah bet ye found some gear for yerself as well. 'N' like as not charged it tae yer boss's account."

"Why, yes, I did. I did. And why wouldn't I?"

"Sure. He kin afford it, 'n' ye wear it well. But how come exactly are ye telling me all o' this? Any o' this?"

Amanda paused, gathering her wits through the mild fog of alcohol. She folded her hands over his and plunged ahead. "Right, well, I've taken it upon myself to make a woman of her."

He laughed and took his hands off the table. "Aye, pure? Fled tae th' other side, hae we?"

"No, no. Not me. I would never..." Amanda blushed at the very thought.

"Then what are ye saying?"

"I...I would like *you* to do it."

Stephen let out a laugh and then turned serious. "Now why would I want tae dae that? And why would ye be asking me tae dae it? Hae ye signed on at th' ponce academy?"

"Of course not. I have my reasons, but I can't let...I can't tell you. I need you to work your charms on her, deflower her and then dump her. As soon as possible. She's kind of sexy in her own way, I daresay. You might enjoy yourself. Boys always do, don't they?"

This was coming out a lot worse than it had sounded in her head.

"Let me see if ah ken what yer saying, Amy." She absolutely hated being called that, which was the only reason he ever did it. "You're asking me tae seduce and abandon a teenager o' yer acquaintance for sport?"

Amanda, who looked stricken, was unable to muster a reply.

"Get tae fuck. Absolutely not. No. I'm certain ye hae a self-serving purpose in mind. Ah won't be a pawn in yer silly game, whatever game that is. Ah don't even want tae know what yer on about — it'll just make it worse."

This wasn't going at all well. At this rate, she was not only going to lose her job, she was going to lose Stephen's friendship — or whatever there still was between them — as well. That hadn't occurred to her as a risk in this scheme, and it suddenly felt significant. She'd never thought of him as having a sensitive side, much less ethics when it came to women. She knew him to be a right cad, but that's what made it easy: she never had to worry about how she behaved toward him; he'd always act worse. His pang of compassion made her feel like a bad person, which meant she also had a sensitive side.

"Did ye really imagine ah would dae this? Do ye nae ken me at all? Why would ye ask?"

"Because you're a bloke?" She didn't intend it to come out as a question, more as an explanation so obvious it did not need stating.

"Ah would hae thought we'd established that. 'N' yer belief is that all blokes are gagging for it enough tae deflower any old virgin brought to them?" (As he heard those words issue from his mouth, Stephen realized that he might not have such an unshakeable basis for his indignation.)

"Stephen, I'm sorry." She exaggerated the lump in her throat into a dry-eyed full-bodied sob. "I'm a mess, I'm desperate. I don't know what to do. About any of it. I didn't mean to insult you, I'm sorry. I was out of order. I'm sorry."

"I'm nae a gigolo. Ah don't shag for sport or dosh, nae that you're offering any o' tha'."

"Liar." She hadn't mean to say that out loud, but she knew enough to find the first part of his declaration hard to, as it were, swallow.

"Jesus, Amanda, you're cold, pure heartless. If ye need a warm body with nae feelings tae leave her miserable, how come don't ye just dae it?" He shifted sharply in his chair, as if his smalls had bunched up. "Ring me if and when yer human heart begins beating again." He got up and left, abandoning the better part of a lovely pint in the process.

AMANDA SPENT a restless night trying to work out how to salvage the mess she'd made. It wasn't yet light when the solution came to her in a dream, like a scene in a movie. She sat up in bed for a few minutes to think about it, then fell back to sleep. At ten, she woke in a panic, conscious of the existence of a plan but unsure if she had thought one up or just dreamed that she had. Once she was able to eliminate that possibility, she set to work recalling what it was. She put on the kettle and sat down to think. By the time the water was on the boil, she knew exactly what she was going to do.

Rather than persuade Stephen to go along with her scheme, she could try and trick him into it. She'd been around enough men to know that there were limits to their free will when it came to shagging, and she was sure Stephen could be counted on to be weaker-willed than many. She need only maneuver him into an irresistible opportunity with the girl and let nature egg him on to action. It was brilliant, and it might even work.

Although some dates on the tour had been postponed, there were still a few shows on the books. Chaz had one coming up in Newcastle — a reliable market for him — on the weekend, a one-off to put some cash in the coffers in advance of the album sessions, which were set to begin the following week. That was where the scene could be set, the actors placed on stage. That would be easy.

She rang Laila and told her that Frank thought it would be good for her to witness the star in his natural environment, a field trip, like. Laila hemmed and hawed, but her reservation seemed to be more about thinking up a story to tell her father than any unwillingness to travel several hundred miles at Amanda's bidding. After a bit, she said she'd figure something out and make the trip. In fact, Amanda noticed with some pleasure, she even sounded excited about it.

The next day, Amanda got on to Stephen, apologizing profusely, begging his forgiveness and, tucked in as an apparent afterthought, inviting him to the same gig, offering tickets and travel as amends for her foul behaviour. She used her best kitten voice as subliminal encouragement and mentioned that she'd be there and possibly up for a bit of "fun." She also dangled the prospect of tapping into a mysterious collection of fine pharmaceuticals. To her enormous relief, he accepted her offer straightaway. They fixed a meeting time on the day and she got busy organizing a car and picking out outfits.

Hit the North

ESCAPING PATERNAL supervision with what I hoped was a knotty enough fib, I turned up at King's Cross Saturday in time for the 3:30 to Newcastle. I had a return ticket, two quid, a change of underwear, a toothbrush and no clue what I was getting myself into.

The last vacant seat in the carriage was by a window, next to a bloke with a *Financial Times*, and faced backwards (as I discovered when it started moving). My stomach got a bit wobbly watching the scenery rippling by, so I pulled the shade, and ignored his harrumph in protest. He turned on an overhead light that somehow pointed at him. I didn't need it — my eyesight was fine. I hadn't thought to bring a book or a magazine, and the trip was around three hours. Boring. I did have my Chaz notebook and a biro, so I opened it and started writing to keep myself occupied, at least until I fell asleep.

> Saturday - Bunking off up north to a concert... it doesn't exactly feel dramatic or glamorous, but I'm a bit scared to be on my own. These boots make my feet hurt. I should have worn trainers. I wonder if Chaz will be good, not that I have much to compare him to other than Roxy Music. It's in some place called the City Hall — will the mayor be there? I hope I can find it alright. I'll have to find a phone to ring dad like I promised I would. I should have written down the details to keep the fib straight.

I stared at it and wondered why anyone bothers. It looked like a to-do list, only not a list. Maybe it would be more fun to make things up. Facing my fears, I suppose. But I gave it a try, letting it spin away from the real world and into the future, a movie I'd never seen.

> This may not make much sense.
>
> There were cars waiting at Newcastle Central when we got there, and we made for the hotel with photographers and

punters in hot pursuit. Filthy and old, Newcastle strikes me as a city people move away from.

A lot of judgment from a girl who'd never been there. But I was away and free to imagine the rest of the night from there.

The show was fine — 3 encores! — but dinner afterwards was soooo W-E-I-R-D. They packed us off to a posh Italian that must of cost hundreds and barely had a light on. It was like eating under the covers. I had wine and they all kept topping up my glass. And, get this, I was the belle of the ball, even though it wasn't me who had just played a gig, or me what was paying the bill. Still, they all focused on me and every time I said something — which wasn't so often — they all listened. And I was talking such shite!

I must have fallen asleep, because the next thing I knew the train was stopped and we were there. I opened my eyes to the sight of a colored bloke in a British Rail getup with his hand on my shoulder. I jerked to attention as my brain worked out that I was not dreaming but waking up on a train that I needed to get off. I closed the diary on my lap — I think the bloke might have noticed that it ended with the words "such shite!" — wiped a bit of drool off my chin and hustled off the train, slamming my knee (no, the other one) in the process.

The clock showed nearly 7:00 and the show was set to start at half seven. I asked someone for directions and learned that it was a twenty-minute walk to City Hall up Grainger Street. I made a wrong turn that cost me a few minutes, but still got there in time.

"There" was an ugly old brick building with white columns and stairs down front. The crowd queuing outside was my age or younger, a rainbow of color abuzz with excitement. I found an usher and asked — as instructed — who to see about the "guest list." I was directed to a window off to the side, told the lady my name and was handed an envelope containing a ticket and a plastic card with a photo of Chaz on a lanyard. When I asked what I do with it, she rolled her eyes. "Put your laminate on, silly. Show it at the door."

"Where?" I was already not enjoying this. She waved to the right, and off I

170

went. As I neared the shuffling line, a girl in a Chaz shirt pointed to the plastic thing around my neck and asked where I got it. She even offered me a tenner for it, but I told her to piss off, feeling a bit special for all of it. There was a hard geezer at the door. I pointed to the pass and he waved a flashlight at it. "Now you behave yourself," he said, opening a side door marked "PRIVATE: NO ACCESS" and motioning me through.

I went down a short corridor that reeked of smoke (and not cigarette smoke) and an open door at the end of it. I didn't know what I was supposed to do or where to go. I was thinking of turning tail and trying to find a seat in the stalls when I saw a familiar figure with an arm in a sling and headphones clamped over his ears. I puzzled on that one for a minute and then tapped his good arm. "Hullo — Will, isn't it? What are you doing here?"

"William." I guessed by the cold, puzzled stare that he didn't recognize me, but he did take off his headphones — with difficulty, given his demi-armlessness, and say hello, in a bored, nondescript way. His voice was very low, not much more than a whisper.

"Are you here with your mum?" He grimaced slightly at the sound of my voice.

"No, why would she be here? And how do you..."

"Then what are you doing here?" I don't usually ask rude questions of strangers, but I felt nervous and alone. So much for manners.

"I'm at uni here." He leaned in toward me. "Do we know each other?"

"My name's Laila. We met at over breakfast at your mother's house in London in June. Maybe it was May. I was sick and dossed there after a Chaz bash. I'm sure you don't remember. I barely do." He was a bit better-looking than I recalled, especially with the ear muffs off.

"Oh, right," he offered with no conviction. "Are you one of his...?" He trailed off, letting his whisper vaporize in the air between us. I guessed — or maybe hoped — he was going to say "fans." I shook my head, not wanting to be any of the things he might have in mind.

He left it at that and relaxed. Maybe he was as uncomfortable here as I was. "Quite horrid back here, innit?"

171

"I don't know, it's my first one. First backstage. Second concert. I don't make a habit of it. I did see Roxy Music at the Marquee. Nearly killed me to do it." I left it vague. Sounded more impressive.

He frowned and shrugged.

"What's happened to your arm?"

He looked at it before replying. "Fell off my scooter, didn't I."

"Ouch." That was the best I could manage. I offered him a shrug. "I suppose I should be getting to my seat. Not sure how to get there."

He waved the uninjured arm in the direction of a stocky bloke with a beer gut and long grey hair, in a blue denim jacket, with beat-to-shit military boots, a roll of gaffer's tape on his forearm like a workingman's bracelet and chains hanging everywhere. He was busy berating a skinny kid in a Who shirt standing by what I guessed was a rack of lights. "Get a fuckin move on, you dozy fuckin cunt. You do know the fuckin show is tonight, right?"

William worked his ear-things back on with his good arm and brought his mouth close to my ear. It had grown loud around us. "See that bloke? That's Fuckin Phil. You'll want to get on to him. He's Chaz's roadie. He'll know where you should be." He winked at me, and I burst out laughing. I may be a happy herbert, but I knew when I was being wound up. "OK, right. Very funny. But what's his actual name? I'm not walking up to your man and saying, 'Excuse me, are you Fucking Phil?'"

"No, for real, that's what he answers to. I promise, you'll be alright. I swear. Tell him I said he was the guv'nor. He'll get a kick out of that." I checked his face for a suppressed giggle or a shred of malice and saw nothing. He looked sincere, and I didn't have a lot of options, so I decided to give it a go. I walked up, braced for a catastrophe and opened my gob.

"Excuse me, are you Fucking Phil?"

"What?" His bellowed reply curdled my blood, but there was no emotion in his face, just a bit of scrunching and a finger pointed at a hairy ear. He hadn't heard me. I turned the volume up as high I could go. "Are. You. Fucking. Phil?"

"That's rrright. And who the fuck might ya be?"

172

"I'm Laila, William said you were the guv'nor." I thought to point him out, but he was not where I'd left him. Instead, I held up my laminate. At the sight of it, Phil unleashed the most extraordinary demonstration of swearing I had ever heard in my life. I tried not to smile at the torrent of profanity. Now, I'm no angel, but I've never heard anyone use so much filthy English before. It hardly sounded like swearing the way he did it.

"Fuckin hell, you're the fuckin bint Mandy had some fuckin cunt call me about. Good fuckin thing you made it. You'll fuckin want to be coming with me. She wants you in the fuckin wings" — he checked the watch hanging from his belt — "and Chaz is on in six fuckin minutes. Give me your fuckin bag and don't fall behind." He waved a torch at the carpeted floor, and, like a cat, I followed the light. As we made our way through a maze of turns and stairs in near darkness, the torch was the only way to avoid tripping over the cables and tape and gear that covered the floor. The trick, I realized after my second stumble, was to plan my steps by what I could make out in front of him as we went. "Watch it here," Phil whispered over his shoulder just in time to keep me from doing a header over a rolled-up rug.

He stopped short. "Here." He waved the torch at a clear spot on the floor. "You stand here. Do – not – fuckin – move – from this spot, right? I'll come and fuckin fetch you when it's fuckin done and get you to the fuckin hotel. The Royal Station, right?" By the time I could eke out a reply he was gone.

I looked around, careful not to move. I was to the right of a curtained stage, at the back of which was a staircase leading to the pipes of a church organ. There were rows of amplifiers surrounding a drum set near the back; a few feet behind the curtain stood a row of microphones.

The voice of an unseen compere came over the PA. "Ladies and gentlemen, welcome to Newcastle City Hall. I see a lot of faces who were right here last month for Bowie, what a night that was, but tonight we've got something really special for you." I could only hear the crowd roar as I watched the musicians took their places. "For the first time this year, direct from London, the rocker's rocker, the man who didn't sell the world, the number-one star of rock and roll, I give you the one, the only, Chaz Bonapart! Let's hear it!"

An even greater din went up as the lights came down. The curtain soared out

173

of sight, and the band began playing. Chaz ran out, waving a silver guitar in the air. Past him, I could make out the left side of the stalls and part of the balcony. It was a handsome theater, far nicer inside than out.

A towering blur in a blue suit, Chaz stood on platform heels, his hair teased up in a wild mane; the overall effect was a stringy giant. The rest of the band was similarly kitted out, but there was no question who the spotlight followed. He waved the band to a stop and grabbed a mic. "Right, then. Here we are. You Geordies look brilliant! How 'bout we get a bit of rockin', what do you say?" The punters roared in assent and surged into the aisles, rushing down as far as they could against the futile resistance of the middle-aged ushers, who quickly abandoned any attempts to shoo them back and vanished from sight.

A song began, and so did the chanting. The music was loud, but the crowd was louder. They kept up without pause — "CHAZ! CHAZ! CHAZ!" — until the first song finished and he yelled "Thank you!" As if to fill the energy dip, the crowd rushed forward again, more powerfully this time, many with outstretched arms. I once saw Catholics in Rome on the telly do that, reaching out toward the Pope on his balcony. Freaked me out a bit then and did again now.

I would wet myself if I had to stand up there before a theater full of lunatics rushing at me, a dizzying riot of screams and shrieks, but it didn't seem to bother Chaz one bit. When I could see his face, he looked calm, patiently taking it all in. I bet the Queen understands this kind of adulation. Two lines into the next song, which turned out to be "Prime Number," a girl in a silver shirt began scrambling onto the stage. She wasn't even standing up when she began a beeline for Chaz. A tackler flew out of the wings to intercept her, but she beat him to the target and had her arms wrapped around Chaz's waist, her head on his thigh, when the roadie came to pry her off. A boy in a pink shirt landed at Chaz's feet and was carried off. More followed, all the same. Amazingly, the musicians didn't miss a beat, or drop the jolly smiles they all wore, rolling right into the chorus, oblivious to the impromptu scrimmage surrounding them. I could see Fuckin Phil, on the other side of the band, rub his forehead with a bandana, nodding vigorously.

I didn't find what Chaz and his lads were doing that exciting — it looked too much like panto and the sound was a muddy mash. He made a lot of faces while he played. I wasn't really getting it, but I was deeply impressed by the audience's completely thoughtless hysteria. Whatever the music sounded like, if it got that kind of response, I could see the point. They were getting what they paid for from him, but they wanted more. In their beseeching need, the outstretched arms made the fans look like infants being separated from their mothers. That thought made me sad. When I used to watch sad movies with Mum, it was the weeping what got to me, not the story. So here two-thousand kids were going completely mental, and that hit me a lot harder than whatever rubbish Chaz was singing about.

The show looked strange from the side, lots of forward and back motion to the microphones, but I kind of got swept up by it all anyways. I stared at the kids down front, the ones who were most into it, and I couldn't see exactly what it was about for them. I mean, you go to a slasher picture and it's the blood, right? But some aging berk bangs out silly songs at ear-splitting volume and that turns people into raving zombies frothing at the altar? All a bit odd, if you ask me. I tried to feel around inside if I shared any of their giddy abandon, but it weren't there. Maybe I got no feelings.

As each new song started, the crowd surged forward, the waves of enthusiasm cresting and receding through the non-stop roar. They were all in it together, a body of random individuals who needed to find each other, and Chaz was their leader. He made them a group, a team, a class, a club. They didn't need to be friends with each other, they didn't need to be the same color, religion, age, sex or class. They just needed Chaz to be the sun they could all revolve around. Together in their individual regard.

With that rolling around in my bean, it struck me that unlike them I didn't want to be part of something bigger, to have allies and teammates who thought about me in the same way. I had no desire to share an idol that defined and propelled us, from gig to gig, single to single, *Top of the Pops* to the *Old Grey Whistle Test*. I didn't need or want a Chaz in my life. It seemed sad to see a theater full of people, each of them with a face, a name and a personality, and think of them as being one thing. What a drag to be so obvious. I was nobody, but I've got no desire to be bound for someone else's glory, thanks all the same. When I thought about it later, it struck me that, beyond the basics, I didn't need anyone in my life. And maybe, it hit me for the first time ever, a bit of shock that I even thought this, I liked it that way.

In an hour it was all over, and he ran off the other side to even more crazed screams, followed by stomping and another round of "CHAZ!" cheers. They came back on and started playing again, even more zizzed-up then before. I was wondering where I was supposed to go next when Phil appeared, tugging on my arm. "The fuckin cars are out back, and you need to be in fuckin third one down. And make it fuckin sharpish, yeah?"

I did as I was told and was soon seated in a car the size of a swimming pool, sunk into a cushion of leather the color of milk tea. There was a glass wall behind the driver; William with the broken wing was there, across from me, erect and looking as awkward and out of place as I felt, along with a batch of other people in fantastic gear with drinks in their hands.

"Hello, again." Surprised at hearing him speak, I nodded, trying to think of a reply. My ears felt like cotton wool that had trapped a bee, and his voice was soft. After an awkward pause that might have ended the conversation right there, he said, "I've recalled our first meeting. What's your name again?"

"Laila." It suddenly felt strange to say it.

"What did you think of my...of Chaz? Makes quite a racket, doesn't he?"

I had to strain to hear him while being sure not to bump his injured arm. At least he wasn't wearing the ear gear, so he seemed able to hear me alright.

"Yes, I suppose. I guess I enjoyed it. Where did you get to?"

"Oh, I never watch the shows, the volume is too much for me. There's a TV thing in a room in the lower basement, with the sound down very low. I had some biscuits and tea." Which did nothing to explain what he was doing here and why he knew people who worked for Chaz. I guessed his mum back in London was one of those.

"Do you know where we're going now?"

"No clue. Out for an adventure of some sort, I reckon. You'd best buckle up." He put on a friendly smile.

A PROCESSION of four black motors on the A69 followed the curves of the Tyne past places called Stella and Blaydon, Ryton, Wylam and Clara Vale. They had been going for maybe twenty minutes when the motorcade crossed a small bridge and pulled up at a castle in Prudhoe.

It was an uphill walk from where the car stopped, and some of the women had a rough time negotiating the pebble road on their platforms. One turned an ankle and was hoisted up on Fuckin Phil's back and carried, like a child, to the entryway, where she made a miraculous recovery and danced her way inside.

Bright lights illuminated the grounds, almost to the point of daylight. The castle was kitted out like a movie from the French Revolution — guillotines, flowers, ladies in hoop skirts, men in thigh-high leather swashbuckler boots with peacock feathers in their felt hats. The waiters were dressed as peasants and soldiers, all carrying Champagne bottles. A pony wandered the lawn, clad in a blanket with Chaz's face on it. There was even a girl in chain mail with a sword who I think was meant to be Joan of Arc.

IT WAS DARK inside the castle; candelabras provided the only illumination. Fortified with a glass of wine, I found a remote corner and retreated into it. William had gone missing again, but that was not as pressing a concern as how long I'd be stuck in this insanity and how I would ever find my way back to 20th century London.

"Hullo there, hen." I squinted up into the dark to see Stephen. His hair was a right mess (odd for a bloke who works in a salon, right?). "I jalouse it's nae a proper Chaz Bonapart bash unless you turn up." He smiled warmly, but I was too surprised to manage a reply, clever or otherwise. "Have ye seen Amanda?"

I focused on the accent, liked the feel of it in my ear, and heard myself — not consciously, I swear — trying to copy it. I don't think he heard; the room was noisy. "No. She said she'd find me at the gig. But then she didn't turn up."

"Right. She and ah took a motor up together but as soon as we got tae th' hotel she placed a call and dashed off tae handle some family thing. Did ye ken her folks bide 'ere in Newcastle? I've nae seen her since. How'd ye like th' show?"

"Alright, I guess. I didn't see you there."

"No, if she couldn't be arsed, neither could ah. Ah suppose it might be rude on my part, but who gives a toss. Ah ken some folk in the city and we had a meal. I don't much fancy Chaz. I'm pure here as a lapdog. Amanda lured me all this way on th' promise of showing me a good time but has failed miserably in that regard sae far." He laughed amiably. "Sae it goes."

He looked into the cavernous lobby in which we were meant to be reveling. I stared at his face. "They say it's grim up north, but clearly tha's nae th' case, is it? Quite a place, quite a do."

"Yes." I was not going to impress anyone with my conversational abilities, but if he was willing to go on, I was more than happy to listen and agree.

"I've no scooby why they'd go sae over th' top all th' way up 'ere. Ah suppose it's to keep his nibs entertained, or inflated, as if he needs any additional smoke blown up his arse. Perhaps it's a pure distraction. Ah should think a wee supper at some swank establishment would suffice, but evidently nae. Instead they lay on Fellini bloody Satyricon. Ah suppose Amanda is tae blame for all of it. Few girls ken how tae spend other people's dosh so enthusiastically."

I nodded vigorously without understanding much of what he'd said. "I don't know anyone here but William, and I haven't seen him since we got here." The noise forced me to shout this bit of information as if I were cheering on the rugby team at school.

"I've nae idea who that is, but you ken me, I reckon. That's got tae count for something." Another friendly smile. "Can you believe this madness? Just because he has th' gall tae call himself 'Bonapart'? I expect there'll be cake."

I laughed along without knowing what was funny and suddenly felt that not-fitting-in feeling.

"Silly berk didn't even get th' spelling of 'is name right. Napoleon built a bloody empire, 'n' all this one's done is to sell a few records to bairns who don't ken the difference. Hardly seems fair, now does it?"

What I know about Napoleon could fit on a pin, so I wasn't about to discuss it. But Stephen was awfully fit. And talking to me as if I were an actual person.

"What *is* yer name?"

"Laila."

"Like the song?"

"No, lie-LUH!"

"I'm Ste..."

"Yes, I know." I probably didn't need to say that so quickly.

"Fancy a dram?" Without waiting for a reply, he was gone. When he didn't return, I went to the bar to see if there was a queue but there were only a few people there, he not among them, so I got my own drink. There wasn't much of a choice, so I pointed at the glass in someone's hand and said, "I'll have that." It was pale green and tasted like Allsorts.

The room began turning, so I found a bare stretch of wall in the path of an air vent and held on for dear life. Some of the partygoers had cleared out, which meant I was at risk of being stranded out here. I took a few deep breaths and calmed down enough to start looking for Fuckin Phil or Amanda or William or Stephen or anyone else who might get me to the hotel.

The music was loud, some throbbing twaddle about boys and girls all around the world. I couldn't guess if the voice belonged to Chaz or not. The PA accentuated the beat and made the room — or maybe it was just my head — pulse in time with the colored lights, which looked like candles, or were meant to, on the walls. Without really thinking about it, I started moving along with it, kind of swaying my arse side to side and waving my arms about.

"Well, well. Keek who's gone all *Top of the Pops*! Git doon and git with it!" It was Stephen again, a drink in each hand. I didn't realize he'd been singing along to the music ("Boys and girls all over the world") when he stopped and said, "Which d'ya fancy?"

I gulped. "I haven't worked out the sex thing yet...do I need to pick between them?" He arched a brow and looked around as if he'd been tapped on the shoulder. He wrinkled his nose and nodded at the drinks in his hands.

"Nae, silly. Dae ya want th' buck's fizz or th' rum and coke?"

"Sorry...I thought you, erm...bucks fizz, please." I must have blushed the color of beetroot.

"What d'ye think ah was on about?" I didn't bother answering, it was only going to make things worse. I didn't expect he'd care anyway.

The song's chorus played again, and the penny dropped. His eyes crinkled in recognition as he smiled. I downed the sweet drink in a go.

He stepped back and gave me an appraising look, bottom to top. When he was done, without any visible reaction, he leaned toward me and said, "Look, there's something ah hae to tell you." That in and of itself was a shock, unless, like, I had a disgusting bug in my hair. "Let's go someplace where we can talk." I thought we were getting on alright where we are, but yes was the only word I had for him at the time. I would have done anything he could think of.

"Ah gather we both hae rooms reserved at the Royal Station Hotel. It was Amanda's original plan that ah put up for th' night in her wee brother's room, but when she run off she said she'd booked me in at th' hotel instead. Her parents can't stand th' sight of me, and ah feel much th' same about them. Quite provincial, nae that you'd imagine our lassie could come from such stock. Quite a reinvention. Not that any o' this should matter a whit tae you."

Not hardly. I was lapping this up. Jealousy, curiosity, excitement, the sheer thrill of having a proper conversation with this super-fanciable boy...I was a high-voltage electric socket buzzing with energy.

We walked outside to the cool air. I anxiously wanted to know what he needed to tell me, but he didn't seem in any hurry about it. "I'll get a taxi. Unless ya need tae be sick or use th' loo." It felt like a test of my mettle and my instinct was to soldier on, but my body insisted otherwise.

"Yeah, good idea. I'll be quick. Will you wait?" I hoped that didn't sound too anxious. Or hopeful. I didn't know if he'd be there when I got back, but there was no way I could get in a car at the instant. I rushed back into the fray, not sure where I'd find a bog in a castle. I felt better on the way back outside, and better still when I found him not far from where he'd been.

I don't know how he organized a taxi, but there it was. I spent the ride back into town staring out the window, thinking up lists of possibilities and responses for how the rest of the night might go. I realized I was just dreaming — nothing was going to happen that wouldn't just as likely take place in my bedroom at home, but at least I had something fresh and relatively real to fantasize about. My seesaw was definitely shifted in his direction; I barely gave a thought to what Amanda was getting up to. Or William.

He still hadn't told me what he needed to tell me when we rolled up to the hotel.

"Fancy a drink?" I couldn't believe that I'd said that, especially to him. And at my age. I immediately felt like a fool, or at least a fraud, since that was an adult thing to say and I was by no means an adult.

"Actually, ah dae. Would you care tae join me?" That was mighty suave, turning it around so he was the one doing the inviting. Regardless, this sounded much better than getting in my pyjamas and writing in my diary. And probably puking. And I was still desperate to know what was on his mind.

We went to the hotel bar, a sorry old pub that had seen better days. The publican, who was mopping up, chucked us out as last call had come and gone. I was relieved that we were done boozing, but disappointed that the night was about to end with more questions than answers. From the looks of him, Stephen was as knackered as me, and probably didn't need any more drink in him either. He said maybe it was best that we call it a night. We went to the desk, said our names and were given keys shackled to metal discs the size of my palm to rooms on the second floor (me) and sixth (him).

I had to trudge down a long passage to reach my room, where I found my bag, miraculously, sat on the bed. It was exciting to be in a hotel room of my own for the first time and I aimed to enjoy it. I pulled off my clothes, all sweaty and reeking of smoke, and got under the covers, intending to have it off with myself. But after a few minutes of watching the vertical lines of the wallpaper circle around me like a carousel, I was asleep.

INSIDE ROOM 606, Stephen was surprised to find a pint of Macallan in his room, along with a not-quite-apologetic-but-at-least-conciliatory note from

Amanda. He had half expected to find Amanda in his room but found the whiskey a more appealing prospect. Drink would require no consideration or patience; the pleasure it gave him would last longer than a ride.

Two miles away, curled up in her old bedroom, anxious about the impending drama but confident that her parents were well off to dreamland, Amanda felt pleased with herself for having squeezed in a long-delayed visit to them on Chaz's tab. It did seem fair to her, since she was here on his behalf. Armed with a tepid instant coffee to ensure that she could stay awake as long as needed, she stared at the clock she'd had since childhood. When she couldn't stand it a moment longer, she rang the hotel and asked for Miss Russell's room, hoping that events taking place well out of her view had played out more or less according to plan.

Laila sounded confused, drunk and half asleep. Amanda hoped she would not pass out before she finished "explaining" that she'd just hung up on Stephen, that he'd drunk too much, they'd had an awful row and he was threatening to bed the first decent-looking female he happened upon as a way to punish her. She'd meant to pretend that she hoped for sisterly agreement about resisting loutish behavior and leave it at that, but instead laid it on thick, moaning how hurt she'd be if Stephen did find someone else. As frosting, she let slip that she'd asked if he'd seen Laila and he'd seemed awfully curious to know more about her. With that, she rang off.

Ten minutes later, during which time Laila really thought she would be sick, Amanda was back on the line. "I wasn't going to tell you this, but I've been worrying about this all night and, as you are my responsibility, I feel I have an unspoken pact with your father to prevent any moral transgressions on my watch. And I have to warn you, I may have accidentally given Stephen your room number. He sounded awfully drunk and said perhaps he would make a woman of you tonight. Yes, that's what he said. I know, isn't it ghastly?"

Laila choked on whatever words she was trying to form and wondered, through the fog, what she would do if he did. The supergirl courage that had come on without warning in the past was nowhere to be found, and although she felt a rush of sexual feelings, she guessed she would not go through with it even if the opportunity presented itself. Not that it was going to. She'd thought of nothing else since encountering him at the party, but layers of why-nots and what-ifs had tied her mind into a knot.

She tried to focus on what Amanda was saying. "...before, just to get me upset, and I know he would never in a thousand years do it, but you know men. They can be so vicious when they're hurt and take things they don't even want just to punish the people who means the most to them. I know he'd feel so guilty that he could even imagine doing that to me, so I just need your word — because we're such good friends, sisters, like — that you will make sure he keeps it in his trousers, if it should come to that. Will you promise me that? I'm sure you feel you owe it to me." Using her own shittiness as bait in a trap might have troubled a girl possessed of greater self-awareness or more capable of shame, but Amanda didn't consider her mistreatment of others in any way regrettable, just a piece of who she was, the woman the universe needed her to be. She might not have been to the manor born, but the manner was hers through and through.

Plus, she was desperate. "I know it's absurd to even imagine that he would want to sully his reputation with a plump teenager, but you know men. Oh, sorry," she laughed drily, "That's not quite true, is it?"

While listening carefully to make sure Laila hadn't nodded off, Amanda reiterated that this was a familiar and altogether hollow threat, that she knew he would not do anything about it but was still hurt by his suggestion of the most ridiculous and offensive assignation imaginable. She made sure Laila registered the word "offensive."

As motives go, emergency repairs to a bruised ego are a formidable force; the chance to punish a rival in the bargain can be irresistible. Amanda knew the recipe well, but thought it needed a dose of desire, so she added a quick list of Stephen's bed skills, which now had more value to her than they'd had in the moment. Too much of that stuff was overly wet and sloppy, seemed a bit pointless and was occasionally chafing. While she went on about licking and pulling and squeezing into the phone, she prayed he wasn't too drunk to deliver the goods, as it were.

She could hear Laila breathing. It was time to start the next motor., and she rang off with a brusque closer. "Go back to sleep and forget all about it. Sounds like you need the rest. We'll talk more back in London. Perhaps I can find you some wally your own age to keep you company."

Laila looked at the phone for a good long time after the line went dead, fuming at the way she'd been spoken to and thinking that if she wasn't so groggy and exhausted she might well see about punishing Amanda for her meanness. In her bag was a bright red lipstick she'd got from Boots and hadn't tried. She'd never seen the point, but it suddenly felt like the most defiant thing to do. She circled her mouth and inspected the result in the bathroom mirror. As she was trying to decide if it looked smart or pathetic, she felt a sudden storm in her belly and threw up in the sink, splashing sick all over.

Unable to guess whether Laila would bolt out of her room in search of Stephen or cry herself back to sleep, Amanda waited a half-hour and then rang his room, which she had carefully chosen to be a good ways from Laila's. Reception was slow to pick up and reluctant to disturb a guest at this late hour, but she made it sound urgent and after a brief delay the phone was purring in her ear. Stephen answered groggily, which was a good sign (if not a surprising one, given the liquid anaesthetic she'd left for him). Larding on the needy anxiety, she asked if he would be a dear and look in on Laila, who she said had rung her in a panic after waking up with a stomach ache. "Poor kid, all my fault, I'll be on my way in a minute, it's a long ride...it'll take a while to arrange a taxi, my dad's motor is in the shop, I'm ever so worried, I feel terrible, would you *please*, just until I can get there? Here, write down the room number...have you a biro?"

In his blurry condition, as Amanda hoped, Stephen didn't ask many questions, and the ones he did manage were brushed off by repeating the room number and stressing the urgency of his response.

Stephen tugged on the bottom of a blue shell suit and a faded Arsenal jersey; after a glance in the bathroom mirror to see that his hair was more or less presentable, he went out into the passage, hoping no one would see him in this sorry state. The lift operator had long since packed it in, and Laila's room, he was annoyed to discover, was four flights of stairs down and a long corridor away. He was breathing heavily and not at all certain what he would find or have to do about it when he arrived at the designated door. Holding a kid's head over a toilet and providing a bit of reassurance was one thing, but if she was in need of more serious medical attention, he'd ring 999 and bugger off.

THE KNOCK SCARED the piss out of me; at first, I thought I was dreaming. I'd fallen asleep after Amanda rang back, but the noise jerked me awake in a flash. Fear took hold as I came to my senses. The knocking continued, then I heard a whispered voice, slow and slurry.

"Laila, it's Stephen Dowery. Open the door."

I jumped out of bed, my heart racing from the surprise, and had my hand on the knob when a chill breeze reminded me that I only had knickers on. I remembered being sick and thought I might be again. Panicked and lost, too confused to locate either my clothes or the light, I pulled the top sheet off the bed in the dark and wrapped myself in it.

I opened the door a crack. My head hurt. Stephen looked rough, his eyes more closed than open, wearing a ratty top and blue nylon pants. "What's wrong? It's the middle of the night," I said, blinking at the lights in the passage.

"Uhh...Amanda...said...you..." His eyes opened and he took what I assumed was a look at the fright I must have been. "What happened tae yer face?" He put a hand up to where I'd smeared the lipstick before being sick. Without thinking, I raised mine to intercept it, the wrong one as it happened, the one crucial to holding up my improvised sheet costume, which promptly slid off. I reached down and grabbed the sheet back up around me, but I'd been on full display and it was clear he'd noticed. I blushed crimson.

"Oh my," he said, far more alert than he'd been a moment earlier. I half hoped he'd just pretend that it hadn't happened, that he'd just go away and I'd never have to see him again. And what was he doing here anyway?

"We'd best gae inside." I gave him a look which neither of us could have correctly read. He coughed and smiled. "Ah think I've locked myself out of my room." It sounded like a fib, but there was too much going on all at once to judge that. He closed the door and leaned against it. I sat on the bed, wrapped up to my nose like a mummy. I pulled a pillow into my lap for good measure.

"That's quite a figure you've got. Ah would nae hae guessed." Perhaps that was meant as a compliment, but it sounded like an insult. I covered my eyes with my hands as if that could help him unsee my bits or whisk me away from the profound embarrassment I was feeling. He smiled at my panic and that calmed me a little. I didn't feel like I was in any danger.

"Sorry ah said that. Right, are ye ill? Did you ring Amanda?"

"I threw up in the sink a little while earlier, but I'm alright now. Just a headache. But how would I ring Amanda? I haven't a clue where she might be."

"Kind of what ah assumed. That's good. The not-ill bit. Do you ken what's going on here?"

At the moment, I felt stumped by everything. "About as well as I understand calculus."

He looked puzzled.

"No, not in the slightest."

He smiled. "It's all her doing, ya ken? Lady Titless is nae your friend, but ah expect you've worked that out by now. She's playing at it sae she can use me to use you."

"Who are you talking about?"

"Oh, you are thick." He didn't make it sound like a criticism, not exactly. "Amanda, silly. Compared to ye…"

I knew full well who he was talking about. And I had my own suspicions about her. But knowing that she might not have my best interests at heart didn't change my feelings about her pale skin, our kiss, shopping day or a dream I'd had about a cuddle with her. I wasn't intentionally trying to sound dumb, I just wanted to know what he thought of her. Calling Amanda names seemed childish, but I did register, between his remark to me and his description of her, his interest in the female bits between chin and belt.

"Do you ken why I'm here?"

"Sorry, blank again." This time, I smiled to indicate that I wasn't trying to be difficult. I was being useless without any effort.

186

"Let me start at th' beginning." I might have been nodding off, or looking a bit glazed, because he came over and shook me gently. "Stay awake for this, it's important." I snorted and forced my eyes open wider.

"Ah ken what she's got ye daein'. Sort of. Ah gather ye haven't got a handle on th' songwriting yet, and she's in a bit of a state over it."

I wasn't ready to be completely honest about what Amanda had told me in the shop, so I resorted to the original version. "It's not writing, it's market research." I told him about the list I'd made, and the book at the library, and the records I'd listened to. It was clear the pop racket held little interest for him, but he did seem concerned about how I might find my way through the maze and put one in the net, as it were. Laila United F.C.

"Look, Amanda hae a plan. An awful, mean plan. She coudnae bring herself to spill it all tae me, and she's nae got th' bottle tae come directly tae you, but the idea in a word is she thinks if you have sex it'll help you help them. Words for songs. For Chaz. Virgin sacrifice, ah called it, and ah told her it's nae on."

I took this in without comment, as I couldn't possibly think of what to say. I was getting more confused by the minute.

"In her daft scheme, your introduction tae romance will find its way intae songs that will — what's th' word I'm looking for here? — resonate with your peers sae her talentless boss can record them and get 'im back intae th' hearts and minds of weans. Aye, that sounds pure like a master stroke."

"Really? Will it work?"

"Nae, ah hope not." He regarded me strangely. "Tune up your antenna, lassie. Ye and ah will nae get on if you take seriously every word ah say."

"So you don't think it would help me think up clever ideas for songs if I had it off with someone? Neither do I, but I'm not against proving her wrong." I didn't actually say that, but I did consider it for a second. Instead, what came out was, "I don't see what the one thing has to do with the other."

Before he could reply, I excused myself for a pee. I closed the door and prayed he couldn't hear me. When I returned, he was on the bed and motioned me to sit beside him.

187

"I've certainly met a few lassies whose minds function as a remote outpost of their fannies, but I'd like tae believe you're nae one. You're a bit young tae be jaded and cynical, too smart tae use your body tae make your way through life. If that were th' case, you'd have far greater challenges tae face than cracking th' pop parade. Would ah be correct in assuming that you're nae, as Hendrix once put it, *experienced*?"

I would have liked to have had a clever reply, at least a proud declaration of my growing skill as a self-pleasurer, but at the moment a discussion of my virginity was simply not on. Especially not with the lovely boy I had dreamed would relieve me of it. It was all so daft and confusing. Words failed me, and the rush to my head emerged as tears. I had enough problems without being fucked over for the sake of a 45. This couldn't be how Bolan did it, right? How scary and sad, and what was he saying about my twat? The lucid me might have taken all of this in clearly, or at least asked the questions that would clarify what he was on about, and worked out what it might mean to me, but none of the above. Instead, I felt overwhelmed, scared and sad. At first he looked away, as if I deserved privacy while I fell apart, but then put his hand on my cheek and said, "Look, this is grown-up stuff, and ah nae think you're ready for any o' it."

I probably should have agreed with him, but bloody-mindedness (or maybe it was pride) prevented me from facing facts, and I endeavored to argue the point. "How did Amanda reckon I was to learn about love? I assume she's in a hurry to get on with it. She wouldn't be having me wait for some spotty git in the fourth form to ask me out, would she? Don't I get a say in this? I'll shag who I fancy, thank you very much. Did she say if she had someone in mind?"

He gave me a disgusted look but withheld the insult of my intelligence that probably should have accompanied it. Be grateful for small mercies.

"Me. I'm supposed tae be yer bad boy. But tha's nae on."

"Of course not." I had no idea why I said that, but the laugh that followed was strictly nerves, not because any of this was funny. I couldn't say anything else, as it was impossible to enunciate with my jaw gaping open. I put a hand to my crown to check that it hadn't blown off. How could something be so wrong — and so blindingly obvious? This topped all the fucked-up things I'd ever heard, except Mum's death. So I couldn't have one of the two things I wanted most in the world because the boy who had given it to countless other girls without a moment's thought was having a crisis of conscience over his not-really-a-girlfriend's effort to pimp him out to save her job? We were in a bleeding hotel room, it was the middle of the night, neither of us was sober and I was wearing knickers and a bedsheet. Talk about plucking defeat from the jaws of victory. This was pitiful. My tears flowed freely. I must have looked a fright.

"But we both ken I'm nae going to do it. It's bloody wrong. A girl your age needs friends, nae lovers. I mean, sure, you're EF and all, but tha's nae th' point. A quick ride in a toilet stall won't break your heart, and ah think you deserve better."

I sniffled and coughed, but at least I was able to stop crying. "F what?"

"E-F. Eminently fuckable. It's what wee jimmies say about fanciable females."

"I am? Really?" My face turned red and I'm sure other parts of me did as well. I was soaking wet down there, I mean I felt it, but without sending off an exploratory hand, I had to go by unfamiliar sensors reporting to a most unreliable command centre. I'm sure I was. This line wasn't helping his side any. And who would appreciate being called desirable as part of an explanation why said desire was in no danger of being satisfied? It was just wrong.

I couldn't stand it anymore; my sense fuses all fried and left me on autopilot. I grabbed his head and kissed him as hard as I could. He didn't do much in return, but he didn't push me away either. He let me do what I wanted until I was done. He didn't look pleased or angry, but I felt as if I'd gotten away with something, like nicking candy from a shop. I guess I felt a little ashamed, but I'd enjoyed myself as well.

He didn't seem bothered about any of it. "I'm sure there are plenty of laddies gagging for a go at you. But you shouldn't let them unless you pure like th' bloke. You dinnae wantae be one of those girls." (How did he know that? I didn't even know that. And I might well have a different opinion on the subject.) "How about tha' wee William lad? He seems crackin'. And it doesnae hurt that his da's a rich pop cunt. You could dae a lot worse than a life of luxury, eating crisps an' peepin' telly in a bathrobe all day."

189

"Wait, who's a rich pop...er, cunt?" It felt strange saying that.

The surprise he registered made me feel silly without knowing why. "Really? Ye nae ken tha' Chaz is his faither?"

My mouth gaped open, as much from the surprise as from the realization that I should have known it all along. "No, but that does explain a few things."

"I expect sae. That apple could nae hae fallen further fae th' tree, could it?"

"Yeah. Not that I know Chaz, in person, or William neither. Seems nice enough but a bit of a pill. And, no thank you, all the same. I'm not interested. He's not my type." As if I had a type. I wondered if I truly thought that or was simply declining the offer so as not to seem easily fobbed off.

"Sae...back tae Amanda. Honestly, she's a total shit, and she's gone and over-stepped this time. Ye can't just screw with people's screwin'."

I liked the sound of that, but I was of two minds about the substance of it. In truth, I didn't think I would mind being screwed with in the way he meant, not that I had any clear idea what that would be like, or what obligations it might hold for me if there were another human present. Anyroad, being pushed around, having my own wishes and desires interfered with in one way or another — wasn't that being screwed with as well? — was pretty the sum total of my life at this point. Pulling some enjoyment out of it seemed like a sound arrangement. But then again. I couldn't think of a reply that I believed enough to say out loud, so I waited for him to continue. A distant rumble of thunder filled the silence, which stretched out for what seemed like forever.

"She thinks we're going tae, y'know, ball. Here. Tonight. Tha's wha' this is all aboot. She arranged for us tae be here, and then pulled this stunt tae get me in your room with th' expectation tha' I'm a laddie an' you're a lassie an' we'd — ah would — dae wha' comes natural. An' it didnae hurt tha' ye made such an impressive show of yer wares. But that was pure nae her doing."

"No, that was all me." We both laughed. It felt easy, like none of this was a big deal anymore. It felt like we were mates, sharing silly secrets.

I wiped my nose with the back of my hand. I didn't want to imagine what I looked like. It was the middle of the night; I'd been drinking and crying and puking, and here I was in a hotel room... Maybe in the morning... My mind was going a mile a minute but getting nowhere. If nature had a shag in its plans for us, then bring it on. But I felt, looked disgusting. I wouldn't touch me if I was him, not when he could get anyone he wanted. But still, I'd never felt so independent and rich with opportunity. Setup or not, when was this ever going to happen to me again? I banged together all the bottle I could scrounge and said, in a small, wavery voice, "But what if that's what I want?"

"You're knackered. Ah doubt ye ken what ye want beyond a proper kip. Ah may be a cad, but ah don't intend tae fuck up your life for th' benefit of some pish artist an' his lady in waiting. Ah reckon ye deserve better."

I couldn't agree less, but if kissing him didn't clarify my opinion about that, I didn't have any other tricks up my sleeve. He wasn't going to participate in it, so it wasn't going to happen. Perhaps someone older and more experienced would have known what to do, but I was utterly lost.

Fortunately, Stephen was not. "Nae reason tae worry. I've got a plan tae help ye teach her a lesson, nae to fuck decent folks about for nae good reason."

I didn't know what to say. I didn't want to teach her a lesson, I wanted her to fancy me and take me shopping every fortnight. I wanted him to take me his arms and make a woman of me. And I wanted Mum to come back and hold me and tell me what to do. I was asking way too much of the world and I knew it, but there you go. A part of me understood that this was growing up, working it all out and seeing where you fit in with the rest of it, but that didn't make me stop being a kid, one who didn't have a clue what I was entitled to, or who I could count on — other than Dad — or what anyone thought of me.

How are you supposed to sort out what stuff means? Is a kiss a big deal or no big deal? What about a shag? I didn't have a big sister to ask these questions by the time they occurred to me, and I gather it's not done to inquire of other party, as it were. You're just assumed to know? Maybe it was like field hockey. I had the distinct expectation of a ball aiming at my head, and I didn't know whether to catch it, bat it back or duck out of the way. So I just stood my ground and let it hit me.

"Ye just hae tae trust me here. Ah ken her a lot better than ye do."

191

I was jealous. Of him for her, of her for him — Christ, of everybody about everything.

"I'll tell her we did what she wanted us tae dae." (What I want us tae dae. To do.) "But you're grand because we won't hae done it. Dae ye ken? Later on, I'll tell her that I've given ye th' push. And you'll go along with it all, yeah?"

Here we go again. People maths. Romantic equations and sexual quadratic variables. Sorry, Miss Russell, but you're falling way behind. You'll have to stay after class to catch up.

"But what about the songs? I don't see how any of this will help."

"You're on your own there, I'm afraid. Ah can't dae it, but then again na one's asked me. And just because I'm passing up an opportunity tae take advantage of ye here doesn't make me your guardian angel. I'm nae screwing ye, but I'm nae your fairy godmother either. Or your boyfriend."

I had been sent to the back of the line in his waiting room. He went to the door. "I'll be off now. When ah wake up — if ah wake up — I'll bang up some bollocks tae tell Amanda. You'll still have tae use your imagination tae give Chaz what he wants — and I surely hope it's just ideas, nae flesh, he wants fae you. Ah may be a bit of a mad lad, but he's a filthy old sod."

The door closed. I stared at it, fantasizing that it might reopen to a better result, but instead was swamped by thoughts of all the problems I couldn't solve (or even face). Now I had to pretend to be a woman of the world, without actually being a woman of the world. The man I wanted to fulfill my wildest fantasies had come up with an inarguable reason never to lay a finger on, or in, me. Amanda was going to believe that she had me under her thumb, thanks to a scenario that would also give her full licence to hate me for supposedly shagging her boyfriend, and then she was going to have the pleasure of ordering Stephen to dump me. At which I was expected to be devastated. Which I already was, in a way. But not that way. I was being screwed coming and going, with nothing to show for it save a ruined (or would that be improved?) reputation. I tried to make myself feel better the only way I knew, but I was far too tired and overwrought to get a fire going. I closed my eyes and fell asleep.

I had more success on that score in the morning, which improved my mood. Other than the rain pissing down, life didn't seem so terrible. Complicated, challenging, but what's the worst that could happen to me? No one ever went to prison for disappointing a pop star. Heading home on the train, I read what I'd written on the way up and felt foolish at how far reality was from my imaginings. I stared at my pad, trying out titles and writing down little rhyming bits, just to get in the mood, to get the feel of it, putting down whatever came into my head.

"What I Wouldn't Give"
You make me crazy, you're so lazy
She's got you, I want you, I can't have you, boo hoo
Your truths are false, I know you lied
I tried, I tried, to keep it all inside
I know I've got my pride, that I can't hide
I thought you were a friend
But now I know you lied

I stared at what I'd written most of the way from York to Grantham, and while I saw the cleverness in the last bit, how I'd shifted things around to be different from the actual facts, I hated what these words meant to me. On one hand, I was expressing things I felt, on the other, I was admitting that it — *they* — had gotten the better of me. Writing these words of useless longing only underscored how puny I felt. I tore out the pages and jammed them into a pocket.

STEPHEN OVERSLEPT and barely made the train after the one he'd been booked on. Amanda had an all-but-silent breakfast with her parents and then waited for the phone to ring. When it didn't by the time of his train, she went back to bed for a bit and then caught an afternoon train back to London. She arrived home in the evening, changed into pyjamas, opened a bottle of gin and settled on the bed, phone nestled in her lap. There was no answer at Stephen's flat, and her impatience to hear the details of his cherry-popping tryst was quickly amplified by her inability to reach him. Although a runaway imagination was not atop any list of her distinguishing features, she concocted several wild scenarios to explain his unlocatability.

193

She rang British Rail to confirm that no trains from the north had gone off the tracks. She turned on the telly to see if the Beeb had word of an earthquake or a tsunami that wiped the city of Newcastle off the map. She even rang The Royal Station to confirm that Mr Dowery had, in fact, checked out. Then she began considering the possibility that he and that tart had liked screwing so much that they dashed off together for a holiday in Majorca. Or perhaps he had gone off on a bender as a result of what she'd made him do and was face down in a ditch somewhere. Or her father had got wind of what had happened and done Stephen GBH. She considered ringing the Geordie hospitals but instead tried Laila, who might give her some clues as to what had transpired. It took a few tries, but the girl finally picked up.

"I just rang to see that you got home safe, and that you were feeling better." Laila sounded quite a bit worse for wear, which was either encouraging or otherwise. "Alright, yeah." Her voice was distant, flat, a question-answering tone that Amanda could tell did not sound happy. Which could mean anything. Perhaps Stephen had already done the whole mission, start to finish. That would be smashing.

Amanda dared not ask any leading questions, or even bring up Stephen's name for fear it could implicate her as a schemer, but she was dying to ask. "Was the hotel alright?"

"Yeah, lovely. Ta for that. Excuse me, but I have to go."

Amanda, unaccustomed as she was to having calls cut short, contemplated the scenario she'd arranged and tried to guess at its likelihood for success. Perhaps the girl had turned him down and sent him packing. At least Laila hadn't said anything about rape. Actually, she hadn't said anything about anything.

By the next afternoon, Amanda was pacing her flat, impatient for Stephen's report. Her confidence in the plan had evaporated, and panic about it — and what it needed to achieve — had set in. She wanted to speak to Grace but couldn't bear the certain gloating and the unlikelihood of any reassurance about its success. When the phone rang, she threw herself at it.

Stephen thanked her for the lig and apologized for not ringing sooner. Then, as if the gratitude he showed needed to be balanced by a shake of vinegar, he enumerated the indignities he'd suffered on the trip home. The train was

194

crowded, he ran out of fags, the bar car had only Carlsberg, which he couldn't abide. He was recounting a pointless anecdote about a woman who thought she was on the train to Blackpool when Amanda finally lost the last bit of her self-control and fairly screamed, "Stephen, did you shag the bint or not?"

"Quite a schemer, ye are. An' a liar. Ye tried tae set me up to do wha' I told ye ah wouldnae. Anyway, ah coudnae. Th' lass ye sent me tae see in Room 309 looked like my gran, with false wallies and th' reek o' bairn powder. Nae my type at all."

"309? You were supposed to go to room 209. Laila."

His reply, a loud chuckle, made it clear he was taking the piss. Winding Amanda up was always good sport, but she didn't take it well, and he had to hold the phone away from his ear as she shared with him — in no uncertain terms — her displeasure at his unavailability and her curiosity about what had happened with Laila. Still, he couldn't resist playing out the line a little more. "Ah dinnae ken who that is, now do ah?"

She eventually stopped being cross and he stopped acting silly. Rather than answer her question, he proposed they meet for a drink.

The pub where they convened was just up the road from his flat — as he'd been the one doing favours here, the least she could do was save him the nuisance of traversing London to deliver his report. And, of course, drinks were on Chaz. The Bell Jar was of recent vintage, modestly appointed and not yet fully bathed in the classic fug of older establishments. Among its other attributes, there was a fit barmaid, a decent selection on tap and a fruit machine that seemed, at least to Stephen, not entirely ungenerous to its supplicants.

Amanda, eager to hear the details of her brilliant success, greeted Stephen warmly and bought the first round. When she returned to their table, glasses in hand, she was perplexed by the sour expression she saw on his face.

"So, tell me all about it. Mission accomplished?"

Stephen shrugged. "Ah don't ken that she fancied the night that much."

Assuming he meant sex, Amanda had half a mind to offer her own thoughts on the subject but held her tongue.

"She was well bladdered when I got tae her room."

"Yes, and then?"

"I dinnae think ah should be tellin' ya wha' happened." Stephen looked down at his glass and went silent.

The rest of the evening, which ended abruptly a few minutes later, was a duel to a draw. Amanda pleaded, commanded, all but begged to hear that her young charge was now a woman and would soon be a weeping lyric fountain, but Stephen — who found tormenting her in this way the most satisfying thing they'd ever done together — danced, ducked and dodged around the question, never saying they had, never saying they hadn't. Given her ghastly behavior regarding all of this, he felt she deserved nothing less.

The 'It' Man

"A BLOKE rang for you a little while ago, luv. Steve something or other. He left a number. I jotted it down. On the table."

I raced to find the note, which was on the cover of an old copy of *TV Times*. This was exciting news. I only hope Dad doesn't...

"Laila, who is he? Sounded too grown up to be one of your school chums. You do have school chums, don't you?"

He'd come into the kitchen and taken up a post leaning against the tea chest. He wasn't quite in the way to get out, but I'd need to slide by him, which would look as evasive as I was about to sound. I rifled through a dozen possible explanations in my head, none of which held any promise of putting his mind at ease. Lacking anything better, I opted for a version of the truth.

"Dad, I have to tell you...about something...I'm...involved in."

He looked horrified. His face fell, he went pale, he coughed — the works. At least he didn't upchuck. It was obvious that he was bracing for a statement that would involve one, if not all, of the following: pregnant, nicked, doctor, in debt, in love, expelled, joining a Satanic cult or moving abroad. Well, he was about to be greatly relieved.

"Here's the thing. I found a girl's bag on the Tube, then I found the girl it belonged to and returned it to her."

I checked for signs of trouble and saw none. His visage was entirely blank, hopelessly unprepared for whatever adult responsibility he might be called on to take. "Turns out she is in the employ of a major pop star who currently finds himself unhappily out of synch with the collective subconscious of Britain's spotty generation." (I didn't make that up. It was something Mr Guy said.)

A laugh of nervous relief got stuck in his nose and came out as a piggy snort. "I see. And what's this got to do with my little girl?"

"You haven't even asked me who the pop star is."

"And who, pray tell, is this culturally disabled musical icon? Paul McCartney? Gary Stardust? Gilbert O'Shaughnessy? Tim Jones? As if I'd know a Womble from an Osmond..."

"Chaz Bonapart."

"Truly?" I guess he registered my surprise. "I'm not as wet as you think I am, Laila. Erm...I know who it is. Matter of fact, we went to see him once, your mum and me, when we were first dating. At the Marquee, I think it was. Bloody awful."

"Really? Well, that's who. Chaz. And what it's got to do with me is they asked for my help sorting him out so he can get back to writing hit singles. He's been in a bit of a dry spell, or so I'm told. Not sure how I'm to contribute, but it seems like a laugh. And pays a little."

I had to pray that making light of it all would distract him from putting two and two together about my absences and other dubiously explained behaviour this summer. He was clever, so I didn't have much hope, but then he seemed a bit hypnotized by what I was telling him and maybe couldn't wrap his head around anything more than the here and now. I hoped he'd been good about taking his pills; they slowed down the thought process a bit and made it easier to slip shots past him into the net.

"So...who is Stephen?"

Blast, not slow enough. As this was proving to be trickier than I would have liked, I called an internal emergency and lied. "He works for Chaz. He's like a minder, a gal Friday, see? Fixes appointments and suchlike. Does hairstyling." At least the very last bit was sort of true. I hoped he would pick up on the dishonest clues I was sprinkling.

"He's light in the loafers, is he?" Score one for my side.

"How would I know? He's just a pretty boy who works for Chaz and wears a lot of perfume." It sounded like evidence to me, but I couldn't come out and say it. Even though I knew I was lying, I couldn't bear to say that my make-believe boyfriend was a poof. Still, leaving Dad with that impression was most helpful.

"Right. I'm off to bed." (*Laila United F.C. departs the pitch victorious!*)

I rang Stephen's line as soon as I could hear snoring. I took a couple of deep breaths as I listened to the pips, but that didn't calm me, they made me lightheaded, like I'd just run up a flight of stairs.

He also sounded strange, like he was otherwise engaged. For all I knew about him he might well be. He asked how the trip back was, and I told him it was alright, just that my head hurt the whole way. I didn't know what else to say, and we fell silent long enough I thought he might have rung off. He hadn't.

"I'd like tae speak tae you."

"You are speaking with me." It was all I could do not to try and mimic his accent.

"Don't be a smartarse. In th' flesh. Are ye free th'morra evening?"

I didn't dare enquire if he was asking me out on a date, but I could tell myself that's what it was. A Laila first! As casually as you please, I said that I would indeed be free tomorrow.

"Right, then. I'll pick ye up at half seven. Where d'ya bide?"

I gave him the address on Milton Road W3 as if it were the most natural thing to tell a devastatingly gorgeous straight Scottish bloke asking me out.

"East Acton, yeah? Ah hope it's in th' *A–Z*." He chuckled, and so did I. I wondered where he lived. If things went my way, I'd find out soon enough.

I started to say that I'd meet him out front, since it had struck me that another monumental Dad-diverting project would be required, but the last thing I wanted to do was sound complicated or confusing, so I just said thanks and goodbye and rang off. It was all I could not to scream out loud.

The scenario I cobbled together for Dad wasn't that complex after all, and it worked like a charm. With a little prodding from me, he was out the door to watch the football down the pub by half six, which gave me time to shower, put on what I'd spent the whole day picking out, get lipstick on (after a couple of clumsy tries) and chew three sticks of spearmint gum.

I sat on the edge of the couch, wound up like a spring, worrying more as the appointed time came and went. When the doorbell rang a little after eight, I jumped up and felt the blood rush to my face. I counted to five, got control of my breathing (not my pulse, which was away) and then opened the door. No one was there. I looked down the front path and there was a yellow Triumph convertible. I gasped and sighed in one go. He signaled me over and I got in.

"Fancy th' cinema?"

OK, that was a shock. Of all the ways I'd imagined that Stephen and I could spend an evening together, the pictures hadn't come up as a thought. I'm not that big on cinema, but I wasn't about to put up a fight, and the thought of a couple of hours spent sat next to him in the dark sounded better than decent.

"Sure, I'd like that. What are we going to see?"

"Let it be a surprise."

It was a surprise alright to be sat on folding chairs at the London School of Economics Student Union. "I've got a mate," was his simple explanation for access to the offbeat venue, but no one who fit that description turned up, so it remained a mystery. Stephen paid my 50p admission (he was let in free) and waited for me to plop down before taking his seat.

The Union hall smelled of burnt toast with a side of mildew; the room conscripted into service as a cinema held various student types in rumpled shirts and unfortunate haircuts sitting on their anoraks as well as several glammed-out fops wearing makeup and smart King's Road gear. Stephen excused himself and returned with two plastic cups of shandy.

"What are we going to see? There weren't any signs or posters in the passage."

"It's called *Performance*, and it stars Mick Jagger. Of th' Rolling Stones. I stayed away when it came oot, but ah thought ye might enjoy it."

"Oh really? Do you reckon I'm into the Stones?"

"You're not? How *fascinating*." He stretched out the word so long it sounded sarky, but it also sounded dead sexy, like a cat purring. I couldn't see how my lack of interest in those crusty old farts could be of any note, but I let it go. "Also, I've been told more than once that ah bear some resemblance tae th' other star of th' film, James Fox, and I'd like ye tae tell me what ye think. So take a good look now." He cocked his head and grinned as a star might. Free to stare for innocent reasons, I drank deeply and enjoyed it mightily. As the lights went down and the projector started up, I gave his profile a last glance and then turned to screen, curious to see what would happen there.

I didn't understand any of it. It was meant to be shocking, with a gangster and a rock star and naked bodies. I didn't know you could show so much skin in movies, but then I'd never been to any that would merit an X-cert. The acting was dead rotten and it all looked awfully tawdry to me, but I did like hearing that there's no rules about who can do what to who when it comes to sex. Did Stephen suspect that side of me? Did he have any of that in himself, and is that why he brought me to see this? I couldn't ask him any of that, but I sure would have liked to have known the answers.

The guy who wasn't Jagger was called Chaz, which was funny enough, but then one of them said something that stuck with me: "The only performance that makes it all the way achieves madness." The credits rolled over a departing Rolls Royce. I waited for Stephen to speak. I didn't reckon it was my place, and I didn't want to sound like a prat if there was no need to. But we walked to his motor in silence. He opened the door for me like a proper gentleman and I got in.

A short while later, the movie undiscussed and all but forgotten, we were seated at a tiny round table in the back of a dark, quiet pub with two pints of bitter and a cloud of cigarette smoke. He offered me one, but I said no. And I didn't dare look at the time.

"I've been thinkin'."

This was promising. "Yes?"

"Ye ken what Amanda tried to get us tae dae in Newcastle?"

How could I forget? "Yes?"

"She's gagging tae ken fae sure if her little plan worked."

"You haven't told her?"

"Ah ha' nae. Left it vague. Ah said when ah went tae your room ye were groggy and pissed and we had a blether and that helped you relax and get back tae sleep. Ah left th' rest o' it tae her dirty imagination. Ah may have used the word 'satisfaction,' but ah didn't quite say if we had or we hadn't. I'm sure she believes we did, given tha' she thinks o' me as a rutting rabbit who cannae control hisself. It's a credit tae you that she reckoned I'd find you shaggable. As, in point o' fact, did ah. Do, if ye wuz a wee bit older. More meat on th' bones than ah generally go in for, but well fanciable all th' same."

Being spoken about like a prize sheep by a wool-allergic vegetarian was both thrilling and disgusting. This was more maddening by the minute. I wish he'd just shut it and leave me to suffer without making it worse.

"It was funny listening tae her try tae hint around without coming straight out an' asking." I couldn't imagine why she wouldn't, given that it was all her idea in the first place. "I didn't tell her we were both so bladdered we wouldnae remember it if we had. Maybe we did! Did she ask ye about it?"

"She only asked me if the hotel was all right."

"I made certain she couldn't find me for a couple of days, sae she was just fishing tae see if you'd tell her on your own. She's got just enough breeding nae tae ask ye direct. Ah wager she's playing it cool until she reckons it's time for me tae give ye th' chop and thus launch ye into th' land of melancholic creativity. I'm shocked she has nae introduced you to absinthe or th' poetry of that French bloke, Rimboo, yet."

It was ridiculous to imagine being hurt by the end of an affair that was never going to begin. I already ached about it not starting — what did I care about the nonexistent rest of it? Unless it meant his hands on me, his body on mine, his tongue in my mouth, there was nothing in this charade for me but disappointment and frustration. The whole business was just stupid, and it made me mad on top of being randy. I had trouble concentrating on his words, I just wanted to grab his hands and pull them against my chest. I wanted to know what it would feel like to have him squeeze my tits so hard...

"...complicated than ah realized at th' time. Ye alright? You've gone a bit red."

I'd been sexdreaming and had nothing to add to whatever he'd been on about.

"I'm fine nae having it off with ye — at th' very least I'm not ready tae have

202

lassies selected an' sent tae me. But I need ye tae help me get away with th' fiction that we are trysting every chance we have."

I checked to ensure that my mouth wasn't open. "Ah cannae have it getting out that ah turned down a ride on principle. Chaps like me, aye, we're not meant tae have them. Principles, that is. It's part of our appeal. Bad boys, we are, th' kind ye don't bring home tae mother."

I thought to note the irrelevance of that but didn't bother to say anything.

"Second, ah don't want anyone ah ken to think ah could be kind and decent tae a lass without getting something in return. Reputation, you'll come tae ken, is a fragile thing. And if it gets around that ah have a good side, all th' girls will expect tha' fae me, and I'll be well fucked. I'd hae tae be 'orrid tae them even when ah don't wish tae be. Do you ken what I'm telling you?"

"No, not really." I didn't want to come off like a dolt, but none of this calculation referred to anything I'd ever thought or done. He might as well have been explaining astrophysics. But I did get that we weren't going to do anything, and I was going to pretend that we did so that he could have a clean shot at getting a leg over on other girls. The romantic illusion I was nursing popped like a balloon. I was just being messed about again, because what I wanted didn't matter, what they expected was me to do what would be best for them. Bollocks to them. I didn't sign on to be a hospital aide, I wanted love and sex, and those things kept moving further out of reach.

He laughed, kindly enough that I could almost forgive him for what he wasn't doing and we he yet was asking me to do. "Look, ah ken you're getting shat on a bit here, and I'm sorry about tha'. But ye bring a muckle brotherly side out in me. I've got two sisters and ye remind me o' th' younger yin. Ah don't want ye tae feel taken advantage of, nae by me, at least. Ah can't control Amanda and her squadron of flying monkeys, but ah can look after ye as best ah can."

"What's her name?"

"Whose name?"

"The sister that I remind you of."

"Oh, aye, Isla."

I started. "How do you spell that?"

"I-S-L-A."

"That's funny."

He looked mildly perplexed. I guess he didn't find anything odd about the coincidence. He put his hands over mine. They were large, and soft, with shiny, neatly done nails and long, elegant fingers. "So, as ah say, it would be grand for me if we pretended tae be getting it on. Can you handle that?"

I wasn't sure how to answer that. I was more than ready to do the exact thing he was asking me to not do and then lie about doing. I couldn't think of anything else I'd ever wanted so badly. I could feel it from my nipples to my knees. But I understood it was hopeless. Some part of me, eager to please, didn't want to be a problem for him, or a disappointment. Rather than try and put that whole mess of conflicting emotions into words that I could say out loud, I just nodded.

"Whatever Amanda's told ye, ah think they're wanting ye tae dae more than just gie 'em ideas."

I looked at him quizzically. "What do you mean?"

"Dae more. Really get your foot in th' door, make some proper dosh an' have a bit o' a say in th' youth culture of th' kingdom."

"How can I do all that? I'm just a kid."

"You seem like a right clever lass, an' this is a brilliant chance for ye. It's nae every wee schoolgirl what gets asked tae help a rock star write songs. Dinna let them take ye lightly, hen, gae oot there an' make a name for yourself."

I'd never had anyone talk to me like that, to encourage me and make me feel like I could do more than I'd ever expected. In his version, I come out the winner. I loved him at that moment, like I'd never loved anyone but Mum. Whether he was talking shite or making absolute sense his enthusiasm filled me up and carried me away. And he wasn't done.

"Right. Ah ken a writer for the *Times* fae the shop. She's smart as a whip. Ah can take ye tae meet her. We talked about th' music business th' other day, she an' ah, an' she reckons th' words of a song need tae be as dumb as ye can make them. Well, maybe not stupid, but you've got tae catch them off guard sae they don't see th' gears working. Ah think she could gie you some ideas about it. Ye won't have tae explain anything more than th' idea that ye want tae try your hand at pop an' hear what she has tae say about it."

My first thought was why would I want to meet a girl Stephen is, was, or might be keen on? But I didn't know how to say that without feeling pitiful. "Right. Thank you."

"And ah ken a geezer who played bass in one o' those poxy blues bands a few years back. He got turfed out for being too pop-minded. For a couple of spliffs — which ah can supply — he'll tell ye all he kens. Might be useful. Sae long as ye keep all o' this atween us. If you tell Amanda, she'll have my bollocks on a plate. So it has tae be our wee secret. *One* of our wee secrets." I nodded enthusiastically. After all the bitter disappointment I'd been forced to swallow, this sounded promising.

"Aye, an' one more thing. Come round th' shop th'morra afternoon 'n' I'll hae someone see tae yer locks. Ah think we kin gie ye a smashing look. It'll be a good laugh."

Let's Get a Bit a-Rockin'

FRANK WAS GREETED at his office by a stack of <u>urgent</u> (*!!!*) messages from Howard, demanding a meeting at the studio "aye zap," whatever that was. Frank smiled to himself, allowing the American his deluded power play. That was the English way, to let the Americans make a stink and then go on as planned. He had Laurence fix a time the next afternoon and send a split of the best champers to him at Olympic as a goodwill gesture.

There was no sign of good will when he arrived. Howard all but pulled him bodily into the control room and chased the tape op out.

"Looky here, Frankie. Your boy's come a cropper. He doesn't have enough songs for an album. You said he was ready to rock and he's not. I don't know what the hell game you all are playing at. Maybe your CBS overlords don't mind paying for this place 24-7 until the cows come home, but I've got other projects in the pipeline, so if he's not ready, and you can't tell me when he's gonna *be* ready, then I'm going back home to the U.S. of A. and you can find some limey cocksucker to wipe your boy's ass."

"Oh really?" said Frank. Winding him up was so easy, it was like the key on a metal toy. Mustering up a modicum of curiosity, none of which he possessed, he asked evenly, "And what projects might those be?"

Howard scrunched up his brow to concentrate. "I've got to be back in LA for the Bread album that I'm just doing for the bread (har har). And then Black Sabbath and James Taylor are waiting in the wings."

"Not together, I hope. I can't imagine they'd get on."

"Look, don't be a jerk, Frank. The point is we can't make this record without songs, and Chaz keeps stalling. Now does he have 'em or not? I can ring someone, maybe JT even, if you want me to see what I can do, but that's not my job, and we both know it. And you don't want me to have a piece of the publishing, I'd wager. I assume you've got a piece of that, so I also assume you're gonna get this problem squared away. What's that you Brits say, sordid?"

Frank knew just how to play this. It was heartwarming to see actors following a script they'd never seen. "Just leave it to me, Howard. We'll have you on your way to your Bread or whatever it is in plenty of time. And you don't need to ring — who was that you said?"

"JT. 'Fire and Rain.' Now, *he's* a genuine artist. Even the Beatles think so. After all, they signed him."

"That's gone well, hasn't it? That bastard Klein has lately been running Apple into the ground. I trust your Mr Taylor is well and clear of that chap."

"He's fine. His cheques clear, I can tell you that. Maybe I should look into the finances of Burgher and see if you're medium or well done."

Frank waved a dismissive hand in the air. "There's no need for any of that. You'll be paid, I assure you. And as for your other concern, the next time Chaz turns up, he'll be ready to record four certain chart smashes. Your job is to make sure they achieve their full potential."

"And when will that be?"

"Give him a couple of days. Why don't you piss off to Paris or someplace and I'll see to the bills. Be back here a week from Monday, shall we say?"

"All right. But basics need to be done by Friday, otherwise this goes on the back burner. And the band had better know the material. None of that messing around in the studio waiting to find a groove, got it?"

"Of course."

AMANDA ASKED ME to come by the studio. When she rang about it, she talked to me like I was a person, not a rag to polish her shoes with. I said I would take the 283 bus to Barnes, but she laughed, called me absurd and organized a car for me. Despite his usual concern about me going someplace he didn't understand to spend time with adults he didn't know, Dad thought it sounded like a good experience for me and didn't make a fuss.

SW17 was a part of London I scarcely knew, and there was nothing that I saw through the car window to inspire a more extensive inspection. The weather was warm, and I'd rather have been outside than in, but in I went. The woman in reception at Olympic didn't even ask who I was, buzzing open a gate and waving me in with a friendly "second door on the right." The walls were hung with gold albums. Amanda appeared and brought me in to the control room, which was smoky, loud and crammed with gear. She waved me into a black leather couch at the back and left. No one paid me any mind, and nothing seemed to be happening. The American was nowhere to be seen.

Two blokes were hunched over the audio desk, turning knobs and punching buttons. A third, seated by the tape machine, kept making it whirr and whizz, playing the same bits back over and over. Loud. The wall beyond the desk was wall to wall glass, looking in to a large, dimly lit room scattered with wires, instruments and microphones. I had a *Lord of the Rings* flash about how far one could safely pursue a quest, and when it was wiser to turn back.

People came and went, but nothing much seemed to be happening. Spliffs were smoked, beers were drunk. It looked like a lot of people working half-heartedly at getting very little done.

Amanda returned after a while, handed me a can of Coke and sat down, saying nothing. With the music blaring from the hob-sized speakers hung on the walls, conversation would have been difficult, but I was wondering what I was doing there and would have liked to ask.

A few tedious hours in, by which time my bum had fallen asleep, musicians assembled in the other room and had a bash — or at least attempted to. The drummer was hidden behind a box of colorful panels with booms hanging down like spider legs. The bass player kept going over and talking to him. I guess the mics weren't on, because it was all a silent movie to me — arms waved, heads shaken, mouths opened, but no sound. In all, they appeared to spend far less time playing than not playing. The lads at the desk had a way of listening to a single instrument at a time, so when there was music to hear, none of it sounded like a song, just odds and sods. Around midnight, bored and exhausted, I found Amanda kipping on a sofa in reception and woke her to say I had to get home. She walked me out to the car and told the chauffeur to take me wherever I said.

Haircut & Attitude

I TOOK Stephen up on his offer (I would have emptied the bins if he'd asked) and got a brilliant shag with style to burn. He did the shampoo, and I loved the feeling of his hands on my head, the closeness to his chest. It was all I could do to keep from rubbing against him like a cat. And then he wouldn't take any money, which was just as well, since I don't have any, and the prices at the shop were dear. I'd still have to think of what to tell Dad.

Afterward, we went outside so he could smoke, and I agreed to the plan, more or less, he'd laid out. In a haze of clueless confidence, I suggested he leave the details of our supposed bunnybungling to me. Rather than risk crossing each other's stories up, if he kept things vague, that would free me — wide-eyed clueless me, supposedly in thrall at my unbelievable good fortune — to tell Amanda any old bollocks about what we were getting up to. Basically, I'd been telling her what I thought she wanted to hear: like an X-cert creative writing course. (I should have written it all down, there was probably a dirty book in it.)

Feeling spiffed and smart, I went to see Bryan in Chelsea. I guess he's becoming a friend, but he's also cute, not traffic-stopping gorgeous, but nice in a comfortable, ordinary sort of way. I like seeing him, and he seems happy when I turn up as well. I wonder if he's got a girlfriend. I'm not sure I want to know, but maybe I could get Stephen out of my head if I put someone else in there.

There was no music on in the shop when I arrived; Bryan was in the back, shifting LP boxes and putting price stickers on polythene sleeves. I was about to tap him on the shoulder, but he was whistling a tune and then sang a few lines.

> *Only lovers left alive*
> *We've made our getaway*
> *Find a place where we can hide*
> *Maybe things will change another day*

I stood in the doorway and listened until he was finished.

209

"Hello..."

He turned his head around to see me, smiled and got up.

"Great haircut, man. You look super cool."

"I do? Thanks. What were you singing? Who's it by?"

"Who's it by? No one. Me."

"You write songs? I didn't know that."

"Not whole songs, just bits. There's a tape recorder at the flat and I sing them onto it when they come to me."

"That's so cool. I'm kind of interested in songwriting as well, but I don't have much to show for it as of yet. How do you come up with ideas?"

"There's a cinema in Queensway that shows vintage classics. I look at the ads and when I see a title that makes me imagine something I like, I make up a part of a song to go along."

"We...I went to see *Performance* the other night."

"Oh really? Amazing, right?"

I didn't have much to offer as a critique, but I needed to know more about his songwriting technique. "Do you see the films first?" This was starting to sound like the secret formula, and I needed details.

"No, I don't care for movies. Never have. Strictly a music fan. I just guess what it might be about from the title and the picture in the ad. Or the posters."

"Melodies, too?"

"They're mostly borrowed, but I change them up a bit. Like Bob Dylan did."

"Let me hear some more! This is so cool."

"OK. This one came from a sign on a stove in a restaurant I once worked at."

> *Ignite the pilots*
> *Set them free*
> *Flame on, my children*
> *That's the way for me...*

"I like the sound of that, but I don't understand…"

"No, me neither, but I think it's cool that way. The songs I like the most aren't about things I know about, they kind of speak a language of their own, from a world out there in the rock and roll galaxy. If the words sound cool, that's all I care about."

I grinned but I still didn't really get it. "Lyrics don't need to make sense?"

"Nah. No point. If rock lyrics had to make sense, there would not be half as many records released. They just have to rhyme now and again."

"I see," although I didn't. I didn't dare ask the question for fear of sounding thick: but how does someone know a good song from a shit one?

"And then there's this one I read in an agony aunt column. A girl's boyfriend left her when she got pregnant."

"How's it go?"

"I've just got two lines."

> *You never knew me, you scarcely cared*
> *Thought you were cool, but you're just really scared*

"I like that. Sounds tough."

The shop was quiet, so he had time for me. I asked how and when he came to England, what his family back home is like, that sort of thing. Then I promptly forget what he told me. Didn't mean to, I was really curious and interested, but I couldn't hold on to it in my head. I should have written that down.

On the ride home, I looked to see what *I* could use for ideas. A candy wrapper. Rain. Bank adverts. A girl dressed in a bright red slicker. She wasn't hard on the eyes, either, so I made up a few lines in my head, and mushed them around till it didn't sound stupid, then I wrote them down.

> There's a dolly with a brolly
> She's not the one you're looking for
> Why can't you see me?
> Right outside your door

At home, I kept noting words as they popped into my head. It was hard keeping up with the rubbish that flits through there. Like chasing butterflies, only with a pen rather than a net.

"Spots and Periods"
"Spots and Blobs"
"Blobs and Spots"
"Spits and Spots"

I remembered some of what Bryan had said and put that in my book as well. I tried perusing the *Express* for useful movie titles, but I wasn't inspired by the likes of *A Day in the Death of Joe Egg*, *Under Milk Wood* or *Carry on Matron*. But I did find two (*I Want What I Want* and *Something to Hide*) that I jotted down for later consideration.

Other stuff in the paper was better. Allowing fragments to matter rather than trying to think big thoughts was a big help, and I owed that to Bryan. I was still beavering away at it, thinking about what I'd got — which wasn't much, but it wasn't nothing — when Mr Guy's weird assistant rang and told me to come by the office Tuesday.

I TURNED up as ordered and I found Amanda with him, looking tense. If she noticed that I'd had my hair done she didn't say. As if he weren't there, or capable of speech, she announced that Mr Guy wasn't impressed with what she had shown him. Well, then, it was unanimous (but I didn't say that). In his words, it was a lot worse than "not impressed." I'd passed a lot of tests by a hair and reckoned that's what would happen here. I didn't care if he was impressed: just give it a check mark and send me on to the next form, alright?

He held photocopies of my lists in his hand, and slapped at them while he spoke, pursing his lips as if he was drinking down medicine. "Look, this rubbish is no help at all. This plan isn't going to work if that's the best you can do." If he noticed my lip quivering a bit, he didn't let on. But then he brightened.

"No matter. Inadequate guidance I reckon." He smiled as he smoothly pushed my failings off on Amanda. "The problem is it's gotten a little more complex than that. Unfortunately, and I mean that in all sincerity, Chaz spent the weekend hatching a plan for a concept album — about vegetables, don't you know. I don't imagine he will need your help with that." (*So long as the shops stay open*, I thought.) "I'm afraid he's about to go all Syd Barrett on us, and we can't have that." I ignored him ignoring my look of ignorance and waited for the rest of his speech to see if any of it had anything to do with me.

"I have to confess, when I read your — inverted commas — lists I was ready to knock this idea on the head, but I like you, Laura, and we're going to stick with the plan for now. Maybe crank it up a bit, raise the stakes a bit, you see, and watch as you rise to the occasion." I worried that might entail. I had no way of guessing how far he'd push to get what he wanted out of a person.

"Have you got anything else to show us? Maybe you can just tell us what you know, and Amanda can jot it down."

"Pardon me, but I'm no stenographer." He shot her a look and handed her a pad. She was now a stenographer.

"Actually, I've got some bits and bobs that might be useful, I dunno."

"Well, get to it, lay them on us." He did a little hip shimmy for punctuation. I pulled out my book and read what was there. "What I wouldn't give..."

"What you wouldn't give for what, luv?"

Amanda hadn't moved, and certainly had not written anything.

"No, that's something I thought of. Maybe you can use it."

"Use it for what? A letter to Santa? An employment application?"

I felt small and stupid.

Amanda waved a hand in the air, as if dispatching a bad smell. "No, wait, I think I see what she's on about." My heart filled, and I awaited her comment expectantly. "It's like the kernel of a song idea. What if the chorus went something like, 'Your reason to live comes from above / What I wouldn't give for a taste of your love?'" She screwed up her face, as surprised as the rest of us at what had just come out of her mouth. "So maybe it's a song about a girl who fancies a priest, and he won't touch her because that would go against God."

213

Mr Guy put a hand to his temple. "And you imagine that thing could be a hit for Chaz, do you?"

Her face fell, but she recovered quickly. "No, of course not, but you see how this could work. If she has ideas, ideas that sprout directly from the mind of a genuine child, then maybe they're representative of a nation of spotty children. All we have to do is find a way to work them into usable form. Go on, Laila, give us another. I trust that isn't all you've come up with in all this time."

I went for it, in a halting singsong of the sort a six-year-old might employ.

> There's a dolly with a brolly
> She's not the one you're looking for
> Why can't you see me?
> Right outside your door.

Mr Guy shook his head disapprovingly. "The meter's fucked. It doesn't scan." Amanda scrunched up her nose in concentration. It was disturbingly adorable. "No, wait. That could be something. How about 'She's the dolly with the brolly, the one *I'm* looking for.' Do you see?"

"Hmm. You're quite a pair, you two. Two brains, one mind." I wasn't sure if I liked how this was turning out. "Are you writing all this down? You're going to need a rhyming dictionary."

I interrupted him. "Spots and Blobs."

He glared at me, with a smile this time, and I relaxed a bit. "What in bloody hell does that mean?"

"I was thinking of, y'know, pimples and periods. Actually, it should be 'Blobs and Spots'."

"Uh huh." He laughed uncomfortably. "I can't imagine Chaz singing about those things any time soon. C'mon ladies, *think*. What's the first thing that pops into your lump of lead?"

I'd heard that phrase before — Aunt Ruth says it. She says a lot of those rhyming things that don't make much sense to me. I could never remember them from one visit to the next, but out of the blue a batch came back to me. And I said them out loud, like reading from a dictionary — "Apple pips, Rosie

Lee, Beetles and ants, Buttercup and daisy," an idea began to form. "Rosie Lee" — that meant tea, but it could be a person. And "Beetles and ants…"

Mr Guy perked up. "Oi, you're not an East Ender, where'd you learn those?"

"My auntie Ruth in Dagenham. I can't always make out what she's saying, she uses a lot of them words."

"How old is she?"

"I dunno, ancient — 60, 70 maybe."

"It's a dying language, but the old-timers won't let it go. I heard it from my father and his mates when I was little. What was the last thing you said?"

I couldn't remember, but Amanda's receptors were functioning. "Something about ants and beetles."

"Beetles and ants. Pants. Knickers. Hmmm. We could do something with that — a tune about insects we could sling right past the censors. Chaz could sing about sex on *Top of the Pops*. That would be a howl. The men don't know …"

"Sorry, what don't men know?" I was lost in all this, not sure if what I was saying made any sense, but Mr Guy seemed pretty hopped up about it.

"What the little girls understand.'" He reached out and patted my cheek. "Exactly what we're trying to accomplish here."

Amanda beamed, but Mr Guy didn't. "I dunno, that stuff's so old-fashioned. Like the Kinks' 'Harry Rag,' about fags. Can't have him sounding like he's living in the '60s, trotting out Eddie Cochran licks for a generation too young to know and eager to erase the past. It's like they're allergic to yesterday."

I found a blank spot in my book and wrote "allergic to yesterday." I spotted some lines of Bryan's I'd written down. Under the gun, I skipped the usual mental once-over for humiliation potential and read them out loud.

> *You never knew me, you scarcely cared*
> *Thought you were cool*
> *But you're just really scared*

I didn't really care for how that sounded. The conspicuous hurt, the frustration, the futile resentment. *Please love me or I'll be mad at you.*

Mr Guy bolted upright, his eyes wide. "What's that? Where did you get that?"

"I made it up." I surprised myself at how easy it was to claim that.

"Let's hear the rest." There was no rest. That's all Bryan had. I'd tried adding to it but crossed those lines out and now I couldn't tell whether they made sense or not. I sensed I was squandering an opportunity for a big score here, but I opted for the safe play. "Haven't got any more yet. Just that bit."

"No, there has to be more. Let it carry you along. If you were singing it, what d'you reckon the next two lines would be?" He reached for a piece of stationery and started writing furiously, no longer relying on Amanda's secretarial skills.

Words flitted at me like bugs. Amanda glared, like a girl who'd been snubbed at her own birthday party.

"How about 'I wanted a friend, you were a frog'?"

"No call to insult the French."

"No, but maybe 'frog' isn't right. Hang on, let me think. 'I needed a prince, you were a toad.'"

Mr Guy still looked unhappy, so I kept riffing: "Need a shoulder to cry on? Then pull off the road."

He nodded. "Very clever. Might be good for something. Let me see if I've got it all down." Mr Guy, who'd been scratching at a pad on his enormous desk, read it back:

> You never knew me, you barely cared
> I thought you were cool but you were just scared
> I needed a prince, but you were a toad
> Need a shoulder to cry on? Just pull off the road.

"Fuck me, that's good. Loaded with double *entendere*. I think I smell a hit." I thought I could smell something else. Mum would have never put up with me being so negative.

I'd never seen Mr Guy look happy before, and it was a bit disgusting. Amanda leaped up and, after a feint in his direction which she evidently thought better of, gave me a weak hug. I felt over the moon and clever enough for *University*

Challenge. I knew it would be forgotten as soon as I was on my way, but I was thrilled at the idea that they liked my idea. "Brilliant," said Mr Guy, clapping his hands together and then pointing one of them at each of us, as if he were the conductor and we the orchestra.

"Of course, it's nowhere near a song. Just an idea for a verse. It'll need a lot of work. You guys should spend time together and see what else you can come up with. Laura's ideas, and Amanda's interpretations. Maybe that's our formula. Let's the three of us meet up again in a couple of days and see what else you've come up with. I'll get on to my contacts on Denmark Street and see who's got a spare melody on hand that I can buy for a song." I chuckled at the wordplay. "Thanks for coming by, errr..."

"Laila. You're welcome."

"Amanda, hang on a tick, I'd like a word."

I WAS DROWNING in music: the albums Bryan recommended and the singles Amanda kept sending. I was supposed to dissect them (like frogs?) to work out how the good ones fit together, what makes them connect with the kids. I thought that was the stupidest thing anyone had ever told me to do, and I'd been in school long enough to have been handed a load of idiotic assignments. She said it wasn't her idea. As if that mattered. Still, I listened to the first few all the way through until discovering it was more fun to flick them like plates. I put a bunch of dents in the walls and ceiling of my room before I thought Dad would get mad, so I stopped and went back to playing them.

I started being able to hear what was going on. It was a bit like knowing the lines of a show on telly before you heard them spoken. It wasn't like a formula, exactly, but there were routines beneath the surface that guided bits here and there and I could sort of guess what needed to come next, what would sound good. It was a strange feeling, like X-ray hearing. I wondered if I had some sort of gift for this bollocks or was I just catching up to information millions of kids my age already grasped?

Either way, I finally felt ready to confront the chore I'd been assigned and thought maybe this time I'd be able to crack it.

217

Rock and Roll Homicide

THWACK. BOOM. *Thwack. Boom. Thwack.* Boom. Boom. *Boom.*

"Oh for fuck's sake, man, it sounds like a drum kit. What more do you want?"
Eddie Fortis, the guitarist in Chaz Bonapart's band, smoothed his mustache as
he glowered over the top of a *Melody Maker* at the back of Howard Moore's
head. "Can't we just get on with it?" The producer ignored him, as he had done
to the utmost degree possible since the sessions began. One of Howard's
habitual strategies was to treat guitarists like shit: it keeps them in their place
and they usually play better when they think they have to prove something.

Psi the Clock continued his alternation of snare and kick drum, a rifle shot and
a wrecking ball that boomed out through the speakers in the Studio 2 control
room at Olympic. Behind the mixing desk, like one of those bird toys that dips
its beak in water, Howard repeatedly leaned in to press the talkback button
and issue instructions to the engineer beyond the glass, who adjusted the
angle and location of a half-dozen microphones poised around the kit.

"Tell Psi his snare is tuned a little high. I don't want it so crisp." Psi put down his
sticks, pulled a key from his shirt pocket and started adjusting the drums,
tightening and loosening the rims, hitting one each time and listening for the
sound he wanted. When Howard gave him a thumb's up, without dropping his
gaze, Psi gave the key another turn.

The red wall phone purred and was answered by the tape op, a lad called
Maurice, who handed Howard the receiver. After a brief call, he handed the
phone back to the tape op, who put it back on the wall and then returned to
reading about what Hunter S. Thompson had to say about George McGovern
in *Rolling Stone*. Howard didn't notice that Psi had abandoned his station.

"Hey, didja see the article about me in there? Says I'm the producer to watch."
("It'd be a far sight better if you were a producer to hear," thought Maurice.)
The youngster thought the Yank a pompous ass but knew better than to voice
his derision. He'd already copped an attitude after Howard saw his name on a

tape box and pronounced it maw-*reese*. Worse, he'd begun calling him "Shevaleer" ("I bet you were named after that old French dude").

"They told me next time I'd be on the cover."

"Over Chaz's dead body," Eddie snickered.

Howard stared into the studio and saw that it was vacant. "I guess now would be a good time for a dinner break," said Howard. "Hey, where's that loco you guys go to?" Maurice and Eddie exchanged glances but said nothing. "Y'know, the pub where your gang chows down."

Howard's longtime engineer, a laid-back black hippie from Pittsburgh named Greg, stifled a laugh as Maurice mucked in. "Oh, it's just up the road. Make a left out the door and go straight. Can't miss. The Bull and Stick."

"Yeah, whatever it's called. I'm going there. Make sure you get that drummer back in here in an hour, and someone call that manager of Chaz's and tell him he'd better have some lyrics for whatever that fast song in D is called tomorrow morning." He strode out, running a hand dramatically through his flowing grey mane and punctuating it with a fey shake of the head.

Maurice and Greg looked at each other and cracked up. "Not my job, mate," Maurice said to the door. Eddie shrugged. "I'll ring Frank." Greg pulled a leather pouch out of his rucksack and headed for a storage room in the cellar where he could light up without interruption or any obligation to share.

Several hours later, as the clock slid past midnight, Psi returned without a word of explanation and resumed his hammering. Neither Chaz nor Frank had been heard from, Eddie was nowhere to be found, and Howard was fuming. He sent Psi home and got on the phone to his agent in Los Angeles, ordering him to get hold of Chaz's manager and exact a promise that his artist would be fully prepared to sing the actual words of an actual song with an actual melody in the morning. And, no, he didn't give "a fucking shit" what time it was or who had to be woken up in the process. And, no, he wouldn't be in the studio until "that fucking shit" was present and prepared to record vocals.

Chaz turned up the next afternoon and feigned indignation at Howard's absence. Greg rang the hotel to let him know and had to listen as Howard raged down the line. Ultimately, he thought better of forcing a standoff and ordered, "Keep him busy. I'll be right there. Call me a car and don't say anything to Chaz about where I am or when I'll be there."

Chaz was all la-de-da, swanning about the studio as if looking in on party preparations. "So how are my drums sounding?" he asked Psi.

"Right and proper, guv'nor. Just the way you like 'em. Moore's engineer is clever enough. He speaks our language and has the suss to know how to get it. We've got four basics done, and they sound ferocious. I especially like the chorus of that slow one. Dead catchy, it is. We'll knock out the rest in a flash as soon as you show us the songs. Basically, we're done with what can be done at this point. Next move is yours, guv. Have you got a song to sing?" Chaz looked around the room and noticed, evidently for the first time, that Howard was not present. "Where's that wally producer? Has anyone seen him?"

Greg promised Howard's imminent arrival, adding an ill-considered apology that he really hoped wouldn't be repeated to his boss. He asked Chaz if he'd like to hear anything, or would like a tea, anything to hold his attention for a few minutes. He didn't, and — causing Greg a fair bit of concern — vanished.

To everyone's relief, Chaz was again in sight when Howard turned up, red-faced and huffy. He offered Chaz a toothy smile and got back a look that didn't convey anything in particular. As casual as you please, he asked, "So what's on tap today? Guitar overdubs? Percussion? Strings?"

Howard was certain Chaz knew full well what was expected of him and could only pretend not to know how long it had been expected of him. "Your vocals, man. We've got rough mixes on four basics but they're not going anywhere until you replace the guide vocals with a real track. With words, y'know. Are you ready to rock?"

Rather than reply, Chaz fired up a spliff and inhaled it languorously. "Did I tell you to mix anything?"

Shock, indignation, resentment, anger and determination ran across Howard's face like a cartoon. When the circuit was complete, he fairly hissed, "Playtime is over, Chaz. Time to get down and get with it. You're spending your own money, man, and you probably can't afford as much as this is going to cost. And I don't have an unlimited window to babysit you. Or take your shit."

Chaz was unfazed by the raw display of hostility. If anything, his voice grew a bit sing-songy. "Oh, you Yanks. So blunt, so greedy. Everything has to be on your schedule. You didn't win the war singlehandedly, you know. Right, Psi?" The drummer chuckled at Chaz's audacity, to wield a glib version of world history as an excuse for his dilatory exertions.

That only inflamed Moore further. "I've got other artists lined up waiting for me to make hit records with 'em. I can't name any names, but they're chomping at my bit. Did you see my article in the *Rolling Stone*?"

Maurice snickered. What Howard was crowing about was a couple of lines and a quote in *Random Notes* from a lig for some artist he'd worked with who was a favourite of the magazine's. Howard pointed a thick finger at the teen. "Get out, asshole. Don't come back until you can respect your betters." Maurice slunk out and Howard turned back to Chaz.

"You need to do vocals for that fast thing in D. Now."

"I would prefer not to." Psi, who was watching this drama unfold, had no clue if Chaz was quoting Melville or had randomly plucked the classic literary dodge of passive-aggressive resistance out of thin air.

Such disinclination was more than the American could stomach. "Not up to you, cocksucker. You sing or else."

Moore had no idea how deep Chaz's reserve of deadpan aplomb ran. One brow suitably arched, he replied, in a plummy tone rich with false curiosity. "Really? Or what?"

"Or I'll get Shevaleer back, have him pack up the multis and ship 'em back to LA on the next flight. You can come over and get 'em there, or you can start recording again from scratch."

Chaz conveyed a bored shrug without bothering to move a shoulder muscle. It was uncanny how such profound disdain could be so subtly transmitted. "A couple of basics that you took the liberty to mix. I'm sure those could be recreated in short order. Psi's a fucking genius, aren't you?"

"Yeah, well, you won't even have all the — what do you call it? — wonking that turned some of your shit ideas into actual song type things. There must be thirty or forty, maybe even fifty, hours of your musical drool, and I'll take all of it. You'll have nothing but a huge goddamn studio bill. And my invoice. How do you feel about that, you stupid fuck?" Flecks of spit were coming out of Howard's mouth; his porcine complexion was shading crimson.

Unaccustomed as Chaz was to being spoken to in such a manner, it pierced his shell of nonchalance. He was suddenly a word or two away from ringing Frank and taking a shit in his ear for hiring this bellend and then leaving him to endure such unwarranted abuse. Frank should be the one listening to this rot.

However. While he was rarely inclined to acquiesce to, much less be bullied by, anyone he didn't respect, need, like or wish to shag, in an unexpected burst of logic and proportion, he found within himself the presence of mind to recognize the benefit here of maintaining the peace. He took a deep breath and presented an ingratiating grin that encapsulated a gamut of ideas: we're all mates here, just messing about, no harm done, jolly good and all that.

"Oh, alright," he said softly. "Just winding you up, mate. There's no reason not to get on with it. After all, that's what we're all here for, innit? Give me a few minutes to get myself in the right head space, yeah? Then we'll get it done."

Chaz's quiet capitulation left Howard, overdosed as he was on adrenaline, speechless and nearly out of breath. He nodded weakly and left the control room. Chaz's smile vanished as he whispered to Psi, "That clown has me over a barrel. I haven't got the lyrics sorted for that song yet." He looked concerned, even stricken: two levels of emotion Psi had never seen in him before.

"You'll be all right, guv'nor. Just jot some bollocks down. You can fix it later." Chaz nodded enthusiastically. As Psi watched in mild horror, Chaz mimed a creative mind in crisis, a series of spasmodic facial tics which suggested a painful toilet episode concluding without result. Psi held his tongue, even as he felt a surge of pity rising in his gut. Frank instructed him to await a clear signal that Chaz knew he was drowning before handing him the life preserver. This surely was that. Psi counted himself in and cleared his throat. "Erm..." The drummer smiled, a rarity for him, and, Chaz thought, not a pretty sight.

"Can I have a word in the other room?" Chaz looked confused but followed Psi into a cavernous adjoining studio used to record orchestras. Walking to the grand piano in that grand room, Psi rested a worn leather satchel covered in stickers and rooted around among the sticks, gaffer's tape, salves and timetables. With as sheepish a look as he could manage, he plucked out a sheet of A4, neatly typed but with a large red "X" lightly drawn across it. (As Frank had explained to Psi, it had to look like a rash idea he'd thought better of, not a memo neatly prepared for Chaz's signature. The "X" was probably too obvious and formal a gesture, but at the present it served the purpose.) Psi handed the page to Chaz, who gave it a myopic squint.

"'Soldier to Cry On.' What's this then?"

"It's lyrics. To a song. 'Shoulder to Cry On'."

"Whose song?"

"It's yours, guv." Chaz mouthed the words silently and then looked up at the Clock, who — despite years of practice — couldn't gauge his reaction, favorable or otherwise. "And who wrote this?"

"I did. Come to me in the bath. I've been around your stuff so long I reckon it's soaked in me. I was listening to the roughs and worked it out to the melody. Not that I can do what you do, but I think the rhythms of it are in me 'ead."

Chaz nodded. Psi pressed on, feeling bad about the lies he was telling. "I didn't think it was anything, but my missus liked what I'd done and got on me to show it to Frank. He said he wouldn't waste your time with my bathwater. That's what he said. Said you might think me a right cunt for pushing in where I don't belong. I know you don't need help from the likes of us. That's why he crossed it out and give it back to me, told me to never show it to you. I wasn't going to, but if there's any chance it could be of any use, well, there you are… No harm done if you don't want to know. I wouldn't forgive myself if I didn't try and be of use to you, mate."

Chaz had not heard Psi say this many words at a go in all the years of his employ, but surprises were abounding, and he paid that part of it little mind.

"Of course I don't need help, we all know that." Chaz stared off into space for a long while, tapping his fingers on the piano. He fired up a spliff and took a deep drag that threatened to spill ash on the Bosendorfer. Psi spotted a teacup and put it on the piano as an ashtray. Chaz stabbed out the joint and looked Psi straight in the face. "But this is a special situation. I do need to sing something to get this bellend off my back, and these words aren't any worse than the rubbish I hear on the radio nowadays. And, as you say, I can always do it again later. But I do think I might keep 'need a shoulder to cry on, just pull off the road' — that's almost clever, you old tosser."

"Ta much."

"And what do you want for it? I expect you to be reasonable here. After all…"

After all, what? Psi thought, surprised at the suspicion. He had never asked for anything other than his wages.

Frank would square it, Chaz knew, but he wasn't the trusting sort, even with old colleagues, and wouldn't want to be trading one barrel for another.

"Don't want nothin', guv. Glad to be of service, if I can be. Drummer's credo, that's what it is." He had no idea where that came from, or even what it meant. There were plenty of fellows he knew who'd steal your sticks out of your hands given half the chance.

Chaz sighed, a long, sad exclamation of frustration and anger, resentment and fear, gratitude, relief and shame, all rolled out in a single breath. "It's not much, but I can see a faint glimmer of a spark in there. What have you been doing, you old perv, shagging schoolgirls again?"

Funny how the guilty always assume everyone else is equally corrupt. As much as he wanted to headbutt Chaz for such an offensive suggestion, it was easier here to fold than argue. "Yeah, something like that." And then laughed, a rickety old man's laugh, to be sure Chaz knew that he knew they were both taking the piss.

"Right then, make yourself scarce and let me get on with this. I'll see if I can't turn it into something that berk will listen to. Who knows, maybe it'll even be a B-side. Maybe it will shut his gob for a day or three."

Psi smiled broadly, a glorious display of the sorry state of English dentistry.

"One thing, mate. No need to mention any of this to Frank, right?"

"Right." Psi drew a finger slowly across his mouth. "Shtum." He strolled to the jacks, pleased that Frank's plan had worked just like he'd said it would. A thing of beauty, it was, like an errant penalty kick curling back in for a score just beyond the goalie's outstretched gloves. He collected his battered old briefcase and prepared to head home. Passing Studio B, he could see Chaz in front of a boom mic, a Gibson acoustic in his hands, eyes closed and his mouth open wide. With the silence of the soundproofing, it almost looked like a smile.

I TURNED UP at the shop just as Bryan was finishing. He took off his smock, and we went down to the basement. I hadn't mentioned the meeting with Mr Guy. There were stools and a guitar in a case. It smelled dank and felt wet.

"What are we doing down here?" I was thinking this might be exciting.

"I've sort of written a song. It's called 'Equal Opportunity Idiot.' Kind of Dylan meets the Stooges. I want you to tell me if it's any good. I was thinking about this girl I once knew, and it came out meaner than I wanted it to."

"Can I hear it?" Truth be told, I wasn't thinking "what a clever lad" or imagining he really wanted my advice or opinion. No, I was hoping it was an idea I could hand off to Chaz. I was already conjuring up a better title.

"Uh, sure. I'm not very good on guitar, so don't take the piss." Bryan coughed to clear his throat and then began strumming so violently his right hand was a blur. I couldn't make out all the words, but it started off something like this:

You deserve your rights — that I see
You're a smart girl, proud and free
But your equal opportunities don't give you the right to mistreat me

There was more I couldn't make out until he sang:

You stupid jerk, you almost ran me down
Dropping your packages all over town...

I stopped him. "Wait, what are you talking about?"

"I was crossing Fulham Broadway this morning, and a messenger blew through a light and nearly creamed me. Missed me by inches. After that I thought up those lines and added them to the song — Laila, what's wrong?"

I was shaking, tears streaming down both cheeks. I hadn't told him about

225

Mum, it just hadn't come up. (I didn't know anything about his parents, and I sure as hell wasn't bringing him home to meet Dad, so not really a topic of conversation.) But there I was, having a full-scale freakout at the thought of losing another important person in my life to one of those Triumph-straddling shitheads. I wanted to tell him, I really did, but the words didn't come.

"Wait, are you upset at me for writing a song?" I wasn't. Maybe I was. I felt my guard go up. He was trying to steal Mum's martyrdom from me. And *he* was writing the songs *I* needed for Chaz. A shitty corner of my ego that I didn't know gripped me; I didn't know I could feel so competitive. I should have explained myself. I bet he would have been cool about it, but I couldn't bring myself to try him. I ran up the stairs and out of the shop. I got shot of the entrance and then wrote down the lyrics as best I could recall (not the last bit) and tacked on some of my own.

PSI THE CLOCK was asleep when the doorbell of his Maida Vale flat rang. But in short order the curtain by the door was pulled aside and his face appeared in the small side window. He grimaced when he saw who it was.

"What do you want, you old poof?"

"I just want to say thank you. Let me in, will you?"

Psi was naked save for beige support hose up to his knees. He looked down and said, "Gi's a minute, would ya, guv?"

He returned in loon pants (still no shirt) and opened the door, leaving it open as he walked ahead of Frank back into the flat.

"For what?"

"For what *what*?"

"What are you thanking me for?"

"Don't bullshit me, Psi. I heard that you worked your mysterious drummer mojo on Chaz and got him to cut a demo of that new number. Howard was purring like a kitten with a bowl of cream when I rang him this morning. And Chaz seemed well pleased at what he called his 'bolt-of-blue inspiration'."

"Didn't take much of an effort, just the right timing. As in all things."

"And the penny didn't drop?"

"Nah. He ain't got a clue. He swallowed the bollocks I told 'im." Psi instantly regretted the phrasing of that, especially when Frank chuckled.

"Brilliant. Just as I hoped."

"You're a fucking evil genius, you are. Your plan was spot on. Is there anything else, guv, or can I get back to what I was doing?"

"Right. Can you swing by the office at week's end to pick up another lyric to slip under Chaz's nose? I expect I'll have one sorted by then."

Psi stiffened. "Sod off, Frank. That was a one-off. I'm paid to hit things, not be the fifth columnist in your shallow talent pool. And I don't like being made out as a drummer so thick I'd be happy to write lyrics for his nibs without any compensation or credit. Do it yourself. Or get one of your toadies on the case."

Taken aback less by Psi's negativism than by the surprising display of vehemence, Frank considered arguing that Psi didn't deserve any credit, since he hadn't had any role in writing the words, but then realized where that might lead and muttered an apology for presuming. He promised to make it up to Psi, apologized again and beat a hasty departure. This Rube Goldberg device he'd bashed together in his mind was working exactly as he had imagined.

Back at the office, Frank had a word with Amanda. "That first bit went down brilliantly. I gather Chaz reworked a track they'd already cut so it fit the new words. I heard the demo and I think we're really back on track. It's not quite 'School's Out,' but it's on the pitch. I love that Chaz cut exactly the words we gave him. I gather he made a big fuss to Psi about insisting on doing exactly the opposite, but then, rather predictably I'm afraid, faced facts and relented."

"And he believed that Psi didn't want money or credit?"

"That's what Psi said. But here's the rub: for reasons I can't go into, we can't use Psi as our conduit again. I've got another idea. That is, of course, provided whatshername keeps coming up with the words. That's your job. See to it."

And see to it she did. Three days later, she delivered the lyrics for a combative song called "Equal Opportunity Girl" ("Girl, your equal opportunities don't give you the right to mistreat me") that he loved straightaway. A bit of misogyny worked for the Stones in the '60s, Frank thought. It might do for Chaz as well.

IT WAS FRANK'S TURN to be asleep the next time he and Psi spoke. Joe was away visiting family, so he had stayed in town, at a flat in the company leased in Knightsbridge. He had turned in early and was dreaming about Dirk Bogarde when the phone rang. He sat up in bed, eye mask pushed up to his forehead.

"Frank? It's Psi. Sorry for ringing so late. I got the number from Laurence. Guv, things have gone to shit at Olympic. It's a right mess here."

"It's fine, Psi. Give me details. What's going on?"

"The American cunt. The producer. He turned up and demanded that Amanda, or that little friend of hers, be there. When no one lifted a finger, he went spare. Then Chaz turned up, and he wasn't having any of it. I thought they were going to square off and have at it like the men they aren't."

"What little friend of Amanda's?"

"That girl we're not supposed to know about. I don't know her bloody name. The one with the words."

"I see. And do we know what Howard wanted with them?"

"I dunno. What do all those American cunts want?"

"I'm sure I don't know, but what's that to do with anything? I'm not running an escort service here."

"I wouldn't know, guv. I just play the drums."

Frank took a conciliatory tone now that the nature of the problem was becoming clear. "And who did Howard ask?"

"Me. I was the only one there. Well, except for the engineer and a tea boy. They couldn't help him, and I denied knowing anything."

"Good man."

"That berk ain't got a clue. He reckons he's bloody Phil Spector or Brian Wilson,

228

and he's just a jumped-up fader jockey with a big mouth. But I did like his boots. I'd fancy a pair like that."

"I'll see about that the next time we're in the States. You can't tell Chaz this, it will put paid to the last bit of his bottle, but Howard is repped by the guy who does Slade in the States, and I made a deal for Chaz to go out with them in the fall. Co-headlining, like. The second British Invasion, some bollocks like that. Howard was part of that deal, so we're stuck with him. But as for supplying him with bints, that's just not on."

"Are you sure, Frank? He's fucking useless, that one. I can produce records better than him. Minus all the misery. You should have hired me."

"Yeah, maybe. You're the ultimate no-drama drummer. Let's keep it that way. Maybe you could have it stenciled on your kit. Alright, thanks for the report."

"You could pay him and tell him to fuck off while I get it done."

"You're overlooking the elephantine ego. He may be a greedy, useless shit addicted to bints and blow, but he'd sooner take it up the arse than have us impugn his professional abilities, such as they are. Colonial resentment., I expect. I know his kind, and they're absolutely terrified of being humiliated. Americans still believe God has graced them with superior everything. Take that man down a peg and he'll land on the floor, screaming like a baby."

"Swiftly followed, no doubt, by Chaz."

"Now, now, Psi, that man has done very well by you, and you ought not be casting aspersions on his mental stability."

"What do you want me to do?"

"Just keep Chaz away from Howard until I can get there. Yeah? And see if you can't have the tapes of anything that's more or less complete moved to the boot of your motor, yeah? Just for a day or two until I can sort this git out. In case it all goes pear-shaped, I wouldn't want to get in a tug of war over Chaz's exquisite efflorescence." Psi grunted and rang off.

Frank tapped the cradle and awaited a dial tone. He rang Laurence and told him to arrange transport to the studio with a stop to collect Amanda on the way. A short while later they were in a car on the way to the South Bank.

Amanda, who was wearing no makeup and had jammed a floppy hat on her head to cover the hair she hadn't had time to wash or style, turned to Frank, hoping to hear what he expected of her in this absurd late-night mission. The situation was dire, she understood that, but the explanation of what was to be done about it struck her as a little, well, vague. Not that she could say that.

"We've got a couple of interconnected problems here. We need more lyrics from that girl, we need the tapes to remain at Olympic, we need Chaz to get a grip and we need Howard to calm the fuck down. Ideally, I need a bit of time to get this sorted." Frank lit a Silk Cut. "What about the girl?"

Amanda was slow to reply, although she had no doubt about her answer. "Uh, no, I don't think we can deliver Laila on a plate to him. For one thing, he's disgusting. For another, I've fixed her up with a lad for inspiration, and it's going to mean a lot to the album if you leave me to work that scenario through without the Yank screwing it up."

Frank looked curious, so Amanda pressed on. "Telling her to suck that git's cock would ruin everything. Plus we could all go to jail. She is underage."

That possibility intrigued Frank — he could solve this dilemma by stitching Howard up. But no. For all his time in Soho, through all the shit he'd seen and done before latching on to Chaz in the '60s, he'd never forced anyone, male or female, into sex. He found the idea distasteful. And, of course, there was the likelihood he'd be tarred in the process. That wouldn't do at all. Still, he needed a way to mollify Howard. "Yeah, you're right. The man is appalling, and we're already paying him a fortune. Not to mention the first-class airfare back and forth and the blow. Will *you* do it?"

She blanched. "I will most certainly not. Why don't *you* do it? Stop the car."

"Don't get shirty with me, young lady." Amanda braced for a barrage but was cut off with a laugh. "Oh, for fuck's sake, I was just taking the piss. I would never..." Amanda stopped herself from pushing the idea back on her boss and then played along as he began a comical game of "why don't we get..." They worked through a parade of well-known figures, male and female, living and dead, and fell about laughing. After a bit it stopped being funny, and Frank resumed the serious business of planning his next move.

The songs were getting sorted, so long as he could continue to get Chaz to accept outside help. Chaz was lost and miserable, but that was his own bleeding fault, and whingeing about Howard was just a diversion. Howard was useless, Frank knew that, but the MD at CBS liked him, and his name on the credits would be helpful with the gatekeepers of American radio, whoever they might be. He could wind him up enough to make him fuck off back to LA and cool off, but that ran the risk of the tapes going missing, or another project coming up and it becoming impossible to get him back. He could surely find a groupie who'd be game for a romp with the producer of Masterband's *Now You're All Mine*, but that wouldn't be enough to see this through to the end. Unless he was willing to risk a huge row with Chaz, giving that twat another point on the album would mean cutting down his own share, and Joe wouldn't take that well. He really had his heart set on redoing the swimming pool.

They reached Church Road and glided into a parking spot between a violet Rolls Royce Corniche and a Volvo P1800. "Wait here. I'll just be a minute," Frank said. The driver wandered off to have a smoke.

Frank stopped in the doorway to exchange a few words with a curly-haired fellow in a leather fringe jacket and then disappeared inside. A few moments later, an extravagantly dressed man erupted from the same entryway, bellowing "I Get Around" with barely a semblance of the actual melody. He lurched down the stairs unsteadily and, spying Frank's car, sauntered over and climbed in the back seat, where he flashed Amanda a toothy grin.

"'ello, 'ello. Who've we got 'ere? What's your name, dear girl? And while I must say the pleasure is all mine, I must enquire what you're doing in my motor."

Before Amanda could reply, the door opened again, and a uniformed chauffeur reached in. "Keith, you've got into the wrong car. Yours is the next one over."

The man looked perplexed. "Dear boy, that simply cannot be. I know my motor as well as I know my dear mother."

As the driver attempted to extricate his employer, he said, "Apologies, Miss. He's got one that looks a lot like this. Erm, well, had one. It went in the swimming pool. C'mon, guv, you're in the wrong motor. Come with me. Time to toddle off."

The man regarded them both with curiosity but made no progress in getting up or out. "Very well, dear boy. It's about bloody time. And bring her along, why don't you?" The chauffeur stood back, his arms outstretched.

Amanda was still contemplating the prospect of being kidnapped when Howard staggered into view, holding a blood-soaked towel to his face. Although muffled, his yelling was clearly audible in the otherwise still outdoors. "Help, help, I need an ambulance. That crazy mofo hit me and I'm bleeding to death! Help, call 911." With his chauffeur's attention diverted, the man in the seat next to Amanda did a slow-motion roll out of the car and onto the gravel. The driver looked down and helped him into an upright position, seated against a tire.

Frank emerged, walking swiftly to his car. He looked down. "Oh, hullo, Keith. I trust you're doing well?" The drummer grunted a reply as his man got him on his feet to guide him toward the correct vehicle.

Frank looked back at Howard, perhaps fifteen feet away, and shouted, "An ambulance is on the way. You'll be well looked after, and I'll see to the medical bill. Oh, and by the by, Chaz shan't be requiring your services any longer."

Keith, who had stopped to watch, howled with laughter. "Francis, you crazy fucker. Did you twat this berk?"

Frank looked fondly at the drummer, with whom he'd spent more than a few ridiculous nights looning about. "I did indeed. Broke 'is fucking beak, I'd expect. Some gifts you never lose." Keith smiled broadly and got in his motor, which pulled away, music blaring from an external speaker.

Howard took the rag away from his face. "I'll sue you, you bastard. I'll call the police and have you thrown in jail. You're nothing but a common hoodlum and you're going to rot in jail for the rest of your life. This isn't rock and roll, this is attempted homicide."

He sat down, hard, on the stairs, head back to stanch the flow from his nose. Frank started to put two fingers up but thought better of it. He laughed lightly and signaled the driver that he was ready to head home.

Raw Power

I SPENT a lot of time at the shop, partly because I fancied Bryan, but more because I was idea-poor and he was like the song dole, handing out what I needed to get by in my make-believe job as a fountain of pop tuneage. I don't think I was stealing his ideas so much as using them to inspire my own (even if whole bits of his did find their way into mine now and again). I don't think he cared, but I didn't make a point of mentioning it. It would have been better if he wrote more, but as it wasn't important for him, lacking both purpose and reward, he didn't make much of an effort. I wish I'd been clever enough to entice him into action, but there you go.

Shuffling through the covers in a bin of German imports by bands with weird names — Grobschnitt, Guru Guru, Neu!, Kraftwerk — kept me busy while he waited on a South American tourist who'd been off studying pygmies in the jungle for three years and wanted to catch up with the music he'd missed. Bryan loaded him up with cassettes, which he said was a naff way to hear music. Sixty quid in all, I heard when they totaled him up at the till, and the guy didn't flinch. He just pulled out the readies and went off with a big sack of tapes. Bryan came over as I was inspecting the back cover of *Phallus Dei* by Amon Düül II and — after mentioning that the title meant God's willy — asked me to come by his flat Sunday. I was chuffed to be invited and said I would do.

He shared a dodgy dump in Fulham with two members of a Dutch blues band who rehearsed in the front room but were nowhere to be seen; I half thought Bryan might have arranged my visit around their schedule, but maybe I was just flattering myself that he wanted us to be alone. He didn't seem to have anything momentous planned, just a listening session and my introduction to pot. I didn't tell him I was a drugs virgin.

We sat on the rug. His spliff-rolling technique didn't produce a smooth, even piece of work, but my curiosity — and the desire to join him in doing whatever he was into — was motivation enough. I coughed a lot, but then the feeling was lovely. I was not just relaxed and happy but felt like I was in the right place with the right person. We smoked some more, and I could feel myself loosening up, lowering my screens, as it were. Then it hit me how different things were. I think Mum would have liked ganja.

There were instruments stood up in various corners of the room; he said they belonged to his flatmates and that he was not supposed to mess with them. But a black guitar was occupying the one comfy-looking chair in the room, so I picked it up to sit down. The feel of it in my hands — the weight, the balance — hit some medicated pleasure centre and, feeling a bit like a child doing dress-up, I strapped it on and paraded around like the rock stars on telly. He didn't say not to, so I kept at it as he put on a record.

"Wow, Laila, you look cool with that Rick. Like it belongs there." His voice was raspy and slow. But he seemed really high, so I didn't take it that seriously. The guitar pressed uncomfortably against my chest, but Bryan gave the strap a tug to lengthen it. "Better?"

"Much, yeah." The instrument, which was lighter than I expected, now hung around my stomach, and I had to hunch over to get my hands around it.

I tried striking poses, but I was too stoned to make my body reliably carry out mental directions, so they came out wrong. Which, under the circumstances, made them even more right. I made silly scrunched-up faces like I'd seen one of those blokes do. Bryan walked me over to a mirror and we both fell about at the sight. I pointed at my reflection and howled, "What a wanker."

"A right poseur. But so are the rock dudes who get paid for it."

"What you reckon they're thinking?" I yawned and realized how hungry I was.

"I'm sure I don't know. Maybe working out how to pull girls." He winked at me and smirked. "Hungry?"

I was. He put an LP on, an import by an American band called Big Star (great name) and went out for beers and crisps.

"So, tell me, how do pop stars decide what to make songs about?" It sounded stupid saying that, and Bryan looked at me blankly. I needed to understand, and he was the only person I knew who I could ask.

"What do you mean?"

"Is it like real life, made up or just what they think people want to hear?"

"I dunno, Laila. You'd have to ask them. Some of the great songs are definitely about stuff that did happen — the Lovin' Spoonful did some of those, the Mamas and the Papas, and I expect Bob Dylan was angry enough at whoever led him to write 'Positively 4th Street.' But it's probably different for everyone. I don't think David Bowie's actually been to Mars, right? Most songs are about sex, romance, love, loneliness, that sort of thing."

"Hmm. Do you reckon you need to have done those things to write songs about them?" I was starting to understand what game Amanda was playing at with me and Stephen.

"Yeah, I'd say so. When I was a kid, all I thought about was what girls were thinking. Not just thinking about girls and all, but trying to think like a girl, to think about what they were thinking about. I wanted to be in their thoughts, though I don't believe I ever was. But after a while, maybe I was fourteen or fifteen, I realized that their minds were the most important thing in my life and that I hadn't the first clue about what was going on in them. I knew what I thought about them, but it was all like a dream, since I couldn't get any real knowledge to replace my illusions."

"I don't follow."

"There were a couple of girls I was completely crazy about..." He stopped in mid-thought as a chorus kicked in and sang along, only what he was singing and what they were singing didn't match up. I must have looked confused, and he shrugged an acknowledgment. "I forgot the words."

"You did? I thought you knew everything."

"Hardly. I'm only starting to get how much I don't know. About a lot of things."

I smiled to cover up my confusion. "Tell me more about the girls."

He frowned and then brightened. "So I spent hours, millions of hours, trying to imagine who they were, what they were thinking. I got the idea that if I knew, I might have had a chance with them, see? But I could never work out what anything they said or did meant. I had no context. Like, one of them, this girl Kit, gave me an album for my birthday — my mom organized a party and I got up my nerve and invited her. That was already a shocker. She wrote something sweet on the back." I frowned. "Of the album."

"Right."

"But I never knew if that was just something her mom had told her to do, or if it was something she'd done before just out of, y'know, good manners. In those cases it wouldn't have meant what it looked like it meant. But then I thought maybe it was teenage girl code that I had a chance with her. What did I know? I was thirteen."

"What did she write?"

"I don't remember."

"You forgot the words? I doubt that. Come on, tell me. Or better yet, show me. I bet you still have it, carefully preserved in one of those polythene bags from the shop. I expect you carry it with you wherever you roam."

"Actually, I don't. Have it that is. I donated it to the Salvation Army a few years later, along with my model, you know, uhm…trains. Seemed like a good idea at the time. I kind of wish I hadn't now. Or at least I did for a while." He blushed.

I started feeling sleepy, enveloped in a heavy fog, the thick kind that makes everything go slow. I kicked off my trainers and stretched out on the floor, imagining I was a very big cat with very soft fur. I rolled on my back and looked at Bryan upside down.

"Go on, tell me, what did she write? I know you haven't forgotten those words." I don't know why I was so sure about that, but I was.

"OK." He closed his eyes. "'Happy birthday, Brine.' She either didn't know or care how to spell my name, so she was comparing me to salt water."

"That's not all of it, is it?"

"No. She wrote 'Thirteen is my lucky number. Prey it's yours, too. Love…Kit.' Only she spelled it p-r-e-y."

"Still, that sounds pretty encouraging. Did you ask her out to see just how lucky the number thirteen might be for you?"

236

"No. Since she spelled 'pray' wrong, I thought it meant I had no prayer with her. Which I'm sure it didn't. But I was intrigued by the ellipsis."

"The what?"

"The dots between 'love' and her name. It left her meaning hard to discern. I worried over that for a long time."

"And you ended up doing nothing. What ever became of her?"

"No clue. We moved away the next year, and that was that." He got up and changed the record. "Now this guy makes faces, and he doesn't even play guitar." He handed me the cover — *Shades of a Blue Orphanage*. The picture on it was three little kids, and I didn't recognize the band's name.

"What's this?"

"Thin Lizzy, they're Irish. The main guy, the bass player, is black. When I saw them at the Marquee he had all the rock star moves. They were seriously exciting. But a spade with an Irish accent..." (That didn't sound so odd to me.)

We listened through a few songs. Hard rock with macho lyrics, done Gaelic green. Didn't do much for me, but Bryan seemed pretty into it, singing along here and there. When the side finished, he said, "I never knew what was inside a girl. I still don't."

"Wait, are you saying you've never...?"

"No, I didn't mean that." He laughed sheepishly and blushed. "I have. What I mean is that I'm still in the dark about how or what they think."

I kind of wished he didn't keep referring to girls as they. *I'm here, and that makes it a you, doesn't it?*

"That's why I listen to records by female singer-songwriters. I hate the music, but I keep listening for insights, the chance to learn what's in their heads."

"And that's why you buy their records?"

"Well, no. At the shop, I just play the records I want to hear."

"So if I wrote a song you might want to hear it to learn more about the mind of a fifteen-year-old British chick?"

237

"Absolutely!" He put on another album and sat down on the floor beside me. I rolled over and put my chin in my hands.

"Wouldn't it just be easier to ask me? I'm not a recording artist and maybe I'm not the most girly girl you know, but I'll try and tell you what I know. I have some experience, you know."

Maybe he heard me, maybe he didn't, but his answer went off in a different direction entirely.

"This is giving me a thought. Maybe I'm the same as everyone else. Just for the sake of argument, imagine that I'm a typical English boy...and say you could write songs that made me believe I was being let in on some profound secrets about girls —"

"Then the songs would maybe help you pull girls."

"Getting a leg up to get a leg over, as it were."

We were both in hysterics, rolling around on the floor. He tickled me, and I tickled him back. Suddenly we were in each other's arms. It was very warm in the flat, and I was sweating. A lot. Still, I'd never felt so comfortable with a boy, or anyone for that matter, and in a spark of enthusiasm, I kissed him. A real kiss, wet and sloppy, with tongues and teeth and lots of squirming. I grabbed his hand and pulled it between my legs, to the place that was suddenly in desperate need of rubbing.

Things proceeded quickly from there. I pulled off my jumper and, after giving him a moment to ponder the possible, unhooked my bra. I'd never shown a lad my bits, so this was probably a bigger deal for me than it was for him.

We were on the carpet, which smelled of cat piss. I had a Durex I'd pinched from Amanda's bag. Lucky I'd satisfied my curiosity by opening the other one she had so I had an idea what's what; dunno why I'd brought it along. There was no pain or, I assumed without interrupting the match for a quick looksee, blood — I guess all my solo work busted whatever needed busting. In fact, some of the feelings were familiar from my solo career, but this was way more exciting. The spring in my belly tightened and tightened, making my toes clench and the inside of my legs vibrate like a rubber band. Something was building up inside of me, not from one place but happening at every point on my body, happening beyond any ability to control or detail it. I thought this must be what drowning is like, a cataclysm that overwhelms the senses, the mind, the body. My cavernous desire grew until suddenly, without warning, I tensed and clenched, sucking in my breath and holding it as if I'd been thrown in the deep end of the pool. I weirdly flashed on Amanda's face and then, in a bunch of violent spasms, I was emptied of all the need, the want, the excitement, it all released at once as this crazy noise came out of me — I can't even describe it, kind of an anguished growl that began urgent and faded into a purr of contentment. I felt as if my body had been chucked into a warm pudding, and I relaxed, enjoying the feel of his weight on me. I felt completely satisfied.

I couldn't wait to do it again.

I COULDN'T STOP thinking about it — all of it — when I got home. I was awash in possibilities, in a new life, one with shagging and a boy who liked me and reckoned I was clever and could teach me about rock and roll. And then I remembered "I forgot the words" and got out my pad to write it down.

> I forgot the words.

I thought I'd best claim it straight away.

> By Laila Russell

I chewed on the end of the biro for a while, wondering what to do with it.

> You forgot the words but you surely knew
> The bees and the birds and now we are two
> I won't forget a moment of this
> And better yet the way that you kiss

It all sounded sappy and needed a twist of something. Given the state of my head at the moment, I realized it was going to need words that I wasn't feeling.

I turned a few pages back and found the words I'd written down after seeing that film. Yearning, burning, turning, learning. I couldn't recall why I thought of them at the time, but now I could hear them in head. I saw them as the last words in four lines of a verse. And I had an idea what those lines might be.

239

> Send me away yearning
> I may be young but I'm learning
> I could go up in flames and lose myself burning
> Or pack you off and watch my life turning

Then I scratched down:

> Good things must end
> Love's for the birds
> So, to you my friend
> I must say goodbye
> But when I try
> I forget the words

I read it back a few times, even tried singing it out loud. I changed the title to match the words. I knew it wasn't perfect. It probably wasn't even good, but it was a start. I felt like I was getting the hang of it. A line that could mean different things, a twist at the end, emotions and a story. I wasn't there yet, but now I had a map of where "it" might be. Two great feelings in one day.

AFTER THAT, Bryan and I were like boyfriend-girlfriend, screwing a lot but also plotting an imaginary future in the music business. He reckoned that he would make a good talent scout, or maybe a producer, and he believed — despite the evidence to the contrary — that I could play in a band and maybe be a singer, even though he'd never heard me vocalize anything beyond the orgasmic battle cries I'd mustered in his bed.

We went to shows together, at places like the Rainbow, Marquee, Ally Pally, the Roundhouse and the London Astoria. We studied what the other kids wore and egged each other on to try and dress like them. We spent time (more than money) down Carnaby Street and in the trendy shops in Kensington High Street and the King's Road, trying on all the top gear we could never afford. Too Fast to Live, Too Young to Die had this crazy rocker stuff that we tried on, but retro wasn't our speed; we were strictly looking forward. Occasionally, we'd splash out and buy something. It was ridiculous fun, like playing dress-up dolls with each other.

240

We took it further, not quite dressing the same but sharing gear and matching our looks up when we went out. We were about the same size (except for the curves I had and the broad shoulders I didn't) and both favored loose-fitting gear, so it was a snap to swap. That bit about which side the buttons on a man's shirt go? Didn't matter to me at all. When we shopped, we both had to like a thing before we'd buy it, since we'd likely both end up wearing it.

The clothes were a good laugh; we felt strange and smart at the same time. We learned words and ideas from each other, using our individualism to build one character in which we were equal partners. It was a bit frightening to feel myself becoming more like him and he like me, but it was also kind of wonderful, a reassuring bond in a fortress that kept the world out. I wondered if that was what it was like to have kids.

The best thing about sleeping with Bryan — well, the second-best thing — was knowing that I didn't have to try and be anything other than who I felt like being at any given moment. That was good enough for him, which made it good enough for me. His acceptance stoked my self-confidence. I loved feeling effortlessly cool, just myself. And bollocks to everyone else. I'd never felt that before, and it was as overpowering emotionally as the sex was physically. I lost myself in both of them, and it was absolutely lovely. Of course, a wiser version of me would have spotted the risk in that, but I didn't.

The downside to blurring the borders between me and him wasn't clear to me, but I must have sensed it. Bryan had opinions about everything, and while he didn't get on me if I didn't agree, I heard myself saying things I didn't believe because I could tell he liked it when we were "in synch," as he put it. Then it got hard to remember what *I* liked and what I only *said* I liked to keep him from that sour look he put on when we didn't agree. I didn't say anything, but it soon got to be a drag, and made me wonder if my ideas were crap compared to his. He wasn't like some mindfuck cult leader, but he had a pull on me that was hard to resist, and it was sucking out bits of me.

I DIDN'T KNOW where things stood with Amanda and Chaz and Mr Guy. She'd "let" my make-believe romance with Stephen go on for more than a month — leastways she hadn't said anything to him about ending it. (I had to take his word on that.) I couldn't guess her mind: she'd been so greedy for whatever was supposed to spill out of my saddened soul after he kicked my heart to bits...but then it never happened. He hadn't heard any more about it and neither had I. Maybe she thought I was doing enough for Chaz in my supposed state of bliss, which had nothing to do with who she thought it did. Maybe she'd been sacked and hadn't told me. Or she thought a breakup might boomerang, turning me into a wreck too miserable to find an idea in my head. Maybe she imagined I might drown Chaz's future in lager.

Stephen reckoned she'd simply forgot. We got to joking about the tragedy of our breakup, and what we'd miss the most about our "relationship." That was a mistake: he said our conversations, I said his cock. I thought I was being funny, but it came out sounding ugly.

When I wasn't thinking about something more useful, I wondered if her ladyship had ever been dumped. I didn't reckon she had — when you look that good, and conduct yourself with such poise, who would dare? No, I guessed she'd done the dumping in her life. I didn't really understand what she and Stephen were, or had been, to each other and how it had ended. Of if it had. He wouldn't say. (In my darkest moments, I could imagine them in bed together, having a cruel laugh at my expense.)

While faffing about with "I Forgot the Words" some more, I got the idea for a song called "Make-Believe Boyfriend." It would be of no use to Chaz, of course, but that was all right. Poofs are becoming so trendy and all, but it still wouldn't do for him to sing that, now would it? I could change it to "Make-Believe Girlfriend," but then, for me leastways, it'd be about Amanda, and I might have to explain why I'd write a song like that. Don't give yourself away — that was something Dad said.

I considered telling Bryan about Amanda and her crazy plan to get me inspired by having it off with Stephen but never had the nerve. That was another me; it had fuck all to do with him. And then there was the other thing. Just because he and I were having it off didn't cancel out my crush on Stephen. But he wasn't interested in me the way Bryan was, so there was no harm in keeping that secret. I didn't tell Stephen about Bryan either: no reason to announce that I was spoken for. It was no bother to keep Dad clueless, but it took a bit of effort to ensure that Amanda was in the dark about all of it. And none of them knew I also fancied her something rotten. I was careful not to introduce the ones who didn't already know each other — that felt like a sure path to unwanted complications.

Stephen rang me from time to time and we made up stories for me to tell Amanda. Winding her up was a total laugh. According to my reports, we did it in a changing room at Biba's, under a tree in Hyde Park and in a hire car parked behind Harrods. It sucked talking about the sex life we weren't having, but things were good with Bryan in that department, so I mixed the two up in my head and didn't feel deprived. Still, we would ring off and I'd need a wank, sometimes two, to get him out of my head. And from time to time, despite Bryan, I still had fantasies about him. A couple of times I woke up from a dream where we'd been going at it and thought maybe it had actually happened. I thought about him once or twice when Bryan and I were in bed. I started really resenting him for holding out on me. To hell with Amanda and her stupid plan, I just wanted him to screw me and get it over with. Shagging Bryan was all well and good, but Stephen was my white whale, my rock and roll fantasy, and I longed to get my hooks in him. Plus, I was starting to worry that I needed it more than Bryan did. And seeing Amanda in the pale flesh still sent me sliding down a different path of hormonal confusion.

But in the meantime, I was collecting song ideas, mostly thanks to Bryan. It wasn't just the sex, it was him and his clever ideas. I listened carefully and was getting better at giving them a bit of a twist this way or that, so that the words I gave to Amanda to give to Mr Guy to somehow get Chaz to use (I still didn't know how and didn't want to know) were more like what they wanted. Plus, it made me feel like less of a whizz girl. I occasionally tossed in a line that sounded like it could be about Stephen so Amanda could believe — without asking me, of course — that her "brilliant" plan was working.

I started saving back some of what we were coming up with. I didn't have a purpose in mind, I just felt like they were getting too much of me. They'd stopped saying anything about my words; shoveling the best ideas Bryan and I had into Amanda's hands never to be seen or heard again, well, that was just too unsatisfying for me. I wanted more.

243

The one bit of joy I *did* get was a fortnightly cheque for fifty quid. That was a lot of money, and I dug having it. I felt bad about Bryan not sharing in any of the profits since he was doing a fair bit of the work, but he did have a job that paid him, so I put that thought aside. And I bought him a pudding now and again.

With Chaz fading out of my life, and without admitting how far I'd already gone down that road, I told Bryan I wanted to try writing songs on my own. I thought he might take it as a putdown, but he was surprisingly keen on the idea. Then he mentioned a mate who worked for one of the record labels that he knew through the shop who knew some legendary figure with a crazy name I'd never heard before, and Bryan said he bet she (!) knew a lot about song-writing and might have advice I could use. Bryan said his mate would fix a visit, which he did, well after I'd already forgot about it. So one Sunday we met up at Victoria Station and he introduced me to his friend Matthew. Neither would tell me who or where we were headed to, but I didn't mind the bit of mystery.

The Liquid Poetess

WYNIFRED CELESTELESTER was a luckless eccentric. Rather than be celebrated for her colorful character, as was common to English of a certain age, she had been ignored — alright, outright shunned — and reduced to a tatty life on the fringe of destitution in a houseboat that was sitting low in the brackish swamp of an estuary near the reservoir in Walton-on-Thames. Over the course of a 40-year career as an avant-whatever artist, writer and musician, she'd produced loads of paintings, sculptures, happenings, an Indian food cookbook, a collection of limericks (in Braille) and a dozen albums few people had heard.

I had no idea what to expect when we — Bryan and me, joined by his friend Matthew, who was a friend of hers — went to call on her. I'm not sure what the purpose was, something to do with inspiration and songwriting, but they said it would be worth my while. I forgot until I was putting on my shoes to go meet them that I was told to bring a gift. In desperation, I grabbed the only thing I had of any value: the 45s from Amanda (leaving out the ones I liked). I found some wrapping paper and bashed together a package tied up with string.

The ceiling of the boat was covered with ornate psychedelia from stem to stern. Canvases, stacked like newspapers, were everywhere, a visual report from the border between startling ingenuity and dementia. So were fag-ends and squeezed-out tubes of paint.

She was dressed in a cobalt blue nun's habit (where in ding dong bell does one obtain such a vestment?), her face painted a frightening shade of yellow, with a green-dyed rabbit on a leash by her side. Color was clearly an obsession. Under a blue skullcap fringed in jangly bells, she appeared to have small springs tied into her long grey hair. Her eyes were a watery, translucent match, with brows died green. The rings on her fingers — enough tarnished metal to make her look ready for medieval battle — were jaggedly cut, crudely bent old cutlery that looked risky at best. I asked myself how — and with the next breath, taking in the smell of the place, if — she could wipe herself.

245

"Matthew, how much did it cost you lot to come down here?"

Matthew looked at Bryan, who — over my protests — had funded this expedition. He answered, "Roughly four pounds for the train and one for the taxi. And then we'll have that again for the return."

"Hang on — so you spent all that to come here — and what? To learn the cost of truth or flatter yourselves for your youth?"

He didn't have a ready reply to that remark.

"All in all, I would have preferred you sent the money instead and leave me be. I'm not running a training college here."

We looked at each other and wondered if we'd wasted a trip.

"And the young lady?" I shivered as she fixed me with a penetrating gaze.

Bryan answered for me, trying to be chivalrous, I suppose. "She's the reason we've come, ma'am. She's...she wants to be a songwriter, and Matthew says you know a lot about that. I guess we're hoping you could share some tricks of the trade. A leg up to the younger generation."

"You young people make me larf. You've not got a clue about ignorance, have you? You think you know everything and the rest you'll pick up as you go. I know it feels like that, but you're dead wrong about it. I taught at uni for a few years back in the day, filling gullible minds with what I thought was true, valuable information and ideas. Then it dawned on me that I didn't really know more than they did, so I turned the tables and had them teach me. That wasn't right either, so I knocked the whole thing on the head. And came out feeling terrible about believing that I knew things. Since then I have devoted my life to sharing my ignorance with the world, making it clear to people what I don't know rather than rabbiting on about what I once imagined I did. Or do. You should do more of that. It's like confessing your sins."

Bryan turned to me and made a go-on-then gesture. "She's brought you a little gift." I pulled the package from my bag and handed it to her. She put it on the floor behind her chair without so much as a nod or a wink, but it didn't look like I could safely take it back.

"I've brought some biscuits," said Matthew. "And those choccies that you like."

246

He held out a cello-wrapped box of candy and a brightly colored tin. "I'll put the kettle on, yeah?"

"Very well. I suppose that'll be alright." We talked for hours, long past my eagerness to learn from her or consider the value of what she was saying. Very little of it had to do with songwriting. Clearly, focus was impossible for an old-timer living alone with an abiding sense of loss about her standing in the cultural firmament. Unprompted, she told us her life story. She was a spectacular storyteller, able — even at her age — to go down long digressions and still find her way back to the central narrative.

Her bitterness ran close to the skin, but her depictions of outrageous snubs and inexplicable mistreatment had the ring of truth. Without knowing why, I felt a lot of sympathy for her. At the core of everything she told me was a bit of quashed faith, of genuine surprise at the way things turned out for her. Maybe she was just absurdly naïve, or so full of herself that she could only understand failure and disdain as the fault of others, but that wasn't the way it came off. As the afternoon wore on, she made more and more sense.

She drifted off after a while, her lips moving in soundless words. Waking up, she stared off into the distance and said, "Nothing anyone says really matters to me. If I believed in myself, maybe it would, but I have nothing to defend, nothing to cling to, nothing to support. Say what you will, it makes no difference to me."

The more she talked, the more I started believing that I was really getting to know her. I got the impression that no one had taken this woman, with her reputation for bizarre-going-on-offensive behaviour, thorough unreliability and haughty disdain for those who accepted societal norms, for who she really was, a shy, insecure artist, in a very long time.

Once she had got it in her head that songwriting was the issue for me, she pulled out and put on an old album by Marc Bolan when his band was still known as Tyrannosaurus Rex, his "acoustic hippie elf period," Bryan called it. I didn't much like the way it sounded — too simple — but I could really hear the words and follow the melodies.

She showed us some of her clippings, a trove divided about evenly between triumphs and attacks. There were vindictive reviews and puny sales reports, fan letters and ornate foreign editions. It was hard to gauge how she viewed all of it: I sensed a vicarious pride in the hurts stronger than what she expressed for the small victories. I got the feeling she was viewing all of it from a distance, an offhand observer of her own existence.

"In my life, no matter how low I have pushed my expectations, or allowed them to sink, there was always someone with a new way to disappoint me. The inescapable suspicion, of course, is that I somehow do it to myself, restoring my optimism as a way to measure my unhappiness, but I'm just guessing. And I certainly can't imagine why I would do that. The child who takes off his glasses and steps on them before the schoolyard bully gets to break them may be denying the other that cruel satisfaction, but the results are the same. I can't do the calculations on shame and humiliation in those circumstances, but then I never grasped the appeal of *haru kiri*, either. The degree to which we control our own fate must be imprinted from birth and displayed like a banner to those adepts who manage to manage the things others of us cannot."

"Sorry? I don't follow." We were speaking to each other as if the others had vanished, although they were seated right where they'd been.

"What I mean is, maybe we're like penguins. Beyond the superficial aspects of appearance and manner, perhaps each of us has a genetic setting for the amount of control we can exert as our lives go on. Think of it as self-actualizing confidence, if I must sink into new age gibberish for a jot. Accounting for acts of god like disease and bouts of banality..." — she smiled for an instant at her digression — "...you are what you believe you can become. And that gets conveyed to those whose acquiescence, or cooperation, or indulgence is necessary to its achievement. If you're a sure thing on your way to the magic kingdom, the world steps aside as you boldly stride to the gates. If the deck of cards your soul holds has been set to never deal a winning hand, no one will let you pass no matter how clever you are. They can't be fooled, faked, bullied, beaten, enticed or erased. At least not by you. Maybe it's nothing more complicated than being a tiger as opposed to a mouse. Lions eat what they want, don't they?"

"Yes, but they don't get to be king, even if that's what their hearts are set on."

248

"How do you know?"

"I guess I don't. Check."

"But foiled dreams are universal. Everyone has something they desire and don't get to have."

"Are you sure? My hunch is that God, or whatever she is, has set it up so that everyone gets exactly what they want exactly to the point that their internal mechanism has been set to get it."

It was getting late. The sun was down, and the breeze through the houseboat was chilly. I looked over nervously at Bryan. She might be able to teach me something useful, but time was running short and I was starting to feel anxious about getting back.

He sensed my concern. "Miss CelesteLester," he ventured mildly, "our friend Laila was hoping you could give her some practical advice about writing… songs. You've got such a vast catalogue, you're obviously very skilled in that department. Any tips you can share with a talented newcomer who is becoming very devoted to her craft?"

She slowly looked from face to face, her frown suggesting that she had no idea who we were or why we were sitting there with her. Perhaps the sunset had disoriented her, or she had drifted off. None of us knew whether she was *compos menti*, or just managing a reasonable facsimile of lucidity.

"Writing songs is like taking a crap," she said. "Sometimes you just sit down and the bomb bay opens, emptying your hold with effortless ease. But then there's those mornings — mornings? — yes, when you push and squirm and strain and plead for your bowels' meager offering. That's songwriting. Don't worry if you have to force it, it will come out just as good in the end. Easy is easy, but hard is also alright. And pay some attention to what goes in, as it has a direct role in what comes out. Don't stint on the experiences life can offer, dear. Your ideas need to be fed."

When Bryan asked how she felt about her fans, she turned serious.

"Do you children know where the word fan comes from?"

We looked at each other. I suddenly felt as uncomfortable as I do when called on in class to talk about a chapter in a book I hadn't got around to reading.

"In colloquial parlance, it's a diminutive for fanatic. Like religious loonies or political zealots. Wild-eyed crazies who set their blinkers on a single belief and ignore everything else: the truth, reality, the grave contradictions of life. That's how they — you lot — are seen. As idiots who only know the one trivial thing they've chosen to believe."

We looked at each other again, weighing what she said against the utterly harmless view we had of pop fans: kids who liked a singer or a band. That didn't sound so ludicrous, but she was chipping away at our foundations.

"If you were smart, you'd change that for yourselves. Make 'fan' short for fantasy, not fanatic. You're into that rock and roll music. It's all just made-up piffle. Why not have a laugh? Don't take it so seriously. Create your own world. Dream things up."

"I thought writers, even songwriters, were supposed to write what they know." That was Matthew, who had not displayed much interest in what she was saying until now. Wynifred sputtered and laughed, her eyes growing wide with, I won't say amazement because it seemed unlikely anything would surprise her. I guess it was amusement. Or indignation. "Don't be thick," she said. "Who could possibly give a toss about what you know?"

Bryan and I looked at each other, since I'd been living in that particular faith for months now. The church of Chaz, as expressed in the minds of punters.

"If you're still fixated on the crap you young people listen to, you've still got the wrong of the stick. The kids who follow the stars aren't seeking a messiah, someone to believe in and be guided by, they're after a fan-*tasy*, a dream of life better than school and bangers and mash. Wasn't that the point of *Tommy*?

I wasn't sure what to do with any of that (except to wonder what fan-*tasy* might have to do with fan-*ny*), but what struck me from meeting her, I thought as we made to leave, was the purity of effort, that she was her own creative taskmaster. CelesteLester, who enjoyed neither critical nor commercial acclaim, had compromised nothing to the expectations or desires of others. It was, I imagined, the faith that kept her going, not any external affirmation. I didn't know if I was up to that challenge. It was just twaddle for tots, as some wag had called the current songs on the charts.

I asked about that. Seems I was dead wrong. She was, as she patiently explained, motivated in quite the opposite direction. "No, no, no, I always worry about what people will think. My aim is truly to be loved, bought, praised and serialized." Surprising, that was, but reassuring. My instinct was to resist desire, that it was weak to want things or to care too much. But if she saw it the other way, maybe I could put my hand out and try to take what I could for myself as well.

Let It Slip

IN HIS STATE of suspended uselessness, Chaz was lost to some witches' blend of depression, insecurity and inertia. The album wasn't done; indeed, it was on the verge of not existing at all. While ordering his solicitors to summon up a rain of legal shit over the whole project, Moore had somehow got onto Chaz and managed to convince him that the work they had done was "audioally defective," had some sort of ambient room acoustics issue that would "really fuck up the mastering." It was undoubtedly because he'd not been able to purloin the tapes and was seeking to do as much damage as he could. As a result, Chaz was convinced it all needed to be cut again, but — to Frank's consternation — evinced no enthusiasm for going back in the studio and doing it. His boat was sinking in the middle of the pond with a paddle that he couldn't trouble himself to use.

Frank suspected that the producer knew what a shit job he'd done and wanted to cash the cheque without having to endure any public scrutiny of the work he'd barely done, which was sure to stiff and would hardly add any gilt to his crap-plated résumé; selecting that berk had been a big mistake. Nothing but misery. He blamed record company anxiety and the irrational assumption that what worked for one artist would work for another. Frank promised himself never to go that route again.

As satisfying a reminder of the way life used to be as it was to sort out that Yank with a headbutt and a hearty fuck off, that luxury cost him dearly — the lawsuit, endless bollocks from the label and Chaz being dropped from the Slade tour. (The jolly postcard from Noddy — "wish yu wuz heer" with a picture of the Grand Canyon — didn't make that any easier to swallow.) Chaz reckoned Frank was to blame for all of it, but it hadn't led him to any hasty moves. In this moment of crisis, Frank was still his lifeline, he'd said.

"I expect we can salvage an album out of this mess, Joe, but what's the point? If it gets a lukewarm reception and dies in the forties he'll be done for."

"I agree. You don't want to sling second-rate rubbish out there."

"Chaz has just about lost interest in the whole thing."

"Right, and a poorly received record will make him lose all hope. You'd need an act of God to set him back on track. I don't suppose Bowie wants to write another 'All the Young Dudes' and give it to him?"

"That's not about to happen. No, it's down to me, as it always has been."

"Feeling a bit sorry for yourself?"

"No, just out of great ideas."

"Well, what have you got? Is it fixable?"

"I'm not sure any longer." Frank ran a hand back over his scalp. "I've got a few reels of scratch mixes in my office. I'll take a run into town and have a listen."

Later that afternoon, Frank was at his desk in the Burgher office. He threaded a tape on the Akai deck and wriggled the Koss headphones onto a comfortable spot. A pad and pencil were at the ready. He lit a fag and pressed Play.

The older songs, take after take of the ones Chaz had written before losing his way, were hopeless. They didn't sound like anything else going this year, just retreads of past failures. (Maybe he could put them out under a pseudonym and bill it as some great lost late-'60s band.)

As the second reel wound off, the hopelessness of the situation overtook him. He poured and drained a drink. There were two more to play, and he avoided them a long while, wondering if he could bear any more misery. He finally made it through half a tape labeled "CB basics, no vocals, no EQ": there were some catchy bits on there, a few strong chord patterns and some solid playing, but they weren't identifiable songs, just instrumental beds that would need a lot more work to be anything. The other box was identified only by a drawing of a circle with spots and a "P" in the centre.

Three minutes later, grinning ear to ear, and feeling better than he had in weeks, he rang Psi. "I just played 'Soldier to Cry On.' I thought that had only got as far as an acoustic demo. But this is absolutely blinding. Do you know how or who it got finished by?"

Psi chuckled down the line. "Yeah, guv, I do."

"Tell me, man!"

"Well, I listened to what Chaz did with the song I gave him. I hated to think of it going to waste when the Yank buggered off. So, for a laugh, I took it round to this eight-track my mate owns in Islington and overdubbed drums, handclaps and some percussion. He put reverb on the guitar. I got my mate from Strawbs in to add a Fender Rhodes part run through a fuzzbox. Did it on spec, so it cost a shepherd's pie and a couple of pints. Some American band was in at night and had hired one of them Mellotrons, so I used that to add strings and a choir. I had my mate mix it. You owe him 250 quid if it gets released."

The vocal Chaz had laid down the night before it all went to shit with Howard was the singular result of a black mood, lack of enthusiasm and a wicked hangover, an unselfconscious display of such louche dissipation that it could have been patched in from Mordor. Having misread the word "shoulder," he sang "soldier" instead, even though it made no sense.

Frank had to stifle a laugh — pretty much nothing was as it should have been, but the cumulative effect was formidably weird and rather seductive. As soon as Psi rang off, he got on to Chaz's product manager at CBS, who loved it and quickly agreed to a rush release — along with renewed pressure on Chaz to deliver the album. Frank tested the new and improved waters for an increased budget and was turned down flat.

They could still bung an album together from what they had and release it, but he knew that would be a waste of time and money. The production was shit and the performances uninspired. Maybe the songs could be revisited, refreshed, recut. But they'd have to pay for the time out of their own pockets, which were not too deep at the moment. Chaz had hardly worked in a year.

Frank rang Psi about his mate's studio, which would be a lot cheaper than returning to Olympic.

"Yeah, no problem. We can get it for a song. He needs the work. And this is the best part: he's an ace engineer, and he comes with the room."

Frank chuckled dryly. "And it *is* a proper recording facility, right, not a jumped-up gaff like Joe Meek's? I don't relish the idea of asking Chaz to sing in the loo."

"No, no, it's a real studio. Small, to be sure, but the whole band can fit in the room at a time. And there's a baffled off corner Chaz can use. It'd be fine. And it's within your budget." Psi smirked to himself.

"Let me think about this before I suggest it to Chaz. I don't know how he would feel about recording in a cupboard."

"If you want, guv, we could do the basics there and then somewhere posh for the vocals. Chaz never has to know. If he doesn't faff about, you make it clear to him that the clock is ticking, he could probably get it all done in, I dunno, twenty hours. You can afford that. And then back to my mate's for mixing."

"Interesting." Frank thought to himself there were a number of ways he could bury that cost, provided it didn't amount to too much. They'd already spent £85,000; another five grand could be got away with. But not much more. "We'd need to find a producer who can do it on the cheap as well. And not talk to the press. We can't have it getting out that Chaz cut corners."

"How about letting me do it, guv? What've you got to lose?"

"I suppose you're right."

AS IT HAD BEEN weighing on me more of late, I felt I'd best come clean with Bryan before things went too much further. I told him about Burgher and Chaz and all that — not in any great detail and without mentioning his unwitting participation. I threw in a little about the nonsense with Stephen. Bryan was amazed and, I'd say, amused by the first bit; not so keen on the second. I promised I'd end it, as harmless as I assured him "it" was.

I didn't really want to burst that soap bubble fantasy in case there was some chance of it turning into real life, but when I thought about it, it pissed me off. All of it. I couldn't have him, I couldn't have her, and I was playing make-believe about all of it. It wore on me, like a pair of trainers that didn't fit right, but I didn't know what I could do about any of it. I wanted Stephen and Amanda to feel a bit of the misery they'd put me through. I decided that rather than just feel like they were done with me, I'd best be done with them. I needed more control over my life.

Inspiration, they say, comes from the least likely sources, and most often when you're least expecting it. So it should not have surprised me one bit when Dad's telly selection proved provident. He had on a programme called *Pot Black* — blokes in suits playing snooker. Now I couldn't give a toss about snooker, but the thirty seconds or so I caught as I walked through the sitting room hit me like a rock. You send a ball into another ball just so, and the second one takes off, ending up exactly where you want it. Maybe I wasn't understanding the physics properly, but it did demonstrate the obvious. My best hope for getting Stephen was to send Amanda caroming into him. And not in a nice way.

What did I know about Stephen? Nothing really, except that he was the sort of bloke who would agree to take part in a fake romance plot to exploit a young girl's mind, not body. He was Scottish, worked in a hair salon, liked to drink and smoke and had shagged countless girls. Except me. Maybe it was time to throw the fiddlesticks in the air and see where they land. In a flash, it came to me. First off, I had to break up with my pseudo-boyfriend before he had the chance to do it to me. Would I get what I wanted out of it? Who knows? Dad once said you have to dive in the deep end if you want to make a splash. I don't think he'd ever done that, but maybe I could.

When I rang to do the dumping, Stephen creased up. In between gales of laughter, he said nothing like this had ever happened to him before. He called it a mark of outstanding character that I had terminated our relationship without succumbing to his charms. I laughed along but took that as a discouraging sign.

"Sae ye hae nothing tae hate me for."

"Not yet." I hope that sounded the way I meant it, but I couldn't tell from his reaction.

To my complete amazement, when he told Amanda what I'd done, she was furious at me. "You stupid little slag," she raged down the line. "Why in God's name? How could you do that? You've queered everything, you know that? I'll never forgive you." I couldn't imagine why — it's not as if I was still providing her any service.

"What's it to you? Why would you care who I go out with? Anyways, you did the same to him, right?"

"That's none of your concern. You owe..." She let that trail off.

"I don't owe you anything. Or anyone else. We had our thing and I broke it off." It had got so easy to pretend to her that we were having it off that packing it in felt just as real and sincere. At least it did to me.

"I suppose you'll blame me for everything." I did, but I wouldn't give her the satisfaction if there was a million pounds in it for me. And we were talking about different things anyways. "It's none of my doing. Not really."

"What?"

"Nothing. Never mind. None of your concern."

"No, really. Why would you care how he feels about me now? He's only interested in you."

I don't know why I threw that out there except I was feeling witchy, and she definitely deserved a bit of deception in return for all the string-pulling she'd done at my expense.

"How do you know he's still into me?" Her tone softened. I knew that flattery would get to her. She sounded friendly, girlish even. My heart melted a bit, but I wasn't ready to fall for a momentary flash of nice. I knew it could be pulled away in a flash. And we really had nothing keeping us in contact, nothing that wasn't evaporating into the air as we spoke.

It's amazing how the shittiest people in your life, the ones who would gladly sell you down the river for a tuppence, are so willing to believe that they have such magnetism and charm or power that you, of course, like and admire them. It's like a free pass to heaven, proof that whatever terrible things they've done to you have been forgotten, forgiven or — best of all — never noticed in the first place. It lets them believe the horrible fictions of their existence. It must be a treat to have your victim smile and say thank you. Only a monster would fall for that. Wouldn't you see the blood in their eye, hear the sarcasm in their voice? No, not Amanda.

I felt the chance to really explore my creativity here. I pushed my brain into high gear — calculating, scheming, plotting — and out popped a solution. It was like being passed the ball in hockey and seeing a clear shot on goal. All I had to do was say it out loud.

"In bed one time, he called me by your name when he came. That's when I knew I had to break up with him. But he made me swear not to tell you. He'll deny it, of course, so you can't say anything to him about it."

I was well away, drunk with the power of the lies I was telling. "In fact, he'll probably deny that we ever did it at all. That's how embarrassed he is about the whole affair. I think he thinks it reflects badly on him, getting mixed up with a c—...a calf like me. (I made a mental note of that sidestep; might be useful in a lyric.) "You probably shouldn't make any further inquiries about it."

A Soldier to Cry On

BETWEEN THE SHAGGING and what I could fish out of Wynifred's weird encouragement, I found myself coming up with better ideas for songs. My favourite was the dirty ditty "Jack and Danny." I found those names in an American comic book Bryan had and recognized a Cockney rhyme I could use. I didn't show that song to anyone, since it was about my private hobby.

I spotted an advert in the back of *Sounds* for a Chaz gig in September at the Hammersmith Odeon, but the following issue had a notice that it had been canceled. Seemed like that ship was sinking, rather than sailing. Feeling a bit silly and stupid, I stowed the clobber I'd got off Amanda in the back of my closet. The whole episode was starting to feel like a dream, loads of things that happened but probably were never meant to.

The only word I had from Burgher came from Mr Guy's assistant, who rang one afternoon to tell me that I was off the payroll and no longer had an account at the Chelsea Drugstore. The first bit was a drag (although not being obliged to them was just as well, what with the term about to begin and all), but the second didn't really hurt. Bryan could play me, or nick me, anything I wanted to hear. That made me think Chaz had finished recording the album, or at least had sorted himself back to doing it on his own without needing the likes of me to muck in. I wondered when it would be out and what it would sound like.

TRUTH BE TOLD, I'd got a bit bored. I wondered if I could do something on my own, not that I had any clue what that would be or how I would do it. Dad told me more than once that Mum's advice was always to stop waiting for things to happen. I don't know whether she meant not to be a lazy sod or not to expect anything. I was leaning toward the latter, getting ready for the grey grind of school and whatnot, when I stopped by Bryan's shop one afternoon in late August. Compared to me, he was totally hopped up, like someone had put leapers in his Bovril. (Or, I suppose, like we were doing it.)

"I've been trying to call you all day, Lye. You'll never believe it."

"I was in the library. Never believe what?"

He vanished into the stockroom behind the tape department and returned with a 45 in a picture sleeve. He thrust it at me. My hand started shaking when I saw it was a Chaz Bonapart single, "Soldier to Cry On." I slid the vinyl out of the sleeve and held it by the edge and the centre, where the label was, as Bryan had shown me. "Produced by Howard Moore," I read. "3:48," I read. "(P) 1972 Elba Songs," I read. "Written by C. Bonapart," I read. What I didn't read was my name anywhere.

"Wait, he didn't bloody write it, I did!" I'd told him about the song, what I could recall of it from that day in Mr Guy's office. I wondered if Bryan realized he'd given me the idea for it in the first place.

"Shhhh." Bryan put a finger to his lips and darted his eyes like a double-O spy. "You said they made you swear to never tell anyone, so it's not like they would print it on a hundred-thousand singles, would they? But did you write it? Maybe they just nicked your title. That's not against the law."

"But that's not even the title. It was 'Shoulder to Cry On.' This way doesn't make any sense."

He wasn't really hearing me. "Let's give it a listen. I've been waiting for you to get here to put it on."

He went behind the counter and took off a mopey girl singer album. He put the record on, changed the speed switch and swung the arm over the vinyl, setting it down with a loud pop. We looked at each other nervously, like you do when the teacher comes down the row, handing out a test you didn't study for.

It started off with strings, like in a detective movie, and then went straight into a drum and handclaps section, with chugging guitar chords. Bryan frowned at a sound that could have been piano. "They did something weird there in the mix," he shouted. "Very cool." When Chaz began singing, I knew exactly what the words were going to be. I mimed along as best I could guess the rhythm. He'd changed "shoulder" to "show-el-jer," which was kind of between what I said and the title he'd given it. We exchanged puzzled looks at that. At the end, a choir moaned in the background as Chaz sang "rah rah hoo hah" over and over as it faded out.

"Oohkay," said Bryan. "That was crazy. I guess if you knew all the words you must have written them."

I made a smug so-it-would-seem face at that simpleton logic as my mind tripped over itself in confusion and excitement. "I guess so, most of them. Well, some of them. At least I knew them, and I've never heard the record before, so either I've got ESP or this is what we came up with in Mr Guy's office that day. Do you think it's going to be a hit?"

All the customers were looking at us, or at least at the record player. One girl, about my age, came up and asked to hear that song again. Then she bought a copy, as did two or three others.

Laughing, he said, "Yeah, I'd say it already is. I wonder how many we got in." He came out from behind the counter and gave me a hug. "Oh, Lye, I'm really proud of you. You're a genuine songwriter!" That was one of the best things I've ever heard about myself. I was proud, too.

EVEN WITH HALF the promo effort that went into "Prime Number," "Soldier to Cry On" did surprisingly well. The press was more than kind: it got Single of the Week in *Melody Maker*. They called it "a surprising leap forward for an old fart whose creative imagination was last seen lolling in the mud at Woodstock."

The single's success was a godsend for Chaz. Frank could finally see an album at the end of the tunnel, but there was a long way yet to go. Most of what Moore had done would have to be scrapped. But they had "Soldier to Cry On," which would have to be included on the longplayer, and one called "Equal Opportunity Girl" that was rough but could be just as good with a bit more studio work. Those two were smarter, more modern, than the material Chaz had come up with on his own. A couple of his songs might be salvageable if redone with better lyrics. Maybe he could send them over to Amanda's girl and see if she could match something clever up to the music. So long as there was a hook in there somewhere, the words and the sound were more important than anything else. Chaz only needed to get out of his own way. Then there

261

were three instrumentals that still needed lyrics and melodies — in his improved frame of mind, Frank hoped, Chaz might be able to make something of those himself — plus the lyrics that were in a folder locked in his desk drawer. There were a bunch of promising scraps and one that was just a brilliant title: "I Forgot the Words." (Maybe John Cage could have a go at that one, he thought.) There were three more or less ready lyrics from the girl: "Only Lovers Left Alive," "What I Wouldn't Give" and "Ignite the Pilots." Those would do nicely, provided Chaz could be conned into cutting them.

He'd get on to those hacks who hang about publishers' offices down Denmark Street; they could pluck a hook, a bit of melody and a middle eight out of their arses for £100, no points promised and no questions asked. Chaz's band could do the rest. But that wouldn't quite tot up to a whole two-sided album. He made a note to ask Amanda how soon they could expect more from the girl.

DAD AND I listened to Radio 1 nonstop and fell about when Emperor Rosko played the song on Friday's *Roundtable*. He didn't seem too keen, but Lynsey DePaul, the one who sang "Sugar Me," was on the panel, and she said the lyrics were "charming." (She called a couple of other things on the show "charming" as well, but there's no way that's not good.) I felt like a million pounds. Dad said he was dead proud of me, and that was lovely as well.

Wednesday morning, I got up early and waited at the newsagents until they put out the weeklies. "Soldier to Cry On" went in at number-26. I was on the charts! I couldn't believe it. Not high in the charts, I know, but in there all the same. Beginner's luck, I suppose, but still. Chaz was on *TOTP*, miming to words I'd, if not quite written, at least came up with enough of an idea that someone else — I didn't know who, although I doubted it was him, despite his name on the label — was able to make a hit song from it.

I had never thought of myself as creative, and I had no clue how to go about being creative. I didn't grow up thinking I had to make or do things, just that I had to get by and keep Dad from going off the rails. Mum was encouraging and all, but she was gone by the time there might have been anything about me worth supporting.

I made it my business to spend the next few days hanging about in the shop, watching to see who bought the record. *My* record. I chatted up a few, just girl to girl, without saying who I was. Most of the punters were pretty useless at answering my questions, but one said she liked singles about her life, that they made her feel part of a new species. That was the word she used: "species."

I'd never felt so good in my whole life. This was amazing, incredible. It was like I'd scored the winning goal in the World Cup and the terraces were roaring with adulation. Dad was dead proud of me. I thought about Mum, what she would have said. What I didn't think about was Bryan. None of this would have happened without him. Or maybe it would. He didn't get me into Chaz's inner sanctum, he just shared some ideas he'd had. I'd done all the hard graft. I suppose he could have been browned off at me for not giving him full marks, but we were young and in love, and anyroad this was just a lark. My giddiness at finally making a mark on the world, even a small one that was not properly credited, blinded me to any ill-will my good fortune may have caused in others.

ALL BUT ALONE in my achievement, success (such as it was) made me intensely self-conscious. About myself. And everything around me. A forkful of beans made me wonder if there had ever been a song on the subject (other than the rude one kids sing). Phone conversations suddenly felt significant; I began taking notes so as not to lose any of the bits that could be useful. I wrote it down, everything that came into my head. I filled notebooks.

A Guide to Amnesia
The Abject of Desire
Nothing's Too Real for My Baby
Absolutely Stupid
Taxi Death
Chips and Chops
Cranium / Germanium
Folding the Clothes, Closing the Fold

I did like the sound of "cranium germanium" but couldn't think of any way to use it and scratched it off the list. Even worse, I imagined that some of the dross could be turned into vinyl.

Leave you behind, chips and chops
You make me sick, you give me the drops
Rah rah rah rah rah rah ray
If only these spots would just go away

I wrote in my diary:

The people in my life now, I can't really trust them, but I've worked out how bad things could be if they fuck me around, and it doesn't really scare me. I don't know where I got all this bottle from, but I know I'll deal with whatever happens. I've come this far with their so-called help, but I think it's really my own graft and wits that've got me here. They're not quite expendable, but I don't think of them as crucial to my life anymore. So long as I don't screw up, I might really make a go of it ~~as a pop star~~. What a laugh!

After a few weeks, things returned to semi-normal. I was still on mental high alert as a would-be songwriter, but to what end?

Out of the Blue

A RARE WARM early-October sun was shining brightly through the kitchen window when I came down Sunday mid-morning to a table set with tea, toast and...the *Melody Maker*? That was novel. (Turns out Dad had sent off for a subscription! I only wish it had been the *NME* because I liked their sarky photo captions better.) I poured myself a glass of Jaffa and picked up the paper, which was open to the singles chart. I was shocked to see an ad for a new Chaz single called "What I'd Give." I wondered how much that had to do with the "What I wouldn't give" lines I'd given Amanda a while back.

"Laila, come in and sit down." Dad was in the front room, a cup of tea alongside the framed photo of Mum on the end table. He sounded serious.

I put a piece of toast on a plate and went to sit on the other chair in the front room — an old wooden thing that felt like school and that no one sat on by choice. I took a bite and got crumbs all over my pyjamas. "Yeah?"

"Laila, I know I haven't been the best dad in Britain, but I've done what I can for you since Mum...left us."

"Get real, Dad. She didn't leave us, she got run over and killed. It's not like she took off with the postman." I looked at the urn over the electric fire. I both loved and hated the idea that my Mum had been burnt to ash and fitted in a crypt the size of a teapot. It was reassuring that she was, in some sense, still there with us in the house, but I didn't need the constant reminder of her death: her absence was bad enough. There was no great spiritual essence in the ash for me, no soul hidden in the dust, or released by fire into the smoke, there to guide me by unseen forces. I wished for it when I was younger, but God never spoke to me, so I stopped thinking he might really be there.

He smiled sadly. "I almost wish she had. Then at least I'd know she was alright. Wherever she was."

I felt bad for what I'd said. I don't know why this was easier for me than him. He loved her, but I came out of her. Flesh and blood and hair and all. If you're

265

gonna measure loss, I think I'd have the striker's spot. But I know how sad it makes him, and I knew better than to make it worse. I smiled, sort of an all-purpose agreement and encouragement to continue with whatever this was going to be about without admitting the impatience I was feeling.

"The thing is, luv, I don't quite understand what you're getting up to these days, and that worries me. I feel like it's my job to protect you. I failed your mother, and I feel doubly responsible for you. You're just a little girl."

"I'm fine. Not to worry." I didn't mean it.

"Really, Laila?" He didn't look at all relieved. I guess it's not within my power to control such things. "If you could just tell me a bit about what's going on with you, in your life these days, maybe I can help or give you some advice. Y'know, a lot of things that look like decisions really aren't that at all."

I had to suppress a giggle. What in jumpin' Jesus does he know about any of it? Decisions. Yeah, I'm sure he's made a few, like whether to get the prawn crisps or the curry ones. Or whether to have another pint before last call. Or whether to have Mum's casket open or closed. I felt a surge of annoyance that I was being asked to make him feel better under the guise of him looking after me. I know he means well, and I expect he still knows a few things more about the world than I do, but this is 1972 and I'm a teenager, so I don't see how he can help. But I didn't want to tell him that. We'd learned about the '60s in class, all that "generation gap" rubbish. What's the point, right?

"That's nice of you, but I'm alright. Just had a laugh faffing about in the pop business for a bit, that's all. That's done now." (At least I thought it was. I really must hear that single.) Still, I liked the idea that he thought I was doing some-thing important enough for him to be concerned.

"I'm so very proud of you. I had no idea creativity ran in the family. Well, your mother was a dab hand at a few things, but me? No, not hardly."

"I didn't know it myself. But there you go."

"Was it just the one?"

"The one what?"

"Record."

"Actually, I don't know. Chaz has a new single out that might be my work as well. I haven't heard it yet."

"I see. And how much do you get paid for doing this?"

"They gave me 200 pounds."

"Well, that's a good amount of money, which I hope you're saving for the future. But that Chaz fellow had a hit record with your words, and I'm sure he'll make a lot more than that. I've heard that Paul McCartney is one of the richest men in the UK, and I'd wager a lot of his fortune is down to songwriting. And this lot of yours, they're probably not skint, either."

"Really, Dad, what's it got to do with you? It's not really work, not like a job or anything. I just scribbled down some words and brought them round. No big deal."

"Laila, I suspect you're being taken advantage of. They're making millions and they're buying you off with trinkets. Like the red Indians and Manhattan."

"I don't see it like that." *Was I the red Indians or Manhattan?*

"You're still a child. I need to look out for you. If you're giving them words they are claiming as their own and making money on, you should share in the proceeds. I once read about the crap royalty deal that Epstein chap got for the Beatles. I'm going to ring Tom Smallwood, we were at school together. He's a solicitor now and I'll ask his advice about how we get you paid. How many songs have you written?"

I wondered about the bits I'd given them, if they'd been recorded and were just waiting to come out. "No, Dad, you can't. I swore that I'd keep my bit in this a secret, and you can't muck that up. *Please.* Mr Guy told me I had to do it for the good of the good ship Bonapart, was how he put it. I told you, 'cos you're my dad, but you can't put it around or they'll be really cross with me."

"Are you still giving them song ideas?"

"No. I reckon they're done with me."

"I'm no communist, but I do believe in a day's wages for a day's work and all that. What's fair is fair. And I'm sure they'll see it that way as well. I'd wager there's a good bit of money in this for you, maybe enough to pay for university. Where would you like to go?"

I didn't answer, although "far away" was what I thought.

"No matter now, you've got plenty of time to work that out."

"You really have to let me do this on my own. Like I said, I'm pretty sure it's over, but if it's not and it ever turns serious, I promise I'll talk to your mate and get you the money you reckon I deserve."

"Laila, that's not it. I don't want money. I just want you to be happy and I want you to be treated fairly. I want you to, well, value yourself. If you've found something you're good at, and you enjoy it, that's brilliant. But you can't sell yourself short and let people take advantage. Your mother would kill me if I let that happen."

I pulled a sad face to show that I wouldn't want that but stood my ground. "I'm fine, Dad, just leave me be in this. I promise it will be alright."

He folded. "I dunno, love. It hardly seems fair, but if you're having fun, I don't suppose it's doing you any harm. Your grades all right, yeah?" I didn't need to answer because he didn't really care. Just doing what he reckoned was his duty to show concern. It's moments like this that I really love him. It's as if he understands me, even though I know he hasn't got a clue. But now and again, what I need him to think and what he comes around to thinking do match up.

But the more I thought about it, the more I saw his point, especially once I heard a lot of the words in Chaz's new single that were already written in my notebook. I talked to Bryan, and he was even keener about it than Dad was. Chaz was living the good life and, in some small way, I was contributing to that. I assumed that the rest of the people who played a part got something for it, so maybe I was being glossed on. In the fantasy conversation I had with Mr Guy he made it out like they were doing me a favour by letting me into their world and letting me find myself. Christ, I hoped he wouldn't say that. It might be true in a way, but it sounded ridiculous. When I protested that everyone else got something for their troubles, what about me, he started in on some rubbish about tender years and child labour laws and the Inland Revenue and pretended that I was better off this way. I got so mad in my head chat that I called him a bastard and spilled an inkwell all over his posh desk before storming out in a tearful huff.

Okay, that wasn't on. I needed a better idea of what it was all about, and I couldn't work it out on my own. I didn't have idea one about even how much people get paid for hit singles. I needed someone I could trust to talk to about it. Instead I rang Amanda. This time I got through.

She sounded annoyed to hear from me and was less than useless as an information source. I guess I shouldn't have expected much better given what I'd done. After a minute or two of snooty condescension she pretty much hung up on me. I assumed that was the end of that for good, but an hour later the absurd Laurence rang and invited me and Dad (?!) to a gig on the weekend as guests of Mr Guy. Mott the Hoople at the Rainbow. This was a huge big deal, as "All the Young Dudes" — which was a real favourite of mine — had been the record of the summer, and the band was about to leave for America. Both shows, Saturday and Sunday, had been sold out for weeks. I would have rather gone with Bryan, but it wasn't up to me and I got why it would be to my benefit to have Mr Guy charm — well, not the pants off — Chives.

Dad worried and whinged all the way to Saturday night, but I gulled him out of his reluctance by calling it a way to meet and judge the people he thought were taking advantage of me. He could see for himself if they were pirates or angels, and maybe talk to them about business. I knew it was a big risk to have him there with all his suspicions and parental anxieties, but I imagined how nice it would be if they all got along.

I did take the precaution of giving him a speech about reserving judgment and not coming on like a D.I. to them. I punched it up with an enthusiastic expression of how much it meant to me that people were taking me seriously, making me feel useful, even clever. I figured he'd suss the value in that and see for himself what was really afoot before coming on like a dad finding his little virgin in bed with the school's worst hooligan.

Come Saturday night, we were collected in a limo with a phone and a bar in the back. I wondered aloud where they'd hidden the swimming pool, but no one found that funny. Most of it was lost on us: Dad wouldn't touch a drop, expecting there'd be a bill and, of course, I couldn't show any interest. Worse, I couldn't look forward to ringing Bryan about the experience: he was browned off that I hadn't picked him to be my "plus one." (He said it should have been him for turning me on to Mott. I suppose he had a point.) Dad and I kept exchanging looks: we were dressed like beggars playing at being posh. It was fun doing something together, a feeling I'd not had for a long time.

The ride didn't take long; in short order, we were stepping out onto a sea of fully kitted glam kids filling Pentonville Road. Amanda found me and, with nary a word, steered us to an unmarked entrance round the back. She was wearing a filmy black dress, with long gloves and a tiara. He looked impressed, but maybe he was just blinded by all the gear and the glitter surrounding us.

The door was opened by a massive bloke with a small head. He stared down at Amanda, perhaps weighing the possibility she might be a royal.

"'Ere, where d'ya fink yer goin'?"

Amanda stretched up on her tiptoes, said a few words in his ear and in we went. An usher guided us to what must have been the best seats in the house: front row of the balcony, dead centre.

"Frank will be along presently," said Amanda, nodding at the two empty seats past Dad.

Once we were sat down, I introduced them. It felt weird to say his name, but I liked saying hers, as if she belonged to me a little. He put out a hand, reaching across me. "Pleased to meet you, Miss." I looked at him and didn't much care for the brightness of his eyes or that crinkly smile. She nodded at him with her usual lack of interest and left it at that.

I paid little mind to the support act, which was called Hackensack; I was looking at the audience, sharp as razors, dressed in the latest gear, with top makeup and hair. The venue was packed and buzzing at the interval, but Mr Guy's two seats were still empty. I wondered who he might bring along, but Dad was saving all his curiosity for Amanda. He asked if she fancied a drink from the bar downstairs, but she said she'd go. He didn't want anything, and I asked for a Coke. "Your friend is very nice," he said after she'd vanished up the aisle.

Amanda was still away when Mr Guy and a bloke called Joe turned up, but she returned a short time later, bearing a tray with three glasses of champagne: I gave Dad a look when I was handed one but he shrugged approval with a grin. It was weird to see him relaxed and pleased rather than lazy and sad.

The interval went on for a long time, and there was lots of conversation between Mr Guy and Dad that I couldn't hear over the DJ music, but I took the headshaking as a bad sign. Just as the music faded down, Dad leaned over and whispered in my ear, probably a bit louder than he meant to, "I think your man here is a poofter, and that's his, y'know, *special friend.*"

Mr Guy smiled at me. I thought he was about to say something, but then it all began. The theater darkened and then, after a hold-your-breath pause that felt very much like the suspended moment right before my climax, the stage blazed on and music began, much louder than before. The band looked as brilliant — platform boots, shiny shirts and trousers, blinding white lights, the singer in his shades — as the crowd, all gilt and flash, and the guitars punched me in the gut. I was battered in the rush: rock and roll energy raced through me, a charge of excitement that — I could see all over the stalls below — was in everyone. "Standing on the corner..." I recognized the song from an album Bryan had played me, but this was faster, smart and alive, full of supersonic style, the sound of right this very minute.

Toward the end, Dad and Mr Guy and Amanda got up and disappeared; Joe ignored me. When they returned just as the interval before the encores ended, they played musical chairs: instead of Joe, Mr Guy, Dad, me and Amanda, it was Joe, Amanda, Dad, me and Mr Guy, who turned to me and said, "Your dad's been telling me a bit about you, Laila. Fascinating." I couldn't work out if he was taking the piss or Dad had made up a pile of shite about me. At least he'd said my name right for a change. Either way, it made me a bit squirmy. "He's also shared his, let's say, concerns about your continuing to assist us in our mission. Cliff, what say we repair to my office for a nightcap and a natter?"

Dad looked at his watch. "No, I don't think so, it's been a long day, and it's high time Laila was in bed." He still thinks of me as a child.

I thought I saw a look pass between Amanda and Mr Guy. "Oh, c'mon Cliff," she said, putting a gloved hand lightly on his forearm. "Live a little." She didn't exactly wink, like they do in old movies, but she did lower her eyes for an instant. She might as well have stuck a power plug into him — he smiled

271

broadly, and said, "Sure, why not. That sounds like a hoot." I couldn't believe how obvious his gullibility was. She was totally flirting with him, and he was buying it whole. What a mug. I wondered if he might start drooling.

"Joe, would you see Laila home in a taxi? We'll take the car and I'll send it to fetch you there as soon as we've been dropped off." We were all, in one way or another, glaring at Mr Guy, but the fix was definitely in. Whatever reservations Dad had about my participation in the industry of teenage entertainment were being vaporized in a romantic illusion. I knew Amanda couldn't possibly give the remotest toss about my father; she was just turning it on to sell a product: me. If I thought he had a Chinaman's chance with her I might have been jealous or disgusted, but it just made me sad to see him played for a fool. Well, he'd be shown that cold cruel mirror in short order, I have no doubt. And then I'll have to endure the whingeing. Christ, it was like watching a toddler with chubby legs who doesn't know what happens when you run too fast. Skinned knees on order, courtesy of our Miss Charles. Just pathetic.

Joe was pleasant company home, but I was pretty upset and not really listening. Swimming in a sour soup of jealousy, revulsion and fear, with no better idea, I rang Bryan. While I truly wanted to tell him every last detail of the gig, he was still browned-off and not keen to discuss it. I said my father was off with Mr Guy, and I was worried what might come of it. He tried to be helpful, but I got the sense we were coming at different things in different ways, so I rang off and got ready for bed. It wasn't until I was brushing my teeth that I realized I'd forgotten to ask him about the new Chaz single.

Dad pulled in about half two; I could smell the fags, drink and perfume on him as he passed my door. At least he didn't stay out all night. I had my light off and pretended to be asleep; he didn't come in my room and I thought better of going to his. I was too upset to say anything until morning.

I told myself I didn't care what took place that night, but the truth is I desperately wanted to know. I couldn't expect an honest answer from Amanda, and I didn't care to hear how he would paint it either. I had my suspicions, but I don't think I could stand to know if it was true. He looked dead rough at breakfast, and I could barely look him in the face. He said he'd been "well and truly impressed by the man" and thought it "wonderful" that Francis, as he called him, was providing an outlet for my burgeoning creativity. (Yeah, he said "burgeoning.") It was what I wanted to hear, but it did make me ill to think how easily he'd been bought off. Mum would have had his bollocks in a bottle if she'd been here. I felt cheap and stupid that he would give me away for nothing more than some combination of a glass of champagne, some flattering words and a cutie's cuddle.

THINGS GOT WORSE. Chives went out a couple of other evenings and wouldn't say where to or who with. "If I told you then you'd know," was his not especially clever way of dodging my enquiries. At least he came home, but he wasn't the same. This man was light, buoyant, upbeat and sunny — four things he'd most assuredly *not* been since Mum died. I had my suspicions, of course, but there was no way I could bring myself to come right out and ask if he was having it off with Amanda. My jealous imagination was bad, but what came with it was even worse. I felt betrayed and denied, competitive and resentful, angry, unlucky and dead useless. Mostly I felt left out. What was wrong with me? What was wrong with *her*? (I knew what was wrong with him.) Why couldn't I get what *I* wanted for once?

A headshrinker (or *The Sun*) would have a field day with this one: *Horny rock teen's father has it off with her lesbo chart crush*. But I couldn't shake it off. I'm not even sure I wanted to. I couldn't bring myself to imagine him naked, having a willy and all, but in a strange way, imagining him in bed with her allowed me to imagine me being in bed with her, using what I knew from Bryan to imagine how it would be with her, what it might feel like to rub her sleek softness, to push fingers into her rather than being the body what gets pushed into.

Seeing him happy every day and not knowing or being able to ask was torture, like starving to death in a cage with food just out of reach on the other side of the bars. There were moments when I was able to shrug it all off, but when you're a teenager drowning in hormones and insecurities, with no control of your environment and nothing but hopeless desires to egg you on, logic and proportion can be hard to cling to. I mean, what the fuck, right?

The fourth night he went out I left a note saying I'd be back in a few days and not to worry. I put up at Bryan's flat. It felt like a badly needed declaration of independence, but it was just a really bad idea: I was a moody cow with no patience or consideration. I couldn't fully explain what was bothering me, so I went at him. Instead of us screwing I did it in the loo with a hairbrush. I was being horrible, I know. But I wasn't alone in being weird: he took the occasion to announce that he was chucking out the "B" and "r" in his name and was to be called Eon (E-O-N) from now on. He got hacked off when I pointed out that he should spell it proper: I-A-N. But no, that wasn't on, it had to be E-O-N. Americans, right? The family name suffered a shakeup as well, turning Bryan Klein into Eon Clean, which sounded to me like an outer space laundry. That really got on my wick, and I told him he was still Bryan to me. That led to a row and so I went home, feeling even more angry and alone.

The next morning, as soon as I guessed she might have dragged herself in to work — and having checked first to confirm that Chives was in his own bed — I rang Amanda at the office. When she came on the line, I didn't even say who it was. "Are you shagging my dad?"

She laughed. Not a nervous titter, like "Oh you've sussed it and now I'm mildly embarrassed," or even a breezy "I'm gonna pretend you didn't say that by making light of it." No, she unleashed a gale of hilarity, choking and wheezing with more volume and unabashed enthusiasm than I've ever heard from her. When that finally ended, she started to say something — I heard the words "little," "idiot," "absurd" and "rich" — and then began chortling again.

That conversation emboldened me enough to ask him as well, sort of dancing around it rather than coming out with it. "So, you like Amanda, I gather. How does she feel about you? She's a bit young, wouldn't you say?"

He laughed nervously, which didn't necessarily portend a lie. Our serious talks always include a generous measure of awkwardness and embarrassment. "Right. I've, uh, seen her, uh, socially, a few times. I gather that's what you're referring to. No harm in that, is there?" He laughed again, nervously this time.

"I dunno, is there?"

"Of course not, Laila. Not that I haven't imagined having a beautiful young girl in my arms from time to time — I'm not that old, you know — but that's not what this is."

"Then tell me what this is. Why are you spending so much time with someone half your age? Someone who isn't me?"

"I'm afraid I can't, love. I do have to admit I find the young lady quite fetching, but what you're implying is not on. Not in the slightest. You'll find out soon enough, and it won't be bad, I promise you. We all want what's best for you, but you'll need to trust me for now."

I scowled but didn't reply. Trust is not one of my favourite things.

"And not that I need your approval, but do you actually expect me to remain single and celibate for the rest of my born days? I love your mother as much as the day I met her, but we've lost her and she's not coming back."

That all sounded better than what I'd fantasized, but none of it explained what was going on. That was still the province of my growing imagination; there was nothing I could do about any of it. I went back to writing in my book, having it off with Bryan — excuse me, *Eon* — and dreaming about Amanda.

Ophelia's Dream

IT HAPPENED one day, without warning. I was sitting in science class, doodling ideas for lyrics in my book, and I suddenly realized I'd made up a song. The idea flew out of me like a budgie freed from its cage. I could hear the music in my head; it was just there. A whole new song, one that had never before existed. And it was mine. All I needed to do was write it down. Preserving the words was one thing, but I didn't have a clue how to write in "tunes." As soon as class ended, I sang it to myself a bunch of times so's I'd remember how it went.

I was going to call it "Amanda's Dream," but I changed my mind about that. Too obvious, too embarrassing. But the rest was spot on, ready for someone to record. I didn't know what to do with it — there was no call for my services in Chazville, and I didn't know any other rock stars in the market for songs written by kids — but I had to tell someone about it, so I went to see Bryan at the shop. He took me into the stockroom, and I sang it for him.

The boys in her class, they all fancy Ophelia
But she can't be bothered with their silly games
They worship her, watch her as works
She can't remember their silly names

She's the one (the one), the one (the one) they all want
But she's not giving herself away
Not to them, not to them
Sad boy, sad boy
Ophelia has a dream – and it doesn't include you

The one in the back, he's called Davy Stardust
His father was famous, back before the war
Rocking on his heels, he hands her a gift
He says, here Ophelia, you're the one it's for

276

Her face is the sun, her voice is a river
She never worries what life can supply
Taking the box, she hugs him and whispers
We'll be friends forever, now let me by

Now the school year's done, but terms are open still
Davy's love remains a hope and nothing more
He dreams of a future with Ophelia
Behind her bolted door

She's the one (the one), the one (the one) they all want
But she's not giving herself away
Not to them, not to them
Sad boy, sad boy
Ophelia has a dream – and it doesn't include you

Many years on, life's taken its turns
For the boy, love still burns
Every time he sees her picture in the color supplement
Ophelia on a pedestal, all alone

She's the one (the one), the one (the one) they all want
But she's not giving herself away
Not to them, not to anyone
Sad boy, sad girl
Ophelia's dream didn't come through

"Wow. *Wow.* What you've got there is brilliant. You're really something. Catchy, too. Where'd you nick the melody from? It sounds a little familiar."

"I didn't. Made it up, didn't I? In my head." I gave him a playful shove. His enthusiasm was great, but I wanted more. From him, from her, from everyone. I thought of how Mum smiled with her whole face when she was proud of me, and that gave me a twinge of lonely sadness.

"You might want to change up the tempo in the chorus so it doesn't drag. I think the whole thing might be a bit long. You'll need to work out the chord changes. Oh, and you should probably add a middle eight."

"A *what*?" I was getting cross at all these complications he was throwing in.

"Oh, that's the other bit, not the verse or the chorus. Musos call it 'the bridge.' It changes things halfway through. For example, let me think, OK, you know the bit in 'Changes' where Bowie goes 'strange fascination fascinating me, changes are taking something or other'"?

"Uh huh."

"That's a middle eight."

"Why's it called that? Eight what? And how do you know that?"

"I have no idea. It just is. Go home and listen to some records, you'll know it when you hear it."

"You're complicating things for me. I thought you'd be pleased."

"I am, I am. Would you like me to take a crack at it?"

I really didn't. It was my song, and I didn't want to share it, not even with Eon. And I resented him for asking. "You'll need to work on the melody some more, it's not quite there yet. Too much like 'Life on Mars'."

It felt as if he was trying to take it all away from me, saying it's good and then telling me why it's not. It's either one or the other, innit? I kept that to myself.

"Y'know what I'd do if I was you? I'd go to the library and take out a bunch of old folk music albums. I bet you'll find some boss melodies in there — that's what Bob Dylan did and shit. It would be easier to write lyrics to fit them, but you could get lucky and find one that will fit words you already have."

"You mean like steal them?"

"Most of those songs are in the public domain. It's not stealing if they don't really belong to anyone. That's why they're folk songs."

"But won't people recognize them?"

"Speed them up to sound more modern. No one who will ever hear your songs will have a clue, and it won't matter if their grandmothers do. What are you going to do with it?"

That was a good question. "Not sure. I can try to get on to Chaz's office and see what they think. But I've not spoken to anyone there in a good while."

278

He scratched his chin, reread the lyrics and frowned. "I don't think this is his kind of thing, Lai. I guess it might depend on the hook and the arrangement, but sensitivity and — dare I say it — a twee approach isn't really up his road. It's kind of adolescent."

My anger boiled over. Wasn't that the point? As an adolescent on loan to a grownup trying to connect with adolescents, I didn't have a way to express that confusion. "Sod off, it's my song."

"I get that, it's brilliant. I just don't want it to die a-borning. What good is a song if no one wants it?" He had a point, but I wasn't so sure Chaz would turn it down.

"You know what I would do if I were you?"

"Take off your clothes and stare at yourself in the mirror?"

"Funny." He sounded as cross as me and began pacing. "What I was going to suggest is that you do it. You know people, I know people. I bet we could do it."

"And what would we do with 'it' then? Get a record label to put it out and make me teenage rebel of the week?" His thin smile meant he caught the reference but wasn't that impressed. I'd passed the stage of being a novice student and such familiarity was requisite, not commendable.

"Yeah, something like that. And why not?" Now we were both pacing.

Later that evening we were screwing, but our minds — well mine, leastways — were elsewhere.

EVEN THOUGH I was thinking about it, I wasn't ready to turn the whole thing upside down. I still fancied the idea of Chaz recording it, mainly out of curiosity what it would sound like. But I didn't trust Amanda and didn't care to ring Mr Guy out of the blue about it. We hadn't talked since the Mott show, and I had no clue what my standing was with them. So, with no other ideas, I rang Laurence and asked him what I should do. I might as well have asked the cleaner for all the help he was. He had no clue what I was rabbiting on about, and I can only understand half of what he *sez* in that ridiculous ax-*sent* of his, but as it turned out, a guy from Chaz's band happened to be there in the office at the moment and Laurence asked him. He knew who I was (!) and said he might be able to help. I didn't have any idea how or why, but the guy — Sky something — offered to meet me that evening at the Wimpy Bar on Charing Cross Road. Sounded sketchy, but I decided to give it a go.

He turned out to be Chaz's drummer, a quiet bloke. Sythe Clot. A strange sort with a stranger name, but he seemed alright to me. He knew I'd had a hand in "Soldier to Cry On" and I finally got told how it came to be called that. He asked if I'd gotten paid for it. Mindful of the speech I'd gotten at home, I asked if he thought I was being messed about. He laughed. "Is the Pope Catholic? I reckon it'll happen again unless you do something about it."

"Why, what do you mean?"

"I suspect you had a hand in some other songs as well: 'What I'd Give' and 'Equal Opportunity Girl.' I know Chaz didn't write 'em, so I expect someone they don't want to acknowledge did. Last time it was you."

"Yeah, those could be mine. Do they have tunes and all? Can I hear?"

"There was a track we never finished for the last album that I thought could be turned to good use if it weren't called 'Rock and Roll Desperation.' I played it for Chaz and suggested he could match the music to lyrics Frank told him he'd found in an old notebook. I didn't believe that bollocks for a minute, but Chaz wasn't a hard sell, as I understood it. So that's how you got another in there. The chords took a bit of shifting around, and it needed a chorus, but the band made it work. We did the new basics for it last week. Chaz laid down a couple of vocal tracks yesterday. We just need to double the handclaps, run it through a compressor and get the chick singers in. I'll get you a cassette." (Damn. I'll have to organize myself a cassette player. Maybe Bryan has one.)

"Do you think I should keep giving them stuff? I figured they won't be needing any more from me. I thought the album was done."

"Ah, well, it's not." He put up a hand and frowned, dropping his head down for a flash. "Don't ask. Total cock-up, that was. In fact, we're in the middle of it again, and I bet he uses your shit, beg pardon, for the bulk of it."

He gave me a look that I took to mean he understand the absurdity of a pop star counting on a kid to write his songs. I liked him, and he treated me like a person, not a child, so I appreciated that as well. I told him I'd written a whole song called "Ophelia's Dream," but said, "I think it might need a middle eight." (It felt ridiculous saying that as if I knew what the words meant.)

"Piece of piss. You just shift down to a minor chord and turn the melody backwards. I'd wager half of them are written in the studio with tape rolling. If you've got a song, and it's any good, you've got Chaz by the short and curlies. Don't you worry about the bleeding bridge."

He laughed, then turned serious again. "Don't be so quick to just hand it over like you've been doing. I co-wrote a song on one of Chaz's albums a few years back and Frank left me off the credits and forgot me when payday arrived. I never got a royalty statement until I threatened to take them to court. I'm never doing that again, and neither should you. It's shameful that man would take such undue advantage. It's not like he's going hungry at night. Well, neither are you." We both laughed, since he'd bought us burgers and I probably had tomato catsup all over my chin.

I asked about the money and almost shat myself when he told me that the one-*third* of a song he'd had a hand in had bought his mum and dad a motor. Well, a used motor, but I guessed that figure would be well above 200 knicker. I showed him the lyrics to "Ophelia's Dream" — I didn't have the guts to sing it for him — and he seemed to like it. (Maybe Eon was wrong about what Chaz would or wouldn't sing.) He said I should get a publisher and a solicitor to protect myself.

It sounded a lot like what Dad had said, that I was entitled to money, that while the ego and the glory might be nice, I was at a big disadvantage and would thank him later "when there's money coming in from a number you can't even recall writing." He really sounded like he had the suss, not just making guesses at things. I felt like I could trust him and even gave him a kiss on the cheek when we parted.

Punch the Clock

A FORTNIGHT LATER, the album was nearly done. As promised, Psi had brought it home for a song and done a brilliant job making the band sound hip and modern, one foot in glam and the other in traditional rock. Hooks, power and credibility. Although they needed some adjustment to suit Chaz, the lyrics they'd got off the girl had a distinctive perspective that you could hear right off, and the tune hacks Frank had engaged had provided catchy melodies to hang the words on.

Frank had been wise to keep Chaz out of the process until all the instruments had been tracked and scratch mixes were in hand. He never even looked in on the Islington shoebox where they worked; Frank had managed to keep its existence, or at least its location, from him the whole time. All that was left was some vocal overdubs, and a few extra days had been booked at Olympic for that purpose. Provided Chaz didn't throw a last-minute wobbly, they were home free. Frank had been to lunch twice with CBS brass to gee them up on the album, and it seemed to be working. Even Chaz was in high spirits, feeling certain he'd get back in the good graces of old fans and summon up a new batch as well. The sun was shining.

Friday evening, three days before final vocal sessions, Amanda was at her desk, hoping that Frank wouldn't give her some big project after his meeting finished. She really wanted a bath and a drink, but she'd been ordered to stay late, and so she had. It was after eight when Psi the Clock blew out of Frank's office, slamming the door behind him and swearing like a sailor. "Fucking cunts, the lot of you," he said. "Thieves." He spotted her and came over. He fixed her with blood in his eye and snickered, "So you're the golden child that got me sacked, eh? Well, good luck to you. We'll have to see how long you remain useful to this corrupt enterprise."

Amanda stared up blankly, unable to manage a reply, sympathetic, angry or defensive. She didn't know what had happened and didn't much care. Frank would sort it, whatever it was.

"Bunch of conniving phonies, you lot. Filled with hot air, keeping that no-talent blimp aloft. Just a bag of hot air, that's all it is. You'll get the shaft soon enough, just wait and see."

In the long and disgraceful history of musician sackings, Psi the Clock's abrupt dismissal was on the far end of mysterious. Was it a drug problem? Was it the meaningless "creative differences" or an offence much further beyond the pale? The public explanation was kept purposely vague; what Frank told Chaz — that he'd walked in, given his notice and fucked off — was unadulterated bullshit. "I gather he (a) wasn't happy in your employ and (b) no longer felt that rock could answer his need for spiritual growth, so he's taken a naff position doing some bollocks for Oxfam. Personally? If I had to guess at what's going on in that mysterious head of his, I'd wager he got a better offer and didn't care to tell you that to your face. All mouth and no trousers, that one."

Chaz, who had gone a bit pale, paced the floor. "I dunno, Frank, I dunno. Isn't there anything...?"

"I'm afraid it's done, whatever the reason. And don't you go and complicate things by speaking to him yourself. That's not on. United front and all. Never know when it could go sideways and turn legal and all. We don't want to be paying for that."

Chaz looked baffled and lost. "I don't get it. I love the Clock. He's a great drummer. He really helped with the new album. We always got on. That's not like him. He's always been honest with me. And he works cheap. Maybe he's just playing silly buggers. Can't we get him back, at the very least to wrap up the album? Did you offer him a rise?"

Frank mustered a bit of feigned empathy for the drummer's well-being. "We all love Psi, mate. Yes, of course I did. Pushed it back across the table without a moment's thought. Said it wasn't to do with money. Personal discretion, doing it for the soul, or so he said. And not to worry about the album: I'll be with you while you finish your bits and then we'll hire a mixdown specialist. Someone really good, with a track record. Psi was never going to handle that anyways. And you don't need him to tell you how to sing, now do you?"

"Not you, neither." He sighed. "Alright, mate, we'll do it your way. I know what I'm doing. Make sure you get the best engineer they've got and give him the

283

tapes so he can work out the room ambience sound and all that other technical bollocks."

"Done. Good as sorted, mate. See you Monday."

Chaz grunted and sloped off home.

Later, Frank explained to Joe how what was supposed to be a quick word with Psi to prioritize the last bit of work on the album had gone sideways and ended in a full-on row. "That twat admitted — he very nearly bragged — that he'd told the girl to demand an advance and points for "her songs." *Her songs*. Bollocks. He had the bottle to tell me I'd best find her a publisher and get a deal done for her songs before CBS could release an album containing them. The album is nearly ready to go — and CBS are dead keen to give it a big push — and this cunt is playing at blackmail to hold up its release. I don't even know what was in it for him. I told him to fuck off."

"Well, it's not as if paying songwriters is out of the ordinary, now is it?"

"Of course not, Joe, but the girl's hardly a professional songwriter. She's just a kid. And what she did is pass along some half-baked ideas that I had turned into material worthy of being recorded, and included on an album, by Chaz Bonapart. Do you think she did that all her own?"

"Of course not. I just mean..."

"Money's not even the real issue. It's a problem, sure, but what I can't abide is the disloyalty. After all this time. And then Psi told the girl she should demand credit on the sleeve. That's not gonna happen."

"I don't get why this has you so wound up."

"I've spent months slipping these songs under Chaz's nose, convincing him that he wrote them, even if he has no memory of it. I can't publicly announce that he didn't. I mean, I suppose deep down he knows he didn't write them, but desire is as good as reality in his case and I've got him a bit turned around about how much he contributed. Plus, he has no idea who his main co-writer is. He's meant to believe that Psi was beavering away on material for his benefit. Or they're old ideas he never completed. Run those credits, even tiny, and that's the end of my professional relationship with him. And probably the end of him as well — it wouldn't do to have people find out his musical strings are being pulled by a chubby teenager from Acton."

"East Acton."

"What?"

"East Acton, is what the father said."

"What difference does that make?"

"A mile maybe. None, of course. Sorry. I know you're coping with an awful lot here. I wish I could help."

"And then Psi threatened to grass us to the press."

"I expect he can just as easily tell her to do it. That's another huge risk. And you sacked him. Maybe that wasn't the wisest thing to do."

Frank snorted and looked at Joe with disgust. "Fuck off, you." He left the house and went for a drive to clear his head and sort through it all. By the time he got back an hour later, he'd got it all sorted in his head, and was more optimistic about the future than he'd been in ages.

FRANK AWOKE WITH a smile and joined Joe at the breakfast table with no mention of the previous evening's unpleasantness. Joe, who knew better than to get on him about pissing off in a huff, poured the tea.

"I've had a blinder of an idea. I've already been on to Giddyap and done a deal. They'll get co-writing credit on the songs she might've had a bit to do with. They're reputable and hot right now, so Chaz will look clever for having enlisted them for his Very Important Album. I'll give them ten percent of the publishing for those songs — that'll earn their silence for no work whatever and they'll pay a quarter of it to the girl."

Joe stuck a spoon in the marmalade pot and smiled at Frank's upbeat mood. "What a clever chap you are. But Giddyap? Perhaps you've mentioned it, but if so, it's gone straight out of my head."

"A pair of Welsh blokes, writer-producers Mike Gideon and Peter Applestone. Clever lads, with a couple of solid hits — a band from Swansea whose name escapes me. I reckon they fancy themselves the next Chinnichap — hence the silly name. But they're angling to really have a go, so I expect they'll jump at the chance to get in with Chaz. They'll assume it's a prelude to writing and producing his next album, and I don't mind helping them to believe that."

"And doing that'll sort out the girl as well?"

"Well, it won't make her rich, but the promise of cheques in the mail should keep her, and us, well clear of bovver. And if her name should happen to appear in the credits on one or two songs, she'll just look like one of the writers in their stable." He stirred his tea and his swallowed down his vitamins.

"She's a problem right now, but there's more innings to come, and I have a hunch about her. She has a knack. It's like she's so simple that her songs end up sounding deep. Hasn't got a clue what she's gotten herself in for, but I don't think she'll wind up badly. Kind of reminds me of a lad I knew at school. Plucky, curious, not sure of herself but willing to face the wind, as it were. I have some ideas about what she might be able to do if I can pull her through this and keep her chin up and her legs crossed."

Joe laughed. "Why, is she a slag?"

"No, that's not it. It's not as if I can read women any longer, but I sense a ripeness about her that makes her seem ready to pop open and gush."

"Oh my!" Joe chuckled at the lurid characterization.

"I can almost smell it on her. She's a goer, or will be once she gets going. And I think I can work with that."

"Lucky she's not your type, or I might be worried."

Frank didn't share the third choice in his plan, the one he was actually working toward, with Joe. He didn't mind being a conniver, but he didn't want Joe thinking him capable of the deceit and cruelty he had in mind. Times when their relationship had stumbled, Joe's insecurities would flare into a lack of faith in him — thanks to parental abuse, he understood — and so avoided deeds and words that would paint him in an unflattering light. Of course it was self-serving, but he thought it generally better that Joe, as an element in his well-being, think of him as an essentially good person.

Swinging Party

THE INVITATION from Amanda, all fancy and formal, arrived on a Wednesday for a do at her flat that Sunday. I kind of suspected Mr Guy pushed her to invite me, although I couldn't work out why he would do that. He's a schemer, that one, a lot more of one than I could ever be. I reckon it's easier to let them who think like that do their string-pulling and plotting until it becomes a nuisance. Then you have to put a stop to it.

I'd not been to her place since the bag business, and I really didn't want to go. It's true that I still harbored a fantasy about getting her in a cupboard and having it off while the music played in the front room, but the more practical part of my brain was still mad about whatever she'd got up to with Dad and knew that I was sure to be treated poorly and end up feeling shitty about her, myself or both of us. Someone should write a song and call it "Love Stinks."

I also understood, when I was honest with myself, that this wasn't really about love. It was a sweet-smelling poisonous pudding made up of desire and greed, jealousy and resentment. I wanted something I couldn't have and being a baby about it. But, good lord, that skin. I just wanted to be a cat and purr all over her naked body.

I turned up with the requisite bottle of plonk as an entry fee and we did air kisses at the door. I was hoping Stephen at least would be there, but he wasn't. Bringing Eon would have risked embarrassment of one sort or another, so I was on my own. Before I'd got a couple of drinks in me I had the feeling people were staring, which I guess was better than being ignored, but I didn't see anyone to chat up and Amanda was being queen bee with a circle of admirers. I wondered how someone like her managed to have friends. I'd only been there a half-hour when I started planning my exit.

"Hullo, are you Laila?" The voice belonged to a large woman wearing garish clothes and enough makeup for a silent movie star.

"'S'pose I am. Who are you then?"

287

"Graziela, Amanda's 'fat friend.' At your service. And you, I take it, must be her pet project."

"Well..." I didn't know whether to be flattered or annoyed.

"As I understand it, she sought your assistance in her work. But you rather turned that on its head, didn't you?"

"Maybe. What's it to you?" I didn't like being asked about this stuff by a stranger. I looked to see if Amanda might be near enough to pull in to straighten the lady out.

"Nothing, really. Just curious. I've always found our girl to be a collection of fascinating paradoxes, so I try and gather what I can to better work out who she thinks she is, which I've always rather thought had bugger all to do with who she actually is. I suppose you could see it as my science project."

The face I made at her was meant to express confusion *and* disapproval, but I guess it didn't.

"Are you alright, dear? You just came over all odd."

"I'm fine. Just wondering what kind of a friend does such a thing. I mean, it's kind of shitty sounding, don't you think?"

"Yeah, well, you of all people should know that she deserves it." She delivered that retort with a smile, grabbing my elbow and aiming me into an uncomfortable plastic chair beneath a shiny arrow on the wall. She went off and returned with two glasses of wine, evidently unconcerned that I wasn't old enough to drink.

"As I've been wondering since Amanda first mentioned your name, was your mother a schoolteacher?"

"Yeah, how'd you know?"

"In Brixton?"

"Yeah."

"So I was right. She was one of my teachers. In either 1961 or '62. I was twelve. My family had just arrived from Italy. Mrs Russell. I remember her quite well. She was lovely."

It took me a choking fit, two glasses of water and a trip to the loo for a private weep before I could properly respond to that. When I finally did, the woman was shocked to learn that Mum was dead. We repaired to Amanda's bedroom — under other circumstances, I would have been fascinated to explore the witch's lair, but in the moment barely took notice — and shut the door. She answered all the questions I lobbed at her. She had a good memory and recalled a lot about Mum, how she looked and acted. She even recalled some of those phrases Mum had left me. I cried a lot. Grace, as she said to call her, said Mum was a great teacher. It was like finding a long-lost relative.

The second time Grace and I met up, by which time I'd decided I could trust her, I told her in some detail about my dealings with Mr Guy. She knew enough about the whole thing that I didn't feel like I was telling tales out of school, but she seemed awfully interested in hearing details and specifics. I didn't know that Psi the Clock had gotten the sack; she didn't know any more about it and said she doubted Amanda did either. That put it in my head that I needed to speak with Mr Guy about a lot of things, and the sooner the better.

We got to be friends. I guess I kind of took her off Amanda, but I never heard anything from her about it. Grace had her own story: arriving in England as a kid who could barely speak English; a brother in the Army stationed in Belfast. She made her dad out to be a bit of a waster, but even though I was mad at mine, I was still loyal enough to Chives to not commiserate. She had a good job at the Italian consulate and no taste whatever in pop music.

But she did show an interest in me, and a sensible view of what a twat Amanda could be. She eventually admitted that it was sort of her suggestion to have Stephen seduce and abandon me. We had a good laugh over that, and she seemed genuinely glad that we had escaped "Amanda's cynical contrivance" (her words) and been mates for a bit. She couldn't, or wouldn't, say what he'd got up to, or what he and Amanda were now to each other. "I never liked him, but I've always fancied him," she said.

"I know what you mean." It struck me that he wasn't the only person in my life I thought that about and wondered why that was. At least I had Eon to keep me from feeling like a misguided loser who couldn't ever get her heart, mind and fanny to queue up at the same window.

Rockit LA

SAVING ME THE trouble, Laurence rang and said Mr Guy needed to see me. I spent a lot of time preparing what I was going to say to get what I felt I deserved. I knew what Psi had told me, but I didn't feel equipped to demand anything from this lot. I figured on stamping my feet and pouting a bit to see how much regard he had for what I'd done. I'd have to ask how much of what I'd given them had got used. I was willing to let the first one go, maybe the second one, too, but I needed to know if they'd found value in the any of the rest of it, and what sort of deal we might strike, if such a thing was possible.

Mr Guy greeted me warmly, which put me on edge. "I quite enjoyed meeting your father. Seems a decent bloke, but he could use a bit more fun in his life."

"And so you gave him Amanda for that," I sneered.

"Good God, no. Nothing like that. Did you really think that? Silly bugger. I just needed to be sure he wouldn't mount any strenuous objections to what I'm about to propose. We need him on our side, Laila."

"Hang on, did he sell me into white slavery?"

"Something like that." He chuckled. "He agreed to a plan I've come up with."

"He didn't say anything to me about a plan."

"Well, no. I asked him to keep it between us until you and I could meet."

If I was suspicious about all the bollocks going on behind my back before, I was twice as worried now. I had never imagined that Chives would sell me out to a stranger, but I guess his loyalties had shifted.

"First off, I've got you a publishing deal." He saw the ignorance pouring off me. "A publisher represents songwriters. They put your songs out there and see that you get paid when your compositions are recorded and sold."

"Go on."

"So long as you let me work out the fine print and all, a company called

Giddyap will be paying you for the songs you had a hand in writing for Chaz's forthcoming album. But I have to warn you, this is an old-fashioned business with its own set of rules, and you won't see any of the money that's coming to you for six, possibly nine months. But rest assured, provided the album does well, you and your father will be able to relocate to a tonier part of London."

"Fucking hell."

"What's done is done, Laila. Now it's time to look ahead. I've had a, an inspiration. It come to me in the bath."

I hoped this wasn't going to be disgusting. "I've got a much bigger future in mind for you, and it has nothing to do with Chaz Bonapart."

"What are you on about?"

"Let me explain. I'd wager Chaz will have a huge hit with this new LP, thanks in part to you, but I've come to realize we were solving the wrong problem by enlisting your help. Keeping him from growing old and in the way is hopeless — it's going to happen. He's the past and you're the future. We can't make him stay relevant to generation after generation of kids. You're so much younger, you can grow up with an audience. He'll be fine, but I've decided to think, to look ahead. I see really big things for you, Laila. We're going to cut out the middleman, as it were. We're going to sell modern teenage music made by a modern teenager to modern teenagers."

"I don't follow." I really didn't.

"You're going to be a rock star."

I burst out laughing. "Fuck off. Don't mess me about."

"No, I'm dead serious. As I told Cliff, you're a talented girl, and I see big things in your future. You being underage and all, I prevailed upon him for permission to pursue it. He gave me the okay and said he would sign the necessary papers when the time came."

"It sounds like I'm being delivered into an arranged marriage. Who's the lucky lad? And when was anyone going to let me in on this?"

"I'm doing it now. That's why I asked to see you. Sorry I neglected to send a car." I stared at him, unsure what any of this might mean. I could feel the heat in my cheeks. "I see," was all I could eke out. Things were moving too fast to take it all in or gauge how I should behave.

"All I did was get his permission to talk to you about a career. And discuss going ahead if it's cool with you. Nothing's fixed. This is your life."

"I thought it was."

"Just to be prepared, I've been on to a couple of my colleagues in the industry, working out what to do with you."

That sounded ominous. I took a breath and tried not to look too concerned.

"How would you feel about being a boy?"

"*Wh-a-a-a-at?*" Now I was getting really scared. Was he running a Dr. Frankenstein lab in the cellar?

"Let me explain. If you want it, Laila, you're going to be a pop star. A *massive* pop star." He spread his arms out for emphasis. I think my mouth gawped open. I burbled out some rubbish, which he ignored. I don't know what I was thinking, much less what I might be saying.

"I suspect you've got star power. You've got what the kids want. We just have to work out the best way to, well, package you for maximum impact." I was trying to imagine what this could possibly have to do with me being a boy.

"Turn around, would you?" I obliged, intensely aware that I'd put on half a stone in recent months. "No, I suppose those" — he pointed at my chest with a look of mild distaste — "rule that out. The press would rumble you in a flash."

Whatever game he was playing at, it felt intrusive and rude. I turned to leave.

"Sorry, I expect I should explain. Something to drink?"

"No, thanks." The room was already spinning.

"As I said, I think you've got a great deal of potential as a performer. The challenge is figuring out how to sell you. As you've no doubt noticed, the glam boys are all acting like girls nowadays. In fact, none of them *are* queer, they just reckon it makes them seem outré or courageous. Now I can assure you from personal experience that being queer, as one is, takes a fair bit of caution and bottle in this country. One has to live one's life, but one has to remain within the law, at least so far as the law is aware of what goes in people's bedrooms."

"And you know all this because you're bent, is that it?"

"Point is boys wearing makeup and women's gear is trendy these days. As you know, stage performers have always used face paint; lately the smart ones have decided to look sharp all the time, everywhere, not just under the lights or on telly. All well and good, a bit of a lark, sure. But I believe that turning that around, giving a girl some boyish style — not butch, more tomboy, like — to confuse the punters in their budding sexuality, might be just the ticket."

"Really?"

"What I'm trying to say is that gender bending can go both ways. Do you know the Kinks song 'Lola'?" It came out a few years back."

I shook my head.

"I thought of it as soon as I learned you were called Laila. Kind of close, don't you think? Well, the song is about a bloke who pulls a bird and goes off with her only to find that she's a bloke. It was a big hit. And Ray Davies is an ace songwriter. A bit old-fashioned for your purposes, but it wouldn't hurt for you to scoff the Kinks' catalogue and hear how the greats do it."

"If you say so." I remember Eon talking about the Kinks a bit.

"Everyone is a bit confused about sex these days, and it wouldn't hurt, when we throw you to the punters, to take advantage of that."

A froglike noise came out of my throat and aptly expressed the confusion I was feeling about the bollocks he was saying.

"I'm not into astrology or any of that rot, but I think it might be a sign. Lola, Laila. A song about boys who are girls and girls who are boys, and who knows what. That will be your calling card — the first girl rocker that isn't exactly a boy or a girl. An alien, but not like Bowie. Screw those poseurs who put on makeup — you could find a way to be mysterious, and that would be your gimmick.

"It's not going to be as simple as putting you in a suit and slicking back your hair. That won't do. Maybe we'll keep things vague, a bit mysterious. Is she or isn't she? Who is...?" He leaned back in his chair and rubbed his bald dome as if it were a crystal ball. "Who is," he repeated. I said it too, getting caught up in the idea of suspense, idiotically wondering who I might be if I weren't me. Finally, he rocked forward and opened his eyes wide, spread his hands out dramatically and declared, "I've got it. 'Who is...Rockit LA?' R-O-C-K-I-T."

"Rockit LA?" It felt funny coming from my mouth, but it sounded like a pop star name. I could imagine buying a record by Rockit LA. (Rockit, Rocket — I swear I never mentioned the Laika thing to him. I didn't even realize the connection until later.) I made the frog noise again. "I'd like that drink now."

I discussed it with Dad and Eon. They both warned it could all end in tears but said I had to try. I'm sure Mum would have agreed. Dad said he'd speak to the head teacher about me and try and sort me some time away from school.

I still hadn't decided what, if anything, had gone on between Amanda and Cliff, but I hated them both for messing me about. Even if nothing happened, they both must have known what it would do to me to worry what they might've gotten up to. And clearly no one gave a toss. So, yeah, on of everything else that was going on in my life, I suppose I was feeling sorry for myself.

Frank, who insisted that we were now on a first-name basis, sent a car to bring me and Dad to Burgher on Friday. He signed the papers, Frank signed the papers. It didn't feel like that big a deal. Amanda wasn't even there. But now I had a manager and, I suppose, a career.

Monday morning, as if a bomb had gone off, my life was blown apart, a feather borne aloft in a sudden storm. I barely got time to pee, what with the musician auditions, rehearsals, costumes, songwriting sessions, stylists, solicitors, chartered accountants — all of it conducted under security that would have done MI5 proud. No one could know what we were doing until I was ready to be sprung on the world. Despite all the fuss focused on me, I felt more alone and scared than I ever had. Dad was there, but none of this was happening to him. With me getting a new name, I finally started calling Bryan Eon, but he quickly got weird, as if it was happening to him. And I still wasn't sure what was going to happen when Chaz's album came out and his song ideas were on it. I didn't have the time to explore how he felt about us, or how I felt about us, or even what was happening to me. I was really on my own. *Face your fears.*

Ready Steady Go

I HAD NO burning desire to become a rock star, no insatiable hunger for fame or fortune. I was content with the change in my pocket, the odd Wimpy burger, a roof over my head. But here I was, standing on the doorstep of a new life. With no way to back out. "Sorry, mate, I was just messing you about. I can't do this music stuff. I was thinking of applying for a place at Boots..."

I stared in the bathroom mirror, imagining my face transformed by powder and paste, and doubted I was someone who could be on *Top of the Pops*. Was I ready for any of this? No way. Would it be fun if it all worked out? Maybe. Tears welled up, but for once I could see clearly through them.

How could I imagine doing this? School was like an afternoon in the park by comparison. I had no qualifications. All risk and no guarantee; if it all goes pear-shaped (as it surely will), where will that leave me? And who would I have to blame? I wanted to ring Eon, but I couldn't do it. We'd said some shitty things to each other, and I didn't want to give up or give in to any of it. I looked at the clock to see saw how long I had before the fairy tale began: less than an hour.

Mum would have encouraged me. She was game for adventure, Dad once said. She never told me that, but I liked hearing it. Life is a package you keep unwrapping was Aunt Ruth's motto. She never explained what happens if it's a Christmas cracker and you end up with ringing ears and no eyebrows.

I put on the clothes that had been delivered to see if I'd feel like a different person. Silver loon pants that felt like the sheerest silk, a loose white shirt with the buttons on the wrong side, a clip-on necktie, a red vest and black velvet jacket. Shoes that could have walked on the moon.

A horn honked outside. Before shifting, I undid the trousers and ran a finger through the soft valley between my legs. By the time the warmth reached my ears I was ready to face anything.

All or Nothing

"A PRESS CONFERENCE? You *are* joking. You think I'm one of those bloody backbench Tory twats trying to explain why I voted for the invasion of Transylvania for the sake of a few votes or my photo in the papers? No, I don't expect I'll be having any of that, thanks all the same. You see me sharing my innermost thoughts on those poor sods chucked out by Idi bloody Amin, is that it? Or is there perhaps a new works project in Hackney that the gentlemen of the press would have me comment on?"

Frank cocked an eyebrow, genuinely surprised that Chaz knew of Idi Amin's existence, much less about the fifty-thousand subjects of the Queen recently expelled from Uganda. He made a mental note to be more alert to what other factual ephemera his client might possess surprising knowledge of.

"Oh, calm down, will you? Would you rather be shut up in a suite at the Savoy while a parade of journos traipse in and out like a Swiss clock, all asking the same questions one after the next until your brain goes soft? You hate that, you've said so a hundred times. And you can't go down the pub with all of them, we'd have a total scene on our hands, and not a good one. What's more, your liver won't appreciate it, nor will mine. This is quick, it's efficient and you're overdue to board the modern media circus train. Grownups do it this way, especially famous grownups like yourself. Christ, the Beatles and Dylan both did it in the '60s, and it worked out for them. Look, mate, you put on some shades and a shiny shirt, say some mysterious-sounding bollocks, wink at the pretty ones, pose for some snaps and Bob's your uncle. It's all done by teatime and life goes back to normal the next day. Nothing could be easier."

"I don't know. It sounds awful — all of them shouting at once, me having to call on them like a schoolteacher. I don't know. How will I know what they'll ask?"

"I'll be there and none of that will happen. We'll play some tracks from the LP, get them jazzed about your new musical direction, however you think we should describe it. It'll be over quicker than a trip to the dentist. You won't feel a thing. I'll get on to my mate at the Beeb and persuade him to send along a crew, maybe we can get you on *The Nine O'Clock News*. That'd sell a few records, I'd wager."

"Will you tell them what to ask me?"

"It doesn't work like that, mate. They do their jobs and you do yours. It'll be fine, I promise."

Resistance to anything he hadn't already done had become natural to Chaz; his unwavering instinct led him to reject, cancel or simply blow off any number of workable undertakings just slightly out of the ordinary and then complain bitterly about the lack of results later on. Frank found it maddening, but that was Chaz. "He doesn't know what's good for him," that's what Joe always says. "You're the best thing for him, and he doesn't even know it. I reckon he thinks of you as an employee."

The connection of cause to result, a good plan to a tangible benefit, was a concept that either eluded him or was a handy spanner in his toolbox of manipulation, a way of making others suffer so he could evade the feelings of responsibility that taking some might induce. Although rarely willing to consider ideas presented to him, he was quick to affix blame (so long as it was not to himself) after the fact. If others could be found at fault, then he could not be held to account, and that suited him up and down. As a result, his default game was firmly passive, pushing others to make decisions for him (or, at least, about him), decisions that he could later rip to shreds without ever investing the effort to weigh them himself. If things worked out, then jolly good, and he would share the credit. If they went tits up, well, then, it just shows you that no one — *not even the people I've known and trusted all these years*, as his stock phrase went — has all the answers. *I let them do it their way and now see what's come of it.* In Chaz's view, his noblesse allowed him to endure his minions' failures with what he wrongly saw as equanimity, despite the occasional bollockings, sackings and lawsuits needed to maintain order.

In the end, Chaz didn't so much assent to the press conference as fail to object strenuously enough to prevent it. And so, in a first-floor hall of the V&A, on a Sunday afternoon no less, less than a week before the end of the coldest, most miserable February anyone could remember, more than a dozen journalists —

297

tousled groovers from the music press, wrinkled smoke-stained hacks from Fleet Street, a Reuters woman flown in from Paris after the agency's London bureau declined to make the assignment, the prized BBC camera crew, a full rack of photographers and a few nobodies — assembled to hear what Chaz had to say. The specific topic of the event, beyond introducing the new album (advances of which had already gone out), had been kept intentionally vague, with tantalizing hints scattered via the media winds that Chaz might have a big announcement to make. In that futile form of socializing groups of people do to when suffering from collective ignorance, the hum of speculation that could barely be heard over the volume at which Chaz's *BoredinSchool* album was being played (much to the consternation of museum staff, who'd not been warned about that aspect of the event) included guesses that he was retiring, organizing a charity campaign of some sort, buying a football club or relocating to America.

Arranged in four curved rows facing a throne-like business rigged with microphones and lights, near which was placed a far less garish settee, the seats were fancy and plush, each set with an embroidered ("CB 73") yellow and purple accent pillow, an advance copy of *BoredinSchool* and a wrapped chocolate in the shape of Chaz's face. Amanda, who had spent a week dealing with a candy maker in Mayfair and then the morning placing them just as Frank had specified, was stationed at the bar, doling out thimble-sized glasses of a very nice 1968 sherry. By 3:00, thirty minutes past the specified hour, all the seats — except the special one for his nibs — were occupied, and impatience was about to overtake boredom. Although the guests had been asked to refrain until the end, most of the chocolates were gone as was the emergency bottle of sherry Amanda had wisely thought to lay on.

Although they'd been invited, none of Chaz's band was present. That was as Frank wished. He knew they would view this event as an unpaid obligation on a day off rather than a public relations opportunity. There was no need to foster resentment on that score. They didn't like him, he didn't like them; that was fine, but he worried they might feel the same way about Chaz.

"Fucking hell!" Every head in the room whipped around to see a copy of the day's *Examiner*, held aloft and shaking as if caught in a stiff wind, in the last row. "Bastards! *Bastards!*" The paper was lowered to reveal its music critic,

who would have benefited from a shave and a coat from the current decade. Judging by the contortion of his features and the ripe apple color of his cheeks, the man was positively livid. As he continued the stream of invective, he became aware of the attention his outburst had attracted, and fell silent, raising the paper to hide his face, just as Frank strode in through a doorway at the front to find himself facing a roomful of backs. Nonplussed, he came to an abrupt stop, which caused Chaz, close behind, to clamp down on the back of his expensive suede boot and give him a thoughtless shove forward. Frank stumbled but righted himself and cleared his throat loudly in the hopes of commanding the attendees' attention before Chaz was able to take in the scene. He clapped his hands together and stepped aside to let Chaz proceed to his royal seat. Like a synchronized swim team (only not all in same circular direction), all heads turned toward the front of the room, followed by a smattering of polite applause.

"Terribly sorry, I, uh, I didn't, uh, mean that outburst. It's nothing, really." Still secreted behind his *Examiner*, Malcolm Pritchett continued his futile — and ill-timed — apology, which caused some further twisting of bodies in the chairs. "Nothing. Didn't want to bother anyone...Just a private matter, nothing really. Not my usual..."

Frank, confused by the interruption, surveyed the room but could not see anyone speaking. As an introduction was now well overdue, he puffed out his chest and announced, "Ladies and gentlemen, thank you for coming. Allow me to present Mr Chaz Bonapart!"

Another small round of applause.

All eyes were now on the star. All eyes, that is, that were not in the head of Malcolm Pritchett, who had thoughtfully lowered the paper to his lap but continued to scrutinize it.

In fact, it was far from a private matter. Unlike certain colleagues at the paper who were valued enough to receive embarrassingly generous notices for their books from carefully selected allies, his latest had been slagged off in a review (that would later be defended as a "thoroughly independent consideration") by Edwin Coolidge, an irascible fossil who, beyond a reputation for carelessness and intolerance, was well known to despise pop culture in general and rock in

299

particular. He'd either been retired or sacked, not that it mattered one way or the other, sometime around the turn of the decade and had not published a word in the paper in years.

Yet there, on page 23A, was the review, headlined "Literature Not Rocked by Dead Roller," dismissing *Mother, I Want to [Blank] You*, the explosive biography of Jim Morrison which Pritchett had spent a year of his free time researching and writing, as a "poorly argued defense of a poor excuse for a man, clearly lacking in talent or justifiable value, whose death provided as cogent a valuation of his artistic merits as any."

That Pritchett had to read this in his own paper, without even the courtesy of a warning or a chance to correct several glaring factual errors, was well past a joke. As much as he had, in the past, rued the *Examiner*'s dilatory standards regarding the arm's-length consideration of staffers' extracurricular efforts, he could not help but feel that he'd been singled out for abuse here. "It isn't good for the paper if one of our own receives a less than warm welcome from our own good selves," was how Norman Jones, the paper's editor, had put it when a mawkish book by the royals columnist about his Irish setter received a rave review. Having read the piece about *his* book for the second time, Pritchett began swearing again, to himself at first, then with more public abandon.

Chaz looked to Frank. "Sorry, what's going on here?" His tone was inquisitive, not annoyed.

Amanda swept in to snatch the paper away from Pritchett, shushing him loudly as she did, then singing out, "All's well, Chaz, nothing to worry about. We're all ears."

"Right then," said Frank loudly, although he was uncertain if anything was right. For a man not given to panic or dramatic shifts in mood, he was suddenly feeling anxious about this whole idea and wished it was over and done. "Thank you all for coming. I believe Chaz would like to say a few words."

"Would I?" Chaz glanced up through his shades, or at least tilted his head in such a way as to raise the possibility that he was looking in Frank's direction. "No, not really." They both laughed, one nervously, the other mirthlessly. Silence held the room for a measure, maybe two. Then, under his breath, he added, mostly for his own amusement, "I would very much like not to say any words, and to not hear any, either. But off we go."

Frank applauded and waved in the direction of Chaz, who was finally able to face the firing squad with a modicum of decorum.

He began with one of those movie star smiles big enough to charm an entire room of tired skeptics. "Hello everyone, nice to see you all. How d'ya like my new record?" The mix of applause and murmured assent did not hide what sounded like an American raspberry; rather, it was Pritchett blowing his nose.

Chaz pursed his lips and pressed on. "I reckon it's my most personal album yet. Not that it should matter to you lot." That broke the ice and elicited a bit of laughter. "I know you couldn't give a toss. The kids, they'll know what they hear, and that's what it's about, innit? A personal message from me to them."

Pens scratched at pads as the headline for their stories presented itself. Chaz lit a fag. A museum administrator rushed over to Amanda and hissed in her ear. The reply was a shrug, and a face aimed at Frank, who was equally disinclined to do anything about it. He made a smoking gesture at Chaz and waved his hand from side to side. Chaz smiled pleasantly and took another puff.

"Chaz, as you say, this is a personal album for you. Tell us what sort of person you are."

"Hmm. Good question. Dunno, I guess you'd have to ask someone who knows. Like 'im." He nodded in Frank's direction.

"And who might that gentleman be?"

"Him? That's Francis Guy, manager, space traveler and noted Buddhist." He pronounced it bud-ist.

"I see. So, if the album is personal, are you the person it's personal about?"

"Of course it is. Who else would it be about, the bloody Queen?"

"What's the album title mean, Chaz? *BoredinSchool*. Is that a play on 'boarding school'?"

"Fuck if I know. I was certainly bored in school, and I most certainly did not go to boarding school." A young man in a smart suit but without a notepad or any other markings of the ink-stained wretch stood and coughed. With the heat rising to his face and the muscles across his chest tightening; Frank felt the countdown to an explosion he knew was about to occur.

"I understand that a certain young lady has been, how shall I put this, contributing to your work."

"How d'you mean?" Chaz's voice had risen, both in volume and in tension.

With that, Blake, the friend of Stephen's who Amanda had engaged at Frank's behest for the very purpose of putting Chaz on the spot, faltered. It had all sounded easy enough down the Ruddy Pirate when Amanda explained what he had to do, but now the curdling reality of challenging, and very possibly angering, one of the biggest stars in Britain was frightening. He cleared his throat and cast a guilty look at his co-conspirators, all of whom kept their eyes lasered frontwards.

"I understand...I understand that you..."

Chaz leaned forward and addressed Frank. "What in bloody hell is this bellend on about?" At that, Blake completely lost his nerve, and scampered out of the room. Frank nodded sharply at Amanda, who followed him out.

Although the plan had gone awry, a pitch was away, and a roomful of alert batsmen were not about to let it hit the wicket without taking their swings at it. Malcolm, already angry and feverish, was first to the post, finishing the question Blake had bumbled.

"So, Chaz, do you have a new girlfriend?" He pivoted slowly to where Amanda was standing and made a face that looked at once both subtle and imbecilic.

Chaz turned back to the microphone. "No, I bloody well do not."

"So the young lady to whom my departed" — he started to say "colleague," but the word stuck in his throat, since he had no idea who the fellow was — "...that fellow was alluding to is a creative figure, not a romantic one?"

This was beginning to sound like a game of twenty questions, but there was no assurance that Chaz was going to stay put for any more of them. His patience, what there had ever been of it, was clearly on the wane, and he began to rise, but stopped when Blake burst back in.

Amanda had made it clear in the other room that he would not be paid for his time if he didn't do what he'd been hired for, adding several inducements she had no intention of honoring. Stood in the doorway, he closed his eyes and said — loudly, in a completely unnatural-sounding monotone — "I understand some the songs on this album were written by a fourteen-year-old named Laila Russell. Is that true." He didn't bother to inflect the last bit as a question or wait for an answer — he was gone again in a flash.

The discomfort in the room radiated in from all corners and froze the participants in a Pinteresque silence. Then one of the writers stood, holding the vinyl close to his face, and exclaimed, "He's got the name right. She's here in the credits! Is she really fourteen?"

Once the ensuing hubbub had died down, an older man in conservative dress raised his hand and waited politely to be recognized. Frank didn't know the fellow, but he hoped whatever was in store would be a run for his side. He signaled to Amanda to call on him.

"The gentleman in the grey suit. Do you have a question for Chaz?"

The man stood up, a show of respect generally ignored by the younger press mob. "Sean Smith, *Luton Reporter*. Perhaps this question has already been answered, but perhaps you'd like to offer your own explanation of why there's a song on your album extolling the virtues of female, erm, well, self-pleasure, given, erm, your gender and the age of your fans."

Chaz glanced at Frank, a stricken look on his face, and then turned back to the interrogator. "I have no idea," he said evenly, "what you're on about."

The man put on his specs and squinted at the sheet of paper he held in an unsteady hand. "Allow me to quote the lyrics to a song titled 'Jack and Danny': 'When Jack and Danny get wet, I go to town, front to back, roll all around, I scream and shout, let it all hang out, I love playing with my Jack and Danny.'"

"Oh please, that's just a schoolyard larf. Mucking about, splashing in a pool. Weren't you ever a child?"

The man blinked twice. "If that's your understanding, Mr Bonapart, then I suggest you pay a visit to the East End, where any urchin will gladly translate 'Jack and Danny' for you."

"Meaning...?" Chaz seemed genuinely curious. He was thinking granny, nanny, little orphan Annie...

"I'm not really comfortable saying it out loud. There are ladies present."

Frank affected a stern look, recalling a priest he'd once feared, and said, "Sean, in for a penny and all that. You've opened the bottle; you'd best see to pouring. Please enlighten us as to what you think it refers to."

"Fanny."

"Forgive me, I didn't hear that. Could you speak up please?"

The reporter looked as if he'd eaten a week-old winkle. He scrunched up his face, which had gone quite red, and said in a clear voice, loud enough to be heard this time, "Fanny. *Fanny*. I trust you'll recognize that as a rude word for the female sex organ, as it were."

"Oh, *bollocks*." Chaz seemed to deflate like a dirigible about to fall out of the sky. "I didn't write that."

"I should hope not, but I don't see how that's the point. You *did* sing it. And tomorrow morning, if I understand what it says here on your bumpf" — he shook the papers in the air with the righteous indignation of a provincial vicar denouncing the opening of strip club near his church — "half a million copies of the album containing it will reach England's record shoppes, with the potential to introduce countless young women to the supposed appeal of onanism."

Whether or not Chaz knew the word, or understood what the man was getting at, he fully grasped that all of this was bad for him.

Pritchett was the next to speak. Arms folded, smiling like the Cheshire cat, he leaned his chair back and, speaking slowly, certain that any answer would yield a juicy lede for his story, asked, "So who *did* write your ode to wanking, Chaz?"

The star gulped helplessly, a baffled look on his face. Frank breathed a silent sigh of relief, his plan having finally come around the track, galloping its way to the finish. He cleared his throat and said, "Malcolm, if I may." He took a few steps toward Chaz. "When he began work on this new record, Chaz came to the conclusion — and, after some resistance to the idea, I agreed — that it was

304

impossible for a busy rock star, caught up in the countless obligations and demands on his time, to stay fully in synch with the rapidly evolving values and obsessions of his core audience. I have to give my star client a lot of credit for his clear-eyed self-awareness and humility, a measure of perception and ego denial that I seriously doubt would occur to, or be embraced by, many of his esteemed peers." Chaz looked at him sharply, not at all enjoying the thought that he might have to accept the existence of peers.

"He felt the need for a reintroduction to the fine young people who make up Britain's record-buying public. I endeavored to assist in this cause by building contacts in that realm and asking them directly what sorts of things matter to them." Frank admired the sound of that: sincere, self-important, sort of commonsensical but utterly outside the bounds of '70s rock star comportment. He imagined, someday, market research would be all in a day's work in the music industry. Meanwhile, the residue of mid-'60s idealism, that hardy foolishness which drugs, money and Altamont had yet to completely snuff out, still deemed such thinking a crass intrusion of business into what had once been called "the dream factory" and a rank form of cultural treachery. He was sure the press would take the bait. He loved the efficient economy of pushing a good idea *and* using the expectation of its rejection to put a shiv in Chaz.

With his trained ear for p.r. bullshit, Malcolm pulled back his rhetorical bow and loosed the sharpest arrow in his quiver. "So, in other words, we're to understand you hired some chick to find out what Chaz should sing about?"

There were gasps as others worked out what had been said and what it all meant. "Not quite, that would have been awfully uncool, and after all we're still following the lead of greats like Lennon and McCartney, Bob Dylan and Brian Wilson, who I believe called his music teenage symphonies to God."

As notes were hastily scribbled, Frank flashed on a childhood memory of spooning porridge into his baby brother's mouth and recalled the sense of accomplish-ment he'd felt at the satisfied smile. Now it was time to elicit the triumphant burp.

"What we did was a lot more sophisticated than that, but simultaneously more naturalistic as well. We're evolving a strategy that may well revolutionize the industry." It was a strange, but oddly good, feeling to say things for the purpose of having them disbelieved.

"So you asked *two* chicks?" That brought a gale of laughter from the journos.

The shouted questions became a blur of noise that could only ignore itself, until Malcolm stood up and shushed the room before asking, for the second time, "Tell us then, Chaz, who did write your songs? Chinnichap? Mickie Most? Jonathan King? Mike Leander's schnauzer?"

Frank could not have hoped for better. Right on schedule, Amanda, who had slipped out of the room at some point, reappeared, a hand gently pressed to the small of Laila's back, guiding her to Frank's side, an entrance as smooth as on a chat show. All eyes fixed on the new arrival, a silvery vision dressed in a Biba rendition of interplanetary lounge wear, all puffed and silvery, her hair buzzed to an inch and dyed platinum, perched on PVC boots with four-inch clear plastic soles.

Before the ensuing furor had settled, Frank clapped his hands and shouted over the din.

"Ladies and gentlemen, permit me to allay your curiosity." The pause for effect quieted the room and allowed a quick check on Chaz, who was wildly looking everywhere but at Laila, pretending to ignore her presence.

"This fantastic creature is, in fact, the primary author of those songs. And now she is about to become a lot more than that. I am supremely proud to launch the newest Burgher Management client and, I am certain, our next great superstar... Meet the future of rock and roll: *Rockit LA!*"

BOOK TWO

Live your lies

The Thing With Two Heads

IT WASN'T the article in *News of the World* that he couldn't be arsed to read; Chaz never got past the headline. All it took to send him over the edge was the semi-clever effort of some anonymous sub ed. By the time he got on to Frank, he'd passed into a state of agitation beyond reason, blind with anger and unable to hear anything but the sound of his own voice.

Frank was in his dressing gown, preparing to retire, when the phone rang. He lifted the receiver to hear Chaz, between loud breaths, reciting the headline with the charged drama of a movie trailer. "The... *Thing*... With... Two... Heads... Chaz the Spaz... Taps... Tatty... Teen... for... Errant... *Brain*." The delivery was as comical as the content, but no one was laughing. Before Frank had a chance to say anything, Chaz declaimed it again, in a poncey lisp this time, augmenting his rage with a topping of gratuitous offence. Frank wished he would stop but didn't dare attempt to cut him off mid-rant, especially if he was willing to stoop so low. While Frank waited, you wouldn't say patiently, Chaz roused himself into gale-force calumny, railing about a dozen things, all of them tied, loosely at least, to the notion that his self-confidence had been undermined and poisoned by forces beyond his control. With Frank, naturally, as the lead culprit.

When Chaz finally stopped breathing fire, he switched to whingeing: about Frank's new client, the debacle of a press conference, something he now hated about the typeface on the album cover and a variety of rotating complaints about this and that. Rather than address it on the phone, Frank offered a load of hollow commiseration and promised to pop by in the morning. There was no purpose in attempting to mollify Chaz at the moment; Frank knew there was more to come, courtesy of *The Daily Sun*. Inspired by the news that Chaz was getting professional assistance from a young girl — hardly a scandal of the Nazi-S&M-party-with-royals measure, but a bit of fluff that sounded compromising enough so long as one didn't give it too much detailed contemplation — the bitter old drunk who sat in the editor's chair dispatched his minions to find a follow-up that would be more titillating to his readers than some rubbish about the writer of songs they wouldn't have heard. Offbeat creative solutions were no patch on downright criminality, pervy behaviour of any form or good old intergenerational shagging. Thanks to the generous dispensing of cash, it didn't take long for a promising rock to be turned over.

A reporter had rung Frank on a fishing expedition about a choir director from Herefordshire whose teenaged daughter had, he claimed, played a different sort of organ with Chaz and was now carrying his child. Whether the story was true or not (Frank rather doubted it from the start), it was a convenient, if random, addition to his own scheming. To maintain appearances, Frank firmly denied everything, declined to make Chaz available and threatened an action.

Fleet Street, he knew, cared little for gentleman's rules or legal suasion, and a salacious celebrity tale — true, dubious, made up or any combination of the three — meant money in the till. The *Sun* could run the story without actually interviewing the girl or obtaining an indignant denial from Chaz. They had quotes from the father, dodgy as he was, that was enough for a story. The pop mags owned by the paper's parent company had photo files of every modern pop star pictured with fans, so that would do for art. Chaz would be stitched up right and proper, and there was ultimately nothing Frank could do to stop it. There was no need to warn Chaz; he'd deal with the fallout once the story hit.

CHAZ'S MAN opened the door with the forlorn look of a surgeon whose elderly patient had just succumbed. "He's not at all well, sir." Frank brushed past him and found Chaz stomping around the cavernous sitting room in a dressing gown, unshaven and uncombed. He looked a fright, like he'd just been freed from captivity. At his manager's entrance, he stopped and turned. "Have you seen this?" He shook half of a tabloid (the rest of which was strewn about in strips on the floor) in Frank's direction.

"No," he lied. "Is there a reason I should?" In the silence, Frank could hear his watch ticking.

"It's about bloody time you turned up to explain what the fuck those berks were on about the other day." Chaz beckoned him to a table and pointed at a front page that had been crumpled and smoothed, possibly more than once.

"Chaz Bonapart Says Off With Their Clothes" over a subhead that added "Aging rock star accused of (re)productive romp with underage schoolgirl." (The abuse crossed the Atlantic: a few months later, *Creem* magazine referred to Chaz as "Sleaze Boner-part" in its gossip column.) Then he squinted at the photograph, which was captioned "Is this one of Mr B's young conquests?"

"Well?"

Frank, who was well aware that any word of explanation would likely set him squarely on the tabloid side of Chaz's fury, was not quite ready to admit that the photo in question — which had nothing whatever to do with the article or the accuser — was taken at the "Prime Number" party at the Rib Room in June. Nor was he about to direct Chaz to the small inside image of the actual teen in question, whose story was as leaky as the Titanic. It would be hard to convince the public (or a judge for that matter) that Mildred Gertzner of Halifax was the nubile teen who had briefly been the sexual obsession of a top rock figure. She was a tiny thing, with thick glasses and the fashion sense of a Welsh farm girl. And she was clearly not six months gone, as the article claimed.

Frank listened patiently to the vituperation and the repeated demands for legal action, as well as the absurd denial that he'd ever taken advantage of a young fan. Surely not this one, but Frank knew of others.

In his most soothing, neveryoumind voice, he said, "Forget about the story, Chaz. I'll get it sorted straightaway, and you'll never be troubled on that account again." One of Frank's rules was never to promise to make a problem go away — with cash or whatever else (in this case, a flash scooter for Mildred and a donation to the choir) — until it was done. He only assured clients that things would be taken care of when he already knew that they had been.

"Thank God for that."

Now that he'd settled Chaz down, he got on to some promotional matters, readying the pitch for his next play. When the time was right, he began, "It's rather funny, what I've got to tell you. In a way, I suppose."

"What?"

"Look at the photo again. I know it's just an accident that the two of you are in the picture together, but it's amusingly relevant."

311

Chaz picked up the paper. "Who is that? Your new client, Rocky the Squirrel?"

"No, well, yes. She was at your party. I have no idea why. Doesn't matter."

"So? It's not like I took her home or anything."

"Funny enough, you did without knowing it. Well, *you* didn't, but she ended up sleeping at the Tally Ho that night. I only learned that recently. She was legless, and Amanda thought it best for all concerned to not have her try and weeble her way home. Willette saw to her."

"My, my, how charming that my employees are so quick to use my house as a crash pad for any ligger that can blag her way into my party. Unbelievable. What kind of operation are you running here? I should fire the lot of you."

"I'm not your employee, Chaz."

"I can still give you the sack. And I should after that stunt you pulled, trotting that bint out at my press conference. I don't appreciate you taking advantage of my fame for the benefit of some grubby little shit you found in the gutter."

"There's no call for that. And I've already apologized for my momentary lapse in judgment. You have to remember, I'm running a business and I have to deploy my resources sensibly for all concerned."

"Oh, so, now I'm one of your resources? You should get your priorities straight, mate. Stick with them what's got careers, not the rubbish you absurdly imagine anyone would give a toss about."

Frank made a noncommittal noise and rubbed his forehead thoughtfully. The conversation was moving in the direction he wished it to. It felt like he was exercising psychic mind control.

"What do you intend to do for music for that one? I can't imagine she has any ideas of her own. You'll be paying through the nose for writers."

"Actually, she's quite a talented songwriter."

"Oh, really?"

Frank forced himself to look at Chaz as he replied. "Indeed. She came up with the best songs on your album." Frank guessed that Chaz had either missed, forgotten or decided to ignore the revelations from the press conference.

Chaz jumped up, red-faced and quivering. "What the fuck do you mean?"

"Where do you think that material, those ideas came from? Did you actually think Psi wrote them?" There was a lot more to explain, but Frank stopped to let the damage work its way in. Chaz stared, his arms waving, his face tight.

"You're telling me that what that Fleet Street fuck said was actually true? No way, mate. You tricked me into recording songs by a nobody? Who gets the publishing on this? *Her?* You'll be hearing from my solicitors. So will she. I'll ruin the lot of you, and then take a giant shit on your graves."

Frank waited a long time, hoping to lower the excitement — or at least not contribute to raising it — until it became evident that Chaz needed to hear something. He modulated his voice to HAL-level calm and spoke as slowly as he could manage.

"First of all, I haven't done anything. I'm just showing you the courtesy of informing you what's happened. Second of all, she's not a nobody, Chaz. She's the writer of a Top 20 single. *Your* single. And she's still in a secondary modern somewhere. A little gratitude might be in order, but I don't expect that from you."

At that moment, the door opened, and for the second time in three days, an androgynous waif in silver trousers, a genderless love child of Ziggy Stardust and Twiggy, made an unwelcome entrance into Chaz's presence, followed by Amanda. *Pull the plaster.*

Chaz stopped seething at the sight of her; the sound of his breathing was audible across the room. When he spoke, his voice was ice cold steel. "What game are you playing at, young lady? You'd best not be stealing my songs."

Laila answered in a voice that was little more than a whisper. "They're not your songs, Chaz."

"What did you say?" He looked over at Frank, who didn't react. "Frank? Please explain to this child who's a tarted-up schoolgirl and who's a proper rock star."

"In a perfect world, Chaz, both of you can be stars. Peter Trowbridge at Massive has signed her. He reckons he can put her out there and turn her into something. She's earned her shot. We'll see, but I think he could be right."

313

Chaz, who was evidently a few beats behind in the conversation, ignored what Frank had just said. "So, what you're telling me is that someone who works — *worked* — for me got someone *else* who worked for *me* a record deal on the basis of *my* hit records? In what trans-dimensional galaxy" (Bowie's success had shamed Chaz into reading Arthur C. Clarke and Robert Heinlein, looking for a character to rival the gold-crusted Ziggy Stardust, but so far all he'd done is acquire a pile of ridiculous jargon that now peppered his conversations) "does that strike you as fair and proper?" He sat down heavily in a chair.

"So tell me, if you haven't done anything, then exactly who is behind this coup d'état? Whose fingerprints will I find on the knife extracted from my back?"

"Actually, I'm going to ask our Miss Charles to look after Miss Russell." Amanda took a step toward the door, but a glare from Frank ended that impulse. She stared ahead with the terrified focus of an acrophobic inching along a ledge.

"My hope here today is to ensure there are no bad feelings going forward, no hidden resentments. I'd really like you to view Rockit, that is to say Miss Russell, as an ally and a colleague rather than as a competitor."

"Oh, you would, would you?"

Truth was it wouldn't really matter. It was just easier for the moment to throw Chaz off the trail and give him someone else to blame. She would be Frank's beard, as it were, the public face of '70s girl power as managed behind the scenes by a shrewd man for the certain benefit of all. Amanda would do the babysitting and the scutwork, and none of the important decision-making, all for a small share of Burgher's take, which was going to be huge. It couldn't have worked out any better.

"Ladies, would you leave us please?"

Amanda and Laila rushed out of the room, grateful to be released. Amanda gently closed the door behind her. When it next opened, a few minutes later, Frank was holding his forehead, which was slick with blood. Well behind him, Chaz stood, clasping his Ivor Novello statue, bellowing *"GET OUT!!!"* over and over like the end groove on an abandoned album.

Frank may have been seriously injured, but he was alert. He looked at the women and shook his head, sending spatters of red onto the floor. Under the circumstances, he was surprisingly calm. Amanda and Laila stood, stunned. "Get in the motor you two and get me to hospital."

IN ACTUAL FACT, I did not have a record contract with Massive at the time Frank told Chaz that. I was told I very well might, but there was no guarantee the offer he said was "on the table" would ever find its way to me.

All the same, two days later, Chives and I were sat in the Soho Square office (which made Burgher look like a right pisshole) of Massive's president, a stuffy bloke in a pinstripe suit and old school tie who looked like an undertaker. We washed Russian caviar (salty and foul) down with champagne (yummy) and were treated pretty much how I always imagined the Queen's daughter must get on. With Frank standing by, grinning like the town idiot, we scrawled our names on a stack of papers that he said would make me rich. I was on a conveyer belt going straight up, and all I had to do was not fall off, which didn't seem all that difficult if it meant living like this and pretending to know why.

In short order, I also had a bio that had fuck all to do with the facts ("she literally has no past"), a glossy 8 x 10 taken under a tree in Regent's Park, a cutout of my face on a stick with eye holes to peer through, a costume designer on retainer, a solicitor, an accountant, a press agent and a binder full of illustrated proposals for licenced merchandise, from T-shirts and badges to scarves, trainers and pink knickers with my new name on them.

As it was explained to me, Amanda would be my sort-of-at-least-in-public manager. Frank, I gathered, was still in charge but did not want to be seen as such, which left me unclear about the details of Amanda's role. I got the message straightaway that her resistance to the idea of working for me — even as part of an elaborate panto — was not to be taken lightly. I expect she expected me to be a complete shit to her, or at least make the effort, and while I sort of understood that I needed to push myself to be less of a loser, I didn't have it in me to be a real boss. So I half-assed it, being hard about the wrong things and looking for guidance and reassurance the rest of the time. Frank said I was just like every would-be rock star in history — a demanding, unpredictable baby in need of mothering. (He'd never asked me about my family life; I expect Chives had filled him in. But still.) I didn't favour the idea of anyone trying to fill in for the real thing quite that way, so I made a snarky remark about Amanda and he laughed, saying that she was as likely to be as good at mothering as sumo wrestling, that he was the loco parent (I think that's the words he used) in my rock and roll family.

There was no way to judge Amanda's loyalty to me, Frank or Dad, who seemed awfully pleased about her supposed role in my supposed career. While it was exciting to have her around a lot more, it was hard to say who was in charge of who. There were times when I hoped we could really open up, get a real sense of where we stood and what we wanted from all of this, and how we could help each other, but she blocked any movement in that direction. I have no idea what I was feeling, but it was never what I wanted to be feeling. Maybe it was the bruises of our past dealings, the deceit and the manipulation, the meanness and the desire. But the stitches on Frank's bonce were angry and red and he still managed to go about his business with ultimate calm, all smiles and promises and no griping over spilt blood. Chaz's name never came up.

First chance I got, I asked Frank, "Is there, like, a musician's handbook or something I should read? An orientation pamphlet?" I was joking, but I also wasn't. It felt like I was about to be dropped into the deep end of the pool without benefit of a single swimming lesson. I suppose people — or at least witches, if I remember my American history — generally float, but I had my sights set a bit higher than not immediately drowning. I felt completely unprepared how to do that. I wasn't expecting to get it completely right, whatever *it* was, but at the very least I hoped to avoid "useless prat" on my rock and roll report card.

> Begging for something I don't even want
> Hand it to me, I'll shove it right back

They made loads of promises — at every turn, some coked-out groover in flares and shades told me what exactly was going to happen, all of it for the good and the glory of my career and, presumably, their coffers, as if there wasn't the slimmest chance of a cock-up or a disappointing result that would prevent it from coming to pass. I never believed a word of it. No one had ever given me anything; what were the chances my life luck could change that drastically? I never considered that I might be in possession of something they badly wanted, something that required no real graft on my part. Maybe this was what being a model or a champion footballer was like. I kept listening for the catch, the way out that would flush me down the shitter and back out into the sea of absolute ordinariness from whence I'd just now arrived, but they had it all sorted, and all I had to do was turn up. In a white fucking Roller, no less.

It occurred to me that Dad had probably worried from time to time that he'd see me carted away in an ambulance or a Black Mariah, not driven around in the lap of sodding luxury. But there I was, bum on the softest leather ever, holding — for one luxurious moment — a cheque that was to be deposited in trust for me. My fanny grasped the significance faster than my brain did; I was wet before it was whisked away. I don't believe I would have stripped off and rolled around in ten-pound notes if given half a chance, but I did think it.

The crash program to turn me into a pop star was sheer madness, a high-speed race to remake me, top to bottom, inside and out. (At least I wasn't X-rayed.) I had a massage, a manicure, a pedicure, skin treatments and a shopping spree that must have cost two small fortunes. Despite my request to have my hair cut by Stephen (I thought that'd be a laugh; maybe I'll get him added to staff), they sent me to Snap Snips, where staff fussed over me like a princess. I did like the hair-washing bit — a cute boy made passionate and wet love to my follicles with the enthusiasm of a baker kneading bread.

I got a drawer-full of frilly knickers, tons of new shirts and trousers, even had a custom brassiere fitting done by a matronly type who reminded me of a teacher I'd once had; that was unsettling on top of embarrassing. I was remade and remodeled. And shifted — installed in a suite at the Connaught, where the bath looked like a swimming pool and the bed was the size of my old bedroom. I was virtually ordered not to appear in public without putting on all the gear and making sure I looked the part; I'm sure the geezer at the desk was a spy under orders to ring Burgher with a report of my appearance every time I passed through the lobby.

I didn't have a single meal that wasn't brought to me there or served in a swank restaurant. Some of what was put in front of me was disgusting, but I never saw a menu, so I rarely knew what any of it was. And I always had to work while I ate: meetings, interviews, consultations. I only found out much later that I was paying for all of it, from an overdraft I knew fuck all about in the first bank account I'd ever had in my sodding life.

School? Dunno what happened with that. I just stopped going one day and that was that. I don't know if I was of legal leaving age or not. I can't imagine Dad was happy, but he never said anything to me about it.

Nothing I did, or had done to me, seemed halfway real, not the guitar lessons, the singing lessons, the band auditions, the costume fittings, the photo sessions. I wanted a girl drummer, that was my idea, but they couldn't find any, or leastways that's what Frank said, because he wanted to get Psi the Clock back to be his man in my band, and that's what I/he got. That was a brilliant idea. I'm glad he and Frank were able to settle their differences and put all of the bovver behind them. I guess it had to do with me in a way, but neither of them would ever admit as much. As Psi said, silver is stronger than blood.

Frank had Amanda arrange a fan club for me, which was absurd, as I didn't, in fact, have any fans. He laughed at me about that and said that didn't matter, that we needed it in place regardless, that simply creating a club would attract members. Moth to a flame, he said. Mott the Hoople's mob was called Sea Divers, so Frank named mine Rockit Scientists. I guess that was funny, but I didn't give it much thought. I was shocked that there were boffins out there who were willing to send along £2.50 for an autographed picture of me (a few of which I signed, dunno who did the rest), a newsletter of made-up rubbish that I made a point of never reading and a discount voucher good for 50p off the price of an album I had yet to record.

I only learned later why Frank was so keen. Joiners got sent a questionnaire asking what kind of songs they liked, options for what kind of gear they'd like to see me in, how much they spent on records, makeup and such. He'd done a deal with some outfit in Soho to make and flog cheap knockoffs of my stage costumes. I never saw a pound from any of that tat. There wasn't anything I could do about it, but it did leave me feeling rotten to be made into a product, another a tin of branded sardines like I'd helped put Chaz in.

The coolest thing that happened in those first few months, the one I will always remember, was meeting Bryan Ferry. I was introduced to him at the BBC Broadcast Centre and I told them I'd seen their Marquee gig, and how I'd almost got killed doing it, and he was fascinated by my brush with Death. I doubt anything else I said made the faintest sense, but I did have the presence of mind to scribble down the name of an artist he said I should check out: Richard Hamilton. Bryan had studied with him at school in Newcastle (of all places) and told me that modern art and modern music were learning a lot from each other — cross-pollination, he called it. He said it would serve me well to understand that. I didn't get how, but I did promise to find my way to a gallery on Grosvenor Square that had pop art on display.

When Frank decided that I was ready to meet the world face first, I did my first live concert: an unadvertised half-hour at a tatty cinema in Bournemouth, facing a dozen spring vacationers come in out of the rain. It's a blur in the old memory banks, but it did take place — I've got a photo somewhere. "Good to get one under your belt," said Frank, who didn't deign to make the trip down with us. I guess he'd been there before. I couldn't remember all the words, the band didn't begin or end any of the songs as one and the PA crapped out not once but twice. Still, between the volume, the spotlight and the sense of belonging, I found it ridiculously exhilarating to be up there, looking down at people, feeling like someone other than myself. I got it, and there was no turning back.

The Saturday Gigs

I WAS IN Frank's office, waiting to see him, flipping through *Sounds* in reception when I noticed the date and realized how long it had been since I blagged my way into Chaz's "Prime Number" lig. Shit, that was a lifetime ago. A couple of lifetimes ago. I'd been a child then, encountering a world I now inhabited for the first time as a complete outsider and now I was...well, nearly a year older, hoarse, knackered and feeling like dog's piss. The drive back from Bournemouth had taken forever, and I'd woken up feeling like I was getting a cold, presumably from putting my face right up against the smelly microphone (as I'd been told to do by the soundman). I had a mind to ask for one of my own that we could take with us and not let anyone else use so I wouldn't risking getting sick every time.

With a nod from Laurence, I went in. Frank started off by apologizing for missing the gig. "Couldn't be helped, y'know." I hoped this wasn't how things were going to be. "How do you reckon it went?"

I know I should have told him it was brilliant, that I loved it, that they loved me and that I couldn't wait for the next one. But what came out was, "Not good. I know I'm crap. I don't know why you think I should be doing this. Maybe we should just rip up the contract and I'll be on my way back to East Acton and we can pretend none of this ever happened."

He looked bemused. Not surprised or angry, just bemused. In my overwrought condition, I rather expected more of a reaction.

"You're not mad?"

"No, I'm not mad. And I'm not daft, either. I never thought you had any enormous musical talent in the, well, in the traditional sense, but you've got more than you need of what it takes to become a star in these callow times. So don't judge yourself too harshly. I'm not expecting you to suddenly give birth to the next *Electric Warrior* or *Space Oddity*. But I am going to see that a bright spotlight shines on you continuously until you arrive safely — and rewardingly, for all of us — at your destination. We'll get it sorted, don't you worry. Just don't lose faith. I — I and you — *you* — can do it. *We* can do it."

I shrugged and sniffled. I guess I'd been crying a bit. He had more to say. "We're different, you and I. Maybe you can't see it, but we are. And the sooner you come over to my way of seeing things, the better."

That sounded ominous. "I probably don't want to hear the answer, but how's that?" His smile might have meant that he knew exactly what I was thinking, or just that he was offering a kind look before giving me a kick in the shins. I expected the worst.

"The way I see it, you want to be somebody. *I* want you to be somebody. Now perhaps we're not envisioning quite the same person, but I think we can agree on a rough outline. And the goal we share. I know this will sound awful, but I want to be on the level with you. It'll save a lot of tears later. I see you as a tool, like a product in a tin that can either sit on the shelves at Tescos and be ignored by nine out of ten housewives or we can put adverts everywhere, do public demonstrations in Leicester Square, skywrite names all over the clouds and do every other bloody thing we can think of to make you the first thing on people's minds. That's what I do, and it works. It sounds worse than it is. You won't have to do anything more than turn up where and when I tell you and do what I tell you to do. The rest of it is up to you, to put all of your natural self into the character we've created for you. Believe it or not, the punters can tell when an actor, even an actor playing a role, is real or phony. You have to believe with every fibre of your body so they will believe in you. If you can do that, then we're on our way to someplace wonderful. If not, then you're just a lump of dross, willing to make a vain try at success but secretly happy to fail just like every other poxy English loser in history. Our nation of shopkeepers is content to close the door at suppertime without selling a tin of beans because we don't believe our beans are especially good. That's the way of the past, Laila, and we are the future, leaders of a land where we know how great we are and believe that we can get anything done we set our minds to."

"How American."

"Quite. I don't know if I ever thought about it quite like that, but I do suppose you've nailed it. Bravo."

The thought of being flogged like washing powder made me want to jump off Waterloo Bridge, but he was, I suppose, right in a way. I wanted to have what he was outlining, and I wanted to have it for who I was, not who he could con kids into thinking I was. We saw things differently, but it might all amount to the same thing. I was a lot closer to believing I deserved a fair hearing, a real chance at success, than I might have been a year earlier. Could I have it both ways? I could see myself doing what I was told I had to do, but that was a far sight different than thinking up that rubbish on my own, or even showing any interest, any belief that it would matter, in going through with all of it. A big part of me just wanted to be left alone, to be counted on by no one for nothing, to be among the living dead, going through life trying not to be noticed. There must be people better suited to this racket, I thought. Maybe we could get one of them to pretend to be me, and I'll just write the songs and hide in a castle somewhere. That's what happened to that sad bloke from the Beach Boys — he dropped out of his own band and took to the studio and his bed. I could see the appeal in that. Except perhaps for the studio part.

"I've learned a few things in my time. The business has changed a lot, but the basics still apply, and if they sound like the Ten Commandments, well, that's because they are. Only there aren't ten that I can recall at the moment." He laughed lightly.

"Fear is crucial — don't stop shaking. If you have to struggle, the audience will appreciate what you're doing for them. That's good. They're scared, too, and want to feel like they're not alone. Otherwise you're just going through the motions, singing words without thinking about it." He paused.

"As a performer, your job is to make everyone watching you love each other because they all love you. Chaz came close, but then he let it slip through his hands. Factions emerged in his following. We won't let that happen. Focus. Discipline."

I know I should have been all agreeable and go-along, nod my head and do as I was told, but that's not how I felt. I suppose I'd been working up to this a long time. Not consciously, mind, but without meaning to I'd saved every bit of shite Amanda and school and everyone else had dumped on me, everything I'd wanted that I hadn't got, every rainy day, every stuffed nose, poor mark, skinned knee. And Mum's death. That box in the back of my heart was well and truly filled with resentment and a vivid sense that I was owed the dignity and decent treatment I'd always been denied. *That's* the moment I realized I wanted to be a rock star. And why.

I'd hit emotional puberty, right there in Frank's office. I felt a force within myself that was new and strong. If I was going to make my way as an adult, I'd need a steady dose of whatever had led me to kiss Amanda and give that skin a kicking. And it couldn't be spontaneous combustion; it would have to be reliably available whenever needed. That was, I suspect, my blurry recognition that adulthood meant thinking ahead to achieve planned-out ideas, having a purpose and a strategy that made good sense and was worth the effort. I didn't realize how long this had been growing in me, but it suddenly seemed like precisely the right point in my life to loose the hounds and get on with the hunt. I tilted my head and shifted my feet to face Frank square.

"I'm not going to do love songs. They're bullshit. Done to death. Let someone else be the sap. I won't play that game. I'll be the girl who doesn't do love songs. That'll be my...thing."

Frank's jaw went tight. He looked around the room, but there was only him and me. "Why would you do that, Laila? Every song is a love song, innit?"

I wasn't really inclined to debate the point, leastways not until I'd given it some thought. I just knew I didn't want to be the one feeding little girls the same poison as everyone else. That won't help them. I doubt it ever did.

A week later, I had another out-of-town gig, third-billed to Mud — a bunch of bored gits in matching blue suits and fixed show business grins — with a band from Newcastle called Geordie (how clever) in the middle at De Montfort Hall in Leicester. Fuckin Phil drove us up in a small lorry with crap brakes and rusted sides. The back was full of rubbish, and he didn't look much better. I reckoned he'd gotten pissed the night before, but that wasn't it. He said he was feeling poorly but was dead set on getting us there and set up before he could catch a nap and be ready for the breakdown and the ride back. Psi rode up front with him, and I was in the back with the lads. I was already getting a hint of what it meant to trudge up and back the motorway, a slog that soon made the actual performance part of this life seem like an afterthought.

Amanda said she would do it, but instead got some telly bird to show me a few makeup tricks, since these gigs didn't merit the full treatment of a proper stylist. Frank said that would come later. I was crap at it and needed someone to keep me from looking like a poxy mime.

The dressing room was small but clean. I was supposed to have one of my own, but that wasn't on. As showtime neared, I asked the others if could have a few minutes by myself, and they were nice enough to oblige. It was getting on to half seven, when we were due to go on, when Psi let himself in, white as a sheet. Before he closed the door, I could hear a siren in the distance.

"What's going on, Psi?"

"It's Phil. He just snuffed it. Right onstage. He was humping a Marshall bottom, put it down, grabbed his chest and keeled over. Just like that."

"Fucking hell." I didn't know what to say. Phil wasn't family, but in a way it felt like he was. I flashed on Dad and hoped he was alright. I thought I might be sick. "What do we do?"

Psi gave me a withering look that still bore a trace of kindness. "We go out and play the gig. That's the way it is. A good, good man, our Phil, but this is way it is. I'll ring Frank and let him know, and he'll get someone up here to help us load out and motor back to London. I'll tell him to get on to Phil's wife and make the necessary arrangements."

So that's what we did. I don't know if we were any good — I was crying and sleepwalking, thinking of Phil the whole time. Fuckin Phil. Toward the end of the set, which was only five songs, my amp sputtered and blew out. I guess it was Phil making fuckin sure we fuckin knew that he was well and truly gone. That only made me sob more. The amp didn't really matter; my guitar was kept low in the mix, not a big part of the sound. Mickey, the guy we'd hired, had all the chops needed — he played all the parts and made it look easy. He had this cool round red pedal thing on the floor called a Fuzz Face that made his guitar sound like a jet engine and, I suppose, covered up any bum notes.

The *Leicester Mercury* had sent a scribbler and a snapper. The review was pro-Mud and anti-Geordie, with barely a word about us, but it did mention Phil's death (I had no idea he was called Phillip Stuart Micklethwaite III) and ran a

324

picture of me. I looked positively awful, a sweaty mess with makeup running down my face like black paint. (Years on, a fair number of punk girls told me that picture was an inspiration to them. Can't say as I was ever proud of that.)

Phil was buried a few days later. I didn't want to go — death and me really aren't on such good terms — but Frank said I had better, so I put on some black gear and turned up. I was shocked to see his two young children and a regular-looking missus. You really can't know people all that well without making a real effort. That thought stuck with me for a long while.

EON DIDN'T MAKE it to Leicester for my second show, not that I could possibly blame him. But then he was "stuck at the store" the morning Phil was planted. It was OK to be on my own, I guess; I felt a bit of guilt that I didn't miss him as much as I ought to have done.

With everything that was going on, we hadn't seen each other, hadn't even talked much, and I had neither the time nor the energy to think, or care, a lot about it. I had the sense that I was leaving him behind. If one were to be absolutely bloody honest with oneself, I wanted to keep this part of my life for myself, and he was the only person, other than Frank — who was going to collect a fourth of my earnings for his troubles — who could reasonably claim to have played a significant part in getting me here.

I was glad for an excuse that didn't have to get all heavy or weird, so rather than see what Grace was getting up to, I asked him to come along when I finally got myself organized to see the art show in Grosvenor Square. In the back of my head, I was hoping to learn something. Or perhaps some of Roxy Music's cool might rub off on me if I went. I said as much to him while we were walking there. He just laughed, and not in an entirely kind way. "It doesn't work like that, Laila." (Funny. He would get cross if I called him Bryan, but I never asked him to call me anything other than my name.)

He was right. I can't imagine how it could. We stared for a bit at a blurry photo of Mick Jagger and some other bloke covering their faces in the back of a car, their wrists chained together. I liked it alright, I guess, but it left me feeling thick, because I couldn't work out what it was supposed to mean or how it might have anything to do with me. Next to it was the same shot but done as a brightly colored painting — that one was called "Swingeing London III." That crap spelling would have gotten me a bad mark in class, but maybe the lesson of the day was that artists don't have to know how to spell.

I made an effort to "study" each artwork, staring as my mind wandered far beyond the gallery walls. I hoped I might get an idea or two, but no. When I felt I'd been there long enough and was ready to leave I turned to look for Eon when I noticed a dark blue velvet curtain covering the back of the gallery: ceiling-to-floor and slightly parted in the middle, with the letters "W" and "C" sewn on in what must have been gold thread. I couldn't tell if it was art or just the way to the loo; I took a few steps and stopped. A girl at the desk must have spotted my uncertainty and came over to say it was alright to go in and have a look. "Are you familiar with the artist?"

I didn't even know who the artist was, so I just nodded politely and went in. Long strips of musty-smelling fabric hung from the ceiling — there must have been hundreds of them — flapped into my face. There wasn't much light in the room, but I could see a glow ahead of me, so I pressed on, coughing at the smell and slapping the strips away as I moved. I soon reached a clearing of sorts, where a bright spotlight illuminated a gleaming example of the finest mod con from Armitage Shanks, with the lid down and the sound of flushing water — or a cheering crowd, or maybe the two sounds fitted together — that got louder as I got closer.

The seat had "L-I-F-T/M-E" painted on it in, so I did. I looked down at the bowl, which contained a pile of submerged vinyl singles. The embossed label on the top one was visible in the water (or what I hoped was water): "Cherish" by David Cassidy. Then I saw what was on the underside of the lid: a press picture of me. I fought my way back out into the main part of the gallery and went to the desk. "Who did you say did that thing at the back?"

"Her name is Wynifred CelesteLester. The piece is titled 'Rocket to the Loo.'"

That explained a lot. "Just one more thing: what's it cost?"

She opened a binder and ran her finger down a list. "75,000. Guineas." That old witch, I thought. I wondered if this was her idea of compensation for the advice she'd given me. Or a warning. Maybe it was a curse against my future: pop music was no better than shit and we were all headed into the sewer. Either way, it was out of order. A handout on the desk near the door had a review from *The Sunday Times*: "CelesteLester's astute attack on the artifice and ultimate worth of pop offers a bluntly effective alternative to Hamilton's showier and more detailed critique of contemporary culture. It's all crap, innit?"

I found Eon outside and sent him back in to look. "Did you see that?"

"Clever old bird, it only took her a minute to suss out the pop racket. From the fringe to the heart of the machine in one easy step. Perhaps you should prepare an invoice for the singles. Or maybe I should."

"What do you mean?"

"She got my number from Matthew and rang me a few weeks after we were at hers."

"What did she want?"

"To know more about you."

"What did you tell her?"

"That you had a new name and seemed well on your way. She was pleased. Maybe that gave her the idea to cash in. I don't think she's had this level of interest in her work, and she's been at it for ages."

"How could she?"

"Oh c'mon, Laila, why should she not? Art is for everyone. Everyone steals and it's all about making money. Isn't that why you're playing at it?"

"How could you?"

"Hey, I brought you to her, and that proved useful to you, didn't it? Life's a two-way street. I don't owe you shit."

I don't know why his treachery upset me so much. In truth, it didn't sound like he'd done anything terribly out of order. But to hear him make light of her plundering and sneering, or to equate my new life with her batshit fiddling, as if *I* didn't also have the right to succeed at something, that was infuriating. We had a right row about it in the street. On the way home, alone, I wondered if the meeting he fixed for us was really for my benefit. We didn't talk again for a long time after that.

Bring Me the Head of Jimmy Osmond!

Barry Wilson goes to meet young sensation Rockit LA and finds her sensational. Snaps by Harry Gable.

Strange times are upon us, boys and girls, strange times indeed. Along with some of the greatest music ever recorded, the charts are filthy with rubbish, the stultifying likes of which have never before sullied the hearing of British children. Sure, it's their fault, but we all know the power of incessant propaganda (not to mention Radio 1), but truly not since the Blitz have we been subjected to more calamitous destruction raining down from the skies. This time, of course, in the immortal words of Walt Kelly, perhaps the greatest American philosopher of this century, we have met the enemy, and he is us.

The foul stench among us on this otherwise fine afternoon is a rotund child from the land of Coca Cola: James Osmond. And a squeaky little bugger he is. His Mormon clan's recent visit to our shores—which caused such a mass cultural delusion that one wag coined the word "screamagers" to describe the participants in such mania—is thankfully over, but the 'orribleness of the music lives on, twice a day (and thrice on Sundays), via our airwaves.

I dare anyone to cite another one-two punch of plastic in the annals of that glorious racket of roll launched by Chuck Berry (amen, brother!) a generation ago that can sink to the ungodly prepubescent depths of naffness currently occupied by "Puppy Love" and "Long Haired Lover From Liverpool". Crippling labour actions have been occasioned by far lesser affronts to the dignity of our fair island. And, what, one wonders hopelessly, did

Merseyside do to deserve being made the butt of this particular slice of xenophobia? (I suppose one could hold the Monkees' "Randy Scouse Git" at least partially responsible. But in fairness to the Prefab Phour, that phrase doesn't appear in the lyrics and the record was called "Alternate Title" in the UK.)

And so we find ourselves in 1973, having lived through the summer of glam (a tip of the derby to Master Ziggy), with highs, lows and in-betweens. It was the beast of times...

Quick thought: glam rock, it's just Elvis Presley and Doris Day, innit?

Which brings me around to confess (I can hear the little sisters' squeals of horror already) that I passed the chance to see little Jimmy O on the box last week, but I had a good excuse. I'd been ordered by my boss to turn up—at an ungodly hour in the morning, when drink and food were both inconceivable *and* unavailable—at the Bond Street offices of rock manager extraordinaire Francis Guy, our 1970s version of Larry Parnes. I was there to have a go – purely in the journalistic sense, mind—at his latest next big thing, a heretofore unknown teenager (female variety) shackled with the absurd name Rockit LA who, to her preemptive credit, has *not* got a song called "Long Haired Lover From Liverpool", is *not* nine years old, is *not* a Mormon (well, she might be: I neglected to ask) and *was* born in London. Plus she's a bird who plays guitar (or so I'm told), which is, at the very least, different.

I read the bumpf I'd been given, but there wasn't a lot there. She's got a band of hired guns, a label deal and a single about to be foisted on the nation. Not much of a back story, just a lot of hype slinging about words like "precocious", "unique", "self-possessed", "original"—you get the drift. And so it was with middling enthusiasm (like going to church only because there's a pretty girl who sometimes turns up) that I arrived, nearly blinded by the morning sun, and announced myself to the girl in reception. I parked in a cozy chair for a bit and then was sent up.

I found the young lady in question seated at a conference table beneath a Hockney painting of a swimming pool (I'm guessing an original, such being the affluence of today's managerial class). She was polite enough, offering a small hand and a shy look that I determined not to find adorable. So, with the blunt ingenuity of the disabled witless, I dived right in, foregoing the evasive niceties of small talk.

As I began setting up my cassette recorder, she suggested we do it on the go instead. Our mobile conversation—I sprung for coffees, but she paid for the taxi back to the office, where she was evidently booked solid for the rest of the afternoon—went on for a couple of hours. Turns out the girl has an actual name (Laila, she demurred on sharing the rest of it), attended East Acton Primary and lives with her dad. She's never been to Los Angeles ("I can't wait to see it for myself!"), or on a rocket for that matter, but that's no surprise. She writes her own songs and never expected to join the pop racket. (So much for failing strivers everywhere.) Inquiries on her discovery, or how she organized herself into a chart-ready career, were met with a stare that could either be taken as blank or opaque. Rock imagery doesn't have to be real and recognizing a fake doesn't make it any less effective. Fantasy can be more real than the real thing, and that she is.

All in, she struck me as a clever and honest character, one who wasn't working out what to say based on how it would play in the papers, but as if she was still working a lot of it out for herself. If I had to hazard a guess, I'd reckon she doesn't have a lot of friends, or has had to fend for herself. That's all about to change.

The 45, "Ophelia's Dream", has all the elements of a hit—catchy chorus, romantic story, handclaps, determined backing vocals and a sporty guitar solo. She's a decent enough singer, but that's not the point. What the record has is that instant feel of transportation, conveying a sense that Rockit LA comes from—

330

or at least currently inhabits—a world we want to know more about. Whoever's pulling her strings has a pretty clear idea of what the nation's youth are into and how to embed it up for their delectation on a small piece of plastic.

The strangest moment in the interview came as we were wrapping up. I thought we'd been getting on pretty well, so I gave Rocky the proverbial push, asking her point-blank if she saw herself as a major new talent with something to say or just a clever bint with a big-time manager and a good gimmick. Now, as my loyal readers know, I've been 'round this track before, and have heard every variation on the cocksure company line, from false humility ("I don't know if I would say that, Barry, there are so many wonderful artists out there and I'm just glad for the opportunity to contribute blah blah") to smug condescension ("I wouldn't be doing this if I didn't rate myself; why should I expect anyone to buy my records if I wouldn't?") to journeyman entertainer decency ("Just a bit of fun, innit? I just hope people get some pleasure out of it"). But I have never before had a pop star in progress burst into tears and plead for my honest opinion of her abilities because "Honestly, I've no clue. Some days I think I've really sussed it out, but others I think my music is just rubbish and they're going to laugh me back to school." (I wrote that bit down as soon as I got outside.) Maybe it's all an act, or PMS lunacy (*Don't be such a twat – Ed.*), but I dunno. She's real in a way today's pop stars rarely are. Despite the silly name and the well-oiled machine backing her bid for stardom, could Rockit LA be the last—or is that the first—honest glam rocker?

Rockit LA, whose date book has been largely unfilled until now, leaves on her first tour of the UK next week. Look out, England, she's all yours!

You Know You Like It

AT FIRST I didn't half mind being caught up in the pop cyclone. I can't say I was a natural — most mornings I woke up half expecting to find myself back in East Acton with nothing on the schedule past a cuppa tea and the breakfast shows. But putting on the mantle of fame, keeping a clear head about what needed doing and setting my gears to be Rockit LA took on a measure of normalcy, like when I first stepped into platforms. I wobbled a bit, felt some discomfort but found my feet, as they say, and it started feeling alright. Fame was like that. I stood taller, felt special. Knew what I was about. I even stopped being surprised when punters recognized me and asked me to sign something.

I liked it.

Without meaning to, I got all caught up in the competition: chart positions, *TOTP* slots, radio play, awards. I became a bit obsessed, checking the papers as soon as they came in to see if my latest release had a bullet or an anchor. I had a blast playing shows, getting treated like a princess one day and a rotting carcass the next. I saw some money, likely not as much as I should've, but Frank looked after me well and I appreciated that. I suspect he was making out like a bandit. We never spoke about Chaz.

I met almost everyone in the business, and some of them were nice to me. I was even nice to some of them, especially the groups who did support for me. I don't remember many of their names, but I made sure not to be shitty to them. They didn't deserve it, leastways not yet. Not even the ones who were full of themselves, who reckoned they were the next big thing.

Roy Wood was an absolute dear to me, like a daft uncle who drank too much but never lost his manners or his charm. He could have brushed me off as a worthless kid, but instead he treated me like maybe I had a right to be on the same stages as him. He even suggested we might work together someday; I heard he had an idea for an all-girl orchestra. The Slade lads were a total trip, on the ride of their lives and loving every minute of it. Beneath the ridiculous

332

costumes, they were all lovely gents, as down-to-earth and decent as they come. They made sure we had a soundcheck every night on our first tour together in '73, and Noddy even came out to settle down some yobbos in the stalls giving me stick in Southend. I learned a lot from them: not to take it all too seriously and to always give the punters their money's worth. Ta much, lads — long may you wave!

The Sweet were off their heads, but a lot of fun. The American Sparks brothers were uptight and not so friendly. I rated their English band, but the stars didn't have time for the likes of me. I was mad for Bowie's guitarist, Ronno — no, not *that* way — and met his missus, who was lovely. He showed me some moves that really helped. I always wanted him to produce my records, but he was so busy with Ziggy and then his solo career. Good on 'im. Bolan? We nodded hello backstage a couple of times, but I never got up the nerve to properly introduce myself and no one else did it for me.

THINKING BACK on it now, I didn't become a bitch overnight, leastways I don't *think* I did. What happened was my place in the world shifted and I found myself seeing things differently. A minor personal adjustment, that's all it was. I can't claim any credit for it. I simply learned that I didn't always have to lose. And that changed everything for me.

It wasn't the transition from a worthless nobody to a successful pop star, no, what made me a new woman was the discovery that writing songs was not so difficult. Once I'd bashed a few together that people seemed to like I stopped worrying about what I was doing, or whether I was good enough at it, and that opened the door: it became a piece of piss to push them out. I could tell when the words went together just right. I was like a safecracker: I could feel the tumblers drop into place. I had a tougher time cobbling together melodies to go with the words. You couldn't just pick notes at random out of books or magazines and see where they led you. I didn't dream tunes the way I did pictures and words. Luckily, I got the hang of jamming: get the band in a studio, earning their wages for a change, and fuck around until someone stumbles upon a hook or some chords that don't suck. The trick was to keep your ears open for it. Otherwise, it's all a waste of time. Once you've got a bit, you keep playing it until everyone's fingers are sore and make sure the tape op gets it all down. Then Psi or the producer or someone else fishes around to shape a song around the new-sounding parts. And I get the publishing. Frank hires some hooks-for-hire hack to polish it all nice and catchy for £500, and Bob's your uncle.

It helped a lot to recognize — and I suppose this was my blinding rock and roll revelation (not that I'd ever call it that out loud) — that what my songs had to convey was attitude, not stories. Kids who felt stuff but couldn't explain it were like moths drawn to anything that could spell it out and give them words for their wishes, their frustrations, their worries. The Who, I gather, sussed that early on and pounded away at it to their substantial benefit. It took me a while to clap on, but love is the dumbest topic in the world to make music about. There are already more than enough love songs in the world. Kids aren't deep thinkers; what they don't understand they can learn from their mates or their big sisters. It's the stuff that makes them feel alone in the world, the concerns they imagine — wrongly, of course — that no one else has ever felt before. That's what songs have to be about. To make them feel less alone. Less confused. Less pathetic. Attitude, courage, standing up for yourself.

The schoolgirl bollocks went right out the window. I had better ideas now, ideas that fairly reeked of commercial potential. The first one went like this:

You didn't notice
Me at the dance
Till we were in the alley
And I pulled down your pants

Mum would have slapped me silly for that, but what did I care. She was dead and I was fighting for my life. Like when I went after that horrid dog-beater — no time to be careful or cautious. Get in there with your best shot, because you only get one. If you don't win in a go, you're sure to be battered. The pop world was no better than the streets. One chance to triumph — make it count or you're good as gone, mate.

So I came up with "Give a Toss (I Don't)," "Got Nothing to Say," "Bollocks to You" (I had to call that one "B2U," which made it look like a Slade song) and

"Let Me Kiss Your Busted Lip." Those fit my new needs far better than the rubbish I'd given Chaz. Frank binned one I had called "Don't Be a Twat."

At first, I let the thought that lots of people rated me fill in for the fact that I didn't really rate myself. I quite liked that — for the first time in my life I wasn't bothered about who I was. I let others sort that out for me. But then it went sour, and their misguided fandom became further proof of how crap I was. That turned it all around, so that I didn't believe what anyone said about me if it didn't line up with the shitty view I had of myself.

When I stopped expecting anyone to genuinely like or care about me (outside of Dad), I stopped trying to be the sort of person people like or care about. I reckoned I had to stick up for myself regardless of how that made others view me. Fuck 'em. Mum would have been horrified. From what I recall, and from what I'd heard, she was a woman with standards, and it was clear I'd fallen well below them. Worse, I stopped thinking about the lessons she'd taught me; first, I started thinking of them as naïve, then I shied away from thinking about them at all, like awful old trousers stowed in the back of the cupboard that I can't believe I ever wore. I knew I had broken with her in some profound way, pushed her out of my present life and left her in the past. Not that there was any other way. Maybe that was what growing up was really about. Or I was just a horrible shit who didn't deserve a mother like that, even if she's the one who left me to make my way without her.

Through the weirdest set of circumstances imaginable, and without much effort of my own, I had found a place for myself in the world. It was up to me, and only me, to make the best of it.

Ghost in the Machine

EVERYONE SHOULD have a personal assistant. Believe me, life gets way better when someone is paid to deal with the bad bits and take away the sort of tedious rubbish that makes my head ache. I recommend it highly.

Mine was a Russian girl named Varda a few years older than me (back then, except for the punters, *everyone* was older than me). She had a crazy James Bond spy accent and, I suppose, from a certain angle, looked a bit like Amanda, only with a shapelier arse and a better sense of humor. (She fell about when I told her how I'd come by my real name.) She grew up poor in a place that's like twenty years behind the rest of the world, but she'd been in England since 1970 and was catching up quickly. In addition to being smart and pretty, she had the courage of an ox and knew how to do all sorts of things. I sometimes wondered if she'd been trained by SPECTRE.

Frank found and hired her for me, I strongly suspected at the time, to keep an eye on me when he wasn't around. But he underestimated the bond two girls traveling together in the vacuum canister of a rock and roll career can forge. We were drawn together like magnets. In no time, she had come over to the enemy side: synchronized periods, shared clothes and endless talks. She ultimately proved better at keeping an eye on him for me than the other way 'round. Yes, we shared a bed from time to time, but no one ever knew. And that wasn't really what I valued her for — except when she had her face in my fanny. At those moments, she was my favourite person in the world.

She handled the hotels and the venues, the roadies, catering, the merchandise guys. She hustled journalists out when they browned me off or bored me stupid; she knew just which fans to bring back to the dressing room to meet me after shows. She even learned how to do my autograph so I didn't have to wear out my wrist doing all the fan club pictures. With her on the case I always had clean clothes to wear and decent food to eat and a minimum of bovver in my life. I dealt with Frank, my chartered accountant, the guys in my band; she did the rest. I don't know how, but she did. And never got shirty or sick or acted stupid. If I didn't know better, I might have thought she was a robot or an alien.

Until Frank brought Varda aboard our merry little pirate ship, working with Amanda was a constant chore. I expect he got V to keep me from killing A. She must have loathed seeing the monster she helped create looming up like Godzilla over Tokyo, but she'd been ordered not to make an enemy of me. I overdid it madly at first, even making her buy me knickers once, but it wasn't nearly as much fun to abuse Amanda as I thought it would be and so I stopped. We had our ups and downs. I never really trusted her, and she never genuinely liked me. Real friendship was not a practical option, so that was that. I didn't hate her; I didn't love her. I couldn't summon any of that up with conviction. I just didn't want to care about her. And I didn't want to be rid of her.

She had taken up with a very pretty but utterly useless Belgian berk who called himself Damniel Dommage and led a ridiculous dress-up group called Soignèe. Looking after a petulant pop singer seemed to keep her too busy to put much effort into my waning career. I would have done something about it if I had thought ahead, but I kind of looked on the whole thing as a natural progression that was drawing to a close. It was fine. I'd grown rather sick of it all.

After dumping that idiot she took on a drippy singer-songwriter from Leeds. I can't remember his name, but he was supposed to be the next Cat Stevens. When she rang to say he was going to open some shows for me I had an inkling that she was using the opportunity to bolster her standing with me, but as usual there was nothing behind the fake sincerity except more fake sincerity.

God help me (since I couldn't help myself), I still dreamed about her at night, imagining that pale, sleek flesh and the chic hair mussed up on a pillow next to my face. I'd written songs about her but always made them about blokes. Dressing butch was one thing, but punters' parents would have burned my records if they thought the lyrics were gay. I didn't want to limit my appeal, so I tried to channel all of my hopes and dreams into songs that kids of any sexual persuasion could wank to.

Hang on to Yourself

SUCCESS GOT EASY. Too easy. (At home, that is. My one venture to America, an expensive promo trip to play a couple of showcases for the satin jacket U.S. label gits and all the liggers they could bribe out of their hovels, was a right mess and set me back on my heels. It was clear my chances of succeeding there were between poor and none. Never went back.) Yeah, I worked my arse off, but there came to be a certainty to my popularity that should have been satisfying and ego-stroking but instead did my head in. The punters didn't care about the records — they'd been sold *me*, just like they'd been force-fed Chaz and Mud and Chicory Tip before me. It didn't much matter what I did, just that I was me. Or rather I was the character they thought I was. Which I wasn't. The game, as Frank repeatedly reminded me, was not to blow it. But who was I, exactly, and how could I accidentally become not me?

The songs spoke to them in code, the gospel of a new church, a lesson in school that they nodded at stupidly and never grasped. Peer pressure — the implacable fear of not being cool — ensured that they didn't question any of it, pretending to understand the flimsiest of ideas or the most complicated. But Frank knew, and I came to believe, that there was an invisible tripwire in the ether that, if I stumbled into, would turn them against me. I knew the more likely event was someone newer and younger would turn up to shove me aside, but he wouldn't say that. He was lying to me, or maybe to himself. I'd done it to Chaz, so there was no escaping the fact. In his telling, the only person who could darken Rockit LA's future was me.

Whether they could comprehend what — if anything of substance — was on offer had very little to do with what they signed on for. They couldn't help but embrace whatever the hit parade was offering. Love him, love her, buy this, watch that. Once the crowd could be turned in the direction of an artist, the golden path ran right up the mountain — until the unseen chasm of disaster opened and it all ended. There was no rhyme or reason to any of it. I don't reckon they sought or received any sort of enlightenment or uplift from the

45s, they just liked the sense of belonging that shared fandom conferred. You wear the badge, you belong to the tribe.

Like a TV programme everyone watches, records were a topic of schoolyard conversation, a passion play with an infinite number of lovers, delivered to the nation's children right under the noses of adults. It didn't feel like mind-control evil, just a harmless perversion of reality. But all the same. I wasn't real to them and they weren't real to me, yet we shared a bond more intense than family.

Even after I'd gotten the knack of it, I still had to wonder what songs were for. What if all the good ones had already been written? Back in the '60s, Dylan sang about the news of the day, but he stopped and thankfully no one else felt an obligation to continue the habit in the '70s. Can you just imagine? "Coal strike what's it for? / Just a bloody bore / Give miners a living wage / Or you will feel their rage." Pathetic, right?

As easy as it was to write songs, it took work to make it look that way, to make fans believe the words had just turned up on cue, all in place and clever, with tunes that dripped down from the sky. There were stars who could convey that divine self-assurance, and I envied them something fierce. When my songs were played back over those huge Tannoys in the studio, I always heard the screws coming loose, the square pegs jammed unevenly into oblong holes.

Words never quite said what I meant them to. Everyone told me they were bang on, but I never believed them. I suspected, maybe I knew deep down, that it was my problem and no one else's; sure, some swot on the *NME* might show off in a review at my expense (and a few did from time to time; it hurt a lot to be caught out when you already knew when and where you'd gone wrong), but the kids didn't know or care about perfectly resolved iambic pentameter or internal rhymes. My band, producer and manager knew better than to undermine my wobbly confidence by shooting holes in my unfilled sails, but I still didn't like being lied to. I recognized shite, and if a lot of what I was coming up was a shade or two better than complete twaddle, I could guess where Bowie or Ferry or Bolan would have made it perfect without expending a trace of visible or audible effort. For a time I believed that was what I was doing, but I lost that confidence as soon as no one dared see it otherwise. I wasn't so naïve to consider it strictly a lack of talent; it took self-confidence to bend wills, to sling a number out there that sounded like nothing that had ever come before and have people go, "Yeah, I like that," not "Ooh, that's not right, is it?"

I wanted them to hear me as if they'd created me. I wanted my music to come from my subconscious: effortlessly perfect. Otherwise, it was just graft. Homework with pay. I wanted it to be hard *and* easy, and it wasn't really either.

If it was all the same to the kids, it wasn't to me. It sucks to have people believe in you when you don't believe in yourself. And what was there left to say? Why couldn't the kids just take what they'd been left and be satisfied? Love, sex, heartbreak, jealousy, desire, frustration — yeah, so? Like there's a new idea anyone needs to hear? Bollocks. One afternoon, in the shower, a green paint chip fell from the ceiling and a month later I released a swervy little tune called "I've Got Space Junk in My Hair (how did it get there?)." Went in at number-eight and moved us all one step closer to the end of modern civilization.

I couldn't work out if I should give it my all or just what I reckoned they would want. Knowing what worked in the charts was a bit like a science experiment — you see what gets the result and then keep doing that. A song is not exactly a chemistry formula, but it does have elements that contribute different things. Like a recipe in the kitchen. Does a song need a bit more spice? Or should it be sweeter? More handclaps? I didn't have all the answers, but it was easy to use the same formula over and over: avoiding variety meant avoiding risk, at least until they go off you altogether. Then nothing you do matters. The temptation to serve crowd-pleasers night after night must be why English mums are so fond of bangers and mash. Who would turn that down? Boring, but reliable.

And while I'm having a go, y'know what else gets on my wick? Those so-called journalists — they're all twats. Stinky inky berks. You sit in a posh hotel room and they traipse in, one after another, with their stupid little tape recorders and their I'm-so-smart attitudes, and you're off to the races in a combination competition and school lesson. The same tired faces every time I put a record out, jobsworths with typewriters, I call 'em. Frank says I should be grateful they turn up, but I'd just as soon be left alone. (He imagines I really care about what I'm doing, and I know I'd be wise not to argue the point.) When they're not insulting you with their supposedly insightful observations and spiky barbs, looking to provoke an outrageous quote they can splash all over their front pages, you just answer the same idiotic questions over and over. *How did you get your name, what's the inspiration for your songs, do you reckon you're more Marc, David or Rod, what's it like to be a blah blah blah...* I might as well have some quotes printed up and handed out to save me the bother. They want me to tell them how clever they are, like making a whore come. Nah, mate. It's strictly business, and I won't give you any satisfaction. The faster you get it over with and the least I have to do, the better I like it. I can't be giving too much of myself away, and the deeper I get into this pop swamp, the more I feel like that's the only thing I have to protect. I had to laugh when one git asked me how stardom has affected my old friendships. As if I'd had any. Didn't tell him that, though. I made up some shite about keeping the ones close who'd always been there for me. I felt a little sad while I said. I wished that were true.

Barry something from *Disc and Music Echo* once asked me about the money, if I enjoyed being rich. Dunno how much I have in the till. Frank does all the deals. There was some talk of having Chives be my fiduciary guardian, but I put the kibosh on that, so Frank looks after it for me. I've got a decent flat, a roomful of clothes and a driver that gets me where I need to be. For all I know, I could be living in a land of hire purchase and they come and claim it as soon as the hits stop. If they did, I wouldn't give a toss. I started with had nothing and I've never expected anything, so nothing suits me down to the ground. Just don't try and take it away from me.

IN DECEMBER, with a new single to plug, I booked a charity show for Oxfam at Hammersmith Palais. Alice Cooper was headlining; I agreed to go on early for the sake of the younger punters who might not be able to stay late. After we played, I decided to hang out and see if the Americans were good live, maybe pick up some staging ideas. Sitting alone in my dressing room, mascara painting lines down my cheeks, I was too shagged to change into dry clothes. The room wasn't properly heated, and I worried about getting sick. And by the realization that this was as good as it would ever be, that it could all slip away and there was nothing I could do to prevent or fix it. I had started thinking again, and not for the last time, that I was crap, that what I was doing wasn't

341

good enough, not really, to bother about. The other acts we shared stages with tried harder and cared more than I ever could. I couldn't gauge talent or accomplishment, only internal drive, and mine never felt fully turned up. Maybe I couldn't gauge my failures either. The kids kept turning up and liked what I was doing well enough.

I needed a shower — I probably smelled like rotting flowers and old chip grease — but I was too knackered to get out of the chair and do anything about it. I said a silent thank you to the bloke stationed outside the door to protect my solitude and keep me from having to explain any of this to anyone. I closed my eyes for an instant and would have fallen dead asleep, or perhaps I did, when I heard the door open.

"Hello, there."

I glanced in the mirror and saw who it was. The fight or flee impulse fed a megadose of adrenaline into my veins but, as quickly as it began, my body relaxed, a flash fire faded to embers. Without turning around, I let my miserable reflection reply. I summoned up what I hoped was a wary but confident look and delivered it into the mirror, as nonchalant as I could make it.

"Wotcha, Chaz. How ya keeping?"

I imagine that was the moment I truly became a star. I didn't feel the panic of an outsider afraid of offending the establishment — I bloody well knew I had offended the establishment. I felt like I'd gone into battle against a terrible foe and emerged victorious. Maybe I was Joan of Arc before anyone lit a match, but in the rush of thoughts that blazed I saw myself as the future and him as the past, acutely aware that the one inevitably becomes the other, and that my vanquisher was out there, in a bedsit somewhere, doing maths homework and carelessly planning my obsolescence. But so what? I'd got tons more than I ever expected and discovered abilities in myself I hadn't even envisioned, so if it all goes *pffft*, who gives a toss?

I did, as it happens. I was enjoying a lot of this, hoped there might be more to come and wasn't prepared to give any of it up until it was taken away from me. Having slain Caesar I recognized how risky a spot I now inhabited, but I had never imagined feeling so protective about keeping it. But, really, what was I

342

going to do with the rest of my life once this crazy bit came crashing down? Go back to school and live with Chives, tending to his needs as he got old and feeble? Go to uni and become a teacher like them? Work things out with Eon, have a kid and move to the country? No, I wanted to hold on to what I'd got for as long as I could; at least I wouldn't have to consider the alternatives.

In retrospect, I suppose I should have been afraid. He could have locked the door and beaten me senseless if he'd been of a mind — he was a fair bit bigger than me, and not completely dissolute (although well on the way). As it happened, he wasn't there for a fight, or really much of anything. Maybe he had something in mind, but he never said. Perhaps he was facing fears of his own. I wasn't sure where his career stood at the moment, or mine neither, so maybe we were like soldiers from opposite sides meeting up after the war and making our own form of peace.

I had, at the time, no clue what he thought about me. I'd heard a few things from people, but who can tell what's real. When he was in the papers, which wasn't often, he never mentioned me. Frank had, of course, stopped working with him, and whatever he knew about Chaz wasn't shared with me. It would have been shitty to ask him, so I didn't. I'd certainly given it a lot of thought. I guess I would have like to have been forgiven, or acknowledged for what I'd done for him, but I don't think he was doing well, and I had to believe he blamed me for that.

I grabbed a towel and dried my face. Then I grabbed my leather jacket off the couch and put it on. He sat down. I offered him a beer. He lit a fag.

Stardom is like a secret society, and there's a comfort thing between those of us who've lived in the clouds. We had a pleasant enough chat about nothing. He asked after Psi, we swapped a couple of road stories — the grizzled veteran having a laugh at the naïve surprises of a neophyte — and then I sucked him off. I had a knack, Eon told me once, and I'd had a bit of practice since then. I was able to keep them on the brink for ages and then send them to the finish without warning. Chaz had a long, thin willy, and that threw me off my pace a bit. It sounds awful, I know, but it was nothing to me, a whim that — when I thought about it later — I realized I'd probably been subconsciously plotting for ages. He was less surprised than I thought he'd be, but it made sense to me after. He even thanked me — well, he did after I assured him that I wasn't aiming to trap him in a Page 3 scandal. I meant that.

I learned a few things that night. I'd never fancied the old sod, and I don't imagine he ever fancied me, but I'd always wondered where the secret to his power lay, and I came away firm in the knowledge that it weren't in his willy. Nice enough, but it wasn't the size of his spigot that made him a rock god, it was something buried much deeper, a belief in his destiny and his value that I could only glimpse at and pretend to have. I went home and wrote a song called "Chase Sin: Thin and In," a nasty bit of pop business that all but used his name. The promo film we made was as rude as the Beeb would allow; I hinted all around it on the chat shows and the single sold by the boxload. I'd wager few girls this side of Hollywood have ever gotten better value for a blowjob.

I'd like to believe I drew the last drop of spirit and desire out of him. There wasn't much left for that tosser to lose, and I took it from him. Seemed fair to me at the time. Now I'm not so sure. I've adjusted my outlook more than a little. At least I haven't been messed about by some kid with a hotshot manager gunning for the air I breathe, just a smelly parade of punks with identikit gear and songs that end before they barely begin. I do admire their bottle, they're down for anything — spit, blood, sore throats, riots — not that I can see how any of that has to do with music, but it's not for me to say.

344

Marc on Ice

MARC BOLAN'S death in 1977 hit me hard, but not for any obvious reason. We didn't know each other, although we'd been on a couple of the same TV shows and chatted once backstage somewhere. Honestly, I'd lost interest in the records he made. Whatever portrait of his fanciable pixie youth he'd stashed away in some sorcerer's attic had gone missing, and for a time there he had the overstuffed countenance and girth of a debauched 18th century royal, laced up like a roast. In his last year he'd slimmed down on a diet of humble pie and even hosted his own series on telly. He seemed to have settled into a more practical existence than the one he'd imagined for himself and then, beyond all bounds and comprehension, realized, but we should have known there would be no easy middle age for the child of Rarn, whatever that was.

It wasn't the loss of a beloved pop icon or the tragedy of a still-young man killed by the negligence of his child's mother crossing a road to greet an unsuspecting tree head on at 50 mph. I'd read that Marc never learned to drive; turns out the smallest choices we make in life can deprive us of it.

No, what connected me to Marc's demise was, of all things, my father. At my fortnightly look-in the end of that September I found him in a right state: unshaved, unkempt, wearing a bathrobe that catalogued meals, sweat and sick. An empty liter of Irish whiskey lay on the floor. I don't recall him falling apart like this when Mum died, but I was just a nipper then so maybe he did without letting me see it.

"Christ almighty, what's going on? Did someone die?" I braced for it to be Aunt Ruth. He was fond of her, I know, but I didn't expect her exit would send him into such inelegant despair.

"Yes." His manly effort to fight back tears crumbled almost immediately, reducing him to blubbering, gasping sobs. "Marc."

"Mark who?" I couldn't imagine who he was talking about. I'd once had a school friend called Mark, but that couldn't be it.

Between sobs he wiped his face with his hands. "Bolan." He pronounced it with the accent on the second syllable (see, I did pay attention in class). I'd never heard anyone call Marc Bo-*lan*, and I'm certain I'd never heard my father mention his name before.

"Yeah, so, what's that got to do with you? And with all this?" He'd apparently harbored a silent admiration for the curly haired boy, but what poured out of him like an overfilled pot of porridge on the boil was a completely daft and impenetrably complicated construction that touched on the perils of stardom, anxiety about my life, guilt about Mum, despair for his lost career, worries about his drinking, his sanity and his finances.

It was an awful lot to absorb. I felt as if I'd been standing in a quiet meadow, enjoying a mild breeze, when a hurricane blew through. At the end of it — the weeping and the shouting, the moaning and the reflection went on for an hour — I'd been carried miles away from where I'd started. He told me things I didn't know, shared concerns I had never heard and left me unsure I'd ever known him at all. Had he gone completely potty?

I took my filial responsibilities a lot more seriously after that, looking in on more frequently, and seeing my role as a caretaker of sorts. I can't say if he benefited from my attention, but I understood that he needed me, and that I couldn't just turn my back. My career wasn't going so well that it required all of my time or attention, so I had neither excuse nor impediment. I was almost grateful for the obligation, not to mention the comfort and safety — was I providing or receiving it? — of family.

Growing up under the cloud of a dead parent, I used to obsess about what I would say when my father dies. I'd make friends call me up and say, "Laila, I hate to be the one to tell you this, but your dad died" so I could get used to the idea. It freaked them out, but it pushed me to think up an answer that wouldn't sound as lame and horrible as what the seven-year-old me said to the bobby at the door — with Mum's handbag slung over his shoulder, that I still remember vividly — to enquire if a Catherine Russell lived at this address and went on say she'd got hit by a motorcycle on Old Oak Road and was in "a bad way," as he put it, down the hospital: "*Fuck me.*"

Muddy Waters

"YEAH, I'M OFF the stage for good. I don't care to live in the mud with those lizards any longer. I've found a way out. Behind the scenes, like, in the artist relations and management game." Chaz leaned in close enough that William could smell how long he'd already been in the pub.

He looked older than William had expected. They hadn't seen each other for several years; Willette's sudden illness and death forced him to leave uni; Chaz had not attended the funeral. Now he was at loose ends, rattling around alone in the great house on Hans Crescent. His father, who was living in a new flat in Belgravia with an American girl half his age, hadn't said anything about altering that arrangement.

"Sorry about your mother, son. I'm sure that was a terrible blow. You alright, then?"

"Yeah, suppose. You?"

"Well, since I patched things up with Frank, put all that bollocks behind us, we're back being a team. Just like the old days." Only now instead of taking a cut, Frank owned the commercial entity known as Chaz Bonapart Ltd., whose custom was using its namesake to lure other old-timers with marketable band associations to be set up with sidemen and sent to Europe and America on Chaz Bonapart's Rock Memories package tours for modest wages. This little scheme had not occurred to him when he set out to woo Chaz back, in fact nothing had, other than flexing a muscle to prove a point, a pyrrhic achievement with no purpose. He didn't care about Chaz any longer, he just set himself a test to see what he could with him. Once the rapprochement got under way, a thought occurred to him in time to make it the centrepiece of their peace treaty. And now he was delighted at the rewarding elegance of selling Chaz's name without the bother of selling Chaz's music. And, after all, who had more of a right to it?

"We've got a company that sets up tours of the States. Plus we've got a couple of hot artists under contract. He's handling the business and I'm the brains of the operation, picking the acts and advising them about life on the road. It's like raising a child, I tell you, I get so proud when they do good."

Stung by the rank obliviousness of that comparison, William looked up from the packet of salt-and-vinegar crisps he'd been inspecting and fixed his gaze over Chaz's shoulder.

"I'm going for a slash."

William closed the door to a stall and fumed. Could anyone be so clueless? There was no reason for him to be here. The man was never going to truly value him. His mother's encouragement now felt sour and wasted; the connection she hoped they'd have turned out to have the sticking power of piss.

Back at the table, Chaz started up again. "I went to see her once, y'know."

"Who?"

"Rockit LA. The little bint who stole my dreams."

William didn't reply. "Yeah, I turned up backstage at the Hammersmith Palais, what a pisshole, to surprise her after a gig. Turned out she needed some Chaz magic in her mouth, didn't she? I gave it to her good, just to prove that I was still the master and she's nothing but a greedy little pig. *Yeah.*"

William grimaced in disgust, not that Chaz noticed. "My acts have shows coming up — I know rock and roll is not really your thing, but it'd be nice if you'd show some support for your dear old dad — so I'll put your name on the guest list. I've got a young glam girl we're calling Faith Adams and a punk combo called Brashcan. We're going to make them the terror of England, like Screaming Lord Sutch but serious as a heart attack." Chaz laughed, more a phlegmy cough than a signal of amusement, and necked sank his pint.

"That's great. I'm sure they'll be great," William sneered. If Chaz saw the disdain, he chose to ignore it. "Christ, I'm tired," he sighed. The lines on his face had deepened, William thought, and his skin had taken on a grayish pallor. Like William, who was showing signs of premature baldness, his hair was starting to thin and he was beginning to resemble Christopher Lee, which wasn't a bad thing in and of itself, but an unfortunate development for a vain former pinup who still imagined himself young and virile.

"So, how's school?"

"I'm done with that."

"Really?"

"Yeah, I packed it in after my mother died."

"That's too bad. But it'll save me some money, I reckon."

"Is that all that matters to you? Did you talk to that professor of mine?"

"Yeah, a while back. Quite a mouth on that swot. Talked my bloody ear off."

"Thanks for that."

"Alright. So, do you think you can come to the gig? It's Thursday week."

"Not really my thing. See ya, Chaz. Look after yourself."

"Oi, lad, can't you call me dad?"

William shook his head. He stood up and left Chaz seated at the table.

White Riot

THE SUMMER of 1980 arrived like a plague. My records were no longer selling that well, and it looked as if Massive might not renew my contract when it come up in the fall. I still had deals with labels in America and Japan, and they brought in more than enough to pay the bills. Given how little decent live work I had lined up, it was hardly worth keeping the band on salary, so when a couple of them booked side gigs I told all of them, save for Psi the Clock, to fuck off. He was a great drummer, but that wasn't his real value to me: he did a lot of the stuff I was useless at, and he was as loyal as an old dog. Reliable as the sun, our Psi was. A man of his word. Plus I liked having an old-timer to talk to, to get some reasonable advice from the other side of the generation landslide. I expect a few people thought we were shagging, but it was never like that. I thought of him more like a fill-in father: a reliable, hard-working, unfucked-up version of the male parent I did have. It made going home harder, seeing what a poor excuse the real thing was, and I did it less frequently.

Frank was still technically my manager, but he and Joe were living in Venice, which left day-to-day responsibilities for me to Amanda. (He'd opened a new office in Earl's Court for his company with Chaz, but that was over and done. Although I'd initially found that move laughable, I took no pleasure in its failure.) Against all odds, she was still employed at Burgher and had even been promoted into a senior role, at which she was more or less competent. We got along alright. We weren't friends, but then we never had been.

I wish I still had Varda; but she was in Paris working as an au pair for some wealthy Russian family that could pay her a lot better than I could. I'd been through a pile of short-term boyfriends and a Swedish girl I quite fancied, but none of them were as clever or useful as I needed them to be, and none held my interest long. I tried hard, but I was never good at faking enthusiasm for very long. Shagging, at least in comparison to the idealized memory I had of my early teen grapples, became a routine bore.

In quiet hours, I wondered what had become of Eon since he'd left England.

We'd meant a lot to each other, and now we weren't even in touch. Americans, they always run home to the land of plenty, innit? He'd sent me a letter before moving back to the States, sad that we'd broken up without a proper discussion or even a row. I waited a long while but finally wrote him back at the New York address he gave me to thank him for what he'd done. I didn't try and explain what happened. What was I gonna say? Sorry, I've got more important things to do than shag you and listen to records together? As accurate a reading of my feelings at the time that may have been, I just couldn't. I told him I hoped he still loved rock and roll. His enthusiasm and knowledge that had ignited and fueled mine, and I didn't want to be the only one to stick with it.

I realized Massive was getting ready to kiss me off when they issued a £1.99 greatest hits LP. The cover was hideous, worse than a *Top of the Pops* package. Things got worse when the chap who handled my A&R hemmed and hawed about "having to fight" for a recording budget. My chances of making a new album, at least for Massive, were small. That was probably just as well: the last thing I needed was to dip a stick all the way down my creative well and find out just how shallow the waters were. I was so skint for ideas that I genuinely considered — just for a minute, mind — making a song out of something a widely loved telly actor I'd dated, who was in fact a miserable shit, said in the middle of a row about his ineffectual performance in bed. "How much effort d'ya expect me to put into it, mate? It's just a fucking hole." Yeah, that'd make a hell of a 45.

The excitement that punk had injected in 1977 was all gone. The spark of rebellion had lit a roman candle, sending bright plumes out in a hundred random directions. I watched jealously from a distance as my contemporaries, all of whom were five (if not fifteen) years older than me, either worked out a stylistic accommodation that kept them in the game without pretending to be something they were clearly not, or failed miserably and squandered their last farthing of credibility by attempting a transformation that was simply beyond their ken. I didn't want to follow them down the bog, so I waited it out, saying no to everything. But then that started to feel like failure. I flipped the switch and started taking every offer that came my way, even free festivals and the like. Speaking like a proper businesswoman, Amanda argued against it for a while (there was nothing in it for her) but then stopped objecting.

Still, it was over the threat of Amanda's dead body (that's how she put it, declining to arrange or attend; Psi sorted it instead) that I agreed to play one of the first Rock Against Thatcher rallies at The Hatrium in Islington. November in London — a fine time for an outdoor gig. Solo acoustic. And at what turned out to be a parade of Oi! bands with me as the token representative of fuck knows what. Was I already a symbol of the past? A de-electrified old fart at twenty-three? The lamb in a wolfen slaughterhouse of mohawks, studs and leather? I was for the cause and all, but still. And, Jesus, the music was god-awful. One outfit's clamor left such an impression that I always thought of them — and every other useless band I happened upon (and I happened upon plenty) — as the Miserable Dipshits.

There was no dressing room as such, just a fenced-off area behind where the PA was stacked up. I'd decided not to bother with makeup or my usual kit so I had nothing to do except tune up, read a book and wait to go on. The sun had set, and they were running well behind schedule, as per usual at these things. One more band to go, then I was on. I hoped the stage was high enough to keep the gob from reaching me. The threat of catching hepatitis haunted the dreams of everyone who toured England in those days.

"Ladies and gentlemen, we've just got a couple more bands. Thanks so much for coming out to support R-A-T today." I could hear amps being switched on and the vicious buzzblast of guitars being plugged in.

"Check, check. Eins, zwei, *drei.*"

"Alright, everyone. Put your hands together for RipdNerv." A mild roar went up. I went back to reading *Valley of the Dolls* as the sound of an amplified chainsaw revved in the air. A few pages later, between songs (I suppose they could have been tuning, but why bother?), there was another roar, this one louder, more ferocious. I went out to where I could see, and what I could see was total bedlam.

An armed mob was pouring into the venue. The marauders set upon the audience, beating and kicking kids, who were caught totally unawares. I looked at the stage to see why the band hadn't stopped playing and got the shock of my life. They were neither addressing the violence nor unaware of it — the singer was egging it on, making punching and kicking gestures.

352

But that wasn't the worst of it. I knew the fucker: it was the dog-beater I'd tangled with in Soho all those years ago. As I felt my guts spin, he looked over and pointed a finger directly at me. He waved the musicians to stop playing and leaned into the mic, still staring in my direction, as if no one else were present. The fighting down front stopped, as if a director had yelled "cut." It was almost comical. Out of the corner of my eye, I could see hundreds of faces in rapt attention. "You see this?" He waved grandly at the crowd and then turned back to face me. "I made this. It's all mine." As the audience followed his gaze it hit me that being the centre of attention could be the worst, not the best, feeling in the world. Over an evil grin he kept staring and pointing at me. "And so are you, right. It's time for a reckoning, little lady." He shoved the mic stand off the stage and then jumped down after it. I lost sight of him in the crowd and froze; a second later, reason kicked in and I legged it for the car as fast as I could. So much for my lovely Martin back in the waiting area; this was life or death: I didn't have to turn around to know he was after me.

Psi, who had the keys, was nowhere to be seen, so I ran to the high street and luckily found a taxi. As we pulled away, I turned around to see that bastard through the rear window, his face a ball of fury, two fingers up and a fat chain in the other hand. I could barely breathe until we were well away.

The Nine O'Clock News had a report on the rioting, which police suspected was the work of the National Front, duffing up protestors and concertgoers to discourage attendance at future events. That was probably true, but there was something about the way RipdNerv acted that felt planned out, like there was some connection between the band and the marauders. In replaying the day's events as I struggled to fall asleep, it seemed pretty clear that the singer knew it was me that night in Soho. Can't imagine how. I was nobody then and it was not like I introduced myself to him. I'd need to get on to the police about this, but I didn't really expect they'd care about a pop star who thinks the singer in another band intends and threatened GBH.

In the morning, Amanda was a smug told-you-so at my description of the fiasco, noting wryly, "It's not as if you were getting paid in the first place." She laughed off my worries about the singer, suggesting that it was a case of runaway ego, imagining that he was after me. I didn't need to add this to Dad's worries, so I rang the only person I could think of, Barry Wilson, the bloke who'd written about me in *Disc*, to see if he knew anything about RipdNerv.

He sounded shocked to hear from me and wasn't familiar with the name but promised to ask around. I gave him the office number and Amanda's name and told him to leave word when there was reason for me to ring him.

A couple of weeks later we met up in Ye Olde Cheshire Cheese in Fleet Street. Quite a place it was, cool and dark, a musty reliquary of history and ink, the site no doubt of countless scoops and scandals. Barry said he picked it because the sight of a recognizable pop musician talking to a journalist wouldn't raise any curiosity there. I didn't tell anyone I was going.

"I'm really surprised you called me. I didn't think we got on that well the first time. And that was ages ago."

"Yeah, well, water under the bridge, that's all it is. What did you find out?"

"A lot, as it happens. Their records are standard ramalama dole queue bollocks. A bit like Crass, I suppose, but harsher. And their politics are rubbish. Down with this, up with that. Nothing we haven't heard before. Singles on a couple of indie labels. No LP yet."

"I don't give a toss about their music. What else?"

"Rough trade, that lot. They're all ex-cons, real hard skins, not the playacting dress-up kind from art school. The main guy is an especially nasty piece of work. He calls himself Death."

"Yeah, I know."

"So why do you care? Not exactly your thing, I shouldn't think. And I wouldn't recommend them as a support act unless you're looking to get yourself banned from every venue in Britain."

I hadn't explained anything, and I guess he didn't know about their part in the Rock Against Thatcher free fest. The papers all had reports that were factually incorrect to some extent. My name barely came up in any of them other than one that called me a no-show. How about an almost-got-herself-killed-trying-to-do-a-good-deed?

"No, it's nothing like that. I once had a run-in with the singer, and I think he might have a grudge against me. I'd like to keep clear of 'im."

"I can well imagine."

"Yeah. The last thing I need in my life is some mad nutter with a prison record and a bunch of thugs in tow keen to settle some imagined score."

"Rilly…"

"Do you think you could do something for me?" I tried to do one of those ingratiating smiles I'd seen Amanda flash a hundred times, but I'm shit at it.

"Depends. I'm not really supposed to be getting in bed," — I shot him a look and he laughed — "so to speak, with the artists I write about, but I'm not averse to a little mutual backscratching."

I was in no mood to dicker. "No terms, no backscratching. I just need a favour. If you won't do it, I'll find someone who will."

Perhaps he liked the idea of my being in his debt; he capitulated without further debate. "OK, sure. Tell me what you need. If I can, I will."

"Can you interview them and see how serious he is? About me."

"Ooh, sounds grim, but I expect I could sell my editor on the idea. A punk out of time, or some such shite. Alright, I'll see what I can do."

"But keep my name out of it. I don't want you sending him my way by mistake."

"Rilly."

"How soon do you think you can sort that? Another round?"

"I'll do what I can. Ta."

Barry rang maybe a month later to say he'd not been able to get hold of anyone from or around RipdNerv. "It's as if they've vanished off the face of the Earth. Nothing in the gig guides. The press officer at the label that put out their last record says they don't have a phone. If they've got any money due, I doubt they'll see it any time soon. I got on to Bushell and friends of mine who follow Oi! and while they've heard of the band no one has a number or an address. I guess whatever bit of action they had going, it's over and done. Perhaps they're all in prison. Or in America. I'm sure they'd go down a storm there. I mean, Christ, even the bloody UK Subs get work in the colonies."

"What if they just changed their name? Become, I dunno, Funky Bulldog?"

"That would be a crap name. RipdNerv at least conveys a vibe."

"That's not my point."

"Sorry. I suppose you're right, they may've done, but then we're even less likely to find them."

I headed home even more wound up than I'd been. It's like when a scary noise wakes you up. Just because it stops doesn't mean whatever made it is gone.

The Tree of Death

I DON'T RECALL what led me to go look at the tree. Or why I thought it would be a good idea to bring my dad along. I knew he needed my help (not that he would ever get around to asking for it), but no idea what I could do. One brief bout of dutiful daughterdom ended when he had a go at my "unwise choices." We rowed and I stayed away for a good while. I felt bad, but I was too wrapped up in my own life to make the needed effort to get past the aggravation.

Losing perspective on my life cost me a realistic sense of his as well. I can't imagine how hard it must have been to have your wonderful young wife killed, leaving you to raise a weird, unhappy kid alone. And then for her to become an overnight superstar while your life stumbles along in a haze of depression and medication and drink. That would've done my head in as well. But I managed to save myself, so why couldn't he? My thoughts about him always seesawed between resentment and guilt.

So while I was busy being useless as a daughter, I took a notion, as the fourth anniversary of Bolan's death neared, that we should pay a visit to the site of his demise. Maybe it was just a way to break the ice and get to talking again. We hadn't so much as mentioned Marc's death since 1977, and I never did understand why it was so important to him. Or me. I'm not one for churches, monuments or shrines. No religion or spiritual mumbo jumbo — if I can't see it or smell it or hear it, you won't find me taking it seriously. Real life was real enough. Yeah, rock and roll is all exaggerated bollocks, but there are living, breathing people making it. Even if the surface is all jumped-up illusion, there's got to be something of real substance in there. There was nothing to learn from a damaged tree beyond what I, and millions of others, already knew. Visiting the scene of a tragedy was not high on my list of fun things to do.

We fixed it for a Sunday in September. I collected him in a motor that belonged to a mate. Mine was having its brakes seen to, and I saw no reason to tempt fate in Barnes with the chance of a fatal repeat performance. He came to the door looking a bit rough, unshaved in a frayed jacket and ancient NHS specs. I was surprised at how much older he seemed, like his pages were turning faster than the calendar. He smiled when I called him Chives; no one else knew him by that name any longer.

Still, I was a bit surprised how good it was to see him. While I often thought of him only as a reminder of what I'd had to survive as a kid, in the flesh he was the last connection I had to my childhood and Mum. Looking at him, even the sorry sight that he was, hit me like a brick: I was six again and we were a regular little family, full of hope and completely blind to the calamity awaiting us.

He didn't ask why we were going; I didn't offer one. Not that I could've; I didn't know myself. I knew what had happened: the terrible newspaper reports were hard to forget. I didn't expect to learn anything, and the day out meant blowing off a rehearsal that we sorely needed for an Irish tour. I should have been working, not wasting time on a silly pilgrimage. But there I was on a gloomy afternoon, sniffling from an incipient cold, stood with my dad and a pair of sobbing Japanese girls before a solid sycamore with a large shoulder-high dent. It was an ugly affront to nature, a sad souvenir of waste.

What did I want from the tree? That's a tough one. Maybe my subconscious sensed some residue I could absorb, a vibration from the past. Maybe I just wanted to feel scorn for the supposedly divine. Really, though, it was just hard to accept that an idol of millions, whose fanciful utterances once altered the course of countless lives, could be erased as if he'd never existed.

By a tree.

I felt bad for the tree. It had survived and was carrying on, sapped but unbroken. It's a shame trees can't express themselves — *The Sun* would have gotten quite a story from the one that killed Marc.

Right, so I was having a kip as I usually do that time of night, and out of nowhere this bleedin' motor bangs right into me — just about here." (A branch waves down to point at the middle of the bare trunk.) "Of all the trees in the forest, as my mate likes to say, I had to be the one she found. It hurt like the devil. I lost loads of sap. It took the emergency lads forever to pull the bleeding fender off me. I'm just lucky there wasn't a conflagration. Would have done me right in. I guess I was tougher than 'im. Cor, I never want to go through that again.

Nature put that guileless tree there ages before Mark Feld appeared on Earth, long before his purple Mini, a modest motor for a most immodest man, flew out of the night, its driver overly oiled from celebration or just too full of life's wonder to follow the road carefully. We walked back past Gipsy Lane, a name that might have amused Bolan were he looking out the window when Gloria swerved to the left. A bit winding, perhaps, it didn't look dangerous. Countless people in every possible state of mind and sobriety had managed it without incident. Not Marc's missus. She slipped up and lost her man for it. And fans lost their faded star. But blaming Gloria wasn't the point. She loved Marc. She was raising his son. Love doesn't save people. It didn't save Mum.

A passing Cortina beeped at us, either in fan solidarity or at having to navigate around gits in the road. I put up two fingers for the benefit of his rearview and returned to my pondering. Chives chuckled at my cheek. I guess my adulthood had never fully registered on him; what a grown-up woman might say or do was probably still filtered through the little girl he had fixed in his memory.

Chives didn't say anything the whole time we were there; I suspect he was giving me room, or maybe he just didn't give a toss and was too polite to be impatient about getting home. I suggested lunch so's we'd have a proper chance to talk. It looked like he could use a proper meal.

Lunch was alright. We talked, but it was awkward, a clumsy dance around any matters of consequence. I reassured him that I was doing alright, surviving the ups and downs of my career. I lied and said I had a steady boyfriend. Dads like to know that male responsibility for their daughters has been handed off to a decent bloke. I asked how he felt about the tree, but his interest in Bolan seemed to have dropped off the chart; so much for the staying power of pop. He swore that everything was fine with him.

A couple of times, when he asked me a question about this or that, I slipped into interview mode, and spouted some rubbish I'd probably said a dozen times in *Smash Hits*. It's impossible to tell what people want from you, especially when they don't really want anything at all. People like me, we build a shell to protect ourselves from the constant onslaught, like one of them *Star Trek* proton shields, but it can't be shut down with an order from the bridge. I felt bad about it; he didn't deserve to be talked to like that. He'd changed my nappies, after all, not drunk my champagne.

He didn't eat much of the steak and chips he ordered. I had a salad. When his food had gone cold, I stood up, threw a tenner on the table and said, "Right, I'll get you home." He was startled but didn't protest. When he asked the waiter to pack his dinner for takeaway, I wondered if he was skint or just too lazy to cook. I flashed on a vision of him as an old-age pensioner, living out his days in some awful doss-house, asking to be wheeled to the loo. I swore not to let that happen to him. He didn't have anyone else, and I was still in a position — if I didn't piss the rest of what I had away — to provide for him. I saw him slip a knife and fork from the table into his coat pocket; rather than say anything, I left an extra fiver to cover it.

We rode back to Milton Road in silence. The traffic was bad; Chives dozed off for a bit but was awake when I parked. "Looks like you have an admirer, Laila." I looked past him into the rainy twilight but didn't see anyone.

"What are you on about, dad?" I hoped that came out kindly, not sharp.

He squinted out his side and then turned back to me and smiled. "They come by from time to time, especially the Orientals, stand outside and take snaps. I just stay in the house and don't answer the door. There was a young chap hanging about last week — he followed me to the off-licence at the top of the road, said he was a fan of yours. He looked all right, but I told him to piss off, and that was that."

"Well, thanks for that. And sorry for the bother."

"I'm really proud of you and all, but I have to admit it can get to be a right nuisance."

"Do you want to see about moving house?"

"No, it's alright. I live a quiet enough life. I don't need to escape further into the void. At least not until it's my time." I studied his face to make sure he was at least half-joking, that he had no more expectation of dying in the near future than I did of buying him a new flat. I should have done that when I could have afforded it.

He got out of the car and came around to my side. I rolled down the window. "Do you want to come in for a cuppa, luv?"

"No, I've got to get back. Things to do an' all. Thanks for coming out. It was really nice to see you." I meant that, but it probably didn't sound like I did. Stardom can screw you up in so many ways.

"Alright, Laila. Keep me in your heart. See you soon. Be well, alright?"

I nodded and sneezed. The head cold which had been threatening all week was roaring into action. A chill shuddered through me. I started the engine and put up the window. The heater started pumping out nice warm air. Dad was putting the key in the lock when the windscreen exploded in my face.

Take Me Down to Hospital

ALTHOUGH I could grasp where I was, I had no idea how I'd got there. My memory of the experience was (and remains) a blurry mess, probably due to the concussion and all. I read about it in the papers and spoke at length about it with D.C. something or other, but as for actual recollections of my own, well, no, not really.

What I came to understand is that instead of what I was going to do — that is, drive away feeling awful about my sad dad — what I got was a huge gash on my face, glass in my eye, a brick in my lap and blood fucking everywhere. I guess the impact knocked me sideways, into the gearshift, which is apparently how I broke two ribs and collapsed a lung. Somewhere between the uncomprehending shock of terror and the unadulterated pain, I managed to pull myself back up, open the passenger door and fall onto the roadway, where a car came to a stop maybe ten feet short of running me over. I must've passed out at that point. Two days later, I came to, surrounded by more blinking and bleeping devices than any studio I'd ever been in.

Crazed Fan Killed by Star's Lion-Hearted Dad

By Derek Clarke

(September 23, LONDON) As hundreds of supporters stood vigil outside Hammersmith Hospital, Scotland Yard today released details of its investigation into the violent assault on a pop singer in East Acton Sunday evening. Laila Russell, 23, who is better known as Rockit LA, was parked in a borrowed Citroen in front of her father's house on Milton Road when she was attacked with a brick and seriously injured. She remains in hospital with broken bones, serious facial wounds and a concussion. Doctors are pessimistic about the chances of saving her right eye.

362

"We're ever so worried about her," said Bonnie Buckworth, 19, of Sussex, holding aloft a pink scarf bearing the singer's name. "My mates and I got here as soon as we heard and we're not leaving until we know she's alright. She's so awesome and we all used to totally love her records. We want her to know we're here for her."

The attacker, 28-year-old William Poole, suffered a fatal stab wound to the neck. He was declared dead upon arrival at London Bridge Hospital. D.C. Jack Lancaster said the motive for the attack, and the circumstances of his death, are still being investigated.

Cliff Russell, 48, the singer's father, was arrested without a struggle by officers of the Met at the scene. In a court proceeding yesterday, he was charged with voluntary manslaughter with provocation and remanded to HMS Prison Belmarsh in Thamesmead. According to a neighbor who was questioned, he stabbed Poole with a steak knife after seeing his daughter attacked.

Poole, a college leaver and resident of London, was the son of Arthur Trundle, who was a popular singer known as Chaz Bonapart in the 1970s. According to sources, he had some role in Laila Russell's early career. Authorities are pursuing enquiries to determine if either he or his late son had a personal relationship with either Russell. Poole's mother, who was never married to Trundle, is deceased.

The accused is due in court Monday.

When the pain and drugs allowed it, I thought a lot about my dad. I didn't in a million years imagine he'd have it in him to stab anyone, but there you go. I was desperate to speak with him. I did hear from Aunt Ruth after she visited him in nick. She said he was under suicide watch, and I suppose they might have been right to do that. He wasn't exactly celebrating life before any of this. Me, I could have used any form of escape. My body was a mess of sutures and plasters and drips and painkillers that didn't much help. And one working eye.

The other one was covered by layers of gauze. The doctors offered a lot of unreassuring "everything will be alright"s and "awaiting a specialist's opinion"s when I asked; I was pretty sure things were worse than they were letting on.

The occasional chant of my name from punters gathered outside didn't make me feel any better. Neither did the daily visit from D.C. Lancaster, an insistent bastard who I wasn't very nice to. First, we got the ownership of the borrowed motor sorted out — no, I was not driving a stolen car. Then I told him what I could about the times I'd met William and what I cared to share about Chaz. Finally, he started updating me on his investigation.

Chaz's weird son had been both the attacker and the victim; I hadn't seen any of it. I expected it would have been that mad fucker from RipdNerv. I'd been wary, maybe even a bit paranoid, the whole time since that Rock Against Thatcher thing, but there was no evidence he'd gone any further with it. It seemed an awful long time to bear a grudge, but I've met and talked to a couple of those hard cunts, and some of them are so bloody-minded they're like steamrollers, going through life in a straight line without a second thought until something bigger blocks their path.

But it wasn't Death that almost killed me. It was a uni swot with earmuffs. I never thought that kid had anything against me, or that he was the type to throw a brick. Maybe he was doing the business for Chaz. Well, it hadn't worked out too well, had it? I'd have to ask Frank what he could tell me about any of this. I wondered how Chaz — and William's mum, who'd been so nice to me once — were coping.

When I was well enough to hear it, D.C. Lancaster gave me his rundown of the case. Reading from a small notepad, he said, "After the object was thrown at your vehicle" — "*into* the vehicle," I corrected — "Mr Russell (your father) rushed from his door to your aid. That's according to several of his neighbors, who said they witnessed both attacks. Mr Russell said, under oath, that he was afraid the thrown brick was not the final part of Mr Poole's plan of attack, which Mr Russell attempted to prevent him from carrying out and causing the victim (you) any additional injury by tackling him to the ground. Mr Russell and Mr Poole then engaged in what one witness described as 'a right punch-up.' Mr Russell said that Poole was a strong fighter and overpowered him. At one point, Mr Russell said, he was pinned down and, fearing grievous bodily harm at Mr Poole's hands, produced a steak knife and stabbed Mr Poole in the neck, severing his carotid artery. Despite the swift arrival of medical personnel, Mr Poole was declared dead in transit."

He looked up. "Do you have any idea why your father might have been carrying a steak knife?"

I had to think for a bit — my head was still a cloud of confusion — but then the penny dropped. I explained about the meal and said they should have found a steak in a takeaway container to go with said knife.

I liked thinking of Chives as a tough nut ready to fight and kill to save me; it was a far sight better than a depressed loser still mourning for his dead wife. I couldn't say I wasn't surprised, though. Good on you, Dad. Coming through when all the chips are down.

I did a lot of thinking about death in hospital. As doctors poked and prodded (finally admitting that my eye was irreparably damaged), I contemplated how close I, and Chives, had come to being dead. Sobering, that.

Between the drugs and the boredom, I slept enough to be a cat. I dreamed a lot, too. The pharmaceuticals they were feeding me must have played a part, but I had the same weird dream every night. I'm not too certain about anything that went on that week, so maybe I imagined the whole bloody thing.

I'm in the motor, there's blood and glass everywhere, only I'm not me. I'm Marc. And I'm not thinking about me, I'm thinking about his life. In my head I'm boogieing at the Rainbow, mincing on *Top of the Pops*. Then I'm in the bath and I've got chest hair. Then I'm putting on silver loon pants and a feather boa. I've got to shove my cock down one leg. I'm at a posh restaurant and Cathy McGowan is asking me for career advice. I'm on a plane, flying to America, with Mickey Finn, who wants to see the Grand Canyon before he dies. Yeah, all of that. Then I'm back in the motor, and Gloria's next to me, bloody but not badly hurt, and I'm dying and she's apologizing and begging me not to go. And I look ahead at the tree through our smashed windscreen and wonder what it's called and if it's in pain. Ringo is speaking about me at my funeral. Then I wake up. I've never fancied myself a patch on Bolan or even been that devoted a fan, more of an admirer, so I have no idea what that dream is about. But I'll tell you this — I have never forgotten it, not a millisecond of it. It's like a guilty memory, as if I'd been there and caused the crash.

Frank came over from Italy to visit me in hospital. "Getting on the Johnny Kidd bandwagon, are we?" I had no idea what he meant and didn't care to enquire. (I later found out about the "Shakin' All Over" geezer and his eye patch, so, yeah, haha. *You* try losing an eye and then tell me if that's funny, mate.) In any event, he was quite unbothered when I told him I was packing it in; I don't reckon he's made any serious coin off my back in a couple of years, so it's probably one less thing to think about, if he had been doing any thinking whatever about me. Amanda wouldn't give a toss, that was certain.

Frank ducked and dived when I asked if he had any theories about why William would want to have a go at me. He started to say he wondered if Chaz...but stopped himself and I couldn't prize anything further out of him on the subject. Maybe I should put DC Lancaster on his trail — see how he likes that.

I conjured up crazy theories, none of which had any basis in fact. It was a bit like songwriting. If I'd been a character in some crap Jackie Collins novel, I could imagine that Chaz put him up to it out of some convoluted revenge plot. I don't think that wally ever forgave me for being young.

I pondered why that daft cunt had chosen that day and Dad's house for an ambush. What was the plan? A smash and run so he could tell his mates he'd duffed up a pop star? No one would believe that. So what was it about?

I paid a top solicitor a king's ransom to get Chives' legal matter sorted — the Crown Prosecutor closed the case with no charges being pressed. D.C Lancaster's final report made a compelling argument for his innocence, but it still cost me £3,000 to have it explained to them. You do what you have to, and he was free to get on with his life, such as it was. He seemed a lot older and a lot smaller when he got out. I think he lost a stone in nick.

I HOLED UP IN my flat with a lot of nothing to do. In time, I came to peace with the one-eye thing, at least in theory. It was a nuisance that I couldn't gauge distance accurately and had to relinquish my driving licence. That was fine, I had no desire to get behind a wheel ever again. Also, I had to turn my head to see things off to the right side, which was a nuisance and looked even more ridiculous than the patch.

I'm through with the pop racket. I was getting to that point anyway, and it was only a giggle when I started. I let the rocket ride get to me. I never wanted anything I felt worth protecting; I should never have taken it so seriously. It nearly got me killed, and it's just not worth it. When you focus on chart positions and press cuttings and radio play and ticket sales you can avoid facing the reality of who you are as a person. You just keep running the race that has no finish line. You never take proper vacations, like the postman or the miner, you just keep running on that wheel, trying to make it keep going faster so you can feel special for being allowed on it. Regular life is for losers. That's a funny way to look at thing, innit?

I was haunted by the desperation in those faces staring up at me. I didn't want that responsibility: you don't know how hollow you can feel until people expect you to give them something you know you don't have. It's like getting on a bus without a copper in your pocket — you're sure to get found out. It was alright when it was just for fun, a rush to be in the lights, with this massive sound system and a band that knew its job and could read your mind as well. A huge turbine, and all you had to do was turn your small wheel and magic happened, miles bigger than anything you could do on your own. Yeah, that was cool, but they didn't understand that it wasn't anything more than entertainment, a way to burn off the excess energy of youth. Not the meaning of life, not the word from the mount, not the missing element. I knew that feeling, of needing to jump and down, to snog and shag and break things just because you couldn't sit still. Who has the patience to read a book or sit through a class? We the dynamite their fuses set off, but that wasn't enough for them.

I had a chat once with an older guy whose band opened one of my tours. He was the brains of the group, and he had a theory about us and them. He reckoned bands became their world, replacing parents, government, school, jobs, all of it. They looked at us and they saw themselves, not as rock stars but as kids in charge, unchallenged by authority and drunk on our own freedom. If we could do it, so could they. A few probably started bands when the new wave thing happened, but that wasn't on for the rest of them. When they raised their hands and screamed for us it was as if they were trying to cross into another dimension, one where they'd be strong and unafraid and free. What they wanted didn't really exist, and we couldn't give it to them. Our job was to sell records, tickets and T-shirts and then piss off back to wherever we felt safe. Knowing what we did, we couldn't believe in them the way they believed in us. I always felt shitty about that. Not that it had to be a two-way street, exactly, but you have to be a right twat to be able to shrug off the guilt that comes with being a phony. I tried to make it worth their while, give 'em a good show, hang around afterwards and sign what they wanted, pose for snaps, all that rot, but I always had the sense we were talking different languages. All packed into the same hot dressing room, we were still inhabiting different planes. They stole my stuff, pulled on my hair, chased my car and even came by the house from time to time, but that wasn't the real bother, it was knowing that they saw me in a way I could never see myself. They couldn't solve my problems any more than the booze, the drugs or a warm body in bed could. You want to show me how much you love me? Bring my poor mother back to life. Can you do that for me? I'd really appreciate that, a lot more than a cake with my face on it, or a banner that had my name in glitter. Honestly, mate, you can keep all that. I really don't need it.

It's crap being used as an escape; I didn't realize that singing about being young and dumb signed me up to service as an addiction, a human drug for people too weak or sad to believe in themselves. It took me years to learn how to look after myself — what the fuck can I do for them? Learn how to fight, or cook, or teach. Do a kindness for somebody or find the bottle to batter an evil cunt, that'll ready you for life a lot better than knowing the chorus of some stupid song. Not that I'm recommending violence, mind, I'm not. The world won't survive if everyone is killing each other.

On top of it all, I had to live with the knowledge that some, if not all, of the spotty boys gawping at me onstage had got off looking at, listening to or otherwise thinking about me. An escape of sorts for them, perhaps, but what a disgusting thought. I don't mean to sound smug — trust me, I'd be a lot happier if I were dead certain it never happened — because it's not at all flattering the way you might imagine. Made me feel all sticky and dirty, if you must know. When I looked at myself starkers in the mirror I didn't think, "Ooh, I fancy a go at that, even if I never will have the chance in real life, so I'll find some of Mum's body lotion and see how proudly I can besmirch a tea towel."

The idea of all that splodge being spilled for me eventually put me off wanking for good. It was easy to get laid, but that wasn't the reason I stopped. I felt more grown up by putting self-love in the rearview. In a way, it allowed me to feel separate from the kids, superior, even. I know that doesn't really make any sense, but there you have it. A proud non-wanker since 1982. Whoopteedee!

That just left the rest of my life to work out and get on with. I was not quite twenty-four, happily single, not exactly skint but far from set for life, with a sad homicidal dad, a career in the crapper and not much else going on to keep me busy. Unless there's a dread disease lurking or someone else out there aiming to have a go at me, I've got a long time to live and no clue how to do it.

Look Wot You Dun

THE RED LIGHT on the television camera glowed on. The host — young, blonde, thin as a rail — lit up as well, sending a generous smile at her studio audience.

"Good afternoon ladies and gents, I'm Nina Whelan and this, of course, is *Wailin' With Whelan*. Our first guest today has been writing and talking about the battle of the sexes for, well, not as long as it's been going on, but a lot longer than I've been in the game." She laughed pleasantly.

"Please join me in welcoming the chairman emeritus of the Institute of Gender Research, Mr John Sneed."

The applause, geed up by a manic production assistant, died away quickly, an appraisal that registered on her face as she greeted the middle-aged gent settling into the seat facing her.

"Good afternoon, sir. And how are you today?"

"Fine, thanks. Y'know, Nina, I'm not so old as you made me out to be there. Haha. But no matter, I'm delighted to be on your programme. Hopefully I can shed a bit of light on the different ways men and women see things."

"Based on the column of yours I read in the Sunday *Observer*, I rather doubt it, but I will press on all the same."

The studio audience tittered at the first appearance of a characteristic barb, the consistency of which had led one wag in the *Times* to dub the show *Whelan's Right Cheek*.

"Right, as I understand it, Johnny, you have a theory of some sort."

He frowned at being called that but pressed on. "Quite. See, here's the main thing women don't understand: for a man, each woman he encounters stands in for all women — the ones who rejected him, the ones he lusted after, every shag he's ever had, all the soft flesh he's dreamed of under a waitress or a nurse's uniform, the ones who broke his heart, every movie star he imagines meeting, the one who held him close. His mum. All of it."

"So you're saying we're utterly interchangeable to you lot?"

He laughed nervously. "No, it's not at all like that. I'd say it's more of a symbolic matter. Identity and species, say. Like each dog is different, right, but they're all dogs, right?"

"Now you're comparing women to dogs?" On cue, the audience booed loudly.

"No, that's not my point at all. What I mean is that when you see a dog, any sort, it can make you think of that little fella you had as a boy."

Nina smirked. "I think we can agree that I was never a boy." The audience whooped its approval as she threw back her shoulders for a provocative visual affirmation of that fact.

"You see, that's what I mean," Sneed stuttered. "Your, erm, your —" he aimed a finger timidly in the direction of her bosom — "make men think of —"

Nina cut him off. "...tits? How surprising." A few members of the audience gasped. "You mean to say that you're currently off in a reverie about suckling at your mother's breast a century ago because I also possess mammary glands? Well, I think we've heard about enough. Thank you for...actually, I don't quite know what to thank you for. Perhaps I'll just leave you with the observation that while I also possess an arse, you, sir, are one." The audience exploded in raucous applause as the red-faced buffoon slinked off the set. In the control room, the director stared at the clipboard clutched in his hand, up at the clock on the wall, then back at the clipboard, shaking his head in resignation. At this rate, she'd have at least four minutes at the end to fill, and there was no telling how she might choose to do that.

Nina stood up and curtsied with mock graciousness, then returned to her seat and hushed the crowd. "Now that he's out of the way, let's bring out somebody really cool, someone I'm sure you're just as excited to meet as I am." The audience applauded expectantly.

"You may remember hits like 'Give a Toss (I Don't),' 'Don't Be Daft' and 'B2U,' which was code for a phrase we're still not supposed to say on telly — bollocks to that, I say. Haha! Maybe they weren't big hits, but all the same, we knew them and loved them. Our next guest was a genuine pop pioneer, a woman who let the world know that the men do not have a monopoly on rock and roll. Let's watch this before we sit down and talk to...the one and only Rockit LA!"

Whelan glanced at the suggested questions in her lap and sighed. Has-beens were more fun than up-and-comers: they had better war stories and could drop bigger names. Maybe this one had balled Jagger or Hendrix. Their inevitable resentment and bitterness could be a drag, but then baby bands all said the same dumb shit, and they all believed they were the first to ever think or say it. Unbeknownst to them, they all lived out the same script, which each thought had been written for them.

OcX-RcK, a regional wing of a large TV network, had a small budget and few of the resources of the mothership. What they did have was limited access to London broadcast facilities, which meant better-looking productions and, more importantly, a leg up on attracting national celebrities their local competitors could not. Whelan saw opportunity in the operation, inferior though it might be, and was determined to make the best of it. She liked the work: stars, no matter who, were always good fodder on which to practice and demonstrate her gift for witty snark. She was glad for the job, certain it would lead to bigger and better things and cocky enough not to take any of it too seriously. Idiots could ask the obvious questions; she believed in her ability to connect with characters, not CVs. Like many in her line, she was adept at faking sincerity and make-believe familiarity.

The montage began with a title card "Teenage Rebel of the Week" and then trotted out the usual parade of newspaper cuttings, magazine covers, single sleeves, press photos, TV clips and the usual assortment of wags from the rock press and academia, offering conventional half-truths about rock, women and the rest of it, all set to a mix of hits.

Watching backstage, Laila squinted her good eye at shots from a gig — it was probably not even one of hers — of kids dressed to the nines in colorful '70s style. There was a poster for the *Fan-Tastic Back to School* tour, the long one in '74 that made her a household name in the UK, and an antic *Whistle Test* performance of "I've Got Space Junk in My Hair (how did it get there?)."

As if she'd been brainwashed and fed a subliminal cue, she felt herself falling through a time tunnel, awash in memories of the life she'd left behind. The figure on the screen was her, but — beyond the inescapable physical reality it being her body — it was also not her. There had been a time before, a time she could barely summon from memory, nagging from far away. The shy teenager with the useless dad who accidentally stumbled into the world of pop — it wasn't vivid, but it was still solidly impressed in her mind.

The live footage was decent; she studied her face in close-up, trying to work out when and how a simple London girl had become that exalted character in the spotlight. Bits and bobs rushed through her mind, a personal documentary running parallel to the one being seen by an audience of, what, thousands? Gigs, studios, parties, planes, motorways, restaurants — all the clichés. She felt, more than visualized, the rest of it, the solitude, the frustrations, the crushing isolation that came with being "known and loved" by millions.

Maybe that was the moment it turned for her, from playing a game with no consequences to discovering the cage she'd built for herself and only partly escaped from. It didn't take long, once the shock of the new had worn off, to realize that being trapped by fame wasn't the problem so much as its symptom, the byproduct of a cataclysmic personality split which hit her without warning. She knew who she was when she was alone in a hotel room but, in the presence of fans, their imagination bled onto her, mixing her reality with their illusions. Their expectations of her could be met, she knew, but it took effort; she felt like an actor in a play with a curtain that went up a hundred times a day. She could never know for certain when she was truly offstage and when she was still stuck in the make-believe dressing room, surrounded by supporters who would not let her drop the act. There was no one to blame — she'd gone along with all of it. And now that it was in her past, she couldn't say why she'd ever wanted any of it. But contracts with the devil, no matter how clever one's solicitor might be, don't include opt-out clauses. This was her life.

She heard her name and walked out into the lights. It had been a while since she'd been in the harsh glare, but the dark shades she habitually wore kept it from overwhelming her.

With an outstretched arm, Nina pasted on a smile and greeted her guest, who

373

sat down with a sour smirk and began waggling her right foot nervously.

"Soooo, I understand you have a pretty incredible story to tell us."

Laila glanced offstage, then fixed Nina with a cold stare. "I wouldn't say that."

Nina rechecked her notes, which read "has a pretty incredible story (but probably won't want to talk about it)." Her skill in getting stars to spill had earned her a reputation for being almost American in her brashness.

"Don't hold out on us, Rocky. My viewers would rather hear you tell it than have me repeat all the scurrilous dirt that's been dished on you over the years."

Laila yawned and poked a pinky in an ear. "Suit yourself. It's your show. But please don't call me Rocky."

"I understand you lost your mother at a very young age."

"Umm." Laila crossed her legs and ran her tongue out over her bottom teeth.

"I also understand you had a longstanding feud with the Chaz Bonapart. Perhaps you can tell us more about that."

Laila stiffened; she drew a breath and exhaled slowly. "You keep saying you understand things, but you know you don't. You don't know a fucking thing about me." The producer lunged for the dump button to prevent the obscenity from going out over the air. He hit it within the allotted seven seconds but held it too long and muted the start of Laila's next remark. "...more enlightening conversations with amplifier heads."

Nina took a deep breath and pressed on. "We're going to be difficult, are we? Petulant and surly? Well, I've played the game before with more imposing figures, trust me. I'm not impressed by your attitude. And I can assure you my viewers won't be, either."

The game. Yeah, I've played it, too. And for a lot longer than you 'ave, Goldilocks. I've been jizzed on and shat on by Burchill, Bushell, Kent, Morley, Parsons and others of the rock press in my time. I've sucked up to label heads and promoters, led a band and made my own way since I was fifteen.

Love, hate, it was all the same to them, printing lies about me in service of a lie about their supposed responsibility to an audience. It was my audience, not theirs.

374

These self-important pillocks were just in the way. Sometimes I wondered what they were there for other than to shift fish and chip papers. But I liked the fanzines; they had suss and respect. It's okay when there's not so much at stake.

Now and again I've liked hearing myself talk, even learned a thing or two in the process. But I don't care to talk about my songs. I don't need people picking over my brain, thinking they've got me figured out. Journos hate me, because I won't give them fodder for their theories, or gratification for their egos. Tough nuts, I say. Write whatever you want, I tell them, it'll make sod all difference to me.

Only that was a lie. What they wrote about me was painful. Over the strenuous advice of everyone I knew, I read it all, and it was like being flogged in the town square. It didn't matter whether they loved me or hated me: being the subject of speculation and obsession made me squirm.

It didn't bother me half as much to be onstage; that was more anonymous in a way, less personal. These kids and I had an unspoken deal worked out: I gave them as much of what they wanted as I felt like giving, and they didn't ask me any difficult questions. But even the fan mags bugged me, and I had a press officer to handle all of that. People said I was difficult, weird, a recluse. But that's bullshit. Just because I didn't give them what they wanted, that made it personal for them. Other stars took it all in stride, did what was asked of them and showed a different side to the world than what they kept for themselves. I couldn't do that. There was only one of me. I didn't have a switch to go from pop star to Laila, so I constructed a pop star version of myself, and left it at that.

Why had I agreed to this? Did I think that putting up with this twit for a half-hour would get my career going again? That it would make everything right in the world? There was no balm for the ego in this: being thought well of was never the thing for me. Maybe I've just become one of those Pavlov dogs that turns up and slobbers at the sound of a bell. Maybe it felt good to be thought of as someone worth putting on telly. Some part of me would really like to explain it all, clearly and carefully, to a bright bulb who could really understand, but I doubt that such a person exists. And if they did, what good would come from me telling them?

"My sources tell me — and I am sooo sorry I wasn't there to see it in person, but I was still in nappies, a few years younger than your fans at the time — that your first London concert was a bit of a shock."

It was. The outstretched arms of kids who wanted something from me that I surely was not prepared to supply. What was lacking in their lives that made them so needy, and what made them imagine I was the solution to anything? I have a pretty clear recollection of standing on stage, a spotlight on me that made it all a blinding blur, and seeing those arms, the open hands, the frantic eyes. I tried to think what it had been like for me, and how I could just as easily have been one of them instead of one of me. I didn't feel special, I felt alone. Horribly alone, like when Mum died.

"Dunno. Alright, I suppose. Done a lot more since. A gig is hard graft, even when it looks easy."

It _had_ looked easy. Things took off so quickly — TV, radio, press, all of that — that seven months after signing to Massive I was headlining the Rainbow on a Thursday night. The bleeding Rainbow! The Kinks were there that same week. Chuck Berry, Davie Bowie, Eric Clapton and Status Quo had all played there. Legends, all, and I was just a hype? No, of course, I was nowhere near ready, had maybe a dozen shows under my belt, none of them worth paying to see. I hadn't earned the venue, had nowhere near the fame to warrant it, but Frank called in a favour to "put me on the radar." (I found out later that he'd bought the entire balcony and gave the tickets away outside of a Suzi Quatro show. That made me feel like rubbish. And then the bastard billed me for the seats!) Still, he did the advance work like a wizard and booked a trio from Manchester with a bigger hit than me, a well-organized fan club and no stage presence to open — they were grateful and could sell tickets without making me look like a shitty second.

Frank arranged for the Rainbow's red script logo to be augmented with a spiky-haired spaceship for the evening. The crowd on Seven Sisters Road was young, colorful and supercharged with the giddy recognition of massed tribal power. Anticipation of what waited inside threaded through them: platform shoes, teased hair and thin arms jammed in the pockets of short, shiny jackets made their thin bodies look unnaturally sticklike, as much insect as human.

The badge and poster sellers were doing bang-up business; the ticket touts were making out like bandits. The punters were so young it must have been a first concert for many of them. And their first time being plugged into the adolescent power grid and feeling that jolt of communal hysteria. The ones who were not *content to simply pose and stare got swept up in the connection to something none of them had witnessed. Their energy coalesced in the cool air, tinged with the primal fear of reality bearing down on their sheltered lives. They were tasting freedom for the first time. If only they'd known the risk that comes with it.*

When you're little, you wonder who you are, what life has in store for you. Then one day you wake up locked into an identity you had no role in selecting. I'm not talking about jobs or anything like that, I mean you know if you're the kind of person who pushes or gets pushed, leads or follows, exults or broods, dreams or suffers. A slob or a neat freak, Miss Organization or a master of disorganization. A spendthrift or a cheapskate. It's a mystery how that happens, but it does, and you spend the rest of your days either being that person or fighting desperately not to be that person. My guess is the ones who go off their rockers are like that. Not accepting who you have to be must coil you like a spring, bends you right out of shape. But not everyone can handle the cards they're dealt.

The compere said my name, I heard applause and I was shoved onstage. I forgot some of the words (in the song I'd written about that, no less). I couldn't hear anything coming out of the wedges. To cap the whole sorry escapade off, I came awfully close to doing a header off the stage. The middle bit was a mad blur. The lights blinded me. The band were way louder and played a whole lot faster than they had at rehearsal. We'd decided not to risk it with a guitar around my neck that night, so I had no idea what to do with my arms. I think I clung to the mic stand like the mast on a ship. God knows what my legs got up to. I did remember to breathe. Then, quick as a flash, I was back in the dressing room with a can of Coke and a rough face rag.

Frank said I went down well. I told him my ears were ringing and he had a good laugh about it. He asked me if I'd had fun, and I told him I had because I reckoned that's what he wanted to hear.

"So, tell me, tell everyone, what was it like to be the youngest pop star, the top woman guitarist and the first female in the glam-rock genre" — pronounced as if it had three syllables, zhan-uh-ruh — "in the UK?"

"Well, I wasn't actually any of those things, Nina, so it wouldn't be right of me to comment." The host gazed accusingly at the paper in her lap, then back at her guest, who offered no further clarification.

She laughed nervously. "OK, I'll be sacking my researcher when this is over. But I un..., uhh, so you started out pretty young, right? Let me show everyone your first album." She held up a worn sleeve, borrowed no doubt from an older brother (or mother) of someone on the show's staff. It was simple: a grid of dots, the larger ones red, the smaller ones black, on a blank white background. The title, covered by a Rock On sticker (£1.99, marked down from £3.99, thanks for leaving that on), was *Spots and Periods*.

"What's that mean, then, spots and periods?"

"Ah, come off it, are you thick?"

"No, of course not, I just think our audience would like you to explain the title to them."

"It was for all the young girls out there going through puberty."

"I see. How, erm, artful of you. So how did you get the name Rockit LA?"

"Dunno, my manager give it to me."

"What does it mean? Other than California lettuce?" Nina could not help but notice that Laila missed a beat in replying; no one had ever made the name sound so stupid before. She'd landed a blow, but the champ was unfazed.

"Nothing. What does 'Nina Whelan' mean?"

"I didn't make my name up."

"How do we know that?" Laila grinned and got a laugh from the audience.

"I'm telling you. What's your real name?"

"None of your business." In the control booth, producer Albert Shaw was increasingly concerned about the dead sea of nothingness he was seeing. Nina had faced challenging subjects before, but she was a resourceful girl and had always found a way to draw them out, to get them engaged. (Or, failing that, enraged.) This, however, felt like a zen standoff. All he could hear in his headphones was the imagined sound of viewers clicking off to another channel. To buy time, he told the cameramen to stay focused on Nina and told her to introduce "Soldier to Cry On," a Rockit LA clip from the days before labels would routinely shell out for high-priced videos and artists were left largely to their own initiative and resources. In fact, it was a lip-synched TV performance, poorly shot on a cheap set for some tatty programme, complete with a gaggle of period dancers doing a martial parade routine that would not have been out of place in a Leni Riefenstahl documentary.

While the clip played, Nina rethought her strategy. When it ended, she turned to Laila and said, "I've just had an idea. How about if we do a swap here, and you interview me as if I were you. So you're me, and I'm you, and you have to get me to tell you stuff so my viewers don't change the channel and go off to watch home improvement shows or rugby. What do you say?"

"Sounds stupid. Sure."

"OK, go ahead then." Laila paused and let a smile flicker and disappear. If her hope was to preface what she was about to say with a genial note, it was too fleeting to make the point. "So, I understand you're a total bitch without a clue who likes to tear people down to make yourself feel better."

Nina managed a tight laugh. "Wait, that's not even a question. Are you saying that to me or to you?"

"What's the difference?"

Nina was defeated. She smirked to show that she wasn't scared, even though she sort-of was. In an attempt to extricate herself gracefully, she kept up the switcheroo scheme. "Well, it's been really great to come on your show, Nina. I'm grateful to you for giving me a chance to tell my side of the story, especially to those too young to know who I am or what I've done."

Laila gave her a perplexed look and coughed. She moved to unclip the mic from her shirt and made to rise, but Nina put out a hand. "Wait, wait, we're not done yet. Let me be me again for a moment."

That disarmed Laila, who relaxed and settled back. "Knock yourself out." She waved gaily in the air.

"Why the dark sunglasses?"

"I don't like looking at the world anymore."

"Now we all know that's not the reason," Nina said, her voice drooling with condescension. "Your eye got buggered in a brutal attack by a madman." The audience gasped. Laila had been out of the spotlight long enough for that association to have fallen off the radar, no longer the automatic attachment to her name it had been for a number of years.

"Who was, as it happened, the son of your nemesis, Chaz Bonapart." Murmurs filled the studio. The producer perked up and leaned in toward the console.

"And the attacker was murdered by your layabout father." The gasps that remark elicited quickly turned into loud studio chatter as Laila gripped the arm of her chair tightly. "That's quite a story you haven't bothered to tell us."

Laila glowered behind her shades. "My dad didn't murder anyone, he saved my life. And when that jumped-up nutter tried to bash my brains in, my brave father stopped him. His death had fuck all to do with Chaz Bonapart, and if you want to do know any more about that, you'd better ask him."

"Now this is getting interesting, don't you think?" Nina grinned at the camera, a lupine smile of satisfaction that just needed a raw piece of flesh hanging from it to complete the picture. "Right, I know you basically stole your career out from under Chaz after torpedoing it by claiming to have written all of his hits, but it turns out that's not the only truly rotten thing you did in your youth."

The audience "oohed" gamely at the promise of a shocking revelation. Laila wondered what in the world she could be getting at. Nina held a glossy magazine up to show the camera.

"This is the current number of *International Musician* magazine, which I received by air mail from the States this very morning."

"Never 'eard of it."

"Well, they've certainly heard of you. Some clever dick did his research and came up with a juicy exposé." She paused to let the drama build. She opened the magazine, slipped on a pair of cat-eye specs and pretended to read the article. She put a finger on the page and made an elaborate show of removing the specs and addressing the studio audience.

"Rockit LA, it seems, has quite a chequered past. It says here that the lyrics that she used to steal away Chaz Bonapart's career weren't even hers. She stole them in the first place. Her American boyfriend, a fellow named Bryan Klein, later a big record exec in New York under his nom de rock, Eon Clean, was in fact the genius behind her fraud. He wrote the lyrics 'Only Lovers Left Alive,' 'Ignite the Pilots' and 'Equal Opportunity Girl' — songs recorded by your unsuspecting benefactor, Chaz Bonapart. Here are some of the lines he wrote that you pilfered, lines that any of you trainspotters with a collection of old glam records will certainly recognize." She read the lyrics in a dull monotone.

Only lovers left alive
We've made our getaway
Find a place where we can hide
Maybe things will change another day.

"Can't say as I recall that one myself, but it reached number-eleven. And you claimed to have co-written it with a production team called Giddyap. And then you were introduced — at a Chaz Bonapart press conference, that took some cheek — as, quote, the future of rock, by the manager you took off of him."

Laila sat, dumbfounded. She'd just about forgotten the American who'd turned her on to so many things that now felt like her birthright. She muttered "you bastard" while Nina went on with her triumphant spiel.

"He gave the magazine proof in the form of a letter from you acknowledging it." She turned to the audience and feigned exaggerated shock. "When he learned that you'd given away his precious creations to a fading rock singer, he let you take credit as the secret songwriter in exchange for prostituting yourself to him. How typical of a Yank — anything to get a leg over. And you were well under the age of consent. How awful. Just awful."

Her tone shifted from accusatory to patronizing. "Now that everyone knows what you've done, would you care to fill us in on the sordid side of stardom?"

No, I bloody well do not care to. I'd endured plenty of criticisms in my time — she can't sing, she can't play, she's got a fat arse, she looks walleyed, her name is stupid, all of it — but I'd learned to live with it. My fans didn't give a toss. They could say or write whatever amused them — I was safe and sound so long as the kids stuck by me and I could tell myself it wasn't true. Their insults were nothing but noise, a lonely voice drowned in the cheering. I wrapped myself in the armor of stardom and got on with it. I was fucking Rockit LA, idol of youth!

381

But. Yes, but. But. When I had time to think — which I rarely did, as the roller-coaster whipped and dipped me through the days and months, through the miles and superficial experiences glancing off the shallowest depths of my concern — I knew in my heart of hearts that Laila Russell was no Rockit LA. I was okay with that so long as I wasn't obliged to admit it to anyone other than myself. So while I could ignore the rubbishing in public, in private I never quite felt like it was me on the magazine covers. It was only an invention, a made-up role that I played. Hard as I tried to, I could never become it. Or maybe it never became me.

For a while I was honest with myself about what I took off of Eon — I mean I rationalized it that we, I dunno, loved each other and would always do stuff for each other, and he didn't seem to mind that I was borrowing a few of his ideas, he seemed proud of me and didn't ask for any compensation. The comforts of the flesh, that was as much for me as for him, so it wasn't any sort of a payback. Did I owe him for being my inspiration? True, I hadn't made that part of my myth either, but when you're a star no one wants to hear you acknowledge every git that taught you anything, explained how things worked, or gave you some records. Right?

But time and desire, success and the daily lies I learned to live with, had replaced the receding blur of actual memory with a convenient fiction. I came to believe that it was all my doing, my creative imagination that had gotten me in with Chaz and them. Eon was erased from the equation, not because I wanted him to be, but — when I was finally able to untie the knots of this mess with a shrink — because my belief in myself (well, not exactly myself, but the myself that people knew as Rockit LA), the faith that allowed me to do what I did and convince people that I was real rather than a sad girl trying to be something she was not, rested on the confidence that I had taken off him. I forgot his encouragement, his support, the dream he gave me.

I had to accept the lie that some mysterious essence of Lailaness had delivered me to my destiny as a pop star, that had put me on the magical lift that carried me from thick clueless schoolgirl to brilliantly creative pop goddess. That it was not Eon, not fate, not Frank, not the happenstance of finding a bag on the Tube, not the blind inanity of a vast audience that could be sold anything so long as it came from someone. I knew, at least I think I had accepted the knowledge, that I'd gotten to the moon largely on my own once I got off the launching pad, but I willingly (if subconsciously) allowed the details of that part to be washed away, replaced with a gap where any memories of the actual hows and whys of my becoming a songwriter once resided. A myth of immaculate creation explained everything: I just was. And that allowed me to get on with it, impervious to all the criticisms, the complications and the challenges that being a pop star entailed. I wasn't bothered by any of it. I knew I had the bottle and the talent to be a star, because that's who I was. Only, in this moment, I wasn't.

Like an arrow finding its way through a gap in chain mail armour, this particular attack reached the deepest recesses of my insecurity, destroying the core of my confidence in a flash. Memories of my past had been securely quarantined and this reminder by the one person who was in a position to know, served up a direct contradiction of who I believed myself to be. I'd literally forgotten the truth of the matter, and a reminder of it shook my foundations. I had the sensation of being dropped down a bottomless pit, scraping the walls as they flew by. I knew he was right, she was right and...and...

I had to expel this terror, and the only available target was this ridiculous woman seated a few feet away. I didn't plan my move, it just happened and, as it did, I wondered if William had felt the same thing right before he threw a brick at me.

Laila reached for the magazine in Nina Whelan's perfectly manicured hand but missed as it was yanked away. She leapt off her chair in a lunge for it. It was hard to tell, even after the videotape of those moments had been carefully reviewed, whether she had intentionally hurled herself at Nina or not; regardless, the effect was the same — to knock the host off her chair, causing her leg to be bent at a most distressing angle. As Laila landed on top of her, the tiny microphone pulled off her shirt and landed close enough to record the nauseating sound of an ankle twisting out of its socket, adding that to the permanent audio record of a truly gruesome celebrity encounter.

Nina writhed on the floor, her face contorted in pain, screaming for someone to call 999. While one stagehand did, others gathered to gape at the unnatural angle of shoe to leg. Laila picked herself up, straightened her shirt and left the studio, *International Musician* still clutched in her fist.

On the Beach

I LOCKED MYSELF away. Pulled the phone wire out of the wall and ignored noises at the door. The post piled up and I let it. Depression didn't stave off hunger, so I went out once a day for a takeaway curry and a can of lager, but otherwise I didn't see or speak to anyone. No one could possibly feel what I was feeling, and I had no use for hollow sympathy. Communication was pointless; I spoke a language of personal experience few shared. Stumbling on a memory gap of rejected reality opened a much larger wound for me than being publicly shamed for once stealing a few words from a fuck buddy. I know it sounds outsized and unthinkable, like pulling one brick out from a wall and watching the whole castle collapse. Believe me, I was shocked to discover how upset and unequipped to cope I was with this turn of events. But there you go.

My adult life had essentially been a fiction; I knew that and had (more or less) made peace with it. But now I had to face the possibility that I had lost what had gone before. And as I hadn't yet begun to work out what might come next, I was suspended in the unknown between fantasy and forgetfulness. I needed a core truth to cling to or I was nobody. I wasn't Rockit LA any longer (if I ever had been) and I wasn't the Laila Russell I thought I'd been, either. Which left me with nothing. Since Mum only existed in my clearly faulty memory maybe I'd made her up as well. It was quicksand and I was sinking into it.

I badly wanted to talk to Dad about all of this but couldn't see how that would be good for either of us. He was the one who needed drugs to make it through the day. I didn't want to inflict my pain on him; it would be like visiting a person in hospital when you're sick. And what did I imagine he could tell me about coping with the aftermath of stardom?

When I finally felt ready to see him (or him me), I got a taxi to Milton Road. He'd heard about, but hadn't seen, the Whelan debacle. Looking at the sorry state of him, I couldn't bring myself to talk about the black thoughts I was having, so I put it by and we had a laugh about one more TV interview that didn't go so well.

We got talking about Mum. I'm not sure why I'd brought it along the life advice alphabet she'd done up for me, but I realized I needed to talk about it with him. This was the last tangible thing I had of her, proof real and true that she'd lived and loved and looked out for me as best she could. When I'd pull it out and look at it was like having her back for a minute, even if the realization that she wasn't there only made things worse.

I gave him the page. "Do you remember when she did this for me? The advice thingies?" He stared at it with a puzzled look on his face. He mouthed the words as he read a couple of the lines. Jail your jealousies....Outlaw the obvious...Pull the plaster...Tell your tale ....

"Catherine wrote this?" It was strange to hear him refer to her by name. He turned it over and smiled at the handbill side. "I don't recall. My memory isn't like it used to be. The pills and all." I didn't say that maybe it was just old age. He was, after all, closing in on sixty.

"Yes, for me. Life lessons. She sealed it in an envelope and gave it to Aunt Ruth to hold for me. She set it aside and then forgot about it until I was in my teens. I vaguely remember going to see her when she was poorly and getting it off her then. It's really all I have of Mum. I've tried to live by what she told me here, although I can't say I've always succeeded." I swallowed hard and tried not to cry. It didn't help to see their wedding picture on the shelf past his shoulder.

He turned the paper over a few more times, and then brightened and handed it back. "Oh, yes. Now I remember. It was a school assignment for the teachers one term. She had a real gift for teaching, she did, so very kind to her students. Concerned, like. She really understood them. Gave so much of herself."

"Wait, what do you mean 'a school assignment'?"

"The head, who never liked me, did a training course that recommended it as an exercise to connect the teachers and the students or some such. He came back and made everyone cobble something together. I tried to do one as well, but I was crap at it. Your Mum, she was browned off about having to do it, but I guess she came through. As one always did. How did you come by this?"

I was suddenly shaking and gasping air. I couldn't fill my lungs. In a trembling whisper, I said, "You mean she didn't do it for me? Mother-daughter, like?"

385

"'Fraid not, luv."

"She used to say 'Face your fears, bunny' to me. She was trying to prepare me for life, as if she knew she wouldn't be around to talk to in person forever. And now you're saying it was just a stupid homework exercise? Like writing your name a hundred times?" Tears streamed down my face. I felt faint and gripped the arm of the chair to keep from sliding off.

"There, there, girl. Your mother loved you. I'm sure she was thinking of you when she wrote it."

"Dad, don't say that. You can't take back the truth."

"Yes, you're right." He offered an apologetic smile. "Take back the truth... right, that sounds like one of her things. That she wrote. Really, Laila, you're more like her than you'll ever know."

By now I was sobbing hard. "That's no help to me now. You've ruined it for me. This was the only thing of hers I had that's mine, and now it's not. What makes me any better than any fifth-former she taught in Brixton back then?" He said something about money and fame, but I wasn't listening. I felt the floor give way, like on an amusement park ride. This was like losing her all over again. Or finding out she wasn't really my mother. Or that she had a second family we didn't know about tucked away somewhere. I limped home and locked myself away again.

Weeks passed. I cried and cursed and moaned and drank. I tried, not very hard, but I tried to think of a good reason to carry on. I fought off the idea of topping myself a couple of times. Slowly, amid a mix of fatigue and acceptance that crept over me, I returned to functioning: I was able to bathe, eat, sleep, the lot. I'd read about junkies going cold turkey on their own, and that's what this was like: clinging on to nothing more than surviving until morning. I was a cast-away, shipwrecked on my own island, well aware that no one was coming to rescue me. I surprised myself that I could do it.

A letter from Barry landed on the pile inside the door. He'd gotten a lead on RipdNerv and done an interview with them. I still wasn't ready to see people in the flesh, but I was curious enough to ring him.

"It turns out they've morphed into vegan straightedge peace-and-love types.

386

They've grown their hair long, gone off the booze and drugs and are hanging out with Hare Krishnas in Leicester Square. Unless they're running a scam of some major proportions, I don't think you've any reason to fear them now. I brought up your name — I didn't say anything that might lead them to you — but that one, Death, the one you were asking about, he was all apologetic and remorseful, said he was sorry that he frightened you at some outdoor festival."

That didn't make me feel any better, but it was better than him threatening to batter me. Barry continued, even though I was losing interest. "Oh, and I learned something else, totally at random. We got on to the band's equipment — I do a *London Letter* column for this American gearhead glossy. He showed me their guitars — nothing special, cheap Japanese knockoffs — but the backline and PA were first-rate, way better than their kind usually bothers with. Turns out it all came from Chaz. That old tosser opened his lockup and set them up with Marshall stacks, Neumann mics, lights and all.

"I didn't think much about it at the time other than being one of those odd connections you happen on now and again, but when I listened back to the tape it stuck with me. I couldn't imagine why Chaz would be so generous with a bunch of racist yobbos, so I got onto that bloke Death and asked when the Nerv had crossed paths with Chaz. He said they'd done business together but wouldn't say anything further about it."

My jaw dropped and I sputtered out a whathowwhyhunhwhat?

"Yeah, I agree. Crazy shit." I was too dumbfounded to say anything.

"I couldn't see it right off, but I thought there might be a story worth writing there. I tried Chaz, but he wouldn't talk to me. Neither would his business partner. So then I had a thought and got on to a friend who has a friend in the coroner's office, and I prevailed upon him to take a look at the William Poole inquest transcript. One of the witnesses who testified was this sociology professor at Cambridge — wait, I've got his name here somewhere. Right, here we are, it's Dr. Solomon Hector. He had William in his class and apparently took an interest in him. I did some sleuthing and discovered that Hector wrote a book about the criminal element and the ethno-sociology of pop. I really don't what that means, but it had to do with Chaz somehow, so he must have used William to get to him."

I was trying to follow, but this was becoming a mental house of mirrors, with everything blurred together and distorted.

"I was able to reach Professor Hector and he was very eager to talk. A real self-promoter, that one is. Dying to be on telly and all that. So I ask him what his part in all of this was, and he said he'd got to know Chaz, but it was his former manager — what's his name, hang on, it'll come to me, oh right, Frank Guy, I think he rang me once to complain about a review I'd written — that was his primary source."

"Barry, you've got to slow down. I'm lost here. And I know, well, knew, most of these people. But this is crazy shit. And how does it connect Frank or Chaz to Death? Why would Chaz give his band a pile of equipment?"

"Hector sent William to Wormwood Scrubs to research a paper he was to deliver on the potential cultural rehabilitation of violent offenders. And one of the violent offenders he was told to interview was your man Desmond Fitzsimmons, who was locked up for an incident of hooliganism."

"Who?"

"Death. Fitzsimmons is his real name. My guess is that Death sussed who his old man was and saw where that would get him. According to Hector, when he got out of nick he and William formed a band. They called themselves The Sons of Shite, but that got changed to RipdNerv before they ever played out. I gather William didn't stay long, something to do with his hearing. But before he split, Chaz gave them all his old gear. Set them right up to arrange their own benefits and the like."

"Wow. That is some crazy shit."

William must have done a roll-up of his father's professional resentment and Death's yobbo grudge and added some lunatic element of his own. I wondered what role that teacher of his might have played. I tried to recall the few times I'd met William. It was so long ago. I thanked Barry and put down the phone.

Then I fell apart. The pieces of my life didn't make sense any longer; it was all random bits with no connecting tissue. Events without logic. Simple repairs were out of the question: I started to imagine that I needed to be torn down and built back up from the ground. I just wanted to run away and hide.

I needed to find someplace where I could shed the past and figure out who I wanted to be without having to be anyone I'd been. Chives would miss me, that was certain, but I'd be no use to him if I stayed. This was a matter of life or death. Mine. I had to get out of London. Everything I thought I knew was crumbling to dust before my eyes — and me along with it.

I wasn't Rockit LA any longer — if I ever had been — and I really wasn't Laila Russell either. Which left me with nothing. I still had the magazine from the TV show. I re-read the article several times. Eon was a hotshot A&R man at Epic Records in New York. From the quotes in there, he didn't seem angry about what happened, I could sense from what he said that he'd been reluctant to talk about it. Maybe he didn't hate me as much Nina had made it out. I tried to remember how I had felt about him before the hurricane of my career hit, what we had been to each other. I don't have a clue how people cling to memories of their emotions. But the more I thought about it the more I sensed that he may have been the last real thing that had happened in my life. He could be a starting point to understand what had happened and who I was. It was a long shot, but it was the only shot I could think of.

THE FLIGHT WAS turbulent, but the supper was decent and the older bloke in the seat next to me was skinny and silent. I never learned to sleep on planes and spent the better part of eight hours fretting. Lacking an actual plan of what I might do or say once I got in front of Eon, I seesawed between killing him and kissing him. Maybe both (but not in that order.) My mission, at least what I thought my goal to be, was to punish or plead for anything that might put me back on the road to recovering a part of myself. I needed a new reality. I hoped reconnecting to the past could help me retrace the steps leading up to Rockit LA so I could see a way forward.

I checked in to the Mayflower off Columbus Circle and lay down for a kip. I'd stayed there before, on my first trip to meet the American label and then during a publicity blitz in advance of my one U.S. tour. None of it had gone well — me and America just couldn't see each other properly.

I spent a couple of days wandering the city — catching the rhythm of it, losing myself a bit in the bustling millions. I felt conspicuously white and foreign in

Harlem and anonymous in the East Village. Nobody recognized me, and why should they? I stopped in at the Strand and bought some books about the city. Maybe New York would be a safe refuge for me.

But the real order of business, the one I couldn't put off indefinitely, was getting up the spit to ring him. His secretary was a total bitch — all "what is this in reference to?" and "will Mr. Clean know what this is regarding?" — so I had to leave several messages and then sit on the bed like a tree stump with a pot of Earl Grey, awaiting his return call.

Eon, who I forgot and called him by his real name, Bryan, when he came on the line, was understandably surprised — and, I'd have to say, a bit wary — about hearing from me after all these years. I didn't say right off why I was there, just that I happened to be in town. I assured him that I was not shopping for a deal and did not have a tape I wanted him to hear. I suggested we meet for lunch. He hemmed and hawed, made a big show of checking his schedule (why do Americans pronounce it that way, anyway? — it's c-h, not k) and "penciled" me in for the Friday.

"We'll go to Nirvana. That's the Indian place I go to be reminded of London. It's got a brilliant view. I miss it." Then he switched into a line of professional patter I would rather have not heard. It was exhausting to be reminded of the old hustle. "Did you know there's a band by that name now? They're from Seattle. They're pretty good, but I don't think America is ready for rock that real. Did you bring a Walkman? Where are you staying? I'll messenger over a cassette and you can tell me what you think. It's called *Bleach*. Don't tell anyone, but we're thinking of going after them for their second album."

I prepared myself for lunch without any idea of what I wanted to convey or receive from it. I thought I might figure it out if I went shopping, but everything looked like a uniform that I didn't belong in. I ended up in a white Oxford shirt and a red skirt, with a plaid necktie and the only shoes I'd brought: a beat-up pair of oxblood DMs.

When he came out to fetch me from reception I thought he looked smarter in the magazine photo, but he carried himself with the easy confidence of a man who was doing well and had got accustomed to being right (or at least obeyed) about things. At lunch, he shared stories about what he'd done since returning

390

to the States: working on a presidential campaign, a stint in advertising, a brief and miserable stretch managing a heavy metal band, even a spot of what he called alternative journalism. He was vague about how he came to land a label job, but I think there was someone he'd known from London who brought him along and got him in there. And he'd found a couple of bands that had done well, so he was a golden boy for the moment. He was living on the Upper East Side with a girl who did press for a museum and trying not to think about formalizing their relationship. She wants a kid, he said, and I'm still one. I could see his point. None of us ever really grow up nowadays, we just paper over life's disappointments. Maybe that's just a fucked-up version of what the previous generation did, but it's safe to say no one my age had turned into an adult, leastways not of the sort that raised us.

He asked how I'd been and went, *"Ewww, gross"* when I lifted my shades to show the scar where my right eye no longer was, but otherwise didn't seem all that curious about my doings these past two decades. He knew about my success, but I guess the story of my failure wasn't that compelling.

As I finished the lamb korma (not as good as any in London, but passable) and my second Kingfisher, I realized I was relaxed and enjoying myself as I hadn't in a long while. There was a familiarity between us that a generation apart hadn't erased. He'd been my first and he was a big part of the reason I got into the music business. I could feel some of what I felt back then (not that there was anything to be done about it).

"So, you really didn't come to see me about getting back in the game? Money for a demo? Nothing like that?" I don't think he could see past his limited view of the world and its possibilities. He'd done well and could keep his position so as long as his ears worked and the record business survived. "Nah, I'm done with that shit. I did it, made a bit of dosh, had some laughs and nearly died in the process. That's more than enough for me. Now I just have to figure out the alternative. If there is one." I smiled at him. I hadn't really smiled at anyone in a long time, and sincerity was nice for a change.

"Bullshit."

Nobody who has ever been up there in the lights — the object of adulation and absurd faith, paid to make noise and prance around like an idiot — ever lets go of it completely. Even bands from the '6os were still going up and down the country, playing their old hits in cabarets for pensioners. It's like a disease that stays in your bloodstream and can't be got out. Like poison. Or a drug. And, truth be told, I'm sure my resistance to the Pavlov dog thing would only keep me away for so long. If someone came calling and told me there was a crowd packed into the Palladium cheering my name and demanding to hear me sing "Ophelia's Dream" one more time, I'd probably get out of my sick bed and do it. (And change the title and lyrics to "Amanda" finally.) Good sense told me not to do it, and even better sense told me not to want it, but then I still had dreams about all of it, all of them, from time to time. People I hadn't seen in ages. I shrugged.

He put his fork down and stared right at me for a long time. I felt more of what I once felt for him. It felt natural. I think my cheeks must have reddened a bit.

"I don't know, Laila." He paused to push the hair back from his eyes. "I can't help you. You have to do this for yourself."

I had crossed an ocean to hear what I already knew. There was a recognizable trace of kindness in his face, but a great distance in his eyes.

"Maybe you should write a book or something."

Epilogue: Miss Teen Wordpower

WRITING A BOOK turned out to be quite therapeutic. Yeah, I sort of nicked the title (*20th Century Girl*), which only encouraged wags' suggestions that, like my songs, it wasn't my own work, but bollocks to them. I wrote every bleeding word, and it took donkey's years to finish. It wasn't a big seller, but that was alright. (My publisher got on me about doing a promotional tour, but I said no.) Doing it helped me see some things about myself more clearly, and I collected a few knicker for my troubles. That made it a better deal than seeing a shrink.

Once I had it all down on paper it stopped feeling real, like it had all happened to someone else or never happened at all. Given the state I'd been in, that was for the best. Let it all go and start again. I probably got a fair bit of the particulars wrong, but who cares. I could've gone and interviewed all the people in my old life, but then it would have been their story, not mine.

I haven't seen or talked to any of my old mob since that trip to New York. I had nothing left in my life, and they were why, so it made sense to me not to go back for more of the same. Except for the book suggestion (ta much, mate), going to see Eon had been a waste of time. I decided my old life was finished. I sold everything, left London and bought a cottage in Basingstoke. Got a border collie I named Desdemona and a thatched roof that leaked. I put on half a stone and went back to using my real name. No one was the wiser, seeing a plain woman in a jumper and jeans doing the marketing. Felt a bit like Syd Barrett, I did, only I wasn't living with my Mum and I don't think I was off my head. I did worry from time to time when a glance turned into a stare, but I had a story ready if anyone thought they recognized me from long ago. Solitude and anonymity suited me down to the ground.

I didn't listen to the radio or buy records; I pretty much missed the '90s, musically. I read a lot and would occasionally spot mention of someone I once knew, which always set me back a bit. I gathered that Chaz had some bother with the Inland Revenue, Amanda married a man from the City who died in a plane crash and left her loaded. Eon signed some poxy metal band, made a fortune and went to rehab. Frank started a film company that went tits up. His boyfriend, Joe, got AIDS and died.

Dad would write me now and again. I was careful to reply, offering nothing more than familial pleasantries. You have to look after yourself and, for me leastways, that means letting them go, even the ones you reckon need you, even the ones you're obliged to. I always paid my debts, but sometimes you have to reckon accounts settled and move on. I'm not cross with him, I just stopped clinging to the notion of family as sacred. He kept me from being killed and I kept him out of nick. Fair deal to you, Dad. He'll have to fend for himself as best he can.

There's an old pub called the Stag & Hounds on the Winchester Road. I drop in for a pint now and again. The jukebox is good, and sometimes I take a notion to put in a few coins and hear some of the songs from when I was a kid. (Yes, they have one of my singles. No, I have not.) The other night, I gave "Metal Guru" a few spins. Sounded old, sounded new. I felt old, I felt new. I went home and had a good, restorative cry — for Marc, for myself, for my parents, for the world. The dog kept me company. Good girl.

The next morning, unexpectedly full of piss and vinegar, armed with a strong cup of coffee and a long-stashed box of fresh biros and blank notebooks, I started writing lyrics again. This time, I knew what I wanted to say.

The End...

With Utmost Gratitude...

A lot of people deserve thanks for their contributions, great and small, to this work.

For her eternal support, suggestions, criticism and inspiration: Kristina Juzaitis

For their incredible generosity of time and effort in providing detailed and significant feedback on early drafts, helping me (re)shape it in countless ways: Sharon Mesmer, John Dunbar and Diane Juzaitis

For advising on and correcting the slang: Pete Silverton, author of *Filthy English*

For their valiant, if ultimately unsuccessful, efforts to find a publisher in the U.S. or the U.K. with the vision to see the value here: Philip Turner and Ben Fowler

For their most excellent Englishness and friendship: Alan Fielding, Paul Rambali, Barney Hoskyns, Wesley Stace

Friends & family: Dave Schulps, Frederick Wasser, Jim Green, Linda Robbins, Wayne King, Regina Joskow, Scott Isler, Sara Schoenwetter, Richard Doherty, Glenn Doherty, Shaina Doherty, Ellen Robbins, Frank Robbins, Tom Rubenoff, Anton Alterman, Michael Azerrad, Doug Brod, Evander Lomke, Ken Kurson, Jon Young, Binky Phillips, Fred Goodman, David Fricke, David Browne, Annie and Jonathan, Russell Wolinsky, Phil Panasci, Janas Hoyt, Freda Love Smith

For literary inspiration: Kingsley Amis, John Kennedy Toole, Nick Hornby, Jonathan Coe, Irvine Welsh, Mona Simpson and the 1970s *NME*

For their linguistic influence: Eric Partridge, the dictionary department of Foyles in London and all the British films and TV shows I've ever watched

For musical inspiration: T. Rex, Roxy Music, Slade, Mott the Hoople, Bob Dylan, Who, Sparks, Sweet, Roy Wood, David Bowie, Elvis Costello, Vivian Stanshall, Roger Ruskin Spear, Neil Innes, Dictators, Chris Sievey, Cheap Trick, Lou Reed, Iggy Pop, Suzi Quatro, Kim Wilde, Rolling Stones, Beatles

For bringing me into the world and setting me on the path that got me here: Estelle and Louis Robbins

For this and that: Bruce Harris, Bill Curbishley, Keith Moon, John Leland, Tony Visconti, Steve Gallo, Michael Pietsch, Tammy Faye Starlite, Ki Longfellow, Gavin Petrie, Amelia Fletcher, Mike Stuto, George Studdy, Jackie Cornish, Dave Thompson, Michael Tedder, Sara Palmer, Sarah Lazin

Author's Note

I was born in, and have never lived anywhere other than, New York City.

Growing up, a lot of what I learned about the world came from rock and roll: geography, girls, culture, attitude, style and, most of all, language. When the Beatles landed in New York in 1964, they didn't just bring songs, they brought exotic new words like *fab*, *gear* and *grotty*. While we already had our own street slang in the poor part of Brooklyn where I lived, this ten-year-old loved being handed a second language.

A decade later, the UK music weeklies — *Melody Maker, NME, Sounds* — provided my adult education in British argot. Around the *Trouser Press* magazine office, we used their words (and lyrics we learned from records) to identify with music we loved.

My interest in slang has never waned. I collect dictionaries; I delight at coinages found on television, in books and films. One of my goals here was to indulge that passion, to use what I knew (and research what I didn't) to conjure up a time and place in the natural voices of those who would have lived there. The jargon and expressions may present a small hurdle to reading, but I'd respectfully submit that exposure to unfamiliar cultures can be a positive experience. I doubt *Masterpiece Theatre* would have thrived on PBS as long as it has if programmers worried viewers would be put off by unfamiliar words.

This novel is about things I didn't do, in places I haven't lived (but have been), written in the voices of people very different from me, using words outside my native vocabulary. While some might deem that cultural appropriation, I claim the right of a novelist to write whatever and however she or he chooses.

A few bits and pieces here are based on things that happened to me, and several fictional characters were created with real people in mind. Other than the stuff I made up, the historical details are as accurate as I could make them.

Ira Robbins
April 2020

T REX. "Metal Guru." (T. Rex Wax Co.).

Cheech: If I was marking this on a scale from one to ten, I would give it minus three.

Chong: It sounds like the drummer mixed it.

Made in the USA
Columbia, SC
01 July 2021